INTRIGUE™

edge-of-your-seat suspense ignited by passion

Hostage To Thunder Horse

Elle James

Colby Brass

Debra Webb

Mills & Boon™

First Published 2010
First Australian Paperback Edition 2011
ISBN 978 1 742 55866 0

First Published 2010
First Australian Paperback Edition 2011
ISBN 978 1 742 55866 0

Published by
Harlequin Mills & Boon®
Level 5
15 Help Street
CHATSWOOD NSW 2067
AUSTRALIA

Printed and bound in Australia by
McPherson's Printing Group

Hostage To Thunder Horse

Elle James

Mills & Boon™
pure reading pleasure

ABOUT THE AUTHOR

Golden Heart winner for Best Paranormal Romance in 2004, Elle James started writing when her sister issued a Y2K challenge to write a romance novel. She managed a full-time job, raised three wonderful children and she and her husband even tried their hands at ranching exotic birds (ostriches, emus and rheas) in the Texas Hill Country. Ask her, and she'll tell you what it's like to go toe-to-toe with an angry 350-pound bird! After leaving her successful career in information technology management, Elle is now pursuing her writing full-time. She loves building exciting stories about heroes, heroines, romance and passion. Elle loves to hear from fans. You can contact her at ellejames@earthlink.net or visit her website at www.ellejames.com.

DEDICATION

This book is dedicated to my new grandson, whose arrival into this world was the best incentive to get this book written. Happy Birthday, Cade!

CAST OF CHARACTERS

Maddox Thunder Horse—Lakota Indian and North Dakota rancher, whose love of the wild horses of the Badlands leads to a winter rescue that turns into a long-term commitment to save a desperate woman.

Katya Ivanov—A princess framed for terrorism, on the run from law enforcement officials and a paid assassin.

Sheriff William Yost—The sheriff the Thunder Horse men despise for the slipshod investigation of their father's death.

Richard Fulton—A shadowy criminal who has eluded authorities for a long time.

Tuck Thunder Horse—Maddox's younger brother, the Federal Park Ranger in charge of protecting the North Dakota Badlands and its herds of wild horses.

Dante Thunder Horse—Maddox's brother, and helicopter pilot for the North Dakota branch of U.S. Customs and Border Protection.

Pierce Thunder Horse—Maddox's older brother, the one who left North Dakota to pursue a career in the FBI.

Dmitri Ivanov—Katya's brother, missing in Africa, next in line for the throne of Trejikistan.

Vladimir Ivanov—Katya's cousin, who covets the throne of Trejikistan and resents its move toward democracy.

Amelia Thunder Horse—Mother to the Thunder Horse men, who lost her husband to a freak riding accident.

Chapter One

He'd gained ground in the last hour, bearing down on her, the relentless adversary wearing at her reserves of energy. The cold seeped through her thick gloves and boots, down to her bones.

Alexi Katya Ivanov revved the snowmobile's engine, thankful that the stolen machine had a full tank of fuel. Regret burned a hole in her gut. Somehow she'd find the owners and repay them for the use of their snowmobile. She'd never in her life stolen anything. In this case, necessity had forced her hand. Steal or die.

She'd ditched her car several hours after crossing the border into North Dakota, and she was tired of wincing every time a law enforcement vehicle passed by. But she didn't know where to go. She'd only lived in Minneapolis since she'd been in the States. Instinct told her to get as far away from the scene of the crime as she could get.

Throughout the night, she'd pushed farther and faster, praying that she wouldn't be pulled over for speeding. Not until Fargo did she realize that the headlights following her hadn't wavered since she'd left Minneapolis. Butterflies wreaked havoc in her belly—whether they were paranoia or intuition, she didn't care. Her gut told her that whoever had framed her as a terrorist had also set a tracking device on the body of her car. How else had he found her and kept up with her through the maze of streets in the big cities?

She'd stopped once and taken precious time to search the exterior, but the snow-covered ground kept her from a thorough investigation of the undercarriage. Thus her need to ditch the car and find alternate means of transportation. Out in the middle of nowhere North Dakota, rental cars were scarce, if not impossible to find, not to mention they required a credit card to secure. She hadn't used a credit card since...Katya twisted the handle, gunning the engine. She refused to shed another tear. The bite of the icy wind was not nearly as painful as the ache in her heart. Her beloved father was dead. An accident, according to the news, but she'd gotten the truth from one of his trusted advisors back in Trejikistan. He'd been gunned down by an assassin while driving to their estate in the country.

Immediately after hearing the news of her father's death, Katya had been attacked in front of her apartment building. If not for the security guard she'd befriended, Katya would be dead. The same guard had hidden her from the attacker and let her know that the police had been to her apartment, claiming she'd been identified as a suspected terrorist. They'd found weapons and bomb-making materials there. Things that hadn't been there when she'd left to go to church earlier that day, hoping to find some solace over her father's death. The guard hadn't believed her capable of terrorism. Thank God.

On the run since then, she'd avoided crowded places, sure that someone would recognize her from the pictures plastered all over the local and statewide television.

She'd taken her car, switched the license plate with that of some unsuspecting person and driven out of Minneapolis as fast as she could.

Something slammed into the snowmobile, shaking her back into the present. A glance behind her confirmed her worst suspicions. The man following her had a gun aimed at her. For as far as the eye could see, there was nothing but gently rolling, wide-open terrain without trees, rocks or buildings to hide behind. The best she could hope for was to stay far enough ahead of the gunman to duck behind another hill. As her snowmobile topped a rise, another shot tore into the back of the vehicle.

Ducking low, she gunned the engine and flew over the top of the hill.

The ground fell away from beneath her, as the snowmobile plunged down a steep incline.

Katya held on, rocks and gravel yanking the skids back and forth during the descent into a rugged river-carved canyon. With each jarring bump, her teeth rattled in her head. Her hands cramped with the effort to steer the machine to the bottom. No snow graced the barren rocks, giving the snowmobile's skids little to grab onto. The rubber tracks flung gravel and rocks out behind her.

Katya couldn't worry about bullets from the man following her. It was all she could do to live through the ride.

With a bone-wrenching thump, Katya reached the riverbank. She couldn't believe she'd made it. She wanted nothing more than to throw herself on the ground and hug the earth.

Bullets pinged off the rocks beside her, forcing her

back into survival mode. She raced the snowmobile along the riverbank, aiming for the bluff that would block the bullets. The machine ran rough, the tracks slipping on the icy surface, getting less traction than needed.

With the shooter perched on the hillside, Katya was a prime target to be picked off. If only she could make it to the bend, her attacker would have to stop shooting long enough to follow.

Hunched low in her seat, she urged the hard-used machine across the snow and gravel. A hundred yards from the bend in the river and the reassuring solid rock of the canyon wall, it chugged to a halt.

Katya hit the start switch. Nothing happened. Bullets spit snow and gravel up around her. Katya flung herself from the seat to the rocky ground, crouching below the snowmobile. A bullet pierced the cushioned seat, blowing straight through and nicking the glove on her hand.

At the shooter's angle, the snowmobile didn't give Katya much protection. If she wanted to stay alive long enough to see another day, she'd have to make a dash for the canyon wall, where she hoped to find a place to hide among the boulders.

As if on cue, the snow thickened and the wind blasted it across the sky. She couldn't see the top of the canyon wall. And if she couldn't see all the way to the top, whoever was up there wouldn't be able to see her. Sucking in a deep breath, Katya took off, running upstream toward the bluffs.

The wind blew against her, making her progress slow, despite her all-out effort to reach cover. But once she was around the bend, the force of the wind slackened.

Katya hid among the rocks, bending double to catch her breath.

Her ride down the canyon wall had been nothing short of miraculous. Would the shooter make a similar attempt? Katya doubted anyone in his right mind would. Which meant he'd have to dismount and leave his machine at the top in order to come down and find her.

Without the snowmobile, she didn't know how she'd find her way back to civilization, but she could only solve one major problem at a time. Her temporary respite from being a target was only that. Temporary. In order to stay alive, she had to keep moving.

As she wove her way through the boulders and rocks, the wind picked up, the snow lashing against her cheeks, bitter cold penetrating the layers of GORE-TEX and thermal underwear beneath. Her feet grew numb and her hands stiff. At this rate, a bullet was the least of her worries.

The cold would kill her first.

MADDOX THUNDER HORSE topped the rise and stared down into Mustang Canyon to the narrow ribbon of icy-cold river running through the rugged terrain. He'd tracked Little Joe's band of mares to the valley below, worried about Sweet Jessie's newborn foal. Full-grown wild horses normally survived the harsh North Dakota winters without problems. But a newborn might not be so lucky. Temperatures had plunged fast, dropping from the low forties to the teens in the past three hours. With night creeping in and the snow piling up, Maddox couldn't look for much longer or he might be caught in the first blizzard of the season.

The handheld radio clipped just inside his jacket gave a static burst. "Maddox?"

Maddox fumbled to unzip the jacket just enough to grab the radio and press the talk button. "Whatcha got, Tuck?"

"I got nothing here in South Canyon. How about you?"

"Nothing."

"It's past time we headed back. The weatherman missed the mark on this one. *Wankatanka* grows angrier by the minute." Tuck attributed every change in weather to the Great Spirit.

The Bismarck weather report had called for snow flurries, not a full-blown blizzard. But Maddox had tasted the pending storm in the air. He understood this land and the weather like his ancestors, the equally rugged Lakota tribe who'd forged a life on the Plains long before the white man came. He'd felt the heaviness in the air, the weight of the clouds hanging over the canyons. Maddox knew if they were to find the horses, they'd have to hurry.

"See ya back at the ranch." Maddox clipped his radio to the inside of his jacket and zipped it back in place. Gathering his reins, he half turned his horse when movement near the river below caught his attention. With the snow falling steadily and the wind picking up, he had almost missed it. Maddox dug out his binoculars and pressed them against his eyes, focusing on the narrow valley below. Were Little Joe and his band of mares hunkering down in the canyon until the storm blew over?

Bear, the stallion he'd rescued five winters before, shifted beneath him from hoof to hoof, his nostrils flaring as if sensing the storm's building fury. Bear didn't like getting caught in snowstorms any more than Maddox did. The horse had almost frozen to death that winter Maddox and his fiancée, Susan, had been trapped in a raging blizzard. Bear had made it back alive. Susan hadn't.

Maddox peered through the blowing snowflakes to the bend in the river. His gaze followed the line of the waterway as it snaked through the canyon.

As a member of the Thunder Horse family, Maddox had grown up living, breathing and protecting the land he and his ancestors were privileged enough to own. Over six thousand acres of canyon and grassland comprised the Thunder Horse Ranch where the Thunder Horse brothers raised cattle, buffalo and horses. They farmed what little tillable soil there was to provide hay and feed for the animals through the six months of wicked North Dakota winter. For the most part, the rest of the land remained as it was when his people roamed as nomads, following the great buffalo herds.

Maddox loved the solitude and isolation of the Badlands. He'd only been away during his college days and a four-year tour of duty in the military. The entire time away from Thunder Horse Ranch he longed to be home again. The Plains called to him like a siren to a sailor, or more like a wolf to his own territory.

Now it would take an extreme change in circumstance to budge him from the place he loved, no matter what sad memories plagued him in the harsh landscape. Time healed wounds, but time never diminished his love for this land.

As his gaze skimmed the banks of the river, he passed over a flash of apple red. Orange-red and blood red he'd expect, like the colors of Painted Rock Canyon, but not bright, apple red. He eased the binoculars to the right, backing over the spot. Squinting through the lenses, he tried adjusting the view to zoom in. A white bump near the river's edge caught the blowing snow, creating a natural barrier quickly collecting more of the flakes. On the end of the drift, a red triangle stood out, but not for long. The snow thickened, dusting the red, burying it in a blanket of white.

Poised on the edge of a plateau, Maddox weighed his options. He hadn't found the mares and he still had an hour's ride back to the ranch house. If he dropped off the edge of the plateau to investigate the snowdrift and the red item buried in white powder beside it, he could add another hour to his journey home. In so doing, he risked getting stuck out in the weather and possibly freezing to death.

Instinct pulled at him, drawing him closer to the edge of the canyon, urging him to investigate. He rarely ignored his instinct, following his gut no matter how foolhardy it seemed. His army buddies called it uncanny, but it had saved his life on more than one occasion in Afghanistan.

No matter how cold and dangerous the weather got, if he didn't go down and investigate, curiosity and worry would eat away at him. He might not get the opportunity to return to investigate for days, maybe months, depending on the depth of the snow and how long the ground remained frozen.

With gloved fingers, Maddox tugged the zipper on his parka up higher, arranging the fur-lined collar around his face to block out the stinging snow now blowing in sideways.

He nudged Bear toward the edge of the plateau.

As they neared the dropoff, Bear danced backward, rearing and turning.

Maddox smoothed a hand along Bear's neck, speaking to him in a soothing tone, soft and steady over the roar of the prairie wind. "Easy, *Mato cikala*." Little Bear.

Bear reared up and whinnied, his frightened call whipped away in the increasing wind. Then he dropped to all four hooves and let Maddox guide him down the steep slope into the valley below. With the wind and snow limiting his vision, Maddox eased the horse past boulders and rocky outcroppings devoid of vegetation until the ground leveled out on the narrow valley floor. He urged the horse into a canter, eager to check out the mysterious red object and get the heck back to the ranch and the warm fire sure to be blazing in the stone fireplace.

His gaze fixed on the lump on the ground, Maddox pulled Bear to a halt and slipped out of the saddle. His boots landed a foot deep in fresh powder, stirring the white stuff up into the air to swirl around his eyes.

As he neared the snowdrift, the red object took shape. It was the corner of a scarf.

His heart skipped a couple beats and then slammed into action, pumping blood and adrenalin through his veins, warming his body like nothing else could.

He bent to brush away the snow from the lump on the ground, his fingers coming into contact with denim and a parka. His hands worked faster, a wash of unbidden panic threatening his ability to breathe. The more snow he brushed away, the more he realized that what had created the snowdrift was, in fact, a woman, wrapped in a fur-lined parka, denim jeans and snow boots. Her face, protected somewhat from the wind had a light dusting of snowflakes across deathly pale cheeks, sooty brows and lashes.

Maddox grabbed his glove between his teeth and pulled it off, digging beneath the parka's collar to find the woman's neck. He prayed to the Great Spirit for a pulse.

An image of Susan lying in his arms, hunkered beneath a flimsy tarp, while gale-force winds pounded the life out of the Badlands, flashed through his mind. This woman couldn't be dead. He wouldn't let her die. Not again. Not like Susan.

With wind lashing at his back and the snow growing so thick he could barely see, he didn't feel a pulse. He moved his fingers along her neck and bent his cheek to her nose. At last, a faint pulse brushed against his fingertips and a shallow breath warmed his cheek.

Relief overwhelmed him, bringing moisture to his stinging eyes. He blinked several times as he tightened the parka's hood around the woman's face and lifted her into his arms.

Too late to make it back to the ranch, he had to find a place to hole up until the storm passed. Being out in the open during a blizzard was a recipe for certain death. As he carried the woman toward his horse, he made a mental list of what he'd packed in his saddlebag.

This far into the winter season, he'd come prepared for the worst. Sleeping bag, tarp, two days of rations and a canteen. Trying to get the woman back to the ranch wasn't an option. Just getting out of the canyon would take well over an hour. Two people on one horse climbing the steep slopes was risky enough in clear weather. He couldn't expose the unconscious woman to the freezing wind. He had to get her warmed up soon or she'd die of exposure.

Maddox remembered playing along this riverbank one summer with his father and brothers. They swam in the icy water and explored the rock formations along the banks. If his memory served him well, there was a cave along the east bank in the river bend. He remembered because of the drawings of buffalo painted along the walls. He carried the woman along the river's edge, clucking his tongue for Bear to follow.

The stallion didn't look too pleased, tossing his head toward home as if to say he was ready to go back now.

The wind pushed Maddox from behind and for the most part he shielded the woman with his body. He crossed the river at a shallow spot, careful to step on the rocks and not into the frigid water. He couldn't get wet, couldn't afford to succumb to the cold.

The blizzard increased in intensity until he trudged through a foot and a half of snow in near-whiteout conditions. Maddox stuck close to the rocky bluffs rising upward to the east, afraid if he stepped too far from the painted cliffs, he'd lose his way. Bear occasionally nudged him from behind, reassuring him that the stallion was still there.

After several minutes stumbling around in the snow, Maddox thought he'd gone too far and might have missed the narrow slit in the wall of the bluff. A lull in the wind settled the snow around him, revealing a dark slash in the otherwise solid rock wall.

The entry gaped just wide enough for him to carry the woman through. Once the ceiling opened up and he could hear his breathing echo off the cavern walls, he inched forward into the darkness until he found the far wall. There he scuffed his boot across the floor to clear any rocks or debris before he laid her down in the cavern.

With little time to spare, he hurried back out into the storm to lead Bear out of the growing fury of the blizzard. As darkness surrounded them, Bear tugged against the reins, at first unwilling to enter the tight confines, his big body bumping against the crevice walls. When the cave opened up inside, the horse stopped struggling.

Running his hand along the horse's neck and saddle, Maddox focused his attention on survival—both his and the stranger's. If the woman had a chance of living, she had to be warmed up quickly. Although protected from the blizzard's fury, the cold would still kill them if he didn't do something fast. Once he came to the lump behind the saddle, he stripped off his gloves, blowing warm air onto his numb fingers.

Leaving the saddle on the horse for warmth, Maddox worked the leather straps holding the sleeping bag in place. Once free, he laid it at his feet on the cave floor. Next, he loosened the saddlebag straps and pulled it over the horse's back. Inside the left pouch, he kept a flashlight. His chilled fingers shook as he fumbled to switch it on.

Light filled the small cavern. The walls crowded in on him more so than he remembered from when he was a child. About half the size of the Medora amphitheater, the cave would serve its purpose—to shield them from the biting wind and bitter cold of the storm.

Without wood to build a roaring fire, they would have to rely on the sleeping bag and each other's body warmth—hers being questionable at the moment.

Maddox set the flashlight on a rock outcropping,

untied the strings around the sleeping bag and unzipped the zipper. He placed the open sleeping bag next to the woman. He had to get her out of the bulky winter clothing and boots and inside the sleeping bag.

Time wasn't on his side. He didn't know how long the woman had been unconscious or whether she had frostbite. Maddox stripped his coat off and the heavy sweatshirt beneath, wadding it up to form a pillow. Then he tugged his jeans off and the long underwear until he stood naked, regretting his lack of boxer shorts. The frigid air bit his skin, raising gooseflesh everywhere.

He went to work undressing the stranger, removing layer after layer. When he tugged off her jeans, she moaned.

That was a good sign. She wasn't completely comatose. Hope burned in his chest as he swiftly finished the job of undressing her down to her bra, panties and the pendant she wore around her throat. Nowhere in her pockets could he find any form of identification. He shoved all their clothing to the bottom of the bag, then laid the woman on the quilted flannel interior.

Tucked inside the sleeping bag, she didn't shake the way most cold people did. Her body had given up trying to keep her warm. The lethargy of sleep had numbed her mind to the acceptance of a peaceful death.

Maddox's body fought to live, his teeth chattering in the cool of the cave's interior. He refused to let the sleep of death claim her, as it had Susan.

Before he lost all his body warmth, he slid into the sleeping bag beside the woman and zipped the edges together. Although the bag was made for one large person, he was able to close both of them inside with a little room to spare. He wrapped his arms around her body, rubbing his hands up and down her cold arms and tucking her feet between his calves to warm them.

Cold. She was so cold.

Susan's face swam before him, her lips blue, her tawny blond hair buffeted by the wind, the only movement on her lifeless form. For a moment his world stood still as he stared down into the quiet countenance, the blank stare of his dead fiancée intruding into his thoughts.

But that was years ago. This woman wasn't Susan. For the first time since he'd found her, he studied the woman, blocking out the sad memories. In the shadowy glow of the flashlight, he leaned back enough to stare at the woman so near death he was afraid he might already be too late.

Dark hair, as black as his own, splayed across his gray sweatshirt pillow in large loose waves. Sooty, narrow brows winged outward in sharp contrast to her pale, almost translucent skin. Her hair dipped to a shallow peak at the center of her forehead and her lashes lay like fans across her cheeks. A pointed chin, perky nose and delicate ears completed her perfection.

As close as he was, Maddox caught a whiff of a subtle yet exotic perfume. His breath caught in his throat. This stranger didn't have Susan's girl-next-door fresh looks, yet her ethereal beauty was so profound it sucked the wind right out of his lungs, his groin tightening in automatic response to her skin against his. He hadn't been drawn to any woman since Susan's death. He hadn't let himself be, his burden of guilt weighing heavily.

The woman in the sleeping bag with him was a stranger. A beautiful, exotic stranger with skin the color of a porcelain doll and hair softer and silkier than anything he'd ever run his hands through.

He forced himself to focus on anything other than her physical attributes, shifting to all the unknowns, the mystery and reasons he shouldn't trust her. He didn't know her, she hadn't carried a driver's license or passport. He didn't know her background.

Who the hell was she? Would she live to tell him?

Chapter Two

Kat snuggled closer to the warmth in front of her, nestling her face into the hard, yet smooth surface. Her nose twitched and she slid her hand between her and the warmth-providing pillow, to brush her hair out of her face.

She couldn't move far with what felt like a tree branch draped across her back, holding her close and adding to the warmth. What was keeping her from moving? She opened her eyes to discover the source of her imprisonment.

Darkness so intense she couldn't see a scrap of light made her close her eyes and open them again. Was she dead? Panic shot through her like a lightning bolt. Had she gone blind? She shoved against the hard surface beneath her hands. The band around her waist shifted, tightening.

She pushed up on her hands, straining against the band. "Help." Her voice echoed as if in one of the large cathedrals of her homeland. "Where am I?" She fought to contain her terror. She had managed to stay alive based on sheer tenacity and by relying on her intelligence for the past two days. She couldn't give up now. But why was it so incredibly dark? Where was she?

"Shh." A deep baritone rumbled in the darkness, the surface beneath her hands vibrating. Then she was rolled to her side. She recognized the band around her middle now as an arm as thick as a small tree trunk.

Her heart slammed against her ribs. Had he caught up with her? Was she his prisoner? "Who are you? Where am I? Am I blind?" Her hip brushed against what could only be a man's… "Oh my god, you're not wearing any clothes!" She pounded against his chest, her feet banging against his shins.

"Slow down." The voice rumbled again, bouncing off the walls of the room they were in. "I'm not going to rape you, woman. Let me turn on the light."

With his one arm still holding her around her middle, he reached above his head. Cold air slipped across her skin, sending wave after wave of chills over Katya. She shook so hard her teeth rattled against each other.

Metal clinked against stone, then a click, and light bounced off what looked like rock walls.

Relief filled her as her eyes adjusted to the muted lighting. She wasn't blind. Light beamed across the room, dispelling the terrifying darkness. Then as quickly as the relief filled her it fled. She couldn't move, trapped against the man's chest and cocooned in a bag. Panic threatened to overwhelm her, but she fought it, taking deep, steadying breaths.

The man's other arm slipped back into the interior of the bag, pulling the gap closed, blocking the chilled air from leaking inside.

Despite her terror at being held captive, she didn't want to die of exposure. Until she learned more about the man she lay next to, she'd do well to appreciate the warmth and gather her strength if she had to fight for her life.

"How do you feel?" the man asked.

"Cold. Incredibly cold. And frankly, a little scared."

"You should be scared, but not of me. You almost died of exposure. You'll probably feel cold for a long time."

Her teeth chattered as she tried to form questions. "What happened? Why are we in this bag together?"

"I found you under a snowdrift by the river and brought you here to warm you. I only had one bag, so you had to share with me."

Her face burned. She stared around at the rock walls surrounding her. "Where are we?"

"In a cave."

"In what country?"

The man frowned. "The U.S., of course."

No *of course* about it. She'd been racing across the country for two days, never on a straight route, always varying her direction, hoping to shake the man following her. If the man currently holding her captive was one of the people after her, they could be practically anywhere. She took a deep breath before asking her next questions. "Who are *you?* Who do you work for?"

"Uh-uh." He shook his head. "You've been asking all the questions. It's my turn. Who are you?" His deep, resonant voice filled the inside of the cave with its ruggedness.

Katya hesitated. His avoidance of her question didn't set her mind at ease. She didn't know who she was dealing with and trusted no one with her identity. Especially after what had happened in Minneapolis. She'd been on the road ever since, until she'd been forced to ditch her car and steal a snowmobile. "Am I still in the Badlands?"

"Yes, ma'am. The Badlands of North Dakota, to be exact."

"My name is Kat," she said tentatively. At least she wasn't lying. Kat was only part of her name, but people she'd gone to school with in Minneapolis had used it as her nickname. "Kat Evans." Evans was an out-and-out lie. Hard lessons had taught her not to give out truth until she knew where she stood. Especially with the colossal accusation of terrorism hanging over her. Homeland Security, Customs and Border Protection, the FBI and every law enforcement agency would be on the lookout for her.

She squirmed against his body, extremely aware of her bare skin rubbing against his bare skin. He was completely naked and she was practically naked herself, except for her bra and panties. "Oh, my!" She tried to scoot away from him, hampered by the close confines of the bag they both occupied. A waft of icy air scraped across her body and she found herself pressing against his skin to re-create the warmth she'd felt a moment before.

"Sorry. You weren't awake for me to ask permission. In these temps, skin to skin is best to bring up body temperature the fastest. Yours was bordering on death."

After straining for a minute to keep from leaning into his chest, she gave up and let her cheek rest against the hard muscles of his smooth chest. "Well, then, I guess I should thank you for saving my life."

He chuckled. "Please, don't strain yourself with your gratitude."

With nowhere else to put her hands, she rested them against his chest, her fingers smoothing over the hard planes, liking his laughter and the contours of his muscles way too much. "Point made. I am grateful you did not leave me out there to die." She settled into the warmth of his arms, awkward about their nakedness, but too cold to climb out of the bag.

"You're welcome." He rested his chin on the top of her hair, a position both comforting and intimate. "Nothing like waking up in the dark with a stranger, huh?"

"Precisely."

"What were you doing out by the river on foot?"

She swallowed, hating that she had to lie to the man who'd saved her from freezing to death, but she had no other choice. "I was out snowmobiling and my snowmobile broke down."

The man stiffened. "What about the others in your party? Most tours stick together."

"I got separated. I drove around for a couple hours… trying to find them. That is when my machine quit on me." Her words came out in a rush as the lie grew bigger. What if he didn't believe her? What if he was the man who'd been after her and he was just fishing for more information? She couldn't let on that she was Katya Ivanov, just in case he really didn't know. Surely the entire United States had been alerted to a possible terrorist at large.

"I didn't see a snowmobile." His voice had hardened, as though he didn't really believe or trust her.

"I followed the river to see if I could find help. I suppose the snowmobile is a mile or so downstream from where you found me." She had hoped to hide it among the boulders, but had to abandon the heavy machine where it had come to a grinding and permanent halt, in order to save herself from a shooter's aim.

"The closest town to us is Medora and I don't recall anyone there offering snowmobile tours."

"It was a special tour out of..." she grasped for the name of a larger town in North Dakota. "Bismarck!" she said in a rush. How much bigger could the lie grow? And would she be able to remember all the details?

"Still, most tours wouldn't leave a rider behind."

"I am sure the weather cut them short on searching for me. I will bet they notified the authorities as soon as they got back. Assuming they did not get stranded too." Kat couldn't look into his eyes. Lying didn't come naturally to her, one reason she could never be a good politician. The question was: Did this man believe any of the lies she had just dished out?

"So really, who are you?" he asked, answering her question. "Kat Evans isn't right. You speak English too proper to have been born in America, and I detect an accent."

She stiffened against him. Like it or not, she couldn't tell him the truth. Not until she unraveled the mess her life had become. "I am from...Russia. And as long as we're stuck in this bag, can we leave it at Kat Evans?"

"Why? Are you wanted for murder or peddling drugs to children?"

"No. Nothing like that. I would just rather not talk about it."

"Running from an abusive husband? In which case, I'd offer a separate sleeping bag, but I don't have one."

"No. No husband." She stared across the cave's interior, wishing he would stop asking. "Is that a horse over there?"

"Consider him our chaperone. Bear is very good at keeping secrets. The stories he could tell, but won't, would shock you."

Katya laughed, although a little breathlessly. "I feel much safer, knowing he is here guarding my virtue." And he gave her a good diversion from the stranger's questions and naked body.

"Damn right." The man nodded toward Bear. "Don't tell her about the mare you stole from that stallion, boy. She wouldn't understand."

"I get it. You are trying to make me relax."

"You're brilliant as well as beautiful." His hand brushed against her hip. "Is it working?"

Katya's breath caught in her throat. The way his work-roughened fingers slid across her tender skin, aroused new sensations, making her body more alert, more sensitized to his nearness. "Somewhat," she lied, again. "I have never lain naked with a stranger before."

"That makes two of us. I usually get to know the women I sleep with *before* we climb into a sleeping bag together." His voice lost all hint of humor. "Short of freezing to death in a blizzard, we didn't have much choice."

A shiver wracked her body and she pressed closer to him, absorbing his warmth, her skin tingling everywhere it touched his. "Good choice." She inhaled the earthy scent of leather and male, noting the smoothness of his chest, not a hair on it. His nearness sparked a charge of electric current in her that made her want to explore more of his incredibly sexy body.

When was the last time she'd felt this drawn to a man? Never. The closest she had come was when she had been in lust with a politician's son back when she was nineteen. A time when all was right with her world and her country.

With her future a black hole of uncertainty and danger, how could she be this attracted to a stranger?

In the rock-solid confines of the cave, with the warm glow of a flashlight chasing away the severe darkness, Katya felt safe for the first time since she'd been on the run. Safe enough to think of something or someone other than simple survival.

With her body heating rapidly, Katya fought for something to break the tension and silence. "Is the weather still bad outside?"

"Listen…" He held his breath and cocked his head to one side. "*Wankatanka,* the Great Spirit, is angry."

Katya listened, concentrating on the silence. At first she heard nothing, then a thin, lonely wail whistled through the cavern, carried on a blast of frigid air that had found its way into their cocoon. Katya tugged at the edges of the bag, pulling it tighter around her shoulders, her face pressing close to the man's chest. "I suppose it's still bad out there." She snuggled closer, the lonely sound of the wind emphasizing the chill still present in her body. His warmth enveloped her and made her feel safe and nervous at the same time. "You still haven't told me your name."

"Maddox." His hand spread across her hip, his arm tightening, drawing her closer to his heat. "Maddox Thunder Horse. You're trespassing on the Thunder Horse Ranch."

"Maddox." She tipped her head up to stare into eyes as black as the cave when it had been the darkest. "Pleasure to meet you. Please accept my sincere apologies for the trespass." Her lips curled upward on the corners. "Thunder Horse is a different kind of last name."

"I'm a member of the Lakota Nation. My father's people were known for their strong horses."

"You are a Native American? Is the ranch on a reservation?"

"No, my father's father purchased the ranch from a retiring rancher fifty years ago. Since then, the Thunder Horses have added to the acreage."

As he spoke, his hand smoothed back and forth over her hip, climbing up to her waist and back to her hip, cupping her bottom.

The more he touched her, the hotter she got, her breath coming in short gasps as if she could not quite catch it. With nothing but her bra and panties between her and the large man holding her in his arms, all manner of wicked thoughts filled Katya's head. Her father would be appalled. "Do you have to do that?"

"What?"

"What you are doing with your hand?"

He jerked his hand away. "I was warming the cold skin. But if you're warm already, I can stop."

Immediately, Katya regretted saying anything. The heat his hand generated warmed her in many more ways than she could have imagined. "No, it felt nice. And I am very cold." And alone.

She could hear the echoes of her father preaching to her. Someone of her breeding should never find herself alone and naked with a man not her husband.

Sadness gripped her anew. The father who had driven her crazy with his archaic ideas of decorum could no longer dictate her life. Nor could he hold her in his arms and tell her everything would be all right. Boris Ivanov had been murdered two weeks ago, his limousine ambushed by a lone shooter taking him out in a single shot. The news reported his death as an automobile crash. Katya's inside sources told her otherwise.

A tear slid from the corner of her eye and dropped to the smooth skin of Maddox's chest.

He looked down at her, a frown drawing black brows together. His arm settled around her, his hand resting on her hip, his feet touching hers in the bottom of the bag. "What's wrong? Are you in any pain?"

He rubbed his foot along her calf, the warmth helping dispel the chill of her father's death. She shook her head. "No."

"I checked you over for frostbite. You looked okay a few hours ago."

She sniffed, disturbed in a very visceral, but not unpleasant way at the thought of Maddox inspecting her body while she lay semi-comatose. As his foot stroked her calf, she stilled her father's voice in her head, urging her to draw away. She liked the feel of his feet on her legs and especially his hand on her hip. A little too much for having just met the man. "I'm fine. Really."

"Then why the tears?"

"No reason." She sniffed again. "It's just…" sniff, "my father was mur—died." Katya sucked in a shaky breath and blew it out, attempting to pull away from the man's chest to keep from letting more tears drop onto his naked skin. Hadn't her father taught her better? Never let the public see you express untidy emotion. He had classified tears as unnecessarily messy. "I'm sorry. Ivan—" She bit down hard on her bottom lip and started again, struggling at lying to this man. "Evanses do not cry."

Maddox pulled her back in the crook of his arm. "I'm sorry about your father. I lost mine not too long ago."

Katya settled her cheek against his chest again and tilted her head up to study his face.

"I wish I could have said goodbye."

"Me, too."

High cheekbones, a rock-hard chin, dark skin and longish black hair gave away his heritage. The man could easily step into the past, hunting buffalo and living off the land. Again, his earthiness reassured her in the confines of the cave. He appeared to be in his element, completely capable of surviving in the harsh environment. Unlike her.

Having been raised surrounded by bodyguards, servants and political dignitaries, she had always relied on her social skills to survive. In the Badlands of North Dakota, social skills were less in demand and more of a hindrance. If she wanted to survive, she had better do as Maddox Thunder Horse said.

"How much longer do you think the storm will last?" she asked.

"Weather in the Badlands has a life of its own." He tucked the corners of the bag around them more securely. "Rest. At least, it'll pass time."

Although tired, Katya didn't feel even slightly sleepy. "I guess you are correct. Nothing else to do." Except feel his lovely body against hers. She never would have thought lying with a man could feel so good. With her nerves on edge, she could be awake for a very long time. Awake and aware.

He reached out of the bag toward the flashlight.

Her attention riveted on the light, Katya gulped. "What are you doing?"

"Conserving the batteries." He flipped the switch, plunging them into the inky blackness of complete and utter darkness. Katya's sense of sight consisted of the residual glow of the flashlight, fading as darkness settled around her.

Her body shook, her teeth chattering. Her fingers dug into his skin, the sensation of falling into an abyss making her hold on for dear life.

Maddox eased her fingernails out of his hide and laced his fingers with hers. "Don't tell me…" She could feel his head shaking back and forth over her head. "You're afraid of the dark."

"Sorry. It is a curse, something that has plagued me since I was very small."

"I can turn the light back on, but the batteries will eventually fade, and we might have trouble finding our way back out of the cave."

"Do not concern yourself about me. I will be fine." Trying to keep her teeth from chattering, Katya aimed for nonchalance, failing miserably.

Maddox's other arm tightened around her and he pulled her snugly against him. "Close your eyes and listen."

"What?"

"Just do as I say."

Katya squeezed her eyes shut, blocking out the cave's endless darkness. Now it was just her own darkness she had to overcome.

"Let me tell you a story my grandfather, James Thunder Horse, used to tell us as children." Maddox's voice hummed off the rocks, creating a warmth of spirit no heater or fire could generate. He spoke of a bear lost in the hills, trying to find his way home. Of a sly fox who led the bear farther away from home and a wise old wolf whose ferocity and courage helped the bear discover those virtues in himself. Ultimately, the bear found his way home, depending on the generosity of the wolf, and the assistance of the stars and the sun.

Katya's eyes remained closed throughout the story. Instead of relaxing, her body stiffened with increasing desire, each muscle and nerve intensely aware of Maddox, responding to the rhythm of his voice, the vibrations of his chest in a way she could not have imagined in the palace back home. "You have a gift." A gift possessed by no man she had ever met.

"It helps when you're lying naked with a stranger."

Katya could feel the strength in his body, the tautness of his muscles beneath her fingertips. She had never been this intimate with a man. Confined as they were in a cave, miles from everyone. Alone.

Even when she had explored sex with a classmate in the small school she had attended, she had not felt this close, as though their bodies melded into one.

Her hand slid across the hard planes of his chest, memorizing the texture and shape with her mind, imagining what it would feel like to love a man like this. To let him make love to her.

The heat in the sleeping bag intensified and her hand slipped lower. Would he be as hard all over? Her hand followed the ridges of his abdomen, sliding over the indentation of his belly button.

When her fingertips bumped into the steely velvet of his erection, a big hand caught her wrist, holding it in a vise grip.

"Don't start something you can't or won't finish," he said, his voice strained.

"I have never been with a man in a sleeping bag."

"Then maybe now's not the time to start."

"I must apologize. I cannot seem to help myself. You do something to me."

"You don't know me, and I don't know who you really are."

"What do you want to know? I am a woman. I am unmarried. I do not have any diseases and I am twenty-seven, old enough to make my own decisions." Perhaps she said the words to appease his conscience, but more likely the words came out to quiet her father's voice in her head. Either way, the words were for her more than him, and she recognized them for what they were. Permission to let go.

"Sex between a man and a woman takes two to decide."

He was right. Playing with Maddox Thunder Horse could be like playing with fire. But she wanted the heat he could provide, both outside and in.

Since her mother's death when she was only sixteen, she had been the perfect daughter to her father, playing hostess to foreign diplomats, always doing and saying the right things, never stepping outside the bounds of etiquette. "For once in my life I want to make a decision for myself. For me alone. Not for my father. Not for the people around me." She twisted her fingers around to lace them with his. "I know what I want." Then another thought sobered her. "Do you not find me attractive?"

He sucked in a breath and guided her hand to that part of him standing at stiff attention. "You tell me." His grip tightened on her. "If this is a tease, forget it."

Her hand closed around him. "I am stuck in a cave with a man I find very attractive and who obviously finds me not completely hideous. It is quite dark. We are cold and I am not teasing." She stroked her hand down his length, loving the contrast of velvet and steel. "Make love to me."

For a long moment Maddox hesitated. "This has to be wrong." His hand closed over hers, tightening her grip around him. Then he let go to slide upward to cup a full, rounded breast.

Katya's back arched, pressing her breast into his hand, hungry for his touch, for the feel of his lips against her skin.

Trailing his fingers over her breast to cup her chin, he drew her to him, bringing their lips within a hair's width of each other.

The warmth of his breath brushed across her lips and her mouth parted, a sharp draw of longing tugging at her core.

"I might regret this later, but for now..." His lips captured hers, grinding against her teeth, the force of his claim branding her with a desire so intense it stole her breath away. He moved against her, his sex rigid, pressing into her belly.

She shimmied out of her panties, while he unhooked the clasp on her bra. When she lay as naked as Maddox, Katya's legs fell open, letting him slide between her thighs. He eased her onto her back, settling down over her. Then he thrust into her long and hard, filling her, stretching her deliciously.

Their bodies melded into one, the heat they generated making their skin slick with sweat.

And she wanted more.

She raised her knees, her hands gripping his buttocks, driving him faster, harder, and deeper into her, until she lost all sense of time and place. They came together as two separate people, but now they were as one in body and spirit, riding a wave of sensation so intense Katya almost forgot how to breathe. As she plunged over the edge of reason, she let go of her worries, and clung to the present and his body.

Eventually, sleep claimed her, wrapping her in warmth and security. She was assured of her safety, if only as long as she remained in his arms.

Minutes, hours, days could have passed before she returned to earth, the floor hard against her back, an icy draft cooling her damp skin.

In a half-sleep state, she listened for sounds of the storm outside. Silence filled the dark interior. No wailing screamed in through the cave's rocky entrance.

With consciousness, reason and memories returned. A few hours ago she had woken up with a stranger, sharing his body's warmth, both of them practically naked.

Katya moved, her knee sliding down Maddox's leg, her bare thigh rubbing against his leg. She sucked in a gasp and her naked breasts pressed into his equally naked chest.

She had responsibilities. Her country needed her. Her people expected so much of her. And she'd just thrown it all to the wind to make love to a stranger.

What had she done? Would he understand when she had to leave? For leave she must, just as soon as she could contact her government for help. Katya chewed on her lip, her brow furrowing. Having ditched her car, and lost her identification and credit cards back on the snowmobile somewhere along the river, getting help would definitely be a challenge.

Chapter Three

Maddox lay beside the woman, guilt gnawing at him. He'd made love to a stranger not quite two years since the death of his fiancée. Susan, who'd grown up in the Badlands, who knew the dangers of living on the prairie, who loved the land and wild horses as much as he did. His perfect match in every way. And in every way so different from the woman lying in his arms.

Susan's sun-kissed tawny hair reminded him of wheat and late-summer prairie grasses, wispy and straight, always blowing in the wind. Her eyes as gray as a storm-filled sky. Her long, lanky body strong and adept at riding the range alongside him.

Kat was nothing like Susan. Her hair lay in a mass of long, loose, black curls, emphasizing her pale skin and eyes as light as his were dark. Her diminutive body, though small, had curves that fit perfectly in his palm, a fact that brought on yet more twinges of guilt. How could he compare them? Susan had been his life, his soul mate, the woman he'd planned to spend the rest of his life with. Only her life had ended and he'd resigned himself to continuing on alone.

Yet this dark-haired beauty, with hands so soft they couldn't have worked a hard day's labor her entire life, lay naked against him. The smell of her skin, the softness of her body, still made him hard as a rock.

Maddox stiffened, his hands dropping to his sides, his fingers burning as though on fire from touching her. He jerked the sleeping bag's zipper down, a frigid blast of arctic air biting at his naked flesh. He reached for the flashlight and switched it on.

Kat blinked, her eyes widening as the cool air hit her skin and pebbled the tips of her breasts. "What's the matter?"

"Nothing." Before he changed his mind and claimed her, Maddox climbed out of the bag, reaching back inside for his clothing lodged at the bottom.

In the freezing interior of the cave, he dressed quickly, fully aware of Kat's gaze watching him, and thankful for the effect of the frigid temps on his libido.

Kat pulled the bag up to her nose, her dark eyes rounded, each breath a puff of steam. "Did I do something to make you mad?" She laughed. "I apologize. I have never been this forward with a man. I'm not usually left alone with one long enough." Her eyes widened and she clamped her lips shut.

Maddox slipped into his insulated trousers, buttoning the fly. "Dress inside the bag. We leave as soon as it's daylight."

"Leave?" She shrank deeper into the bag, a tremor shaking her cocoon.

"Yes, leave." Her big eyes reminded him of a scared colt, and he almost softened. Instead, he turned on his heels and edged through the crevice out into the bitter-cold wind.

The sun hovered below the horizon, giving the landscape a steely, washed-out, gray-blue glow. Clouds clogged the sky in a blanket of charcoal-smeared waves of dirty white, churned by the ever-present wind.

Maddox braced himself before leaving the relative shelter of the tumbled boulders to stare up the hillside at the icy terrain. They'd have to climb the rugged sides of the canyon wall to reach the plateau. From there it was an hour's trek on horseback to the ranch house.

As bitter cold and windy as it was, he preferred to get back to the ranch rather than spending another night in the sleeping bag with Kat Evans—or whoever she really was. The sooner he got back, the sooner he could relinquish his responsibility for the woman.

Maddox unclipped the radio from his jacket and flipped the On switch. "Tuck, you out there?" As he waited for any response, he knew he'd get none. The handheld radios had a short range. More than likely, Tuck had made it back to the ranch and was wondering what had happened to Maddox. He hoped they hadn't sent out a search party. With the skies as heavy as they were, they could be in for another onslaught of the white stuff.

Maddox closed his eyes and drew in a deep breath, the frigid air stinging his lungs. He could taste the coming snow, feel it in his blood, chilling him to the bone. It would arrive soon. Too soon for comfort.

Something touched his arm, jerking him out of his trance and back to the canyon floor. He spun, braced for attack.

Kat stood with her arms crossed, the red scarf wrapped around her nose and mouth and her jacket hood pulled up over her hair. Buried in all those layers, her pale face peeked around the edges of clothing, her eyes as wide as icy-blue saucers. "I am r-ready," she said, her voice muffled by the wool scarf.

"Then we leave." He reentered the cave, making quick work of rolling up the sleeping bag. Flashlight in hand, he led the stallion through the entrance and out into the windy gray of predawn.

Kat waited at the cave entrance, stamping her boots in the snow, rubbing her hands along her arms, her gaze darting from side to side as if she feared venturing out for more reasons than the cold wind. "Are you sure we shouldn't stay here?"

One look at Kat and the memories of the night before hit Maddox like a sucker punch to the groin. "We move." He didn't ask permission or warn her. With little effort, he grabbed her around the waist and swung her up into the saddle.

Kat squealed and held on to the saddle horn as Bear reared and danced to the side.

She sat the horse well, despite his nervous dance, as though she'd ridden before. A woman with soft hands who could ride.

Maddox tucked that little bit of insight away in the back of his mind. He'd get to the bottom of Kat Evans when they were safe from the weather. With gentle hands, he pulled on the reins, running gloved fingers over the horse's nose, speaking to him in Lakota, calming him.

Then he set out at a quick pace, leading the horse along the base of the bluffs, searching for a suitable path to climb out of the canyon.

"Aren't you going to ride with me?" Kat called out, hunkered down as low as she could get in the saddle to escape the full force of the driving wind. Her voice barely carried over the roar of wind bouncing off stony cliffs.

"Not until we're out of the canyon." Finally, a break in the sheer rock wall revealed a narrow path zigzagging up the side of the canyon, probably left by elk or big horn sheep. Maddox climbed the hill, the horse close behind him. Kat clung to the saddle horn as they rose from the riverbed up the treacherous trail.

Several times Maddox's boots slipped on loose rocks, sending a tumble of gravel and stones toward the horse. Bear sidestepped and almost lost his footing. Kat's hand flailed out for balance, her face even more pale and pinched than when they'd started up the incline.

Maddox found that the less he looked at her, the better he felt. Only when he had to did he turn to make sure that she hadn't lost her grip and fallen from the horse.

Kat's fingers and cheekbones burned with the cold. Not long after they left the cave, she started shivering and could not seem to stop. She could not afford to waste all her energy, not when she had to use all her strength just to hang on.

She cast a look over her shoulder to the canyon floor, wondering where the man who had been following her had gone. Had he headed back when the storm struck? Or had he holed up as she had? In which case, he would be out looking for her again.

A shiver shook her so hard her teeth rattled. If not for Maddox, she would have died out there, saving the man following her the trouble of killing her.

Where would that leave her country? Without a ruler, without anyone to lead them into democracy, her people would fall back into chaos and warlords would take over. She needed to find out who was behind her father's death. No matter what the news reports said, that car crash had begun with a bullet. A deliberate attack by a skilled assassin.

Whoever was after her did not plan on holding her hand and escorting her back to her country. He had taken several shots at her before she had lost him. Skimming through streams and across barren rocks had taken their toll on her snowmobile, but had bought her much-needed time to escape in an otherwise snow-covered landscape.

She had taken a huge risk crossing Minnesota and North Dakota in a car. The open farm fields and grasslands left little cover and concealment. But she kept moving just to escape the law and the predator tailing her. Only he had been persistent and tracked her every move. She was tired of running, tired of always looking over her shoulder, completely cut off from everyone who could possibly help.

As they climbed higher, the terrain became increasingly more treacherous and their footing more precarious. The more Kat looked back at the canyon floor, the dizzier she got. The canyon wall inclined at more than a forty-five-degree angle, the path they followed less than six inches wide in most places. How she longed to be on foot, rather than perched high on a horse's back, even that much farther from the ground.

Nausea fought with vertigo, making her head spin. Kat squeezed her eyes shut and clung to the saddle horn. Because the stirrups were so long, her feet did not quite reach the footrests, giving her no way to balance her weight on the big animal. With her hands quickly freezing and the possibility of a frightening fall making her hold tighter, she thought the ride to the canyon's rim would never end.

With one mighty lunge, the horse nearly unseated her, clearing the edge of the canyon and arriving on the plateau above.

Kat opened her eyes, the wind whipping her scarf across her face. For as far as she could see, semi-barren rolling hills stretched before her.

Behind her, the canyon cut a long, jagged swath out of the prairie walls blown free of snow, glowing a ruddy red in the increasing light from the muted sun. Every breath of the wickedly cold air stung her lungs and bored through her thick clothing. Chills shuddered across her body and she huddled lower in the saddle, praying for the journey to end, preferably in a hot tub. She groaned. How she would love to sink neck deep into a warm bath and stay there until her skin shriveled.

All the while she had been perched atop the giant stallion, Maddox had been climbing the hill. He had to be tired by now. Was he as cold as she was? Did he wish to be done with this trek—and her?

Several hundred feet from the rim of the canyon, Maddox stopped to catch his breath and speak to the horse in a language Katya did not understand. She assumed he spoke the language of the Lakota Nation.

In the light, she could finally see him. Dark skin, black eyes and straight, thick black hair falling to his shoulders. He tugged his fur-lined parka up around his face and turned to face her.

With the ease of one born to ride, he placed one foot into the stirrup and swung up onto the horse's back, landing behind the saddle.

His arm wrapped around her waist and he lifted her,

easing himself into the seat beneath her, settling her onto his thighs.

Immediately she could feel his warmth through her clothing. Just blocking the wind on one side made a difference. She sank back against him, glad for his presence and the balance he provided on the moving beast.

He did not say anything and with the wind so strong it could steal her breath away, Kat did not speak either.

For several miles, they rode in silence, curled into each other.

The gentle rocking motion of the horse, plus the constant cold, lulled Kat into a dull, half-sleep state. Snow turned to sleet, the tiny hard pellets slung sideways by the approaching storm.

"Don't go to sleep, Kat Evans," a voice said over the roar of the wind.

"Why?" she leaned against him, her eyelids dropping over snow-stung eyes. "I am exceedingly tired."

"If you fall asleep, who will I talk to?"

She snorted softly. "You were not talking." She turned her face into his jacket. "I am so cold."

"We'll be there in less than half an hour."

"I need to sleep."

"Talk to me, Kat," he said, his chest rumbling against her back.

"About what?" she muttered, her eyes closed. She had to keep her secrets, but she didn't have to stay awake, did she?

"How did you get into the canyon? We're miles from the closest highway or public lands."

In her sleepy haze she could not think straight. How much could she reveal? Did she care? She gave a half-hearted attempt at laughter and opted for mostly truth. "I did not see the canyon. I drove my snowmobile over the edge. It did not stop until it reached the bottom beside the riverbed."

Funny how leaning against Maddox, with the soft swaying of the horse beneath her, lulled her into thinking the horrible tumble down the bluff was nothing but a bad dream. Except for a few bruises, she had survived, only to fall victim to the extreme cold and mind-numbing lethargy.

Other than her hands and feet, she was fairly warm in Maddox's capable arms. They did not build men this rugged where she was from. Her brows furrowed. Or she had never met any men who had been built this sturdy. Her father had kept her surrounded by bodyguards and state officials everywhere she went in Trejikistan.

Maddox shifted her weight, pulling her closer against him. "Why were you snowmobiling out this far? Why not closer to Bismarck?"

"Cars cannot follow." She yawned and settled back against him, her eyelids closing for the final count. "Unfortunately other snowmobiles can."

"Isn't that the idea with a snowmobile tour?" Maddox's words were carried away on the wind as Katya slipped into a numbing sleep.

Maddox stopped the horse periodically to tuck Katya's hands into his jacket and adjust her position to keep her from getting too cold in any one place. As he rode Bear through the storm, he went over Kat's words again and again. They didn't make any sense. Had she been out on a snowmobile tour and gotten lost? And what did she mean that cars couldn't follow but snowmobiles could? Had she been running away from something? Was someone following her?

Maddox vowed to get to the bottom of it all when they finally made it back to the ranch. The one-hour ride from the canyon rim stretched into two as the storm settled in around them.

Sleet turned to snow, blowing in sideways, making it difficult for him to see more than two feet ahead of them. At one point, he took shelter in a ravine, the wind and sleet too harsh to be out on the open plains.

Too cold to remain exposed much longer, he ventured out again, hoping Bear knew the way. Maddox couldn't make out any landmarks and the storm only grew worse, nearing blizzard conditions.

Maddox hoped the horse's sense of direction led them back to the safety of the barn and ranch house and not farther away.

When he'd just about given up hope of getting there, the ranch house materialized through the whiteout conditions.

A dog barked, and a light blinked on next to the front door.

Through the driving snow, his brother and a ranch hand raced out into the blizzard toward the horse and the two people sagging in the saddle.

"Take the woman." Maddox handed Katya down into waiting arms. He didn't like others carrying her away, but the cold had taken more out of him than he originally thought.

He nudged the horse toward the barn. When they reached the barn door, he slipped from the saddle, his legs buckling. If not for the horse standing beside him, Maddox would have gone down in the snow.

Three Thunder Horse ranch hands emerged from the barn. One took the horse's reins and the other two rushed to grab Maddox's arms, draping them over their shoulders. His horse taken care of, Maddox let the men walk him up to the house. Once inside, he settled in a chair near the hearth where a fire blazed with enough warmth to thaw even the coldest parts of his body.

His mother, Amelia Thunder Horse, crouched on the floor in front of him and tugged his boots off his feet and the socks with it. "Thank the Lord you made it back. We were so worried. Who is the woman you brought with you? Where did you find her?"

Too tired to answer her, Maddox stood. "I'll answer all your questions later. Where is she?"

"In the guest bedroom."

Maddox stumbled down the hallway, shedding his jacket. When he reached the guestroom, Mrs. Janek, the housekeeper had just finished tucking Kat into the bed, the blankets drawn up to her chin. The older woman clucked her tongue. "She's out. I hope she'll be all right. Do you want me to call the doctor?"

"No, I'll see to her." Maddox stood next to the bed, staring down at the woman who'd called herself Kat. In his gut, he knew she hadn't told him the entire truth. Despite that, he couldn't help the overwhelming need to protect her that came over him.

Tired beyond endurance, he pulled the covers aside and lay in the bed beside her, gathering her into his arms as he'd done in the cave.

"Maddox?" His mother hovered in the door of the guestroom. "Is she okay?" She twisted her fingers together, her brows dipped in a worried frown. "Are you okay?

His eyelids weighed so heavily, he closed them. "I don't know, Mother. Somehow, I don't think I'll ever be okay."

Chapter Four

Lights glittered in the myriad chandeliers hanging from the vast ceiling. Too bright, all merging and blending together as she spun around the room, dancing from partner to partner. In a deep red ball gown, her hair piled high on her head and the world at her feet, Katya smiled, laughed and drank champagne from crystal goblets.

At one point her father danced her around the room. She was a little girl all over again, smiling up at him, proud of the man who ruled Trejikistan and made her feel loved and protected. So relieved to see him healthy and happy, she leaned against him and hugged him tight. "They told me you were dead."

He just laughed and spun her into the arms of her brother, Dmitri, so tall and handsome, his wavy black hair so much like her own. His hands held her, gently guiding her through the steps of the intricate traditional dance of her ancestors. Hands of a doctor, a man meant to do good for the people, with a heart so big he could love every child in their country.

Katya smiled and laughed at him. "Where have you been, Dmitri? We have all been so worried."

Before he could answer, the music ended. Dmitri

tweaked her nose, just as he had since she'd been a small child, and disappeared into the crowd.

Standing alone in the crowd of guests, Katya looked around for her father and brother, suddenly sad, lonely and afraid. The orchestra played a waltz, the music so beautiful it melted Katya's fears and sadness away. As she glanced around the ballroom, the sea of blurred faces parted and one man stood at the center. Unlike the other guests, this man didn't wear a tuxedo or the uniform of a military man. He wore buckskins and moccasins, his long black hair hanging down around his shoulders, a wild gleam in his brown-black eyes.

As if drawn to him by a magical thread, Katya floated across the room toward him, the other guests fading away in a haze of gray. She could see his face so clearly, every line, angle and shadow etched in her memory. When the tall, swarthy Lakota native took her in his arms, he moved with the grace of a lion. At ease in his traditional dress, he waltzed her around the room, ignoring the whispers and comments made by statesmen and their wives, oblivious to the pomp and circumstance strictly adhered to in formal settings.

For once, Katya did not care that she might not fit in, that the man she danced with would draw censure from the exalted guests. Princes, princesses and leaders of foreign countries did not matter to her as long as she remained in the Lakota native's arms. The world didn't exist, except for the two of them.

As the music faded to a halt, the world crowded in. Her father gripped her arm and pulled her away from the Lakota.

"No!" she cried out. "I want to stay with him."

But her father's grip tightened and he led her out

of the palace and into a waiting limousine where her brother sat, shaking his head.

"No! Let me stay. I want to dance," Katya called out.

The limousine sped into the darkness, the lights from the palace fading with each passing mile. Katya looked back, her tears blurring her vision.

When she slumped into her seat beside her father and brother, she could not stop sobbing. "Why?"

Suddenly, the vehicle lurched, rammed by another car speeding along the highway. The limousine spun around and around, the motion flinging Katya around the inside. Out of control, it pitched over the edge of the road and tumbled into a ditch.

The door nearest her flew open and Katya fell into the ditch, facedown, her beautiful gown ruined in the mud.

She lay for a moment, wondering if she had died. But the sticks poking into her hands and face made her open her eyes and look around.

The limousine lay on its side, riddled with bullet holes.

"No!"

MADDOX HAD AWAKENED WHEN Kat first kicked out in her sleep. He stared down at the woman who'd managed to end up in his arms yet again.

Her brows dipped together and a tear slipped down her cheek, even as she slept.

What was he doing? What happened to the plan of dumping her on someone else as soon as they reached the ranch house? She wasn't his problem and he didn't want to be responsible for her.

Deep in a terrible nightmare, she cried out.

And despite his determination not to care, his heart went out to her. She must have gone through a lot, getting lost from her tour and falling into a canyon—not that he completely believed that story. If he hadn't come along when he had…it didn't bear thinking about. He couldn't erase the image of her lying in the snow, her face so pale. He could forgive her lies, but he couldn't forgive himself if she'd died. "Kat, wake up."

"Dmitri, don't go!" she mumbled. "I need you."

His chest tightening, Maddox shook the woman. "Wake up." Who was Dmitri? Kat had told him that she was single. He didn't make love to married women. Or even those promised to another man. Too much about Kat Evans remained a mystery, and Maddox didn't like it when he couldn't get to the bottom of things. An unexpected surge of anger powered through him. "Kat!"

Her eyelids fluttered, then opened. "What? Who?" Her gaze shifted around the room and returned to his. "We are not in the cave." She closed her eyes again and leaned her face against his chest.

A knock on the door drew his attention away from the black-haired beauty lying so naturally in the crook of his arm.

Maddox's mother pushed open the door, balancing a tray in her arms. Amelia Thunder Horse smiled. "You two missed dinner, so I brought it to you. And we have company."

Maddox frowned. "In this weather?"

His mother's smile widened. "You've been asleep for several hours." She set the tray on a table and scooted it close to the bed. "It stopped snowing, and the wind is dying down." Amelia planted fists on her hips and stared directly at Maddox and Kat. "Are you two going to sleep the rest of the night away, or are you going to eat some of this food I slaved over?"

Kat sat up, her eyes wide, her face flushing a rosy red. "I beg your pardon." She slipped out of the bed and stood in the rumpled shirt and jeans she'd arrived at the house in. "Is there someplace I could wash up?" She shoved her mass of black hair away from her face. "I must be a fright."

"Of course." She led Kat to the bathroom. "In here. I'll bring a change of clothes in a minute."

Maddox's stomach rumbled as he sat on the edge of the bed and reached for a fork, painfully aware that he'd gone an entire day without eating. "Who's the company?"

His mother picked up Maddox's discarded shirt, refusing to meet his gaze. "Sheriff Yost."

Without taking the bite of food, Maddox slammed his fork down on the tray, rattling the plates and glasses. "What the hell's he doing here?"

Amelia Thunder Horse shrugged. "Checking on us after last night's storm."

"And is he checking on every other rancher in the county as well?"

"I didn't ask him." She faced Maddox. "He'd like to talk to you and your visitor."

Maddox's eyes narrowed. "What does he know?"

She shook her head. "No more than any of us."

"How does he know she's even here?"

"Tuck mentioned it. The sheriff probably just wants to notify her family that she's all right."

Kat stepped through the door of the bathroom, her

fingers attempting to comb her hair into place. "Whose family?"

"Yours, dear." Amelia smiled and crossed the room. "I'll get a brush and those clothes I promised. You have a lovely accent."

"Mother—" Maddox stood, intending to tell his mother just what he thought of Sheriff Yost, but she cut him off with a stern look.

"Maddox Thunder Horse, you'll speak with the sheriff and you'll be nice." She shot a wry smile at Kat and left the room.

Kat stared across at Maddox, her eyes wide, worried. "I don't have a family for him to notify."

"So you say."

"You don't believe me," she said, her words flat. "Are you going to turn me over to the sheriff?"

"Have you committed a crime?"

"Well…" Her frown deepened.

"Why do I have a feeling that this situation is going to get even more complicated?"

"Because it will." She gave him a weak smile. "I do not have any of my documents on me. I am a foreign national, and I lost my visa and all my identification papers back on the snowmobile in the canyon."

"Convenient."

"I have copies stored in a safe place, if I can just get to them."

"Or you could contact your embassy and have them forward them to you."

She nodded, not really answering or committing to his suggestion. What was it she held back? What was she not telling him?

"Look, whatever trouble you're in, you might as well tell me now. I don't like being blindsided."

"You would not understand," she said, her back stiffening. "You might as well turn me over to the sheriff now. I'll go quietly." She faced off with him, daring him to do just what she suggested.

For a moment, he considered it, certain that if he turned her over to the sheriff he'd be rid of her. But after that night in the cave, he couldn't. Maddox drew in a deep breath and let it out in a long slow sigh. "I'm not going to turn you over to the sheriff. At least not this one, and not now." He stepped close to her. "However, be warned. I don't like it when people take advantage of me or my family. And I especially don't like it when someone places my family in danger of any kind." He tipped her chin up and stared down into light blue eyes so shiny he could see himself reflected in their depths. "Do you understand?"

She nodded, her bottom lip trembling.

Maddox groaned and kissed her, his mouth crashing down over hers, drawing her into his world and wrapping her in his protection. With her wide, blue eyes, pale skin and diminutive stature, she looked as fragile as a porcelain doll, but her strength and determination to survive shone through.

As quickly as he initiated the kiss, he broke it off, dragging himself several steps away from her. To be that close only rekindled the heat and desire he had no control over. "Join me when you're ready."

As Maddox left the bedroom, his mother met him in the hallway, her hands full of clothing and a hairbrush. "I'll send her along when she's had a chance to change."

A last glance back into the bedroom made Maddox's jaw tighten.

Kat stood with her hands clasped together, the dark circles beneath her eyes making her appear waiflike, vulnerable.

Her presence made him hot, cold, protective and tense all at once. If he had any sense whatsoever, he'd hand her over to the sheriff and save himself and his family the grief she was bound to cause. He turned away, wishing he could wash the image of her staring after him from his mind. Angry that he couldn't, Maddox grabbed a sweatshirt from his own bedroom, tugged it over his head and marched into the living room.

His brother Tuck stood in front of the floor-to-ceiling windows, his back to the view of the snowy-white North Dakota hills. The brightness of the snow behind him cast his brother's face into shadows, consuming his expression and making it completely unreadable.

Maddox almost smiled. Knowing Tuck, he'd done it on purpose to unsettle the sheriff neither of them cared for.

The tall, barrel-chested man standing in the middle of the room turned to greet Maddox, his hand held out. "Maddox."

Maddox hesitated, then took the sheriff's grip. "Sheriff."

The sheriff nodded. "Your brother tells me you rescued a woman out in the canyon."

Maddox nodded. "That's correct." He didn't volunteer any more information than was necessary.

"What was she doing out there?"

"Snowmobiling."

"Damn city people." The sheriff shook his head.

"They've got no sense when it comes to the winters here."

Maddox didn't respond, just stared at the sheriff, willing him to leave.

The sheriff's eyes narrowed as if sizing up Maddox's mood. "Mind if I meet her, see for myself?"

Maddox crossed his arms over his chest. "Why?"

Yost's brows rose. "To see if she's really alive. Come on, a strange woman found in the canyon in a snowstorm isn't an everyday occurrence."

"Any reason to believe she might be dead?" Maddox shot back at him.

The sheriff's eyes narrowed again. "No, none at all. We just get so many missing persons reports over the wire that I like to follow up on them if I get the chance. Has she notified her family of her whereabouts? I'm sure they must be worried by now."

"We'll take care of it," Maddox replied.

Tuck left the shadows and joined Maddox in the middle of the room, facing the sheriff. "Anything else keeping you from performing your civic duties?"

"I'm just paying a friendly visit." His frown deepening, the sheriff glanced down the hallway where Amelia had gone. "If you don't mind, I'll wait and talk to the woman."

Maddox strode to the window and stared out at the stark landscape. Even before the chill of the air closest to the window penetrated his sweatshirt, goose bumps had risen on Maddox's arms. "Why did you come here?"

"I came to see if you and your family—"

"You mean our *mother*," Maddox interrupted.

The sheriff's lips tightened. "—to see if you and your family weathered the storm."

"We're fine. Mother's fine." Tuck took another step closer to the sheriff. "Go find some other family to check on."

Rather than leave, the sheriff sat in John Thunder Horse's favorite chair as if he owned it. "It would be rude of me to leave when *Amelia* asked me to stay."

Maddox wanted to tell him to stay away from his mother, even though he'd been the one insisting that she get out and date again. Date, yes, but not this sheriff, a man his father never trusted.

Sheriff Yost was an arrogant ass and he'd done nothing to find their father's murderer. Getting into a fight with the man would prove nothing and land Maddox in jail.

What good would that do? Where would that leave Kat? Not that she'd be his problem for much longer. As soon as she contacted…whoever, she'd be out of there. "Five minutes with the girl and you leave."

Chapter Five

"I always dreamed of having a girl, but it seemed Mr. Thunder Horse was set on giving me an entire tribe of strapping boys." Amelia bustled about the room, her presence a welcome distraction.

Katya was happy for her company, especially since it meant delaying the inevitable meeting with the sheriff. And the more Maddox's mother talked, the less nervous Katya was.

"I worried all night about Maddox, stuck out there in the cold. I should have known better. He's just like his father—tenacious, industrious and a survivor." She came to stop behind Katya. "Well, almost," she said, her voice catching.

Katya turned in the chair and captured Amelia Thunder Horse's hands in her own, the ache of her own loss still burning in her chest. "What happened to your husband, Mrs. Thunder Horse?"

With a half smile and her eyes suspiciously bright, Amelia recalled the accident that took her husband's life. "He fell off his damned horse." She laughed, the sound more of a sob.

"I'm sorry." A tear slipped from the corner of her eye and Katya squeezed Amelia's hands. "I lost my father recently." She stared up at the older woman. "Does the ache ever go away?"

Maddox's mother smoothed a hand over Katya's temple, tucking a long strand of hair behind her ear. "No. But it does start to subside." Amelia's blue eyes swam with tears of her own.

"I hope it does soon."

"It can take years. It's taken Maddox the past two years to get over the death of his fiancée."

A gasp escaped Katya's lips before she could stop it.

"I don't suppose he told you." The older woman stared at her reflection in the mirror. "They were so much alike, both used to the outdoors, both passionate about the wild horses in the canyon, both born and raised in this desolate part of the country. Such a shame."

Katya looked down at her hands in her lap. How did she compete with someone like that? Not that she was competing. The woman was dead, and Katya wasn't staying around to start anything with the handsome Lakota man who'd saved her life. Her main goal was to stay under the radar of the law and live to find out who'd set her up and who was responsible for her father's murder. Most of the pictures circulating in the media were ones where her hair hung down around her face. Usually an asset, her glossy black locks were a dead giveaway if anyone was looking for her. "I believe I'll pull my hair straight back into a ponytail today."

"But you look so lovely with it down."

"Thank you, but it'll be so much easier to manage up."

"I'll be back in a moment with a rubber band." She left the bedroom.

In seconds, she returned and Katya pulled her hair back into a severe knot.

"Only you could get away with this harsh a hairstyle, my dear."

"How so?"

Amelia tucked a stray hair into the knot. "You have the bearing of royalty."

Her heart skipping a beat, Katya forced a laugh. "My brother would laugh. He thinks I am too much of a hoyden."

"Your brother is so wrong. You're a beautiful young lady. I can see why Maddox is so taken with you."

"Oh, please, Mrs. Thunder Horse. We barely know each other."

"Maybe so, but I know my sons and love them very much. I don't like it when someone tries to hurt any one of them."

Katya's lips twisted. "I understand. I won't be staying long enough for that to happen. Your son has done so much for me already. I'd never hurt him."

"I know you wouldn't—intentionally."

"What do you mean?" Katya thought she'd spent enough time in the United States to understand the nuances of American English. But Amelia's words escaped her comprehension. In the short amount of time she'd known Maddox, she couldn't have had that much of an impact on him, nor he on her. Right?

Last night in the cave, she'd made her own decision and had only one regret—that the night hadn't lasted longer.

"Looks like you're all done." Amelia patted her hair. "I can see why my son saved you."

"He'd have saved me if I'd been a seventy-year-old grandmother."

"You're right. That's Maddox for you, always trying to save the world."

Katya laughed. "I can see that in him."

"His problem is usually that he's so busy saving the world, he doesn't remember to save himself." Amelia laid the brush on the dresser beside the pile of clothing she'd loaned Katya. "Are you feeling okay, dear? Your cheeks are flushed."

The older woman laid a palm across Katya's forehead.

Her face burned hotter at the same time Katya realized how much she missed having a woman care about her. Her own mother had passed away right before Katya's sixteenth birthday. For that brief moment, she closed her eyes and pretended this woman was the mother she missed more than ever. Her eyes burned with unshed tears and a lump rose in her throat. Swallowing hard, she leaned away from Amelia's hand and straightened her shoulders. Wishing didn't make things happen. Both her mother and father weren't coming back. Her brother was missing, her country in turmoil and she was alone in the world. She couldn't bring her family back, but she might be able to help the people of her country. "I'm fine, really."

Amelia stared into her face for a long moment, and sighed. "Come on, then. The men will be wondering what's keeping us."

Katya followed Mrs. Thunder Horse down the hallway to the spacious living room with windows reaching from floor to ceiling and a massive stone hearth blazing with a fire. Despite the warmth of the room, a chill feathered across her skin. Maddox and his brother stood near the window, their backs to the room. A man in a law enforcement uniform sat on the sofa. When he spied Maddox's mother, he rose and extended a hand to her. "Ah, Amelia."

Katya only glanced at the sheriff before her gaze sought out Maddox, the man who had saved her from death and lit a burning fire inside her.

His face could have been made of stone, if not for the muscle twitching in his cheek and the way his fists clenched in tight knots. He didn't even look at her, his gaze pinned on his mother and the man kissing her hand.

"Amelia, my dear," the uniformed man said. "Thank you for seeing me on such short notice."

Amelia blushed and pulled her hand free. "Stop it, William. Please have a seat while I get some hot cocoa. Tuck, why don't you help me?"

Tuck shot a glance at Maddox.

When Maddox didn't look his way, he nudged him in the side.

As if noticing others in the room for the first time, Maddox looked at Katya. "Go on. I can take care of things here," he said to his brother, his voice low.

When Amelia and Tuck left, Katya stood in the middle of the room, alone and completely aware of Maddox's barely leashed anger. She prayed that the sheriff hadn't seen the news or gotten notification to be on the lookout for a suspected terrorist. The only photos the police could have would be those from her apartment, all of which had her hair hanging down, framing her face. Katya hoped that by pulling it back, the sheriff wouldn't recognize her. She fought to keep her nerves steady.

"Five minutes, Yost," Maddox ground out between clenched teeth.

Sheriff Yost raised eyebrows at Maddox and smiled at Katya.

She shivered as if a snail had crawled across her skin, leaving a slimy trail.

"Miss..."

"Evans," Katya finished for him.

"I understand you had a snowmobile accident out in the canyon yesterday."

"That is true."

"Were you with a group?"

"Yes, sir."

"Care to elaborate?"

"It was a tour group out of Bismarck." She prayed she was giving the same answers she'd given Maddox.

"Where is the rest of your group, Miss Evans?"

"I don't know. I lost them." She stared directly at the sheriff, squaring her shoulders. "Is there a reason for all these questions? Am I being arrested or something?"

"No, no." The sheriff held up his hands, smiling, although the smile didn't quite reach his eyes. "I'm just doing my civic duty to protect the good citizens of the county by checking on anything out of the ordinary."

Katya nodded. Fair enough. She just wished this inquisition was over. The longer he was there, the more chance of him recognizing her.

"Three minutes, Yost," Maddox warned.

"Miss Evans, you have an accent." Sheriff Yost crossed the room and walked around her. "Not from around here are you?"

"No." Katya didn't look at the sheriff, her gaze seeking Maddox's, her only rock in this island of uncertainty.

"Foreign?"

"Yes."

"Where from?"

"Russia," she lied. If the police had her passport, they'd know she was from Trejikistan.

"Do you have a visa or passport?"

"Not on me."

"Somewhere you can get to it?"

"If you give me a couple days to send for it." A couple days should allow her enough time to get away from here.

"For a stranger in a foreign country, seems a little odd that you aren't carrying legal documents with you."

"I didn't think I'd need them for a snowmobile ride. I didn't plan on being away for more than a day while I was on the tour." Katya couldn't meet Maddox's gaze as she told one lie after another.

"Is there someone who could forward your documents to you?"

"I hope so."

"So do I. If you can't come up with the necessary proof of legal entry into this country, I'll have to notify Homeland Security."

"I can get you those documents," she insisted, trying to keep her voice calm with no sign of the panic rising like bile in her throat. "I just need time."

The sheriff touched a finger to his chin and tipped his head to the side. "Maybe I should place you in holding until that time comes."

"That won't be necessary." Maddox stepped forward

and slipped an arm around Katya's waist. "She can stay here."

Sheriff Yost's lips pressed into a straight line. "I'll have to check with headquarters. They may want me to secure your little houseguest until she can come up with identification papers."

Katya's heart thundered against her chest. She forced herself to remain composed on the outside. "Completely understandable, Sheriff. If the Thunder Horses are willing to host me until my documents arrive, I would be very happy to stay here." Another lie. Katya fought to keep from choking on the lump rising in her throat.

She had to get word back to Trejikistan and seek out some kind of diplomatic immunity until she could figure out what to do. When she had left Minneapolis, all she had was what she took with her to the church. Her purse, a few credit cards and the remaining U.S. currency she had taken out for incidentals the day before. Her credit cards could be traced, so she cut them in pieces and disposed of them. The little money she had was already gone.

Since she had left the Twin Cities, she had not stopped long enough to call her homeland. She would not know who was left—and who to trust—even when she did.

She could try to get in touch with her cousin, Vladimir Ivanov, on his personal cell phone if he had not also been a target of the takeover. Her personal servants back at the palace were only available through palace telephones and they were not secure. She had to try her cousin when she finally had the chance.

Her passport had been in her apartment, probably confiscated by the police to use as evidence to convict her. She could not stay with the Thunder Horses too long, or the sheriff would begin to get suspicious when her papers failed to arrive. If the sheriff kept up with the news, he might be back sooner with a warrant for her arrest.

No doubt the sheriff would check the databases for anything on Kat Evans. If her pursuer was still trying to track her down—if he didn't think she had died in the snowstorm, he might be listening to police scanners in the area. He might suspect that foreigner, Kat Evans, was really Katya Ivanov and come to check her out for himself.

The sheriff gathered his hat and jacket. His eyes narrowed as he looked across at Katya. "I'll hold Maddox Thunder Horse responsible for your whereabouts until I can review your documents. So don't leave."

"Your five minutes are at an end," Maddox cut in. "And so is my patience."

"Careful, Maddox." Yost glared at Katya's rescuer. "This young lady is a stranger. Who's to say you aren't harboring a criminal?"

Katya gasped, her hand clapping over her lips.

"Get out," Maddox demanded.

"Don't push me."

"Or what? You'll kill me, too?"

"Are you accusing me of something, Thunder Horse?" Yost stood, feet braced, his hands rising dangerously close to his holstered pistol.

Maddox didn't answer, his jaw tight and eyes smoldering.

"Here we are." Amelia sailed into the room, followed by Tuck bearing a large tray filled with steaming mugs.

"Ah, Amelia, how kind." Sheriff Yost smiled and reached for one of the mugs.

Maddox got to it before he did, blocking his path. "The sheriff was just leaving."

"So soon?" His mother pouted, settling the tray on the coffee table.

Yost's smile slipped.

Katya expected him to say something to contradict Maddox. Instead, Yost took Amelia's hands in his. "You're as lovely as ever, Amelia. Much as I'd like to stay, I have work to do. Maybe we can get together for lunch in Medora?"

"No," both Maddox and Tuck said in unison.

Their mother gave them both a stern look before smiling at the sheriff. "That would be nice. How's tomorrow?"

"Perfect." He shot an oily smile at both Maddox and Tucker.

Standing beside Katya, Maddox growled.

Sheriff Yost turned to Katya. "Miss Evans, I'll be in touch. Don't go anywhere until we clear up this matter."

"Yes, sir." Katya vowed to leave as soon as she could. If not to keep her identity safely secret, then to keep the Thunder Horses out of her troubles.

Chapter Six

Maddox's muscles remained tense after Sheriff Yost departed. He walked to the window overlooking the front yard, rolling his shoulders in an attempt to release the pent-up anger over the sheriff's visit.

Sheriff Yost's SUV taillights disappeared down the long drive leading toward the county farm road.

"What did he say?" Tuck stepped up beside Maddox and stood at the window with him.

"You heard him. He wants Kat to stay put until he can contact his superiors or until she can cough up her legal papers."

"We should get Dante in on this. As a member of Customs and Border Protection, he should be up on all the passport regulations."

Katya cringed. Another law enforcement official *and* a member of the family? Great, just what she needed.

Maddox nodded, unaware of the panic rising in Katya. "Isn't he due for a visit?"

"Heard Mom on the phone with him yesterday. He was scheduled to fly over two days ago, but the storm grounded him in Grand Forks."

"The weather's cleared somewhat," Maddox said.

"Right." Tuck turned and strode across the living

room. "I'll call him and see if he's headed this way. If not, at least we can get his take."

"Thanks." Maddox remained at the window, his gaze on the road leading to the homestead. The only indications of the sheriff's visit was the anger burning in Maddox's chest and the tracks left in the newly fallen snow.

Kat crossed the room and stood beside him. "I am sorry. I had no intention of staying or causing you any trouble. I should leave immediately."

"No." The one word came out harsh.

Katya stepped back. "No, what?"

"No, you can't leave." He faced her. "I promised that you would stay here."

Kat's lips tipped upward. "I did not get the impression that you cared for what Sheriff Yost said or did."

"True." Maddox's mouth twitched at the corners and then firmed. "However, for as long as your alien status remains in question, I'm now the responsible party. You stay."

Kat's brows furrowed. Used to bodyguards in her home country, she should have been fine with his determination to protect her. But Maddox wasn't a paid bodyguard. He had been a Good Samaritan in the wrong place at the right time to save her. Now he felt obligated to keep saving her.

Being with her because he wanted to be with her was one thing. Being with her because he was forced into accepting responsibility for her was something entirely different. Kat didn't like it. The more she thought of someone being obligated to watch her like a child, the more the idea grated on the hard-won independence she had been nurturing before her father's death. Staying was not an option. Maddox's stubborn determination to detain her placed her and his family in danger.

What if the man following her tracked her to the Thunder Horse Ranch? Would he attack her here and anyone else who might get in the way?

Then there was the criminal element. If the sheriff matched her face with a wanted poster that might be circulating for a suspected terrorist, the Thunder Horses could be in a lot more trouble for aiding and abetting an alleged dangerous criminal.

Katya closed her eyes and dragged in a deep breath. *Think, Katya, think.* She had to leave. But how could she and not implicate them?

Maddox grabbed her arms. "I don't like that look."

Katya's eyes popped open. "What look?" For a moment she feared he could read her mind and see her plotting her escape. Even more frightening was that he might see the desire ignited by his hold on her arms. His hands squeezed her. Instead of trying to break free, all she could do was recall how his fingers had felt on her naked skin.

"You looked like you were thinking."

She forced a laugh, making light of his comment. "Do not tell me you are one of those men who believe a woman should not have a mind of her own."

"Of course not. But if the woman is dreaming up a cockamamie scheme, I can tell you now, I don't like being surprised." His eyes narrowed. "I'm watching you, so don't do anything we'll both regret."

"Fine," she said. Her brows rose and she stared down at his hands on her arms. "Do you mind?"

He let go as though he hadn't realized he was still

holding her. "What do you need to get your legal documents sent here?"

Katya swallowed her flippant response and settled on, "I need to make a long-distance phone call."

"There's a phone in my office."

"I would rather not impact your long-distance bill." She tipped her head to the side. "Do you have a computer with internet service?"

"Sorry." He shook his head. "We haven't broken down and had the satellite internet service installed yet."

Katya's mouth twisted. "Is there internet service anywhere nearby?"

"Closest is in Medora, a thirty-mile drive."

A surge of hope combined with a sinking in the pit of her belly. "Can you take me there?" She knew what she had to do and it did not make it any easier. If she remembered correctly, Medora was a little town on the interstate highway.

"The library will be closed by now," Maddox said.

Katya had not realized how late it had gotten. At least she had a plan forming. The sooner she executed it, the better. She would contact her homeland via the internet and then hitch a ride as far away from the Thunder Horse Ranch as she could get. Maddox and his family did not need to assume the burden of her problems, nor did they need to be accused as accessories to the crimes someone was trying to frame her for.

"You're doing it again." His hands rose to her arms, only this time he rubbed them gently up and down. "What are you thinking?"

She could not meet his eyes. "How much you and your family have done for me, and how much I appreciate it." She could not tell him goodbye without cluing him in on her plan to escape. At least she could let him know he had done enough. "Thank you." She lifted up on her toes and kissed him.

As soon as her lips touched his, his arms closed around her, drawing her into his embrace. The kiss deepened, his tongue thrusting past her teeth to stroke hers.

Lust and longing burned through her, pressing her body closer. If the kiss could last forever, Katya would be content to let it. Reality had a different plan for her. That plan being to escape and leave Maddox behind. She realized that her plan was only half-baked, as her American classmates would have said. If she wanted to get out of this alive and without spending time in jail, she could not keep running. She had to find out who had set her up. She had to go back to Minneapolis.

A flash of fear streaked through her, making her want to press even closer to Maddox. In the short time she had known him, she had completely relied on his strength and survival skills. Going forward, she would have to do this alone.

Kat broke off the kiss and leaned her forehead against his chest. Their lives were worlds apart. She would have to go home and take on her royal responsibilities, running a country in her father's absence. Until her brother was found alive, she was the next in line for the throne. Katya sighed. As if she didn't have enough to worry about. She backed out of Maddox's reach. "This was never meant to be."

"I know."

Katya's gaze met his, unexpected tears welling in her eyes. She reminded herself that Ivanovs didn't cry.

Before they could spill over and run down her face, she turned away and made a dash for the bedroom she'd shared with Maddox earlier, closing the door between them.

Maddox stared after Kat, his lips tingling, his heart thudding against his rib cage. He hadn't planned on kissing her, but he couldn't help himself. Kissing Kat was as natural as breathing.

The sooner he got her out of his house, off his ranch and out of his life, the sooner he could return to normal.

How he could be drawn to such a woman was beyond him. Susan had been open, honest and straightforward.

Kat had lied to him every step of the way, even down to her name. She was holding back information and he'd better find out what it was before someone got hurt.

Maddox hurried toward the office, intent on calling Pierce, his brother who worked for the FBI, to see if he could dig up anything on Kat Evans or a woman fitting her description. It was a shot in the dark, but a shot worth taking if it led to information on the mysterious woman occupying entirely too much of Maddox's thoughts.

After several rings, his brother answered. "Hello."

"Pierce, Maddox here."

"Hey, brother. How's everything? You guys got hit with a pretty bad storm, didn't you?"

"Yes, we did."

"Have a chance to check on the wild horses to see how they fared?"

"Not yet."

Before Pierce joined the FBI, he'd been just as

involved with tracking the wild horses as Maddox. He always asked, as if they were part of the family. To the Thunder Horses, the horses were a part of their family, their heritage.

"Look, Pierce, I need a favor."

"Name it."

"There's this woman…"

"About time, brother. I know how broke up you were over Susan, but you need to move on. It's been over two years and you aren't getting any younger. I want to be an uncle before I'm too old to enjoy it."

"Pierce, will you shut up for just a minute and let me finish?"

"Don't get your boxers in a wad. Shoot."

"It's not like that." Maddox told him how he'd found Kat and his doubts about her name. "She says she's from Russia—that part I believe. She also said her father recently died. Maybe that will help."

"I'll look into it." Pierce paused then added, "So is she really hot?"

Oh, yeah. With hair the color of midnight, eyes so blue he could fall into them, and a body that, well… "It doesn't matter, she's in some kind of trouble. I need to know what it is before our favorite sheriff finds out."

"Gotcha. She's hot." Pierce laughed. "Give Mom a hug. I'll call as soon as I learn anything."

Maddox hung up and stared out at the sky. Darkness settled in early in the frozen northern states. The clouds had all but disappeared, leaving a crystal-clear blanket of stars scattered across the heavens. Temperatures would drop well below freezing with nothing to keep the warmer air from rising. A chill slithered across Maddox's skin.

He stared out at the night, not seeing any of it, his mind on the stranger in his house. Who was she, and why did she have this power over him?

KAT LAY IN HER BED, dressed in the warm flannel pajamas Mrs. Thunder Horse had loaned her, wishing she were lying naked in a sleeping bag with Maddox.

She sat up, punched her pillow and flopped back down. The man had a way of monopolizing her thoughts when she should be planning her next move. For the next hour she forced herself to think about how she would get word of her survival to her cousin back in Trejikistan. Trying to board an airplane with every Transportation Security Administration staff and police element searching for her would be an impossibility. Even if she managed to board a flight bound for home, there was no way to guarantee her safety upon arrival.

She didn't have a clue what was going on back home. Access to the computer in Medora was imperative—not only to notify her contacts that she was alive, but also to glean anything she could from the news about her country and the power struggle that was surely occurring there. Knowing her cousin, Vladimir, he would have taken temporary control. Which made it all the more important that she return as soon as possible. Vladimir's approach to ruling the small nation was exactly the opposite of her father's vision of a democratic society with free elections.

Surely Vladimir would not have time to force the country to move backward into an autocratic state. All the more reason for her to contact him and let him know she had every intention of returning to rule the country and continue to implement her father's dreams of democracy for Trejikistan.

The more she thought about home, the more her heart ached. Yes, she loved her country and wanted to do right by her people. She could not abandon them to her cousin, Vladimir. Not after her father had made the promise of free elections the next year when they had everything in place and candidates identified. She hoped Vladimir wouldn't resist her claim and declare himself king.

Katya would rather not rule her country. She had been happy that her brother meant to carry on his father's work after he performed a humanitarian mission in Africa. Just two weeks before he was scheduled to return, his convoy had been ambushed. Some of his team were killed, but they never found her brother's body. Her father had been devastated, and Katya was preparing to go back to Trejikistan when she had received word that her father had been in an accident as well.

Her mind roiled with all that happened in the past couple of weeks, her heart heavy for her losses. As the hours passed and the night wore on, exhaustion claimed her.

A sound jerked her awake. Or at least she thought it was a sound. She might have been dreaming, but she could not slow the thump of her heart against her chest. Katya's eyes opened wide and she looked around the room. Starlight shone through the gap in the curtain, allowing a narrow blue ray across the room. From her vantage point, nothing moved.

Having been followed and shot at, Katya was not leaving anything to chance. She rolled over in the bed and eased herself to the floor, using the bed as cover and concealment. If someone was in the room, she did not have much of a chance. If the noise was from outside the house, she needed to hide until the source was discovered.

After several long minutes, she ventured to the end of the bed, her gaze darting from the window to the door that connected her room to Maddox's. Should she check out the noise herself or wake Maddox and have him check it out?

Calling herself a coward, Katya chose to alert Maddox. If she investigated the strange sound alone, she had no backup, no way to alert the rest of the family should something happen to her.

Keeping low to the ground, with the bed between her and the window, she crept toward the door. As she reached for the knob, another sound penetrated the thrum of blood banging against her eardrums. Her flight instincts kicked in, she twisted the knob and dove into the room.

"What the hell?" Maddox leaped from the bed and landed in a crouched stance, his fists clenched. He stared down at her, his eyes narrowing. "Kat?"

"Shh…" She pressed a finger to her lips. "I heard something outside."

Maddox grabbed her and pulled her around to the other side of his massive bed. "Stay here."

"No. I can check on it. I just wanted you to know." She tried to get up, but he held her down.

"I know this house better than you do. Promise me you'll stay put." He waited, refusing to move until she complied.

"I promise." She did not like hiding behind the bed when Maddox might be placing himself in danger.

Instead of going to the window, he tiptoed out into the hallway. He moved so stealthily, Katya couldn't tell which way he had gone.

All she knew was that he could be in danger, and it was all because of her.

Several long minutes passed. Katya could not hear or see anything from where she sat, and the suspense was making her crazy with worry. When she could not stand it any longer, she crept out into the hallway.

A light sprang to life in the living area and low male voices rumbled, one of them belonging to Maddox.

Katya hurried toward the sound. When she emerged into the light, Maddox and Tuck looked at her.

"You promised."

"I did stay for as long as I could. What was the sound?"

Tuck stared at her. "Someone was prowling around outside the house."

Maddox crossed his arms over his chest. "Care to enlighten us on who it might be?"

Katya's eyes widened, her cheeks burning. "How would I know? I did not go outside." What was it the Americans said? The best defense was a good offense. She hoped that was the case. She could use a good defense with Maddox glaring down at her.

How could she talk her way out of this one? She had to get to Medora tomorrow before she could escape the Thunder Horse clan. They didn't need to know any more than they already did. The more they knew the more likely they'd be arrested for helping her.

Maddox shook his head. "Not buying it. Try the truth."

Chapter Seven

Maddox waited, anger burning inside.

The way Kat's gaze darted from Tuck and back to him didn't give him any confidence that she would tell the truth this time.

"Really." She sighed and stared at her feet. "I do not know who it was."

Anger exploded in him and Maddox grabbed her arms. "No more lies. I want the truth."

She stared up at him, her eyes an icy-blue, glistening with unshed tears. "I am telling you the truth. I do not know who is after me."

Tuck laid a hand on his shoulder. "Let her go, Maddox."

He ignored his brother, shaking his hand off. "I saved your life in that snowstorm, and you repay me by feeding me lie after lie."

"I am deeply sorry." Her gaze dropped to where his hands rested on her arms, squeezing hard. "I have no idea who was outside my window."

"You said you didn't know who was after you."

Kat stilled, refusing to look up from her feet.

"Is that why you were in the canyon? Someone was after you?"

She squared her shoulders and looked across the room, her gaze never making contact with him. "I got lost and fell into the canyon."

Maddox didn't move and didn't say anything. He'd been having romantic thoughts about this woman, something he hadn't done since Susan's death. She'd been lying to him, and he'd been stupid, knowing she lied and not caring.

He cared now. When it came to endangering his family, he didn't take kindly to a stranger's lies.

"Look, whoever it was is gone. Let's get some sleep." Tuck plucked Kat from Maddox's grip. "I'll stand watch over our guest." He turned to lead her away.

Maddox, unwilling to let go of his anger so easily, removed Tuck's hand from around Kat's waist, but didn't replace it with his own "I found her, I'm the one answering to Yost for her. I'll keep watch."

"You get all the fun stuff." Tuck shrugged. "Have it your way. I'm going to bed."

Kat didn't wait for them to settle the argument. She headed for her room.

Maddox let her go, entering his own room. Once inside, Maddox paced the floor. He hated it when he was lied to. Even worse, he hated when he still felt protective of the one who'd lied. How could she stand there and refuse to tell him the truth, yet still look like the victim?

And what kind of fool was he to continue to play her game? Anger pushed him through the door and into the connecting room.

Kat lay in the bed, the coverlet pulled up to her chin, her ice-blue eyes wide and wary. "What do you want?"

"The truth."

"I've told you the truth. I can't help that you don't believe me."

"You aren't telling me everything."

"I've told you what I can."

He stared at her. Even with the sheet pulled up to her chin, wearing those ridiculous flannel pajamas his mother had given her, she looked sexy.

He strode across the room and flung the blanket back.

Kat yelped and drew her knees up to her chest.

"You're coming with me." Grabbing her hand, he pulled her up and led her to his room.

She yanked her hand free and backed away from the king-sized bed. "I cannot sleep with you."

"Why not? It's not as if you haven't already."

"I know." She twisted a button on the pajama top and backed up another step. "I just can't."

"It's too late to go modest on me. Get in the bed."

"No."

Maddox scooped her in his arms and deposited her in the middle of the mattress. "You're staying where I can keep an eye on you."

She scooted across the bed to the farthest corner, glaring at him. "Barbarian."

"Keep it up, and I'll show you barbarian." He stripped his sweatpants and sweatshirt off and crawled into the bed in his boxer shorts. He rolled over to switch the light off. "I suggest you sleep. And don't try anything."

"Why? Are you going to throw me again?"

"No, but I'm about ready to turn you over to the sheriff."

She sat at the foot of the bed, her arms wrapped

around her flannel-clad knees, her eyes wide, glowing in the starlight streaming in through the window. "You would do that?"

"You haven't given me any reason not to."

"Would it help if I told you it is for your own good?"

"No." He turned away, afraid that if he continued to stare at her, he'd do something stupid, like take her in his arms and make love to her. "I suspect you're in a whole lot of trouble and we've only just scratched the surface."

His body ached with the desire he fought to control. Those damn pajamas had a stronger impact on him than seeing her naked.

Kat sat for a while at the end of the bed.

Maddox feigned sleep.

Eventually, she crawled beneath the covers, keeping as far away from him as possible.

He knew she was there. His body recognized every movement. Her scent filled the air and drove him crazy with need.

Tomorrow he had to do something to get her out of his life.

KAT WOKE TO THE SUN streaming through the window, and the other side of the bed empty. She'd done something she hadn't done in a long time. She had silently cried herself to sleep. She sat up and stared across the room into the mirror hanging over the dresser.

Her hair stood on end, the masses of curls a riotous mess. Her blotchy skin and red-rimmed eyes did nothing to instill a sense of confidence in her.

The door to the bedroom opened, and Mrs. Thunder Horse entered, bearing a tray loaded with food. "Good morning." She smiled brightly and laid the tray on the dresser. "I figured that after all the fuss last night, you'd be too tired to join us at the breakfast table."

"Really, Mrs. Thunder Horse, you are not my servant. I could have come to the table."

"I rarely have guests. Please, let me spoil you a little."

"But I am not a guest. I am just one who has been foisted upon you and your family."

"In my view, that makes you a guest, and this is my chance to pull out the good china. I can't believe I slept through everything last night."

"I'm sorry there was such a fuss."

"Why should you be sorry? It's not as though you invited whoever it was to lurk around outside our house."

"Your son seems to think I did. Or at least that I invite trouble."

"Maddox tends to see only the black and white. Gray disturbs him. It's out of his control and he's uncomfortable with things he can't control."

Katya smiled at the woman. "You remind me of my mother. Thank you."

Amelia's cheeks reddened. "Oh, well then. You're quite welcome. How about some food?"

What Katya wanted most was to know where Maddox was, but she did not want to sound anxious or needy. Not when she planned to escape Maddox's protective custody as soon as the opportunity presented itself.

"Maddox is out helping Tuck feed the animals. He said to be ready when he gets back in. He'll run you to town."

And drop her off at the sheriff's office? A shiver

of apprehension feathered across the back of her neck. Sheriff Yost would lock her up so tight, she would never see the light of day if he knew she was a suspected terrorist. The sooner she left the county, the better off she and the Thunder Horses would be. "Do you have a pen and paper I could use?"

"Certainly." Amelia laid the tray on the bed. "I didn't know what you eat in Russia or what you like to eat in America, so I put a little of everything on your plate."

"I could not possibly eat all of that."

"I don't expect you to. Enjoy. I'll be back with your pen and paper." Amelia sailed out of the room.

Katya picked at the toast and scrambled eggs, her appetite less than healthy. The thought of leaving Maddox did not inspire her to eat. Yet she knew if she wanted to find the man who framed her, she would have to keep her strength up. With that in mind, she forced herself to finish the food and she downed the glass of orange juice.

By the time Amelia returned, she had finished eating and gotten out of bed to dress.

"Here are your clothes, dear. Now, I've got to go finish my grocery list for Maddox to pick up while you two are in town." She paused at the door. "How does baked chicken sound for supper?"

Kat almost cried again. She hated to disappoint the woman, but she had no intention of returning. "Baked chicken sounds wonderful."

Mrs. Thunder Horse beamed. "Good." The older woman left the room, a spring in her step.

She'd be making food for a guest who would not be there if Katya's plans worked out the way she hoped. She quickly dressed in the clothing Amelia had thoughtfully cleaned and returned to her room. Someday she hoped she could return all the favors this family had bestowed upon her during her stay. But for now, survival and proving her innocence took precedence.

She was just zipping her snow boots when Maddox arrived, filling the doorway.

"Ready?"

"I am." She stood, straightening her shoulders.

He didn't say anything, just turned and walked down the hallway.

Katya assumed she was to follow.

Amelia gave Maddox her list and hugged him before he pushed through the door.

She surprised Katya with an equally warm hug, which threatened to bring more tears to her eyes.

A blast of cold wind swirled in, enveloping Katya in its icy clutches. She had not been out in the cold since they'd come in from the storm. The wind chill bit into her exposed skin, sending violent shivers across her entire body. She hurried down the steps and out into the snow-covered drive where Maddox stood next to a large truck with knobby tires.

She rounded the hood to the passenger side and climbed up into the truck. The interior of the truck smelled of hay and leather. The gloves on the seat beside her explained the scent of leather. Beside it was a handheld radio.

Maddox climbed into the driver's seat and started the engine.

Tuck came down the steps of the house with a paper in his hand. "You forgot Mom's list. And I just heard from Dante. He's on his way and will be here in less than an hour."

"Good. Let him know we've headed into town. We'll see him when we get back." Maddox took the list and hit the button to close the power window and block out the blasts of cold wind filling the truck.

Katya huddled in the seat, quietly taking it all in and trying to be as invisible as she could be in the tight confines of the pickup truck.

They made the thirty-mile drive in just under an hour on the snowy roads.

When they arrived in Medora, Maddox parked in the library parking lot and got out.

"I can do this myself," Katya insisted.

"Without a driver's license, they might not let you use the internet." Maddox's dark brows rose. "Got one of those?"

"No."

Maddox led the way into the facility and proceeded to charm the librarian into letting Katya use a computer with internet access without a driver's license or passport.

As she sat in front of the computer screen, Katya wondered how she could tell Maddox to go away so that she could send her message in secrecy. He had been right to be angry with her last night. After saving her life, he should expect her to be forthcoming with the facts. But she did not want him to know anything in case the authorities interrogated him and his family. She had to have time to discover the real culprit.

Just when she opened her mouth to tell Maddox to go get the groceries his mother wanted, a cell phone rang in Maddox's pocket.

Katya jumped. "They get reception out here?"

His lips twisted into a grimace. "Sometimes." He dug

in his pocket and pulled out the phone. "Excuse me." Maddox walked toward the front entrance to the library and out into the street, speaking into the receiver.

Katya breathed a sigh of relief and hoped whoever it was would stay on the line long enough for her to get word to her people. She had spied a gas station not far from the library. A large tractor-trailer rig had been parked there, the driver filling the tank. If she hurried, she might be able to catch a ride with him, assuming he was headed for Minneapolis.

She keyed in the web address of her internet provider and brought up her email. Several of the students in her master's program had sent emails asking her where she was, and when she would have her portion of their group project done. A stab of guilt made her skip past them quickly and click on an email from her former bodyguard.

If she trusted anyone, it was Andrei Sokolov. He had protected her for most of her childhood. Since she had been gone, he had been in a state of semi-retirement, augmenting the team of bodyguards protecting her father. She had been in contact with him, exchanging emails like old friends up until two days ago. The message was short and in her native Russian. "Where are you?"

She quickly typed, "Are you there now?" Katya hit the Send button and glanced over her shoulder toward the glass front door of the library. Maddox stood with his back to her, the cell phone pressed to his ear, hunching his back against the wind.

Please be there, Andrei, please. She rubbed her fingers over the pendant her father had given her, wishing her friend would come online. She needed to communicate with someone from home.

It would be close to nine o'clock in the evening in Trejikistan. Andrei liked to go online and send emails at that time. Hopefully, the turmoil in the country had not changed that. After several long seconds, Katya realized that she'd never have time to wait for his response and still catch a ride with the trucker. She composed a brief message to let Andrei know that she was okay and that she had trouble in the States. She would contact him when she had more information and let her cousin know that she would return to Trejikistan as soon as possible.

She signed off the email, erased the computer's history and shut it down.

Katya stole a glance at the door where Maddox still stood with his back to her. Pulling the paper and pen Amelia had given her from her pocket, she dashed off a quick note of thanks to Maddox and folded the paper. She hurried to the front desk and asked the librarian to give it to Maddox when he came back in.

Then pretending that she needed to use the ladies' room, she walked toward the narrow hallway where the bathrooms were located as well as the rear exit door.

Before she could change her mind, she slipped through the back exit and out into the open. Katya hurried toward the corner of the building and peered around. The space between the library and the next building was empty. She ducked behind the next building and ran to the end. A gust of wind whipped her red scarf up into her face. Temporarily blinded by the scarf, she did not see the person behind her until too late. A gloved hand clamped over her mouth and another lifted her off her feet and ran her toward the open trunk of a car waiting in the gap between the buildings.

Kat kicked and tried to scream, but the wind carried away what little sound made it through the thick gloves. She braced her feet on the car, refusing to let the man shove her inside. Once in, she knew her chances of escaping were slim to none.

The man kicked at the backs of her knees and her legs buckled enough for him to shove her through the opening, slamming the trunk lid over her.

Darkness and the smell of tire rubber and exhaust surrounded her, filling Katya with despair.

Chapter Eight

"Yes, she has black hair and ice-blue eyes," Maddox said into the cell phone, having a hard time hearing his brother, Pierce, over the wail of the wind.

"Pretty?"

"We established that the last time we talked."

"I think you have a problem on your hands, my man."

"Tell me what I don't know." Maddox shifted the phone to the other ear. "What did you find out?"

"One Katya Ivanov, a college student, from a Russian breakaway country called Trejikistan, went missing from her apartment here in Minneapolis two days ago."

"Katya." She hadn't been lying about that part of her name and Ivanov was close to Evans. "So? Why the fuss?"

"Her picture is all over the news in Minnesota, and CNN picked up on it today."

Maddox gripped the phone hard. "What the hell did she do?"

"Bad news, brother."

As if what he'd already learned wasn't bad enough. He steeled himself for more. "What?"

"Authorities suspect her of plotting a terrorist attack based on the weapons and explosives they found in her closet. They have flyers going out to all the law enforcement agencies in Minnesota and all the surrounding states. They want to bring her in for questioning. I have my people digging into her background."

Maddox let out a long breath. "Wow. I guess that's why she didn't want to tell me anything." He shook his head, calling himself every kind of fool. "Great. I was harboring a potential terrorist."

"Not a good place to be, bro. You know I'll have to report it."

"Do that. It's what I get for saving a stranger's life."

"You can't blame yourself. You didn't know."

Maddox snorted. "I knew she was lying."

"But you didn't know about what."

Still, he hadn't followed that gut feeling, instead following lust.

"You have to bring her in."

"Where?" Maddox kept his back to the library, afraid Katya would suspect him of plotting to turn her in. "I can't turn her over to the sheriff. Yost is a sadistic bastard. He'd use this to hurt her and our family."

"If you could keep her away from Yost for the day, I could be there to take her off your hands. I have a buddy with a private pilot's license. He could get me there in as little as five hours."

"Let's do it. She already has someone following her. I'm not sure who it is, but I suspect he chased her into the canyon. I don't know how dangerous he is. You might check and see if it's one of your guys."

"Will do. I'm on my way as soon as I can secure a plane ride. Keep her close."

"Right." Maddox hit the End button, terminating the call. What was Katya doing on the internet? Sending notes to her terrorist buddies? Maddox pushed through the door and hurried across the floor.

"Sir?" As Maddox passed by the front desk, the librarian held out a folded piece of paper. "The young lady you came in with asked me to give you this."

He grabbed the paper, jammed it into his pocket and kept on walking toward the bank of computers. The seat where he'd left Kat was empty, the computer screen blank.

Great, just great. She'd ducked out on him. Maddox ran through the shelves of books, searching for a backdoor, finding it in the aisle with the bathrooms. She had to have gone out this way. She hadn't come through the front.

As he ran out the back, he looked left then right. A man struggled at the back of a dark blue car and finally slammed the trunk. Before the lid closed, Maddox could see a flash of red scarf and coal-black curly hair. He heard a female cry for help.

"Kat!" Maddox ran toward the car.

The man jumped into the driver's seat before Maddox could get close enough to stop him.

The car pulled away as Maddox reached it, only giving him enough time to slam his hand against the metal doorframe before the vehicle skidded out into the street and headed south out of town.

Maddox yanked his cell phone from his pocket and punched in the number for Dante. He didn't wait for an answer, sprinting out onto the main road and back to the library where his truck was parked. Dante's number went directly to an answering machine. Damn reception!

He tried his house. Maybe Dante had already arrived there.

After the second ring, Dante answered. "I just landed at the ranch. Where are you and your hot foreign number?"

"Crank up your bird and get over to Medora ASAP!"

"What's going on?"

"Someone just snatched Kat. They're headed south out of town in a dark blue, four-door sedan."

"How do you know he snatched her and she didn't go willingly?"

Maddox climbed in behind the wheel of his truck, flipped the ignition and yanked the gearshift into reverse. "She was thrown in the trunk. Can you hurry? And bring the handheld radio. Cell reception is nil once you leave town."

"On it. I'll bring Tuck with me. We'll see you in a few."

Maddox flung the phone onto the seat next to him and slammed his foot down on the accelerator. The truck shot forward, the back end fishtailing on the ice.

By the time Maddox had his truck on the road, the car carrying Kat was long gone. He hoped and prayed that the kidnapper didn't turn off the main highway onto one of the side roads.

Kat must have slipped out the backdoor of the library and run into trouble outside. Her attacker couldn't have grabbed her from inside the building without raising a ruckus and alerting the library staff.

Maddox pounded his palm against the steering wheel. How had he let this happen? He'd only been away from her for a few minutes, talking to his brother. Hell, why did he even care?

Kat hadn't planned on sticking around. That had to be why she'd convinced him to come to town. To make contact with her people.

Really. Why did he care? She'd lied to him, tried to ditch him and could be a terrorist. Why was he so concerned that someone had kidnapped her?

An image of her lying naked in his arms, the soft glow of the flashlight shining in her eyes and on her hair came to mind. His groin tightened and his foot pressed the gas pedal to the floor.

She'd reawakened him, reminding him what it was like to allow himself to care again. The least she could do was live long enough to tell him the truth. Had making love to him been a means to an end? Had she only given herself to sucker him into protecting her?

Kat had dragged Maddox from the fog of the emotionless existence he'd buried himself in for the past two years. An existence in which he refused to care about anyone who wasn't family. Maddox now warred with the full spectrum of emotions. Anger, betrayal, fear and… *oh, please, no…*the potential to love again.

Hadn't he been better off emotion-free?

Ten miles outside Medora, Maddox worried that he'd gone in the wrong direction. He hadn't seen the car, even on the long, straight, flat stretches of road. Had the kidnapper gotten that far ahead or had he taken a side road Maddox missed?

Overhead the loud rumble of an aircraft engine and the telltale thumping of rotary blades made Maddox let out the breath he held. The green-and-white CBP helicopter blew past him, following the ribbon of highway.

Several miles ahead, the helicopter slowed and appeared to be hovering or moving very slowly.

The handheld radio buzzed on the seat next to him. He grabbed it and hit the Talk button.

"Hey, it's Tuck. We just passed you and found a dark blue four-door car ahead on the highway." The radio crackled, static blasting in his ear, but Maddox held onto it like a lifeline.

"That's it," he shouted.

"Two miles ahead over the next rise. He's going pretty fast."

"Can you slow him down or stop him?"

"How? You want Dante to land on him? He's already in enough trouble taking the chopper out on non–Border Patrol business."

"Never mind." Maddox pushed his truck past the safe driving speed for icy roads. "Just keep him in sight until I catch up."

"Then what? If we force him off the road, he might crash." The static increased, filling Maddox's ear.

Maddox's chest tightened. No matter how many lies Kat had told him, she didn't deserve to be kidnapped or to die in the trunk of a car.

"We'll figure it out when I get closer." Maddox stuffed the radio into his pocket. As his truck closed in on the helicopter's position, the dark blue sedan came into view.

The man drove like a lunatic with a death wish, spewing snow and ice behind his tires. He slowed and turned off the main road into an area Maddox knew to be filled with ravines and canyons dropping off the sides of the road. If they didn't stop him soon, he could easily slip off the road and crash down a sheer drop.

Dante's helicopter dipped low over the car as Maddox caught up.

The car hit a bump of ice on the poorly maintained road. The wheels jerked to the right, launching the car up a ramp of snow, pitching it over the edge of the road and down into a steep ravine.

Maddox's heart skipped several beats before kicking into an adrenaline-pumping machine. He forced himself to slow gradually on the snow and ice until he could come to a complete and safe halt at the point where the car disappeared off the edge of the road.

Slamming the gearshift into Park, Maddox dropped down out of the truck and ran to the road's edge. Far below in the bottom of a deep crevice, the sedan lay on the passenger side, its front wheels still spinning.

Panic threatened to paralyze Maddox. He pictured Susan lying lifeless in his arms. He couldn't and wouldn't let that happen to Kat. He leaped over the edge and scrambled down the hill toward the mangled vehicle, his breath hung in his throat, his legs shaky and threatening to buckle with each step.

She couldn't be dead. Not Kat. She had too much determination to survive.

A shot rang out, the bullet pinging off the rocks next to Maddox's feet. He threw himself behind a large outcropping of boulders, knowing the trip down the ravine made him an ideal target for someone below. More shots hit the rocks and dirt behind him.

He glanced toward the sky. As if on cue, the helicopter flew over with Tuck leaning out the door, a rifle in his hand, firing at the kidnapper.

The overwhelming rumble of the helicopter was all that Maddox could hear. Soon the chopper eased farther away, following the flow of the ravine down into a small canyon.

With the helicopter noise gone, the sounds of gunfire had ceased. Maddox couldn't see a shooter. He had to assume Tuck's cover fire had chased him off.

Kat could be injured in the trunk, maybe bleeding.

Unable to wait a moment longer, Maddox abandoned the relative safety of the boulder and continued his descent.

As though moving in slow motion, he slipped and slid on snow, ice and rocks, until he landed beside the vehicle.

With the car lying on its side, the undercarriage facing him, Maddox couldn't see inside. No one had shot at him on his trek down the hill, but that didn't mean the guy wasn't hiding, waiting for his chance to nail an easy target.

Maddox eased up the undercarriage of the overturned vehicle and peered down into the interior. Nothing moved. The driver's window was gone, shards of glass scattered all over the seats.

"Kat!" Maddox said, loudly enough so she could hear him, but hopefully not so loud that the shooter could zero in on him.

"Maddox?" Kat's muffled voice sounded from the rear of the vehicle. "I cannot get out. Find the key."

Still up on the side of the car, Maddox felt around the steering column until he found the keys. He yanked them from the ignition, pushed backward and dropped to the ground, glancing around for signs of the shooter.

When he moved around to the back of the car, he

groaned. The trunk lay wedged against a huge boulder. Even with the key, he couldn't get the trunk open.

"Hang on, Kat. I'm going to need more help."

"Hurry!"

Maddox pulled the handheld radio from his pocket and hit the Talk button, praying the helicopter was in range. "Where are you guys?"

"Following your sedan driver. He disappeared into the canyon."

"Leave him. I need your help here." Maddox explained the position of the car and what he needed to get Kat out.

The helicopter rumbled into sight and hovered over Maddox.

Tuck appeared in the door, leaned out and latched a cable to the skid, dropping the coil of cable down below the helicopter.

Dante eased the helicopter above where Maddox stood, the cable dangling closer and closer until Maddox could grab the hook and direct it toward the undercarriage.

He hooked the cable on the car and waved up at Dante.

Tuck, rifle in hand, scanned the terrain below the helicopter.

Maddox climbed up the hill and to one side of where the car rested. "Hang on, Kat! The ride's going to get bumpy again."

Maddox waved to Tuck. Tuck leaned into the helicopter.

The cable tightened, the helicopter straining against the weight of the vehicle.

Maddox held his breath, hoping that by righting the car it wouldn't slip farther down the ravine.

Metal scraped and groaned and the car teetered, swaying toward the helicopter. Gravity kicked in and the car dropped toward the ground, tugging hard on the cable.

The helicopter dropped a couple feet before it steadied and hovered low enough for the cable to hang loosely.

Maddox unhooked the cable from the undercarriage of the car and waved at Tuck who gathered his end and reeled the cable back up into the chopper.

The helicopter lifted higher into the sky and circled back toward where the attacker had disappeared.

"Kat?" Maddox slipped and slid down the rocky hillside to the back of the car and stopped.

"Surprisingly, I am still here," she said through the metal of the trunk.

Maddox fitted the key in the lock and twisted. Dented and battered, the lid didn't budge. He fit his fingers beneath the edges and lifted hard, throwing his back into freeing Kat.

Metal scraped against metal and the trunk sprang open.

Kat blinked up at him, her face bruised, her hair tangled and matted with blood from a gash on her forehead, but she was as beautiful as ever.

Maddox reached for her, pulling her out of the trunk and into his arms.

Kat clung to him, her body shaking, speaking in a language he couldn't understand, her words coming fast and furious.

He tipped her face up to his and stared down into icy-blue eyes awash in tears. Then his mouth crashed down over hers with the force of his anger, his desperation and his fear. He couldn't stop the flood of emotion he experienced whenever he was around her, and he hated himself for his lack of control.

Her hands circled behind his neck and if it was possible, she drew him closer, kissing him back as if they were the last man and woman on earth.

When he came up for air, Maddox pushed aside the intense relief and allowed his anger to resurface. "When we get back to the ranch, you're going to tell me everything. Do you understand? Especially what the hell you were planning to do with the guns and explosives."

Chapter Nine

Katya sat in a straight-backed chair in the Thunder Horse living room as Amelia cleaned the blood off her forehead using a damp cloth. Tumbling down a hill in the trunk of a car had taken its toll on her and she had the lumps and bruises to show for it.

As Amelia worked her magic, Maddox paced the floor in front of her, finally coming to a halt. "That's good, Mom. She can do the rest later."

Amelia Thunder Horse shot a narrow-eyed glare at her son. "Don't you think she's been through enough?"

Maddox crossed his arms over his chest and shook his head, his lips pressed into a thin line. "We haven't even begun."

Undeterred, Maddox's mother dabbed antibiotic ointment on the gash, plastered a bandage over it and stepped back. "She could have a concussion. She really needs to see a doctor."

Katya shook her head, a blast of fear racing through her veins. "No."

Maddox's mouth twisted. "Care to tell my mother why you don't want to see a doctor?"

The harshness of Maddox's gaze sent a chilling wash of despair over Katya, making her feel colder than if she'd been lying beside the river in a bank of snow. For a brief moment she'd allowed herself to rely on Maddox to protect her. But that was over. She squared her shoulders and lifted her chin the way her father taught her when facing her adversaries. "What do you know?"

"That you've been lying to us all along. Your name is Katya Ivanov, you were a student in Minneapolis and you're a terrorist."

Amelia gasped. "Maddox!"

"What?" Maddox pinned Katya with his stare. "It's true, isn't it?"

Katya winced, at once relieved and concerned that he still didn't know the whole picture. What he did know was bad enough. She drew in a deep breath and let it out. "Part of what you just said is true."

Maddox's eyes blazed and he stalked across the wood floor to stand in front of her, trapping her in the chair. He leaned over her, bracing his hands on the chair's arms. "The part about lying to us? Or the part about being a terrorist?"

Katya leaned back in order to look directly up into Maddox's eyes. She held his gaze, determined to give as good as she got. All the while her heart pounded in her chest, her breath catching in her throat at his nearness. "My name and the part about being a student in Minneapolis."

"What are you talking about, Maddox?" Amelia touched her son's arm. "Katya isn't a terrorist."

"Evidence indicates otherwise." He directed his words at Katya. "Doesn't it?"

Anger bubbled up inside Katya. She had been through hell and she was damn tired of it. "Not everything is as it appears. And if you would give me a chance, I will explain."

"You've had more chances than I can count to explain yourself, to tell the truth, but you didn't."

"I did not want to get you and your family involved in my troubles."

"Hate to tell you, darlin', but we already are." Maddox pushed away from the chair and towered over her. "Since we're about as deeply involved as we can get by harboring a terrorist, maybe you can enlighten us."

Katya stood, placing herself toe-to-toe with Maddox. "I came to the United States to go to school, not to blow it up. The weapons they found in my apartment are not mine. Someone set me up. You have to believe me."

"Why? You've lied to me from the beginning."

"I had to." She looked around the room at the faces of Maddox's family. "When I woke up in that cave, I did not know who you were. I do not know who has been following me or why, but he tried to kill me."

"And you thought I might be him?"

Katya shrugged. "I didn't know. I was unconscious when you found me."

"So you slept with the enemy, just in case?"

Katya's face burned, anger making her pulse race with the need to strike back. Dammit, she was the victim, not the villain. "That is correct. Keep your friends close and your enemies closer." She turned to the others in the room, avoiding Maddox. "I am not a monster bent on destroying your country. I am a student who has been targeted by someone, for what reason I do not know." She had her suspicions, but she was not sharing them until she knew for certain. "Go back to the canyon and find the snowmobile. You will see the proof."

"Proof that I was a fool to believe you in the first place?" Maddox ground out, no pity in his gaze for the woman he'd rescued.

Katya swayed, her head throbbing. "Proof that whoever is after me is shooting real bullets."

Amelia gasped, hurrying over to Katya. "Maddox, you've bullied her enough. Let the child lie down. She's been shot at, almost frozen to death and now she's been in a car wreck. I'm surprised she's still on her feet."

"She still hasn't told us why the weapons were in her apartment." His brows rose. "Why—Kat—Katya or whoever you are?"

"I do not know! I am a student and a citizen of Trejikistan, not a terrorist."

Maddox crossed his arms over his chest, his jaw taut, but for a muscle twitching in the side. "Give me one reason why I shouldn't turn you over to the authorities right now?"

"I'll give you one." Tuck grinned. "Yost is the only *authority* in the neighborhood. I wouldn't turn over a rabid dog to that man."

"Tuck!" Amelia admonished. "Sheriff Yost is an officer of the law."

Tuck snorted. "Maybe he should pay more attention to the law."

"Turning her over to Yost will only make it bad on you, Maddox," Maddox's brother, Dante, said. "He won't wait to get the truth."

Tuck shook his head. "The man wouldn't know the truth if it bit him in the—"

"Tuck!" Amelia planted her hands on her hips. "What would your father say?"

Maddox's gaze shifted from Katya to his mother,

his expression softening. "A lot more if he were still here."

"But he's not. And we have to carry on." Amelia sighed. "Why are you all so down on Sheriff Yost? He's been nothing but good to me since your father's death."

Tuck crossed to his mother and draped an arm over her shoulders. "We don't trust him, Mom." When she opened her mouth to argue, Tuck held up a hand. "Don't ask why, we just don't."

Dante stood. "Which comes back to our little problem here."

Katya's lips twisted into a grimace. "By *problem,* I assume you mean me."

Maddox nodded, the frown a permanent fixture on his forehead since they'd returned to the Thunder Horse Ranch.

She sighed, her shoulders drooping with the weight of fatigue and defeat. "I did not put those weapons in my apartment. Someone else did. And I do not know why."

Dante stood with his arms crossed over his chest. "The question is what to do with her until we have an answer. I could turn her in to Customs and Border Patrol as an illegal alien."

Maddox didn't respond.

Katya held her breath. If they turned her over to the police or CBP, she might never learn the truth and be punished for a crime she had not committed.

Tuck moved to the window and peered out. "You'd better figure out the solution quick. Our favorite sheriff just drove up."

"He's here to take me to lunch." Amelia hurried

toward the door. "Relax. I'll take care of the sheriff. Maddox, you take care of Katya. Go out the back, I'll keep him inside long enough for you both to escape."

While Amelia hurried toward the door, Maddox stared across at Kat. "What's it going to be? Come with me, go with the Border Patrol or go with the sheriff?"

She shrugged. "You have to do what you feel is right. If you are so certain that I am a terrorist, you should turn me over to the law. If it makes it any easier, I'll go now." She took two steps in the direction Amelia had gone before Maddox blocked her path.

"No." He pushed his hand through his long hair and sighed. "I don't know who you are or what your game is, but for now, you'll come with me."

"Where?" she demanded.

"I don't know. But you're my problem until I can figure this mess out. Get your coat and gloves. It'll be cold outside."

Railroaded into agreeing, Katya went for her outdoor gear, gathering her coat, gloves and scarf while Maddox spoke quietly with his brothers.

Katya could hear his mother talking to the sheriff and the sheriff's answering murmur. Her pulse quickened, fear pushing her forward despite how tired she was and how much her head hurt.

When she emerged from the bedroom, Maddox met her, outfitted in a heavy winter coat, carrying gloves and a bag. He marched Katya through the house, urging her to silence with a finger pressed to his lips.

At the backdoor, she paused. "I'm sorry I brought you and your family into this."

"No more so than I am." He held the door open and a blast of frigid air blew in.

Katya shrugged into her coat and gloves and stepped out onto the porch. "If you could get me to the interstate, I could leave you and your family in peace."

"You're not going anywhere until we figure out exactly what trouble you're in."

"But you don't have to help me." She stared up into his eyes.

"I'm not. I'm helping myself and my family." His lips thinned into a tight line and he gazed down at her. "If you are a terrorist, we are all guilty of harboring you. I don't plan on my family going to jail because I was fool enough to rescue a stranger."

"You could let me go and claim that I escaped," she offered.

"Or you could be my hostage and I'll turn you over to the police when I know for certain that you are a terrorist."

"And how will you know that?"

"I don't know yet." Maddox pulled the hood of his parka up over his head and slid his hands into the gloves. "For now, you'll stick with me."

She opened her mouth to disagree, but he cut her off with a raised hand.

"No argument." He grabbed her elbow in his hand and ushered her off the porch and across the snow-covered yard toward the barn.

Once inside, he bypassed the horses and headed for the two snowmobiles parked in an empty stall. He laid the bag on the back of one snowmobile, securing it with flexible cords.

Katya shivered. The cool air had nothing to do with the chill spiraling down her spine. The last time she'd been on a snowmobile, she'd almost lost her life. That and the amount of animosity radiating from Maddox made her want to run away as far as she could get. From warm, caring rescuer to tall, cold stranger, filled with nothing but anger and accusations. He was breaking her heart.

How? How could a man—practically a stranger—have such a hold on her emotions? Was it some psychological attraction she felt for him because he had rescued her? It had to be.

It could not be because he was so tall, strong and earthy, the exact opposite of the men she was used to. Or that he accepted the risk of rescuing her, placing his own life in danger. And he had rescued her again when she had been kidnapped.

"Rescuing me is becoming a habit for you, isn't it?" she stated, more to herself than to him.

Maddox shot a glance her way and, without responding, walked to the opposite end of the barn and flung open the back door. A gust of wind whipped through the barn, carrying with it a spray of snow. Then he climbed onto one of the machines and cranked the engine, backed it out of the stall and drove it through the door. "Hop on."

She crossed the interior of the barn, pulling the collar of her jacket up around her neck. "Shouldn't I ride on another?"

"No. I don't trust you on your own." He dismounted and closed the barn door behind her, before resuming his seat on the machine.

"I see." Katya stood, anxiety and something else burning low in her gut. "What if I don't want to ride with you?"

"Tough."

She could not imagine riding behind Maddox, her arms wrapped around him. "And if I refuse?"

"If you refuse to come with me, I'm sure Sheriff Yost would love to add you to the scalps on his belt." His brows raised. "What's it going to be?"

Knowing there was only one answer to his question did not make it any easier for her to give in. She was not known for her easy acceptance of any awkward situation. Her father had called her stubborn. But the choice was clear. She couldn't go with Yost or she would be thrown in jail, no one the wiser for who had actually planted the weapons in her apartment.

If she was to be Maddox's hostage, she had to convince him to help her find the real terrorist—the one who wanted her dead or at least so buried in the penal system that she couldn't get out to go home to Trejikistan. If she could not convince Maddox to help her, she had to find a way to escape from him and get back to Minneapolis to get answers to this mess on her own.

Katya slung her leg over the backseat of the snowmobile, keeping as far away as she could from actually touching Maddox. She could not risk letting her guard down with him. He did not trust her and because of that, she could not trust him. With what seemed like an entire country on the lookout for her as a suspected terrorist, she did not see how she would find the real culprit without help. But she would manage, or die trying.

Maddox revved the engine and shot out of the barnyard, careful to keep the barn between him and the ranch house for as long as possible, thus lessening the chance of being seen or heard until they were too far away for the sheriff to give chase in his pickup.

At first Katya refused to hold on to him, but as they

bumped across the drifts of snow, she was nearly unseated several times and finally grabbed him around the waist, holding on as tightly as she could.

A certain sense of justice filled Maddox, along with a rising need to feel her body against his. She'd been a mystery to him from the first time he'd laid eyes on that damn red scarf blowing in the wind. And nothing she'd said or done had cleared up the mystery surrounding her since. He'd be damned if he let her go until he figured her out. If that meant holding her hostage until she came clean, so be it.

They sped across the expanse of snowy terrain, putting as much distance as possible between them and the sheriff.

"Where are we going?" Kat yelled over the roar of the snowmobile engine.

He didn't answer, letting her guess, as she'd had him guessing since they'd met. That little bit of payback did nothing to settle the thrumming in his veins, the adrenaline kick he couldn't set aside in anticipation of their destination.

An hour later, fingers cold and Kat clinging to him to keep warm, Maddox pulled up to a small log cabin out in the middle of the frozen tundra. He parked the snowmobile behind the cabin in a lean-to built for that very purpose.

"What is this place?" Katya stood, stretching stiffly, tucking her hands beneath her armpits for warmth.

"The family hunting cabin. We come out here during the fall and stay for a week."

"Why here?" She looked back the way they came.

"Hard to find and harder to get to if you don't know where you're going."

The logs were old and weathered a dull gray, the door made of planks held in place by a combination lock. Maddox removed a glove and tumbled the combination, twisting it left then right until it fell open. He removed the lock and opened the door.

The inside was as gray as the outside, only darker. A small table, one rickety chair, and a rough-hewn bed made of carved wood posts with rope strung across was the extent of the furniture. A fireplace, lined with river rock, filled one end of the cabin. Next to it was a footlocker, which could be used as a second chair.

Maddox tossed the bundle he'd brought onto the bed. "There's canned food in the footlocker, see what you can find while I bring in the firewood."

When she didn't move, he stared across the floor. "You do know how to cook, don't you?"

"Yes, yes. Of course I do." Katya hurried toward the box on the floor and lifted the lid.

Once outside, Maddox collected logs. Being alone in the cabin with Katya brought back way too many memories of their night in the cave, memories best left in cold storage. The more time he spent alone with her, the less he was able to rein in his libido. The woman was hot, in or out of all the winter clothing. And one bed between them spelled trouble. Thank goodness they wouldn't be there the entire night.

Grateful that his family kept the cabin stocked, Maddox carried a full load of wood inside and laid it by the fireplace.

Still wearing her coat, and blowing steam as she breathed in and out, Katya had opened a can of beans with the manual can opener they kept in the footlocker.

Beside it was the pot they would hang over the fireplace to heat their food.

"See, I'm not completely useless. But I do need to relieve myself. Are there any facilities I can make use of?"

Maddox glanced over at her, attributing her inability to make eye contact to her embarrassment over asking about a bathroom. "There is an outhouse behind the cabin."

Her brows furrowed.

"An outhouse is an outdoor bathroom. It's either that or expose yourself to nature and the biting wind."

"I'll risk the outhouse." Her forehead smoothed. "Thank you for everything, Maddox." With that, she turned and left the cabin.

Something about the way her last statement came across didn't sit right with Maddox. He tossed the kindling he held into the fireplace and straightened. As he did, a distinct rasp of metal on metal was accompanied by a sharp click.

In the back of his mind, Maddox knew it wouldn't be there, yet he looked at the table where he'd laid the combination lock when he'd come into the cabin the first time. The table was empty.

"Katya!" Maddox raced for the door and shoved the bolt to the side. When he pushed on the door, it remained closed. "Dammit, woman, unlock the door!"

"I will not let you be held responsible for my predicament. This way they will know that I tricked you."

Maddox dragged in a deep breath and let it out, counting to ten at the same time. In as calm a voice as he could manage with anger and panic warring within him, he said, "Katya, don't do this. It's almost dark. You'll get lost on the prairie."

"It is a chance I have to take to keep you and your family out of trouble with the law." She paused. "I won't forget you, Maddox. Thank you for helping me when I needed it most. Thank you for…everything."

His heart pounding in his ears, Maddox hit the door, hard. The metal latch held.

"Katya!"

Chapter Ten

The cabin door shook with the force of Maddox slamming against it.

Katya jumped away, afraid the metal latch wouldn't hold under the force of his weight and anger.

Her heart thundering, she raced around the cabin to the lean-to in the rear. She hoped Maddox had left the keys in the ignition of the snowmobile. Without them her attempt to escape would be hopeless. An hour away from the ranch house, she could not possibly make it back to a highway to hitch a ride before nightfall. As it was, darkness descended on North Dakota early in the winter, making it difficult to see in the shadows of the overhang. To add to her dilemma, clouds covered the sky, negating any possibility of starlight to navigate by.

"Katya!" Maddox's angry cries thundered through the solid log walls.

Katya straddled the snowmobile and ran her fingers across the controls, searching in the dark for a key or starter switch.

As her hands closed around the key, a great crash sounded behind her.

With her breath lodged in her throat, Katya turned

the key and the engine revved to life. She jammed the gearshift into Reverse and backed out of the shed.

Once clear, she shifted into Drive. As she twisted the handle, giving the engine a quick burst of fuel, something heavy landed on the back of the machine, arms closing around her waist.

She screamed, her hand letting go of the throttle.

Maddox's arms circled her waist and yanked her off the seat and into a pile of snow.

She landed with a jolt on top of Maddox. He held tight, taking the brunt of the landing.

The snowmobile slid to a stop, the engine humming, but the machine motionless with no gas to power the tracks.

"Let go!" she yelled. "This is the only way to keep you safe."

"No way. Not until I know everything."

"How can you know everything when I don't even know it?" She struggled, kicking and flailing like a turtle on its back, unable to gain purchase.

"Will you be still?" Maddox grunted.

"No! I need to get out of here. I have to find out who is doing this to me."

"Be still, dammit!" He shoved her off him, letting go for just a moment.

Taking her only chance left, Katya leaped to her feet and ran for the snowmobile.

Before she had gone two steps, Maddox tackled her, taking her down in one inglorious heap, facefirst in the snow. The wind knocked out of her, she could not move or fight him off. He flipped her over and straddled her hips, pinning her hands over her head in the snow.

"No. More. Running," he said through gritted teeth, glaring down at her.

Katya stared up into his eyes. Completely immobile, captured by her rescuer and powerless to escape. He outweighed her and could easily fend off any attempt she made at fighting him. Defeated, she gave in, hopelessly hostage to the way he made her feel. "I never meant for this to happen."

The lines across his forehead eased, his gaze shifting from her eyes to her lips. "Neither did I." Then he was kissing her, his lips slanting across hers, his tongue pushing past her teeth to twist and taste, thrusting past her defenses.

Determined to remain immune to him, Katya felt her resolve dissolve under his savage onslaught. She couldn't feel the cold snow on her backside for the heat burning within. She couldn't fight him…she didn't want to. This was where she'd wanted to be since their first night together in the cave.

When he lifted his face, she gathered air into her lungs and made one last attempt at reason. "You should not get involved with me."

"I know." He smoothed a tendril of hair out of her face. "And yet I can't help myself." His gaze broke contact with hers and he stared around at the snow as though just becoming aware of his surroundings. "Come on, it's getting cold." He climbed to his feet and extended a hand to her.

She laid her gloved hand in his and he pulled her up against his chest.

With his arm like an iron band around her waist, he stared down into her eyes, his gaze fiercely determined. "Promise me that you won't try to run again?"

"Being with me puts you in danger."

"*Kitala igmu taka,* little lion." His jaw tightened. "Promise."

After the past couple days on the run, alone and without anyone to call for help, Katya couldn't resist Maddox's strength. "I cannot continue to rely on you to protect me. You have your own life, and getting involved with me could ruin it."

"Let me worry about that." His gaze never wavered from hers.

Katya sighed, leaning her forehead into his chest. "I promise."

For a brief moment, his arm tightened, then he moving her away from him. "I'll take care of the snowmobile."

Without his arms around her, the cold crept beneath her jacket, making her shiver. As Maddox climbed aboard the still-humming machine, Katya looked on with a mix of regret and relief. Finding her way across the frozen North Dakota Badlands in the dark had been a foolish idea, one born of desperation and panic.

Maddox spun the snowmobile around and parked it beneath the lean-to, purposely pulling the keys from the ignition and dangling them for her to see before he tucked them into his pocket. He led her to the front of the cabin and stepped inside.

Katya entered the cabin, noting the splintered latch where the lock had been until Maddox busted through. "I am sorry about the lock."

"It can be fixed." He knelt by the fireplace, arranging the kindling and then striking a long wooden match across the stones. Before long a small fire burned, casting an intimate glow in the tiny cabin.

She turned away, forcing herself to think, to reason away the yearning she could not seem to deny. Ever since her mother died, she had taken on the role of hostess for thousands of diplomatic dinners and meetings, all the while longing for the freedom to be herself, to be alone with only one man. A man of her choosing.

A smile curved her lips. Funny how this man had not been of her choosing. The situation had chosen him for her. Yet she could think of no other she would rather be stranded with on a windswept prairie.

Heat spread through the cabin and pulsed throughout her body, carried by a rapidly increasing heartbeat.

How could she keep her distance from Maddox Thunder Horse, the tall, dark Native American hero who'd saved her from death not once, but twice? Despite her determination to keep her distance, Katya glanced toward him.

His back to her, he was staring down into the fire. His presence filled the room, broad shoulders, blocking the light cast by the fire, silhouetted with the blaze bright between his spread legs.

He unzipped his jacket and tugged it from his shoulders.

Katya caught her breath as his muscles flexed beneath the stretchy cotton of the long-sleeved shirt he wore. Her fingers tingled at the memory of his smooth, dark chest beneath her hands, the way his skin tasted on her lips. That moist place between her thighs throbbed, achingly aware of his every movement.

When he turned toward her, she could not drag her gaze from his, could not hide what could only be longing shining from her eyes.

Maddox stared across the cabin at Katya. The faint

glow of the fire reflected in her ice-blue cyes and gave her black hair a soft shine, highlighting the waves. Even bundled in her winter coat, the woman held herself like a queen—regal, elegant and yet fragile in the sparse surroundings of the hunting cabin.

Every fiber of Maddox's being cried out to protect this small woman—from the ravages of the weather to the violence of the man determined to abduct her.

When she'd locked him in the cabin, panic catapulted his anger, pushing adrenaline through his veins like pressurized steam. Every possible scenario that could happen to her erupted in his mind, none with a good outcome. First and foremost was Katya lost in the Badlands, only to be found too late to help, her frozen face staring up at him. Her image merged with his memory of Susan.

"What do we do now?" she asked, her voice a hushed whisper in the confines of the tiny cabin.

Maddox could think of a lot of things they could do to pass the time. But he didn't want to scare her or take advantage of her after her tumble in the back of the wrecked car. "You could start by telling me everything you've been hiding from me."

"You already know I've been framed."

"Why?"

"I don't know." Katya turned away.

Maddox closed the distance between them. "I think you do." His arms circled her waist and he drew her back against his front. "Tell me."

At first she remained stiff in his arms. After a long moment, she leaned into him. "My father was…" she hesitated, then continued "…an important political figure in Trejikistan, my homeland, formerly part of

Russia. I received word two weeks ago that he was involved in an accident. There was no accident. He was murdered, and I think the people who murdered him are after me."

"But why set you up as a terrorist?"

"So that if they do not manage to kill me, I could never return to Trejikistan and carry on my father's legacy."

"I thought you were just a student."

"I am…I was, until my father's death. I just wanted to have a normal life, to blend in and be a student, not a political figure with an entourage of paparazzi following me around the rest of my life. I wanted to be me." Her voice dropped to a whisper on the last word.

Maddox turned her in his arms.

She gave little resistance, laying her cheek against his shirt, her fingers curling into the fabric. "Just me."

He tilted her chin and looked down into her eyes, amazed at how brave she'd been under the circumstances. No matter how badly he wanted to push her away and believe the worst, he couldn't. He might be the biggest fool ever, but he wanted to believe her story.

"I'm tired of crying," she said, looking up into his face. "And I'm tired of running." Her chin hardened, her lips pressing into a thin line. "If you want to help me—and I am not asking you to—I need to get back to Minneapolis and find out who planted those weapons in my apartment."

"Are you sure you want to go back where you're probably on everyone's watch list?"

"I have to." Her gaze raked his face. "Do you not see? If I do not, the police will crucify me. I am a foreigner, the media will try to convict me without bothering to get their facts straight. I will never be able to go home again." Her hands clenched in the fabric of his shirt. "My father's death will remain an *accident* while a killer runs loose out there. Whoever did this will win."

For a long moment, Maddox stared down into those bottomless blue eyes. "If I agree to help you, will you agree to do it my way?"

Her brows dipped slightly. "You know you will be labeled an accessory to whatever crime they pin on me. Are you willing to take that risk?"

He nodded. "You didn't answer my question."

The frown furrowing her brow lifted. "I will do it your way."

"Good." Maddox still held her in his arms. "That wasn't so hard, was it?"

Katya sighed. "I still do not like that you are involved."

"I made that decision, not you." He brushed a lock of raven-black hair from her forehead. "Get over it."

"I am finding it very difficult to get over it as far as you are concerned." Her eyelids drooped, the long, lush lashes shadowing her pale irises. When her tongue swept across her full dusky-rose lips, Maddox couldn't hold back.

He had to taste her, touch her lips with his own. His fingers rose to cup the back of her head, lacing through the long, luxurious layers of hair. When his mouth descended onto hers, he took her slowly in a deliberate kiss, one meant to explore, discover and learn everything there was to know about this woman in his arms. He knew so little about her, and he longed to know more. From her favorite color to the name of her first pet, to the places on her body that made her crazy with desire.

Maddox's groin tightened and he pulled away. He wanted her so badly, he was afraid it would cloud his judgment.

Katya's arms circled his neck and drew him back down to her mouth. "Is this part of doing it your way?" She pressed her lips to his. "Because if it is, I will agree to more of this—no argument."

A chuckle rose up his throat and he kissed her hard, before setting her away from him. "You aren't obligated to kiss me."

Her brows winged upward. "Do you think I kissed you out of obligation?" She unzipped her jacket and let it fall to the floor. "My reactions to you have never been those of one who feels obligated." She closed the short distance between them. "More a sense of the inevitable." She stared up at him. "Do you kiss me out of obligation?"

Maddox snorted. "No." His gaze captured her stormy one, his pulse racing, his hands aching to take her back into his arms, but he refused to make the first move this time. If she wanted what he wanted, she'd have to tell him. Taking her, making love to her in this tiny cabin might be the biggest mistake of his life. This woman could be a master spy, a consummate liar, a terrorist for all he really knew about her. But if she took him into her arms and kissed him, she would have conquered him completely, undermined his ability to resist.

Katya's gaze retained its hold on his. "My father never let me be with men he deemed unsuitable. He kept a very tight rein on my activities, not that I would disappoint him in any way."

"And your father would deem me unsuitable."

She curled her fingers around the hem of her sweater

and pulled it up and over her head, tossing it onto the table. "Probably. You do not provide any political value to the equation. You are not from Trejikistan or one of its neighboring countries." She unzipped the snowpants she'd borrowed from his mother and slid them down her legs. "You do not own a fleet of ships or oil wells." Her fingers tugged the button loose on the jeans she wore beneath, flicking it open.

His breath caught and lodged in his throat as her jeans followed the snowpants to the floor.

"You do not have any major political connections. You would be unworthy of my affiliation." Katya strode across the floor, wearing nothing but a black lace bra, panties and the pendant she fingered now.

Maddox's heart fluttered, the ache intensifying in his groin. "You know how to build a man up, don't you?" She didn't have to say a word to make him hot.

"I did not say that I agreed with my father." She stopped in front of him and ran her fingers down his chest to the button of his snowpants. "I loved my father. But he was, after all, a father looking out for the best interests of his only daughter."

"And you found his scrutiny too confining?"

"Yes." She unzipped the pants and pushed them down his legs.

Maddox stepped out of them and kicked them to the side. "And now that your father can't call the shots?"

Her hands paused on the rivet to his jeans. She closed her eyes and sucked in a ragged breath. "I miss him."

Maddox's hand closed over hers. "Don't do this just because you can."

Katya opened her eyes and stared up at Maddox. "I've

been a student in your country for six months. I could have made love to a dozen men by now."

"And have you?"

"No."

"Why me?"

She didn't step away, didn't remove her hand from his jeans. Instead, she stared up into his face. "I don't know. For some reason, you make me feel as though I am living life for the very first time."

That cold lump in his chest he'd given up on when Susan died swelled, filling and expanding to accommodate the blood flowing swiftly through his veins. The rush of emotion was quickly chased by panic. "And you make me feel…again. And frankly that scares the hell out of me."

She raised her hands to his cheeks. "I'm sorry about your fiancée. That must have hurt a lot."

He nodded, unable to voice the amount of pain he'd experienced at the time. His fingers tightened in her hair. "I can't do that again. I won't." His jaw clenched, his teeth grinding away at his memories.

"You don't have to." Her smile softened, her blue eyes swimming in a film of unshed tears. "I cannot stay in your country, anyway. Once I clear up this mess, I have to return to my home."

She'd left him an out. The opportunity to make love with no regrets, no ties, no claim on this woman, or her on him. He didn't have to invest his emotions as he had with Susan.

But what if he wanted to? "Do you have to go back?"

She nodded, her fingers stroking his stubbled chin. "Yes."

He sucked in a deep breath to steady his heartbeat, hoping he could turn it back into stone, although he feared it was too late. "Well, then, we'd better get some sleep." Maddox pulled her arms down from his face and stepped away from her tempting body, clad only in her underwear. It cost him.

Dearly.

"Sleep?" She stared at him, her breasts rising and falling behind the black lace, her arms wrapping around her middle, covering the rising goose bumps.

"Sleep." He nodded to where the sleeping bag lay spread across the ropes strung between the hand-carved bedposts. "You can have the bed."

She glanced at the bag, a shiver wracking her body.

Maddox wanted to take her back in his arms and warm all parts of her body, but he dared not. He couldn't afford to put his arms around her. If he did, he was afraid he'd never let her go. And she'd made it plenty clear to him that she was not sticking around.

One by one, she gathered her clothes.

His pulse thundering in his veins, his body stiff and ready for what he knew he couldn't have, Maddox couldn't watch. He turned his back to her and stirred the logs in the fire, the flames flaring up, sending a shower of sparks across the floor.

She'd done that to him. Stirred the embers in his heart and made him want the flame again. How had he come to this? How had he let himself feel for a woman again? Especially one who came with so much baggage and promised she'd be leaving.

Damn her!

Chapter Eleven

Katya dressed in her jeans and sweater before crawling between the folds of the sleeping bag. She lay facing Maddox, silhouetted in the glow from the fire.

How she wanted to go to him and put her arms around him, bring him back to the bed to make love to her as they had in the cave. But that was before he knew she was an accused terrorist. Before he knew she'd be leaving soon. Before she knew she was falling in love with this tall, dark Native American, whose heart and family were tied to the North Dakota Badlands. Even if she wanted him to follow her back to Trejikistan, she couldn't let him.

She didn't know what awaited her there. With her country torn apart by warring factions, she would be in constant danger, forever looking over her shoulder. And how did she expect the people of her country to follow her when it had taken every ounce of political pull and diplomacy her father could muster to steer the people toward democracy? And what had it gotten him? He'd been murdered, probably by the very people determined to squelch the democratic movement and return a king to ultimate power.

Who would they choose as the leader? Who would

they put in power if Katya decided to stay in America? If she decided to abandon her country, her people?

She gathered the edges of the sleeping bag around her, the thick fabric unable to dispel the chill suffusing her body. Her life, her moral code, instilled by her father, dictated that she return to her country. Without a ruler to guide them, Trejikistan would become a military state. Whoever orchestrated her father's death would take power and ruin the people's chances of a democracy.

As her father's daughter and until her brother returned, she was next in line to rule Trejikistan. She had to assume her position and responsibility at least until the elections the following spring.

Maddox poked at the fire, his broad shoulders flexing and retracting with each movement.

The temptation to go to him grew stronger with each passing minute. If she hoped to get any sleep whatsoever, she couldn't continue to watch him. Forcing herself to be reasonable, she turned over in the bag, turning her back to Maddox and the alluring glow of the fire. She stared at the dark, bleak walls, so cold from the temperatures outside. Even if she didn't go to sleep, she could rest. She'd need to be ready to go whenever they made their next move.

With the pendant her father gave her clutched between her fingers, her eyelids drooped and she fell into a troubled sleep.

Trapped in a canyon, giant boulders blocking her path, forcing her into a maze she could not find her way out of, Katya ran. Her breathing came in ragged gasps, behind her a man with cold eyes followed, closing in on her location.

She ducked inside a cave, crouching low to the floor,

dragging in enough air to keep from passing out. When would this nightmare end? Surely it was only a dream. Soon she'd awaken in her own bedroom.

Katya closed her eyes and reopened them, hoping for the familiarity of her floral bedspread and the clock radio on her nightstand. Instead she awoke to her apartment filled with machine guns, blocks of plastic explosives and someone banging on the door.

"Police!" someone yelled through the wood paneling. "Open up!"

Katya closed her eyes again, wishing for escape, only to find herself back in the cave, the sound of footsteps running toward her. She had to get away. She couldn't let the murderer capture her—her family depended on her to clear their name. Her people depended on her to save them from a crushing military dictatorship.

Katya leaped to her feet and ran for the cave entrance, ready to stand up to the man chasing her or die trying.

As she emerged from the cave into the night air, hands grabbed her, pulling her against a rock-solid body. "No!" she cried, beating her fists against her captor's chest.

"Wake up, Katya!" Her captor shook her. "Wake up!"

Katya opened her eyes to the soft glow of fire in the fireplace and Maddox's worried gaze. Her struggles ceased, and she fell into his arms, her body shaking, exhausted.

"It's okay, you were only dreaming."

"But it felt so real." She buried her face in his neck, inhaling denim, leather and Maddox's fresh-soap smell. Her fingers clung to his shirt, clutching him close to her.

"You're safe for now," he crooned softly, his lips against her temple, his hand stroking her hair down her back. "You're safe."

"No, I am not." She moved closer, her body curling into his. "I will not be safe until the man chasing me is caught, or I am dead."

"I'm here. I won't let anything happen to you."

"You cannot promise that," she whispered into his neck, afraid to let go, lest she wake up to find he was never there.

"I can and do." Maddox's hand continued to stroke the back of her head, threading his fingers through her hair, trailing them down her back.

Slowly, her muscles relaxed and she let herself breathe again. "I cannot live this way."

"No one could. That's why we're going back to Minneapolis to figure this whole thing out."

"When?"

"Soon." He glanced at the watch on his wrist. "I arranged to meet my brother, Tuck, at the highway in a couple of hours when the coast is clear and the sheriff won't be awake to track us down."

She looked up into his face, loving the way the firelight enhanced the rich dark tones of his skin. "How did you arrange that? Does this cabin have telephone service?"

"No. I did it before we left." He stretched his legs out on the sleeping bag beside her, leaning against the cabin's log walls.

"You planned on helping me all along?" she asked.

"Yes."

His warmth spread throughout her body, chasing away the fear and dread from her dream. "Thank you."

"Don't thank me yet. We don't know what we have in store for us in Minneapolis."

"Still, you're putting your life on hold and in danger to help me." She leaned up and kissed his beard-roughened cheek. "Thank you."

Gratitude had nothing to do with her next kiss. She pressed her lips to his, loving the smooth fullness. The closer she moved, the closer she wanted to be to him.

He broke away, his hands still entangled in her hair, the rigid evidence of his arousal pressing into her thigh. "No, we shouldn't."

"No one knows that more than I do." She leaned forward and kissed him again.

"Someone needs to stop before we go too far."

"Would that be you?" she asked.

"Not this time. If you want this to end now, you'll have to say so. I've been wanting to do this since the cave." He laid her down beside him, nestled in the sleeping bag. Leaning over her, he kissed her so thoroughly he took her breath away.

Katya clung to him, her pulse quickening, her breath tight, short spasms, providing little relief to her oxygen-starved lungs. Her fingers shoved at the shirt he wore, pushing it up and over his head, her hands splaying over the hard planes of his chest, feverishly memorizing every contour. Later, when she made it back to her home country, she would have little more than her memories to keep her warm at night.

Her breath caught in her throat and a sudden welling of tears threatened to take over. Dammit, she was done with crying. She had shed enough tears in the past three days to last a lifetime. With so little time left with Maddox, she wanted nothing more than to seize the moment, experience everything she could before she went home—should she live long enough and bypass the legal system to get back.

Maddox tugged her shirt up over her head and flung it over the bedpost. Her jeans came next, then the scrap of silk underwear and lace bra. The chill air pebbled her skin and made her breasts form pointed peaks.

Maddox stared down at her, drinking in every detail. Her pale skin reflected the warm glow of the firelight, her hair held a sheen similar to moonlight on still water. Her legs parted, her knees falling to the sides, welcoming him.

He stripped off the rest of his clothing and crawled into the sleeping bag with her, covering her body with his, settling between her legs. His erection pressed against her opening, but he refused to dive in like an eager teenager.

Katya had insisted that she couldn't stay. Her words hurt more than Maddox cared to admit.

His revenge would come in the form of sensual torture. He lowered his lips to hers, poised a hair's breadth from the temptation of her kiss. When she leaned up to capture his lips, he pulled away.

Instead, he pressed a kiss to her nose, her forehead, her cheeks and trailed a line of tender caresses along her jawbone, nipping and tonguing the pulse at the base of her throat.

His hands smoothed along the regal line of her neck and downward, skimming across her collarbone, edging ever closer to her breasts.

Her back arched, bringing her breast in contact with his fingers.

He tweaked the rosy-brown nipples to a velvety peak, his fingers massaging until Katya moaned.

"Maddox, please." Her body writhed with each touch, her feet churning the sleeping bag into a tousled heap. Her fingernails scraped his buttocks, digging in, tugging him closer, urging him to fill her.

He resisted, letting his lips follow his fingers to her breasts, taking them into his mouth one at a time, tasting the luscious sweetness.

Katya's legs wrapped around his waist, her heels digging into his back. "Please, Maddox," she begged.

"Patience. I want to bring you with me."

"I am with you, oh, please. What you are doing is making me completely insane." Her words came out in breathy gasps. Her feet falling to the sleeping bag, her heels digging in, lifting her hips upward.

When he didn't think he could hold out any longer, Maddox slipped lower on the shifting rope bed, his knees digging into the sleeping bag, finding the gaps between the ropes. He levered himself lower, his tongue skittering across Katya's flat belly and lower to the apex of her thighs.

"Please come inside me, please," she begged, her fingers clutching at his hair in spasms.

He wasn't finished. His tongue delved between her folds, lapping at the swollen nub until her bottom rose off the bed and her fingernails pressed into his scalp.

Her body tensed, then a soft gasp whooshed from her lips. She clung to him, breathing hard.

Only then did he shift up her body and slide into her heated slickness. He thrust deep, riding the wave of his desire.

At last he catapulted over the edge, his body throbbing

to a rhythm as ageless as time. Spent, he collapsed over her, drawing her into his arms without severing the intimate connection.

Together they fell into a deep dreamless sleep, arms and legs intertwined, the sleeping bag pulled up around their shoulders as the fire died.

A loud roar and insistent beeping woke Maddox. He jerked away, stabbing at his watch to silence his alarm. It took several seconds for him to realize the sound was coming from outside the cabin. The roaring wasn't the wind but the revving of a snowmobile engine.

Maddox leaped out of the bed and dragged his jeans up over his hips.

"What's happening?" Katya sat up, clutching the bag to her breasts.

"I don't know."

"Maddox!" Tuck's voice called to him through the thickness of the wooden door.

Maddox grabbed his sweater and flung the door open, letting in a blast of arctic air. "Tuck, what are you doing here? Is it time already?" He glanced down at his watch, the icy wind against his exposed skin making him shake so badly he could barely see the digital numbers.

"Get your clothes on, someone alerted our favorite sheriff that Katya is a wanted woman. He's on his way out to check the hunting cabin."

"How did he know to come here?"

"Heck if I know. I heard it on the police scanner and hightailed it out here as fast as I could." Tuck nodded at Maddox's naked chest and glanced toward the dark interior of the cabin. "Better get her out of here before the sheriff arrives."

"What about the truck?" Maddox asked, tugging his sweater over his head.

"Dante's driving it to our designated location on the highway. He'll take the snowmobile back to the ranch. He didn't dare take the chopper out. As it is, he'll have enough explaining to do with the Border Patrol."

"I am ready when you are." Katya stepped up beside Maddox, zipping her jacket up to her neck.

Maddox could have kissed her already kiss-swollen lips. "Give me a second, and I'll meet you in back by the lean-to." He shut the door, blocking the wind from blowing through the already freezing cabin while he finished dressing in his cold-weather gear.

When he had his boots on and his hood pulled down over his head, he pulled Katya into his arms and kissed her. A quick, brief kiss, but it would have to do until he could kiss her again. And he planned on kissing her a hell of a lot more. So much so that she would change her mind about going back to Trejikistan. With her father dead, what could possibly make her want to return to a country that didn't want her back to begin with?

When Katya walked outside, the full force of the wind hit her, making her step back before she could get her balance. Each time she went out into the cold, it got harder. She'd give anything to sit in a sauna and ease the chill out of her bones. But now was not that time.

Maddox jogged ahead of her and backed the snowmobile out of the lean-to, dusting the snow off the seat.

Katya climbed on the back and looped her arms around his waist.

Without another word to his brother, Maddox raced off into the night, headed toward the highway where his other brother waited. Tuck's snowmobile kept pace at his right, neither rider using headlights.

Katya glanced behind her at the cabin, a dark shape barely illuminated by the sketchy starlight was intermittently revealed by the skittering of clouds across the heavens.

A light blinked on the horizon past the cabin, a tiny light, barely the size of a distant star—only this wasn't a star.

Katya's heart raced, her hands tightening around Maddox's waist. "We're being followed!" Katya yelled and pointed back at the light.

Weighed down by two people, the snowmobile could not outrun the one following. The best they could hope for was to stay ahead of him and arrive at the truck before he did.

Tuck's snowmobile pulled close and he shouted over the roar of the engine, "We should split up. Maybe he'll follow me."

Maddox nodded. "Don't go and get yourself shot. Mom would never forgive me."

"Don't worry. I'll take a punch for you, but forget the bullets."

Despite his words to the contrary, Katya would bet her life that Tuck would take a bullet for Maddox. The Thunder Horse brothers were a force to be reckoned with and they obviously loved each other, even if they did not say it outright.

Tuck split off and dropped back to intercept the other snowmobile.

Maddox opened his machine up full throttle and raced off across the snow-covered landscape.

The last time Katya had been on a speeding

snowmobile, racing away from the bad guy on her tail, she had gone over the edge into a canyon. Between peering around Maddox at what lay ahead and tracking the light of the snowmobile behind them, she could not be still on the backseat.

She wished they did not have to go quite so fast, but slowing down was not an option.

If the man following them was the sheriff, he would throw her in jail, and wait for Homeland Security to come get her and sort things out. And when they did, her quest to clear her name might as well be over. Who would think to look further than a foreigner?

If the person behind them was the man who had tried to kidnap her, she might not see the morning dawn.

Squelching her fear of speed, Katya buried her face in Maddox's back and held on. The bumps and dips were amplified by the speed, slamming them into the earth or making them go airborne off the snowmobile's seat.

Several times Katya nearly lost her hold on Maddox, her body flying into the air, only to crash down when the skids hit the hard-packed snow.

Even while trying to hold on to Maddox, Katya worried about Tuck. Whatever he was doing back there, the light had not wavered once. In fact, it was getting bigger. The vehicle was closing in on them.

Katya glanced ahead. Where was the highway and Dante with the waiting vehicle? Would they make it in time?

Another look behind and the light was closer still. Then Katya saw a shadowy form cross in front of the other snowmobile. Over the roar of the engine, a loud crack ripped through the air.

Starlight glinted off Tuck's snowmobile as he

swerved and raced back across the path of the other snowmobile.

Her breath lodged firmly in her throat, Katya could only watch with a dreadful sense of doom as another crack blasted through the air. Tuck's snowmobile veered to the right and slowed to a stop.

Had their pursuer shot him? Was Tuck bleeding to death in the frigid cold? "We have to go back. Tuck's hurt."

"We can't," Maddox insisted. "The truck's ahead. Once we reach it, I'll send Dante back for Tuck."

"It could be too late. He could bleed to death!" Katya pulled at Maddox's sleeve. "You have to go back. You can't leave him there to die!"

Chapter Twelve

Maddox wanted to turn around and go back for his brother, but he'd promised Katya that he'd keep her safe. He couldn't do that by driving back into bullet range of their pursuer.

Ahead the sporadic starlight reflected off something metallic. That something had better be the truck his brother, Dante, was bringing. When they got to the truck, Dante would go back and check on Tuck.

That is, if they made it there before their pursuer planted a bullet in Katya's back. The only saving grace was that the terrain was bumpy, and steady aim would be impossible. But that didn't rule out a lucky shot—or an unlucky one if it hit one of them.

A quick glance over his shoulder kicked up his pulse a notch.

The snowmobile behind them was catching up fast.

A loud bang sounded over the noise of his engine.

Katya's arms tightened around his waist, her face digging into his back.

Maddox would have zigzagged to make it harder for the shooter to use them as target practice, but anything other than a straight line would slow them enough for him to catch up. With the throttle wide open, Maddox pushed the snowmobile to its limits.

A small beam of light flashed out over the snow. Using a handheld flashlight, Dante guided them to the truck.

Like a sprinter racing past the finish line, Maddox didn't slow down until he passed the truck and put the body of the vehicle between him and the shooter.

Dante stood behind the truckbed, a rifle aimed at the oncoming snowmobile. He fired off a shot.

The pursuer swerved, killed the headlight and pulled a tight circle, regrouping now that the odds were stacked against him.

Maddox pulled the snowmobile up to the pickup and leaped off. "Tuck's down back there. Promise me you'll take care of him."

His brother's eyes narrowed, his grip tightening on the rifle. Their pursuer kept his distance, just out of range of Dante's rifle. Which meant he was also out of range to fire a pistol at Maddox and Katya. "I've got this covered. You get her out of here."

"That's the plan." Maddox opened the passenger door and, keeping his body below the outline of the truck, climbed in and cranked the engine to life.

Katya hesitated. "We cannot leave Tuck out there. He could be hurt."

"I'll take care of him," Dante said, his focus remaining on the snowmobile in the distance. "Go!" he barked.

Katya threw herself into the truck, keeping her head below the level of the windows.

Even before the passenger door closed, Maddox shoved

the gearshift into Drive and shot down the highway, slipping sideways on the snow-covered, icy road.

Katya looked over the top of the seat. "I think the snowmobile is following us. It is hard to tell, he still has his light off."

"Keep your head down. Until we get to the interstate highway, he has the advantage on these snowy back roads."

The truck skidded and bumped across the treacherous path.

Every few minutes, Katya sneaked a peek out the back windshield. "I can't see him."

Maddox didn't slow or lose focus. With the headlights of the truck reflecting off the snow, their night vision would be less than adequate past the manmade illumination. They had to make several turns to get to the highway. The snowmobile didn't. The shooter could cut across fields and head them off if he knew where Maddox was headed.

Katya sat quietly in the seat beside him, slumped low, her eyes wide, brows furrowed. "I hope your brothers are all right."

"They've been through worse." His words belied his own worry as he fought to keep the truck from sliding off the road and into the ditches.

As they neared the intersection of the county road and the main highway leading to the interstate, Maddox slowed to make the turn.

Serving as his lookout, Katya swiveled in her seat, panning the horizon. "On your left!" She ducked.

The snowmobile roared across the road in front of the truck. Instinctively, Maddox slammed on his brakes.

The truck skidded sideways, not slowing any sooner.

A loud pop ripped through the air and the driver's-side window shattered, spraying glass throughout the interior.

"Stay down!" he shouted. Something stung his arm, but Maddox didn't let go of his grip on the steering wheel. He straightened the truck and skidded through the T-intersection, aiming for the interstate, sure that if they could get there, the snowmobile wouldn't be able to keep pace.

On the straight road, Maddox pushed the truck as fast as he could, praying he wouldn't slide off the side. The frigid air blowing in from the shattered window took his breath away. He reached for the heater, twisting the knob to the highest setting to keep them from getting frostbite. Lights reflected off the low-hanging clouds that had moved in from the west—it had to be the small town of Dickinson.

With hope in sight, Maddox increased his speed. As they neared the town, the road had less and less snow until all that was left was the sand and salt used by the highway department.

"I think we lost him," Katya said, looking through the rear window.

Houses and businesses lined the road into the town, and towering lights lit the interstate.

Katya touched Maddox's arm. "If the sheriff knows about me, he will have put out a message to all the law enforcement agencies, especially those along the main routes."

"You're right. Having a busted window won't help, either." Maddox slowed the truck and pulled down a side street, taking a less conspicuous route to the interstate. "We have to ditch the truck."

"How will we get to Minneapolis? Do they have a bus station here?" Katya asked.

"No, they have something better—truckers." Maddox parked two streets away from a well-lit truck stop and behind a large Dumpster.

Maddox dropped down out of the truck and rounded the vehicle to Katya's side. He opened the door and held his hand out to her.

She reached for it, but drew back, her forehead wrinkled. "Maddox, you're bleeding!" Katya slipped out of the truck without his help, her gaze on his arm with the blood-soaked sleeve. "We have to get you to a hospital."

He hadn't realized that he'd been hit. The shattering glass and the wild ride hadn't given him time to think about anything other than getting them to safety. "We don't have time. Besides, it's just a flesh wound." He touched his hand to the wound and fought back a wince. "Let's find a ride." He hooked her arm with his good one and led her toward the truck stop.

As they neared, Katya dug her heels into the pavement. "You cannot go in there. With all the blood, someone will get suspicious. They might call the police."

Maddox frowned. "You're right. But we can't risk you going in. What if they have fliers with your picture on them? If there are any cops in there, you could be caught."

"We'll have to take that chance."

"I'll sneak in and wash up in the bathroom."

"You'll need help."

"Here," Maddox dug in his back pocket and removed his wallet. He handed her a couple of twenties. "Buy a hat to cover your hair and face as much as possible. Get some bandages and meet me at the bathroom door in five minutes."

Katya nodded, accepting the money, her bottom lip caught between her teeth. "Are you sure you are okay?"

"Yeah. As far as I can tell without looking, the bleeding's stopped. I'll be fine. Just stay away from cops." He leaned close and brushed her cheek with his lips. "See ya in five."

Katya tucked the money into her snowpants pocket and entered the building through a side door. The truck stop had a store on one side and a restaurant on the other.

Through the front window, Katya spotted two county sheriff's cars parked along the curb. Her heart pounded against her chest as she moved through the aisles, keeping her head lowered. She found a rack of knitted hats in soft pastel colors. She chose one in rose and gray, colors so very different from her own hair color. Then she found the row with the first aid items, grabbed a box of gauze and medical tape and hurried to the counter to pay, careful to avoid contact with anyone. From the corner of her eye, she located the bathrooms between the restaurant and the convenience store. Now all she had to do was pay and get to Maddox.

A man asking for cigarettes got to the clerk first. Katya stood behind him, her head down, her gaze fixed on the floor.

As she waited her turn, a pair of brown boots appeared beside her. In her peripheral vision she could tell that the man wore brown trousers as well. The same color worn by Sheriff Yost.

A quick glance upward confirmed her guess. A

sheriff's deputy stood beside her, talking to another man in uniform behind him.

At last the man with the cigarettes paid for his purchase and left.

Katya laid her items on the counter, praying that the lawmen wouldn't question her need for gauze and tape. The men were so deep in conversation, maybe they'd completely ignore her.

The one closest to her was saying something about an APB. "Sheriff Yost issued it a couple hours ago. We're supposed to be on the lookout for some Russian woman suspected of terrorism."

Katya's heart skipped a beat at the man's words. She struggled against the urge to run, before the officers realized the woman they were supposed to be watching out for was right in front of them.

The clerk lifted the knit cap. "Ma'am, the hats on the other rack are half off."

"That's okay," she said, keeping her voice low and as American sounding as she could. She had practiced the American accent, wanting to fit in at school. "I like this one."

"There's one just like it on the other rack. Well, almost. Want me to get it for you?" The clerk stepped away from the register.

"No," Katya said, desperate to pay and leave the deputies behind. "I want this one."

The young man shrugged. "Have it your way. But the others are cheaper." He rang up the purchases and took the twenty she handed to him.

Her heart thumping wildly in her chest, Katya tried to fake a calm she didn't feel.

"Not from around here, are you?" the deputy beside her said.

Katya jumped, but refused to make eye contact with the man talking to her, preferring to fix her gaze on the clerk. "Nope," she said as quietly as she could.

"Where ya from?" he asked.

The man behind him elbowed him. "Give it up, Swenson. She's not interested."

The deputy closest to her turned to his friend, a fierce frown pulling his brows down over his eyes. "Shut up, Roe. Let the lady decide." The deputy faced her again. "Ignore the jerk. Where are you from?"

Remembering a movie she'd seen with her neighbor, she forced a response she hoped sounded genuine. "Jersey," she said, laying on the thick Jersey accent from the movie. Thankfully, the clerk handed her change to her. Relieved beyond reason, Katya was about to make her escape.

The clerk smiled at her and delayed her further with, "Really? What part? I have relatives in New Jersey."

Caught in her own lie, Katya's mind went blank. She couldn't remember the name of a single city in New Jersey.

As she groped for a response, the clerk tipped his head to the side. "Newark, I think. My cousin lives in Newark. You from anywhere close?"

"Newark," she said, gathering her items.

"Need a bag for that?" the clerk asked.

"No, thank you."

"Hey, I'm off in thirty minutes." The young deputy said. "Care to have breakfast with me?"

"Sorry, my husband is waiting," she said and hurried toward the bathrooms and Maddox. Not until she ducked down the hallway and out of sight of the deputies did she draw a breath. Then it was only to have it yanked out of her when a hand grabbed her from behind and tugged her into the men's bathroom and one of the stalls.

Her face burning, Katya stood chest to chest with Maddox. "I cannot be in here. This is the men's bathroom. What if someone comes in?" Katya protested.

"We'll take that chance." He had his jacket and shirt off.

Katya's hands, full of the hat and bandages, pressed into his warm, smooth skin. Her breath caught now for another reason entirely.

"Good, you got bandages." Maddox smiled. "You took longer than five minutes."

"Couldn't be helped." Katya eyed the wound.

He had managed to clean the blood off his jacket and hung it on the back of the stall door. The edges of the cut were cleaned as well, but fresh blood oozed out.

"Here, hold these." She handed him the hat and box of tape. Ripping two sterile packages of gauze from the remaining box, she folded one into a tight pad and pressed it against the injury, then laid the other over the first. She held out her free hand. "Tape."

He handed her the box of tape. "Are you a nurse back in your country?"

"No, but I had a brother," she said. "He was constantly getting into scrapes."

"What do you mean *had?*" Maddox's forehead creased. "Did he die?"

"No," she answered too quickly. She refused to believe that her brother was dead. If he was, she had no other family but her cousin, Vladimir. In other words, she had no family. "No, he is not dead. Wc…I do not know where hc is."

Maddox's lips turned up in a gentle smile. "You've misplaced your brother?"

"You could say that. I have not heard from him in months. But he is alive." She stretched a band of white tape over the top of the gauze. "He has to be."

"Now we're getting somewhere. You know that I have three brothers. I know that you have at least one. Any other family I should know about?"

"No. It was just me, my brother and my father." Her voice cracked on the last word and she fought to keep from shedding another tear. She ripped off another strip of tape and plastered it to the bottom of the gauze. "There, you were right. It was just a flesh wound. You probably need a tetanus shot to be safe."

"Yes, ma'am. As soon as you're safe." He smiled down at her. "Thanks." Then he kissed her nose.

How she could get all hot and bothered by a man kissing her nose, Katya did not know, but she could not stop the rush of blood to the lower regions of her belly. She pressed closer to him, her hands sliding over his dark-skinned chest. "I do not understand why I cannot keep my hands off you."

"You don't hear me complaining." He captured her fingers in his and drew them up to his lips where he kissed her fingertips. "Much as I like what you're doing to me, we have to get out of here."

"Right." Katya said, dragging her focus back to the more immediate need for transportation. "And there are a couple of sheriff's deputies out there."

The outer door to the bathroom swung open.

Katya stepped up on the edge of the toilet seat and

squatted down so that whoever came in wouldn't see two sets of legs in one stall.

The door next to them opened and closed.

Maddox pressed a finger to his lips, slipped his shirt and jacket on, then slid the lock open on his stall door. Before she could guess at his next move, he grabbed her around the legs and lifted her up.

She swallowed a scream and held on as he carried her through the stall door to the exit.

Once outside the door, he dropped her on her feet. He took the hat from her hands and stretched it down over her hair, tucking the long strands up underneath. "There. Now we have to find a ride."

Maddox led the way through the restaurant, head down, eyes averted to avoid being recognized.

The deputies were sitting in a booth in the far corner, laughing over coffee and breakfast. The one who had hit on Katya looked up, his eyes narrowing at Maddox.

Pretending she didn't see him, Katya moved on to another booth as far away from the deputies as possible.

A group of truckers sat between Katya and the deputies, their loud voices and laughter enough to drown out any conversation Maddox and Katya might attempt.

"Aren't you afraid the deputies will question us?"

"We won't find out where the trucks are going if we don't eavesdrop on the conversations."

Katya sat with her back to the lawmen. Maddox faced them and the truckers. He stared toward Katya while he surreptitiously studied the truckers.

"Haven't seen the wife in a week." An older gentleman with a weathered face and graying hair twisted his coffee cup in his hands.

"Lucky dog." The man with his back to Maddox, with

strawberry-blond hair and freckles running together on his arms and neck, waved at the waitress with his mug.

"Unlike you dirtbags, I actually like my wife." The older man sipped his coffee and grimaced. "She makes a better cup of coffee than this swill."

"You're probably the only man I know who still gives a crap about his ball and chain." The man in the booth beside the older gentleman had the gravelly voice and heavily lined face of a smoker.

The gray-haired trucker shrugged. "She puts up with me and she's still as pretty as the day I met her."

The waitress swung by with a steaming pot of coffee.

"Where is this wife of yours?" The younger, freckled man set his mug on the table for the waitress to fill. "Might need to pay her a visit while you're out of town."

The men all laughed.

"She's out of your league, Red."

"How do you know?"

The man in the booth beside the freckled man, nudged him in the side. "Any woman in her right mind would be out of your league."

Ignoring the younger men's antics, the gray-haired man looked over at the smoker. "Where ya headed?"

"Spokane."

"I'm going the other direction." The older man stirred sugar into his coffee. "I'll be in Chicago by nightfall. Only have to make a quick stop in Minneapolis."

Katya's gaze connected with Maddox's and he mouthed the word *Bingo*.

After topping off the truckers' coffee mugs, the

waitress stopped beside Katya. "You want a menu, or do you already know what you want?"

Maddox stood, keeping his torn sleeve out of sight of the deputies in the corner. "We've changed our minds. Come on, darlin'."

The waitress shrugged. "Don't blame you, the food here sucks."

Katya slid out of the booth and preceded Maddox out of the restaurant and into the convenience store.

Without saying a word, Maddox purchased shrink-wrapped breakfast biscuits and a couple bottles of orange juice, all the while keeping a watch on the gray-haired trucker in the restaurant. Whether or not he knew or liked it, the old guy was their ticket to Minneapolis.

As he paid the clerk, Maddox could see the trucker zipping his jacket and pulling on his gloves.

"Come on, we have a bus to catch." Maddox grabbed the plastic bag with their food and hurried toward the door leading out to where the truckers parked the big rigs.

"Bus?" Katya said, running to keep up with Maddox. "I thought you said we were not taking a bus."

"Just some American slang." He smiled and held out his hand. "Come on, let's get out of sight until our bus driver comes out."

Katya grinned and slipped her gloved fingers in his. Her eyes widened and her smile slipped when she looked past him. She tugged him hard and shoved him behind a large trailer.

"What? Was it something I said?" Maddox leaned over the top of Katya's head as they peered around the corner of the trailer at the county sheriff's car pulling up to the other two parked at the curb.

Sheriff Yost climbed out of the car and scanned the area.

Maddox and Katya ducked back behind the trailer. “We have to get out of here.” He looked around the corner again. Their gray-haired potential bus driver stood talking to the sheriff, looking down at the paper in the sheriff’s hands.

The older gentleman shook his head and took off across the parking lot toward the tractor-trailer rig where Maddox and Katya were hiding.

Maddox swore under his breath. The only man they’d found going their way had gotten the heads-up from the sheriff. What chance did they have now that he would let them in the truck?

Chapter Thirteen

"Sorry, folks, but this is as far as I can take you. From here, I'm on to Chicago." Chuck Goodman pulled the truck into a huge distribution center in the warehouse district of Minneapolis. He climbed down out of the truck and stretched.

Maddox descended to the pavement and reached up a hand to help Katya out of the tall vehicle. They met Chuck in front of the truck. "Thanks for giving us a ride this far."

"You guys did me the favor by keeping me company. I hope things work out for you two. You seem nice enough."

Maddox held out his hand to the older man and they shook.

Katya bypassed the hand and hugged the man's neck. If not for him, their trip might have ended at the truck stop. "Thank you for taking a chance on us."

"Probably wouldn't have if you weren't such a pretty little thing. Can't imagine you had anything to do with whatever stuff they found in your apartment. And even I've heard of the Thunder Horse Ranch. Makes me proud to know someone is looking out for the wild ponies of the Badlands." He shook Maddox's hand again.

"Your wife is a lucky woman, Chuck. I hope we meet again." Maddox waved and led Katya through the gates and out onto the sidewalk.

They left Chuck at the distribution center and hiked toward a convenience store they'd spied a couple blocks away.

"We can take a taxi or the city bus from there," Katya said.

"I want to make a call first."

"Tuck?" Katya shot a glance at him. "Why didn't you borrow the trucker's cell phone?"

"I didn't want any law enforcement officials tracing anything back to Chuck. He did us a favor giving us a lift."

"Right."

At the convenience store, Maddox purchased a throw-away cell phone for himself and one for Katya. "Just in case," he said.

Katya shoved the phone in her pocket and stared out the window of the store at the gray skies and traffic, praying the news was good from the Thunder Horse Ranch.

Maddox finished his call and joined her. "*Wanka-tanka* is looking out for Tuck. He's fine."

That little bit of news was such a relief it lifted some of the weight off Katya's shoulders. She couldn't have lived with herself if something bad happened to any one of the Thunder Horse clan.

"One more thing." Maddox paused, his lips pressed into a thin line. "I told Dante where we'd left the truck."

"And?"

"A man was murdered near the truck stop and his

car was stolen. The sheriff was all over it, blaming us for the murder and the theft."

Katya's stomach clenched. Another crime to add to her growing list. "If they catch me, I will be in jail for the rest of my life."

"You didn't kill anyone, Katya." His hands gripped her shoulders. "Look at me."

Her eyes opened and she stared up into the fathomless depths of his brown-black eyes.

"We'll get you through this."

"How?"

"I don't know, but you have to believe we'll make it through." He pulled her close and held her for a long moment. Then he put her away from him. "Just believe."

Katya stared out the store window, trying not to fall apart. She twisted the chain around her neck, remembering the day her father gave her the necklace—the day she left for school in the United States. He'd wanted her to have something to remember her family back home in Trejikistan. He'd had the thick, white-gold pendant engraved with the family crest. "So that I always know you are safe," he'd said. "And so that you always know where you belong."

And she belonged with her people now that her father wasn't there to protect them from the potential of an unwanted dictatorship. Katya could only guess at who had attempted the coup. Trejikistan was such a small blip on the American news radar that finding any information about the country's upheaval would be next to impossible. If only she could get to the internet again. When she'd been at the Medora library, she hadn't had time. At the very least she needed to check for her bodyguard's response. Perhaps her brother had made his way back home after hearing of their father's death. *If* he'd gotten word. *If* he was still alive. Katya prayed that her brother was alive.

In the meantime, she had to find out who was trying to frame and kill her.

A taxi pulled up to the curb in front of the store. Maddox circled her waist with his arm. "Ready?"

Ready to walk back into the apartment where all her troubles had begun just a few short days ago? No, Katya's chest tightened and the uncontrollable urge to run hit her, panic setting in. The last time she was there, someone had tried to grab her. Would the man who'd been following them find her here? After all the cross-country trekking, she'd have thought she'd shaken the pursuer.

Like a Pit Bull Terrier with his teeth dug in deep, her nemesis wasn't letting her go that easily.

Katya gave the taxi driver directions to the hair salon where she had her hair done, two blocks from her apartment complex. She pulled the knit hat down low over her forehead, the bulky yarn covering her dark brows. If the entire police force of Minneapolis was searching for her, she'd be discovered in no time.

"How will you find out who set you up?" Maddox broke into her thoughts, his voice low enough so the driver couldn't overhear.

"I'm not sure." She hadn't thought further ahead than arriving at her apartment complex alive. Now that they were this close, she didn't have a clue. "I suppose I could talk to the neighbors."

"Does the apartment have a security system?"

"Yes." Katya sat forward, remembering her father's

insistence on staying somewhere that had good security. He'd wanted her to be safe so far away from home. "The apartment complex has a high-end security system. Surely part of it consists of a camera and a digital history of that day."

"If we could get the historical videos, maybe we can find our real terrorist." Maddox grabbed her hands. "Do you know the security guards? Ever talk to them?"

"As a matter of fact, one of them is a friend of mine. Casey Reed. I set him up with my classmate." He was the man who'd helped her escape her attacker and hid her from the police.

"Perfect." Maddox sat back, staring out the window. "Maybe he'll get us in to see the videos."

Katya stared across the backseat at Maddox, her heart swelling in her chest. "Thank you, Maddox."

He turned toward her, his brow furrowing. "For what?"

"For helping me when you really should not." She leaned across the seat and kissed him full on the lips.

The kiss deepened, Maddox's hands circling behind her neck to draw her closer. His tongue thrust between her teeth.

Katya melted against him, wishing the kiss could last forever.

Not until the taxi driver cleared his throat did they break apart. The kiss was everything she could have hoped for and yet it broke her heart into a million pieces. Once she cleared her name, she would be on her way back to Trejikistan. Maddox would be half a world away.

Katya climbed out of the taxi and stood on the sidewalk, her mood as dreary as the Minneapolis winter.

She should not have kissed him, knowing they could never be more than acquaintances. The more physical contact she had with Maddox Thunder Horse, the harder it would be to say goodbye.

They took the side roads to the apartment complex arriving at the rear entrance. "We won't get in without my card key, and that's somewhere back in the canyon with the snowmobile," she said.

"Then we'll go around the front and wait for your friend."

"He works the midnight-to-noon shift. He should be leaving any moment. I have a better idea that won't be so conspicuous." Katya took his hand and, like lovers, leaned into him and guided him a block away from the apartment to a park within view of the front entrance, but shaded by the overhang of trees and bushes.

A metal park bench faced the street and gave them a good vantage point from which to watch for anyone entering or leaving the building.

Katya dropped onto the metal seat and tugged on Maddox's hand. "Sit."

Maddox complied, his glance panning the area. "Aren't you afraid your stalker will make an easy target of you?"

Katya's lips pressed into a line. "Hopefully, he is still back in North Dakota scratching his head." She patted her hat. "And with the disguise, hopefully, he will not know who I am."

"I want to know how he found you at the cabin."

"Maybe he followed the snowmobile tracks."

"I suppose he could have."

A man dressed in a security guard uniform exited the

apartment building, walking toward them, head down, hands tucked in his thick winter jacket.

Katya gripped Maddox's hand. "That's Casey."

Maddox stood, pulling Katya to her feet. "Let's get started."

"What if he is spooked by all the publicity about my being a terrorist?" Katya stared up into Maddox's eyes, pretending that she was his lover for anyone passing by. Her heart skipped a few beats when he leaned close.

With his lips close to her ear, he whispered, "We'll just have to convince him that you aren't."

Katya's stomach tumbled, all her nerves bouncing from his gentle breath on her neck.

Maddox straightened and stepped in front of the security guard, blocking his path. "Excuse me, sir, are you Casey Reed?"

Casey stopped abruptly and backed up a step. "Yeah, that's me."

Katya laid a hand on the man's arm. "Casey, I need your help."

The security guard stared down at her hand then into her face, his eyes widening, a grin spreading across his face. "Kat?"

She darted a glance around the street. "Yes, Casey, it's me, Kat."

Casey's gaze swept the area as well before returning to Katya. "Holy cow, Kat, where have you been? The entire Minneapolis police force and the FBI are all looking for you."

"I know."

Casey shook his head. "What happened? Where did all that stuff come from? Tell me all those weapons and explosives weren't really yours. I never believed it, but the media sounds so convincing."

"No, they weren't mine. I have no idea how the weapons got into my apartment. They were planted while I was out that morning."

"I knew it. When they told me all that stuff was yours, I didn't believe them. You're too nice to be a terrorist. That's why I helped you get away."

"I had to leave." Katya recalled the man who had jumped her on her way back to her apartment that fateful morning. "Someone tried to kill me, Casey. I have been running ever since."

Maddox broke into the conversation. "Look, we can't stand out in the open much longer. We need your help to clear her of the charges."

Casey nodded. "What can I do?"

Katya touched a hand to his arm. "You were on duty between eight and noon that morning. Did anyone deliver anything to the building?"

"The cops asked the same question. We had a furniture delivery scheduled for apartment 627 at nine." Casey ran a hand through his hair. "I watched from the monitor. Everything was on the up and up. They brought in a couch and a love seat. No boxes or anything else. That was all that was delivered that morning."

"Did you actually see them take the furniture to 627?"

"Yeah. They delivered at exactly nine o'clock. I remember because Mrs. Carmichael walks her Shitzu every morning at nine o'clock."

Maddox stared across at Katya. "We need to see the videos of the entrances to the building. If that was the only delivery, they had to have gotten the weapons in during that time."

Before Maddox finished speaking, Casey was shaking his head. "The Feds confiscated every video for the last six months you've lived here."

Katya's hopes sank. "All of them?"

"Were the videos on tape or on a hard drive?" Maddox asked.

"Everything is backed up from the hard drive to tape once a month," Casey said. "We'd just completed a backup when the Feds charged in. They took all the tapes."

Maddox stepped forward. "Do you wipe the videos from the hard drive when you back up to tape?"

"You know," Casey scratched his chin. "I believe we do it a week later, just in case one of the tapes is bad on the monthly backup."

Katya pulled in a deep breath and let it out, feeling lighter. "Can we look for that day, just in case the video is still on the hard drive?"

In the corner of her peripheral vision, Katya noted a Minneapolis city police car pulled up to a stop sign two blocks away. "We need to move this discussion inside." She hooked Casey's arm and moved toward the apartment building.

Casey resisted. "I can't take you in there now. My boss is filling in for me while I'm on lunch break. He doesn't expect me back for another fifteen minutes. Besides, he's very strict about who gets inside the control room."

Katya changed direction, leading the two men to a small bistro a block from the complex. "Then let's get you some lunch and we can plan our next move."

Fifteen minutes later, Casey walked out of the bistro, his steps swift, his gaze shooting from side to side.

Katya regretted having to involve Casey. If he were caught assisting her now, he too could be considered an accessory to a potential terrorist wanted by the police and the FBI. And the poor man was scared to death.

For that matter, Katya was scared. Walking into the apartment building set her up for capture. Casey had given her his master key card. While he searched for the video from that day, Katya and Maddox would perform some illegal activities of their own. It was too dangerous to enter her own apartment, but based on Casey's observation, the owners of 627 were out.

Maddox and Katya were going to check out the furniture they'd had delivered and inspect it for any anomalies.

Katya pulled her collar up over her chin and ducked her head as she strode past the cameras at the entrance and in the front lobby.

Casey's boss had left shortly after he returned from lunch, but they didn't need to leave clear evidence of their visit on the videos.

Katya and Maddox took the stairs two at a time up to the sixth floor.

Maddox slowed near the top to wait for Katya. Adrenaline pulsed through his veins at the prospect of breaking and entering someone's apartment. He'd always lived his life by following the rules. This was outside his comfort zone, but it had to be done. They needed to know how the weapons got into Katya's apartment. Maddox was almost certain the furniture delivery was the key.

"Casey said it was a red leather sofa and a matching

love seat," Katya reminded him as they paused in the stairwell.

With a nod, Maddox pushed through the stairwell door and hurried down the hallway to apartment 627.

He pressed his ear to the door and listened. Nothing. No sounds of movement, voices or music. After taking a deep breath, he slid the master key card Casey had provided into the door lock and waited for it to give him a green light. The locking mechanism clicked and the light blinked green.

As soon as the door swung open, Maddox and Katya rushed inside, closing the door behind them to keep other tenants from looking in while they poked around.

The red leather sofa sat against the living room wall, the love seat stood with its back to the entrance, framing the living area.

Without saying a word, Maddox and Katya rushed to the furniture and pulled the cushions from the seats. Beneath the cushions both pieces looked like most sofas, with a layer of fabric and padding beneath.

"Grab the other end," Maddox said, grasping the end of the couch. Together, they tipped the couch over. Again, nothing looked like a storage place for weapons.

"How did they do it?" Katya voiced the question in Maddox's mind.

"I don't know."

"Should we check out my apartment? It's the one right below this one."

Maddox shook his head. "If the cops or the FBI are looking for you, they might have someone watching it."

"They would watch the building entrances, too. We succeeded in making it this far…"

For a moment Maddox considered her argument.

"We are in danger no matter where we go," Katya continued. "Besides, we might find a clue as to how they got the weapons in without detection."

"Okay, but I go first."

"As they say in the American movies…" Katya stuck out her hand for him to shake. "Deal."

"Deal." He took her hand, pulled her to him and kissed her. Then he headed for the stairwell.

On the fifth floor, Maddox scanned the hallway before edging out. "Stay here until I tell you to come," he said to Katya.

Yellow crime-scene tape crisscrossed apartment 527. Maddox carefully removed one end of the wide ribbon, shoved the key in the lock and pushed the door open.

He slipped through the doorway, into the apartment. Tastefully furnished with solid mahogany occasional tables and a soft, cream leather sofa festooned with colorful cushions in shades of burgundy, pumpkin and apple green, the room should have been warm and inviting. But the place was a wreck. Kitchen cabinet doors hung open, dishes and canned goods littered the polished granite counters. In the bedroom, drawers were laid across the dresser top and bed, their contents tossed.

"They took my photograph," a soft voice whispered behind him.

Maddox spun to face Katya. "I thought I told you to stay put."

"Someone was coming up the stairs. I had to move or be discovered."

Although he didn't want to, Maddox accepted her

explanation. "See anything out of place, missing or different?"

"Other than the fact they went through all my belongings and made a mess?" She sighed. "I do not know." Katya reached for the drawer containing her panties, her face reddening. "It's hard to accept that people have gone through my personal belongings." She glanced around the bedroom and out toward the living area. "Where are the crates of weapons they say I had?"

"The FBI or ATF must have confiscated them as evidence." He didn't know what he'd expected by sneaking into her apartment, but the effort had netted nothing.

Katya released the undergarment she held and crossed to the nightstand, her fingers brushing its surface. "They even took the photograph of my father and brother." She hugged her arms around her middle. "It was the only one I brought with me to America. I feel as if I have been violated." Her gaze shifted to his, her ice-blue eyes suspiciously bright, the dark smudges beneath them more noticeable.

"To be expected when strangers go through your stuff." Maddox wanted to go to her, wrap her in his arms and drive away the fear and sadness. If he did, he wasn't sure he could let go again or stay alert and focus on keeping them alive.

On the dresser, Maddox found a gold-plated hairbrush and let his finger trace the intricate design on its back. "Is this some kind of coat of arms?"

Katya stiffened. "Why do you ask?"

"It's the same as the one on your pendant. Does it have special meaning?"

"The pendant and the brush were gifts from my father. The symbol is our family crest."

"It looks expensive. This apartment looks expensive." Maddox stared around again with a more critical eye. "What did you say your father did?"

She turned away and headed for the living room. "He was an important political figure in my country. Should we get out of here before someone comes looking for me?"

Maddox followed her out of the room. "I suspect you're still not telling me the entire truth."

"Oh, it is true. My father was an important political figure in Trejikistan."

His gut told him there was more to it than that. "He wasn't a terrorist, was he?"

Katya rounded on him, the color flaring in her cheeks. "My father was an honorable man, concerned only with his people—the people of Trejikistan. He would never kill innocents or destroy out of hatred. He was good and kind and respected—"

Maddox grabbed her arms and held her still. "Okay, okay. Your father wasn't a terrorist." He stared down into her eyes, a moment before full of sadness, now flashing with the fire of her passion. How he'd love to make love to her and see her eyes flare with another kind of passion.

Despite their need to hurry, to get out of the apartment building before they were caught, Maddox couldn't stop himself from stealing a kiss.

Just one.

His mouth descended on hers, hard and swift.

Still stiff, she resisted his caress.

Maddox softened his assault, teasing the line of her lips with his tongue, urging her to open and let him in.

A little at a time, her shoulders relaxed, and finally, with a soft sigh, she unclenched her teeth.

He swept in, his tongue tasting, thrusting and ravaging her. She spread her hands across his chest, her fingers digging into his shirt. She stood on her toes, leaning into him, their bodies melting together.

He was the first to break away, but only far enough to trail kisses across her cheek, to take her earlobe between his teeth. "You make me ache."

Her gentle laugh made him even hotter. "I do not know whether to apologize or to be flattered."

"Both. I can't think when you're in the same room. Given the situation, that could be dangerous." He moved her away from him, sucking in a deep breath. "Much as I'd like to continue this conversation, we should get down to the control room and see what Casey has found."

"Agreed." She touched her fingers to her swollen lips and ducked past him into the hallway.

They took the stairs back down to the main level and emerged into the hallway near the door to the control room.

Casey opened it before they could knock. "I saw you coming. Come see what I found." He let them in, looked out toward the lobby and then locked the door. "I was able to bring up the day of the raid by the ATF."

The room contained an elaborate array of screens. Each revealed different floors and community spaces in the building, even exterior corners and the lobby.

Maddox's pulse quickened. "Did you figure out how they got the weapons in?"

Casey's lips twisted. "Yes and no."

A surge of impatience made Maddox want to shake

the security guard. "What do you mean, *yes and no?*" His words came out angrier than he'd intended.

Katya stepped between the two men. "Casey, show us what you have."

The young man sat at a computer keyboard separate from the other video screens, and clicked on a file. "Here. Watch this."

The video played, displaying an almost-empty lobby with the occasional tenant entering or leaving, the image slightly grainy, yet clear enough to make out the faces.

A man entered pushing a dolly with a large box, the size of a love seat. He disappeared from the camera's view onto the elevator.

A few minutes later, he exited the elevator with an empty dolly only to return a few minutes later with another box of a similar size to the first.

"Wasn't the sofa larger than that?" Katya asked.

"Yes." Maddox nodded, his gaze fixed to the screen and what happened next.

"Do you have the security video of the fifth floor about the time he would have gotten off the elevator?"

"I checked. This is the interesting part." Casey clicked another icon displaying the man with the box in the elevator. The man turned his back to the camera, partially out of sight, then a hand came up with a spray can and suddenly the video turned black.

"Where did the picture go?"

"That's the interesting part. I think he used black spray paint. Now listen." Casey increased the volume.

The automated assistant for the elevator sang out, *Fifth floor.* A swishing was then followed by the rumble of a heavy cart bumping over the elevator threshold.

"Fifth, not sixth floor," Katya said.

"And an extra love seat," Casey added. "I was on the phone at that time and didn't catch the additional load."

"Back it up." Maddox leaned forward.

Casey rewound the video to the where the man on the elevator faced the camera.

Maddox poked a finger at the screen. "Stop."

The frame stopped on the man's face, giving a fairly clear picture of him. Blond hair, gray or blue eyes, tall with a muscular build under the gray coveralls of a delivery driver.

"I need you to send a copy of that picture to an email address."

As Casey brought up his email account, Maddox wrote an address on a sticky note pad. "Send it there."

The young security guard keyed in the email address. Just as he maneuvered his mouse and clicked the Send button, Katya gasped.

"Boys, we have company." She pointed at the screen displaying the lobby. Men dressed in blue coveralls emblazoned with the bold yellow letters ATF AGENT entered, carrying scary-looking automatic weapons.

Chapter Fourteen

Katya's heart thundered in her chest like a bass drummer out of control. "Is there another way out of here?" she turned around looking for a back exit, anywhere she could go to escape the law enforcement officials who'd obviously been tipped off by someone.

"No, that's it." Casey nodded toward the door, then his eyes widened and a grin spread across his face. "Wait." He jumped up from his chair and ran across the small control room to the back wall. "If I recall correctly from my orientation, we have an emergency exit somewhere around here, just for the building security force that leads from the back of the control room to the parking garage two floors down." Like a madman, he pushed aside boxes and a copy machine, revealing a small door in the back wall. "I never think about it because we aren't supposed to use it unless it's a real emergency. I, personally, have never actually been down there."

He fumbled with the keys on his massive keychain, fitting one at a time into the door's lock. "Geez, which one of these keys goes to the door? I've never opened the door so I really don't know which one will make it open—*if* I even have the key."

Katya alternated between monitoring the screen and the progress the ATF men were making toward the control room and checking on Casey's progress in the back of the room. "Hurry, Casey. Some of them are headed up the elevator. Two are on their way here."

"I'm going as fast as I can." Casey dropped the ring of keys on the floor and dove to recover. "How close are they now?"

"Outside the door to the control room," Katya said, her voice low. With her insides quaking, she abandoned the screen and ran for the little door.

As she reached the two men standing there, Casey fitted a key in the lock and turned it. The door opened to reveal a metal ladder leading down a tiny shaft into darkness.

"Wow, this is too cool." Casey stared down at the escape route and then stepped aside, motioning for them to proceed. "You two better go."

Katya almost backed away. Dark, narrow ladders into an abyss weren't a normal, everyday occurrence in her life.

Maddox stepped up to the door. "I'll go first." He cupped her cheek. "I'll be there—all you have to do is follow my voice." He pressed his lips to hers in a hasty kiss. "Ready?"

She nodded and waited.

Maddox climbed onto the ladder and lowered himself into the darkness. "Now you, Katya. It's not so bad once you start down."

Katya, her hands shaking, grasped the cold metal rungs and placed her feet on the first step.

A loud banging on the control room door made her jerk and almost lose her hold on the ladder.

"Go," Casey whispered. "I have to shut the door and move the boxes in place before I let the ATF in. Be careful."

"Thanks, Casey. For everything." Katya sucked in a deep breath and lowered herself down the rungs.

Above her, Casey closed the door, shutting out all the light, leaving her in utter darkness.

"It's okay, Katya," Maddox said below her. He touched her foot. "One step at a time, and we'll get out of this."

Katya clung to the ladder, her breathing coming in quick, shallow pants, her fingers in a death grip on the metal rung. "I can't do this."

"Yes, you can." He stroked her calf then guided her foot to the next step. "See? One at a time."

"I am beginning to think this nightmare will never end."

"It will. Keep moving." Maddox coaxed and guided her every step of the way.

After what seemed like forever, dull gray light shone up the shaft from the bottom. Then Maddox was dropping the last few steps into a secluded area in the parking garage. He held his arms up. "You have to jump from the last rung. It's only five feet down. I'll catch you."

Katya climbed as low as she could, then let go, falling the last five feet into Maddox's arms. For a long moment, he held her, smoothing his hands over her hair. She wished she could stay that way forever, in the warmth and security of Maddox Thunder Horse's arms. She looked up into his face. "Do you make it a habit of saving damsels in distress?"

Maddox's expression hardened, his jaw tightening.

"No. Sometimes I'm too late." His arms dropped to his sides and he turned away.

Katya remembered what his mother had said about Maddox's fiancée dying in a blizzard. "You have to let go of the past, Maddox. You did not kill your fiancée—the blizzard did."

"What do you know about it? You weren't there."

"No, and I was not there for my father when he was murdered." Katya touched Maddox's arm. "You do not know how I wished I had been there for him."

He turned on her. "And if you had, you'd be dead, too."

"Exactly. You do not know how many times over the past couple of days I wished I could die and be with him."

"But you didn't."

"I know." Her hand moved up his arm. "Because of you."

"I won't always be there."

"No, but I am thankful for when you are." She pressed her cheek to his chest and hugged him around his middle. "I know you will not always be there. Especially when I go back to my country." She hugged him hard, then pushed away. "But we have to get out of here, or I will never make it back."

Maddox grabbed her hand and stopped her from stepping out of the concrete alcove. "Would that be such a bad thing?"

She gazed back at him, wishing with all her heart that she didn't have to return to Trejikistan. If she had her choice, she would stay with this tall, dark Lakota native on the Plains of North Dakota with his beloved wild horses. What a glorious life that would be. "Yes, I have to return to my country."

Maddox nodded and, still holding her hand, stepped up to the corner of the alcove, peering around the edge.

Nothing moved in the garage, the spaces empty, most of the tenants gone to work for the day.

Maddox tugged her hand, drawing her along the walls, keeping to the shadows. When they reached the exit, Katya yanked Maddox back.

A big, black van stood in the road, against the curb. Several men in the navy blue uniforms of the ATF team stood beside it, talking into handheld radios.

Maddox pointed to a bush close to the exit ramp. He let go of her hand, his gaze on the men by the van, then he ran across the ramp and dove into the bush.

The men at the van continued to talk on their handheld radios, oblivious to Maddox's exit.

Her heart thumping in her chest, Katya focused on the men in the street. When she was sure they were not looking, she followed Maddox, running across the concrete ramp. She dove behind the bushes, crashing into Maddox. He caught her and cushioned her fall, pressing a finger to her lips.

He parted the bushes and stared out.

Katya held her breath. Would this be it? Would the ATF finally catch up with their suspected terrorist?

What appeared to be the man in charge spoke to several men standing in front of him and pointed toward the building, specifically the garage exit.

"Time to move out." Ducking low, Maddox pushed between the bushes and the brick wall of the parking garage until they reached the far corner, leading toward the next building. A small gap between the hedges was all that separated the buildings.

Maddox went first, then Katya.

Someone shouted behind them.

Katya and Maddox didn't look back. They ran down a side street, leaving the apartment complex and the ATF behind.

Maddox didn't stop until they were ten blocks away. He yanked Katya behind a building and they both bent over at the middle, gasping for air.

Katya couldn't get enough oxygen. She dropped to her knees, her head thrown back, pulling in air as fast as her lungs could take it. "What…do…we…do now?"

Maddox straightened, his chest heaving, but closer to normal than Katya felt. "I had Casey send that picture to my brother, Pierce. He's an FBI agent. Maybe he can identify the man."

"In the meantime, what else can I do? I don't have anywhere to go, no one who can clear me." Her lungs hurt, her shins and calves screamed from the effort she'd expended.

"We locate a place to hole up until we hear from Pierce." Maddox looked around. "We should be able to find a motel around here."

"A motel?" she asked, her shoulders drooping. She didn't think she could run another step.

Maddox glanced at her. "We need rest."

Katya nodded, the idea of a pillow and a comfortable bed so very appealing after being on the road all night and chased by a crazed killer and the ATF. "A motel sounds great. Will it be safe?"

"As safe as anything when you consider that the ATF is after you."

She grimaced at Maddox. "You are making me feel *so* much better."

He smiled and held out his hand. "Good, then let's get moving. We aren't out of hot water yet."

She laid her hand in his and let him pull her to her feet and into his arms. "Hot water sounds wonderful. I could use a bath."

Katya guided them to a bus stop with a route to the outskirts of Minneapolis. Keeping her head down, Katya climbed aboard and moved to a backseat where she pressed her hand to her face, pretending to cough. Maddox sat beside her, shielding her from view of the other passengers. He didn't like being in a public place where someone might recognize her.

Maddox found a motel off the beaten path of the interstates and main thoroughfares. While he obtained a key, Katya huddled in the bushes at the far end of the parking lot.

He didn't like leaving her even for a moment, but he couldn't risk a clerk matching her face to the ones plastered all over the television screen behind him.

He'd asked for a room at the end of the building, farthest away from the road, and paid cash. When he unlocked the door, he scanned the parking lot and the street beyond before he motioned for Katya to join him.

Keeping close to the hedges surrounding the parking lot, she moved quickly and quietly until she entered the room.

Maddox shut the door and locked the dead bolt. "Well, now that wasn't so bad, was it?"

Katya unzipped her heavy winter coat and dropped it onto a chair. She stood with her shoulders sagging, and stripped the hat from her head, her long luscious locks falling free in a tangled mess around her face. Her pale face was as pale as when he'd first found her almost dead by a frozen river. The dark smudges beneath her eyes stood out like bruises. Yet, despite how tired and worn out she looked, she was still the most beautiful woman Maddox had ever seen.

"I'm tired," she laughed, her voice shaky, her lips trembling.

"I'll bet." He held out his arms and she fell into them.

For a long moment, they stayed that way, holding each other, the warmth of her body chasing away the chill in Maddox's. A chill that went back to the day Susan died in his arms. She was right. He couldn't hold onto the past, not when the present was kicking his butt.

"You can have the bathroom first."

"Thanks. But I don't think I can move." She sighed and leaned closer.

"I'd help, but I need to place a call to my brother, Pierce, and check on Tuck."

Katya stepped away, her arms dropping to her sides. "That's more important. I'll be quick."

As Katya stepped into the little bathroom, Maddox pulled the throwaway cell phone from his pocket and dialed Pierce's number.

"Pierce? Maddox here."

"Where the hell are you?"

"I can't tell you yet. Are you near a computer?"

"I can be, give me a sec."

A moment later Maddox heard the squeak of what had to be an office chair.

"Shoot, brother," Pierce said.

"I had an email sent to you. It contains a picture of

a man we think planted the weapons in Katya's room. He might also be the man who's been following her and tried to shoot her."

"I'm on it. I'll see what we can do to ID the guy. Can I reach you again at this number?"

"Yes."

"I'll call as soon as I get a hit on your man."

"The sooner the better. We're hiding out from just about every law enforcement agency in the country and this man you're going to be looking to match."

"I know. We even got the heads-up on the girl here at the Bureau. Won't be long before you're on the same dance card. Be safe."

"Will do." Maddox clicked the Off button and sighed. After another call home to make sure Tuck, Dante and his mother were all right, he let some of the tension slide from his shoulders. For the moment they were relatively safe.

The sound of the shower called to Maddox. Knowing that Katya was naked in it made the decision for him.

He stripped off his clothes and entered the bathroom, shoving aside the curtain.

Katya, her face and head beneath the water, rinsing the suds out of her eyes, didn't hear him enter.

God, she had a beautiful body. Maddox stepped into the tub behind her and slid his hands around her waist.

She jumped at first. When she realized who it was, she relaxed, leaning against him. Katya fit him perfectly.

He rubbed soap in his palms and smoothed them over her belly and upward to cup her breasts.

Katya breathed deeply, her chest pushing against his

hands. She reached behind her, capturing his buttocks, pressing him closer, his erection nudging against her.

He tweaked her nipples, drawing them to a hardened point. Then his fingers trailed through the slippery soap down her torso, over her flat abdomen to the thatch of curls at the apex of her thighs.

Her hand found his shaft behind her and stroked him from tip to stem.

Maddox groaned, his fingers dipping into her folds, matching the rhythm of her strokes, flicking and teasing her until her back arched against him.

He wouldn't last long, not as hot as she made him and as good as her body felt against his. Nothing could top that, except being inside her.

As if reading his thoughts, Katya turned in his arms, one perfect leg trailing up over his calf.

He hooked her thighs in his hands and turned her back to the cool hard tile wall of the shower, balancing her as he lowered her down until he nudged at her opening.

"Please," she said, easing herself down until she took him fully inside.

Maddox's breath caught in his throat. "You feel so good."

"Make love to me, Maddox, like this is the last time."

He froze, his hands holding her legs wrapped around his waist. "No. I'll make love to you like this is the first time." He drove into her. "The first of many." In and out, he thrust, the tension pulsing through his body. Desperation, frustration and anger fueled his passion, pushing him harder and faster.

Katya had come to mean more to him than he ever

expected, and he didn't want to lose her—wouldn't lose her. Not after all they had been through together.

When he climaxed, he pulled her close, holding her tight against his body.

Her arms and legs clung to him, her body shaking. They remained this way until their passion and the water cooled.

Maddox set Katya on her feet and they finished rinsing off. He dried her body and she dried his. Maddox carried Katya to the bed, laying her among the sheets, where he kissed every inch of her body. When she tried to return the gesture, he stopped her. "No, I want you to sleep. This is my treat."

Katya lay back, her damp curls splayed out across the pillow, while Maddox explored every inch of her body with his lips. She fell asleep soon after.

Although he could have gone for another round of lovemaking, he knew she was tired and his mind and muscles ached for sleep. Eventually, he crawled beside her and fell into a deep sleep, her body curled against him. Where she belonged.

He couldn't have been asleep for long when his cell phone buzzed on the nightstand beside the bed. Maddox fumbled for the phone, punching at the unfamiliar buttons until he stopped the ringing. "Yeah."

"Maddox, you have a serious problem."

It took him a moment to surface from sleepiness to recognize his brother Pierce's voice. He shoved a hand through his hair and sat up, hoping the movement would jar him more fully awake. "What problem?"

"The man who is after Katya is a professional assassin."

Chapter Fifteen

"What is it?" Katya sat up behind him, pressing her naked breasts against Maddox's back.

He sucked in a deep breath, completely awake, adrenaline firing throughout his system. "Who is he and who would have hired him?"

"Richard Fulton, alias, Rick Masters, alias, Patrick Delaney, and the aliases go on. We suspect him of at least twenty assassinations and those are only the ones we know about. He's at the top of the FBI's Most Wanted List."

"Damn." Maddox sat back, sick to his stomach. "What do we do?"

"You can't keep her safe by yourself," Pierce said. "You need to let me help."

"I can't drag you into this. I've already implicated the rest of the family in Katya's problem—no need to drag you in as well."

"Just my knowledge of this has me fully involved. Let us help. We have the resources to figure this thing out."

"The ATF hasn't figured it out yet. How can the FBI?"

"I have a vested interest, brother," Pierce's voice

dropped, low and insistent. "I can get my boss to buy in. We bring in the girl, Fulton will follow."

"Use her as bait?"

"No, provide her protection."

"The way this guy has followed us, he'll find her."

"Not where we'll hide her. We can set her up in a safe house with dedicated agents to guard her. Then we can set up a phony safe house and let it slip that she's there. He'll come after her, we'll get our man and Katya will be cleared."

"Sounds like you have this all planned out."

"Either way, Maddox, she's not safe out on her own."

"She has me and she's still alive."

"Fulton is a professional. He always gets his mark. It's only a matter of time."

Maddox held the phone to his ear, but he didn't respond. "Let me think about it. I'll call you back."

"Maddox—" Pierce shouted into the phone as Maddox hit the Off button.

Let someone else protect Katya? Every one of Maddox's brain cells screamed, *No!* But he wasn't alone in this. Katya had a say in what she wanted to do.

"I only caught a little of that." Katya pulled the sheet up over her trembling body, her eyes rounded. "An assassin?" She shook hard, her fingers clenching the sheet to her breasts.

"Richard Fulton." Maddox ran his hand through his hair. "From what Pierce said, the man is a paid assassin and extremely dangerous. He's on the top of the FBI's Most Wanted List."

"What did your brother suggest?"

Maddox stared across at her, his chest tightening. "He

wants to put you in a safe house and use you as bait to catch Fulton."

Katya didn't utter a sound, the only indication that she heard him was a slight widening of her already rounded blue eyes.

"My gut feeling on this is no." Maddox twisted the phone in one hand. "We've managed to stay safe this long, we can continue doing what we've been doing while the FBI looks into the video we sent."

"How long will it take for them to clear me of suspicion?"

"I don't know."

"I don't have time to wait for a full-fledged investigation." She dropped the sheet and crawled across the bed to Maddox where she kneeled beside him. "I can't expect you to protect me forever."

He frowned and opened his mouth to protest, but she placed a finger over his lips and then replaced it with her mouth. She brushed a kiss across his lips and pressed her cheek to his. "I want to go to the safe house, Maddox. But I want it on the condition that I am freed of charges and sent back to Trejikistan once they capture the assassin."

He slipped his hands around her waist and pulled her onto his lap. "What if I can't let you go?"

"You have to. I am not your responsibility and no matter how this ends, I cannot stay." She reached up and cupped his cheeks with her hands. "I have to go home."

Maddox stared down into her eyes. Anger, fear and something else battled in his heart, making his chest hurt. He captured her hands in his and squeezed them hard. "If that's the way you want it." He stood, lifting her with him to set her on the floor.

As much as he wanted to drag her naked body back to the bed, he didn't. She wanted to leave, and he'd make it possible. As she'd stated from the very beginning, back in the cave on the ranch, *no strings.* "Get dressed. I'll arrange a transfer point with the FBI." Too bad the strings he'd allowed to grow were now choking his heart.

HOURS LATER, KAT STOOD at the window, staring out at the group of cars leaving the small house perched in an isolated location west of Minneapolis. Maddox had left well over an hour ago after he had seen her settled in. He had not wanted to go, but she insisted. Better to cut the ties now. If all went as planned, she would be back in her country within the week.

The four men positioned at every corner remained outside.

"You should be safe here." Pierce Thunder Horse laid a hand on her shoulder. "We've leaked word that you are at the other safe house. We have an entire squad of agents surrounding it, ready to capture Fulton as soon as he makes his move."

Katya didn't respond, her gaze on the now empty road.

Pierce's lips tipped into a small smile. "Maddox didn't look too happy about leaving you with me. What's up between you two?"

"Nothing," she replied. Her life was back in Trejikistan. Her people needed her leadership to see them through the next few months in preparation for their first election. Maddox had a family and a ranch to go home to. She had a country to lead into democracy.

"If it makes you feel any better, Maddox looked pretty miserable."

Why did Maddox's brother insist on poking at her wounds? She frowned and captured Pierce's gaze in his reflection in the window. "Why would that make me feel better?"

"He made me promise to take good care of you."

"He would do that for anyone. Maddox is a good man."

"True." Pierce nodded. "But he seems a little hurt that you chose the FBI to look after you rather than him."

"I do not know why. I have only been trouble to him since he saved me out in the canyon."

Pierce chuckled. "Yeah, I heard about some of that from Tuck. I didn't think you'd come to the FBI for help. What changed your mind?"

Katya avoided Pierce's gaze in the window's reflection, preferring to stare out at the dirt road leading to the remote cabin. "Maddox."

"He did? Maddox convinced you to turn yourself over to us?"

"No. I did it for Maddox. I could not continue to lead him on."

"How so?"

"I have to return to Trejikistan." She straightened her shoulders the way her mother had taught her so long ago. *You are royalty. Act like it.* "It is my duty."

"And he didn't want you to go?"

She nodded.

"Did you tell him why you had to return?"

"No." She hadn't wanted anything to change between them. Had he known who she was, he might have been like everyone else and looked at her differently, like a freak or someone who was too fragile to even think for herself.

"Did you tell him about your family?" Pierce persisted.

Katya's heart skipped a beat and she turned to face Maddox's brother. "What do you know about my family?"

"I just got your dossier on my way out the door to pick you up." He held a file in his hands and flipped it open. "Seems your full name is Princess Alexi Katya Ivanov. Daughter of the late Boris Ivanov, king of Trejikistan."

She sucked in a deep breath and let it out slowly. "Did you tell Maddox?"

"I didn't have time to read the dossier until we were on our way out here."

"Don't tell him, please." She knew she had to leave, and she didn't want Maddox's opinion or memories of her to change because of a stupid title that would mean nothing in a few months.

"Why not?"

"I came to America to be me, not Princess Alexi Katya Ivanov. If Maddox chooses to remember me, I would prefer him to remember me as just a girl, a foreign exchange student, not a princess from some faraway land few people in America had even heard of." She took Pierce's hands in hers. "Please, don't tell him."

Pierce stared down into her eyes. "I'm beginning to see why Maddox has fallen in love with you."

Katya shook her head, her hands falling to her sides. "Do not be foolish. We have not known each other long enough for him to fall in love with me."

"He left for home with the most wounded-dog look

on his face I've seen in a long time. What else could it be?"

"Not love." Katya turned to stare out the window again.

Pierce started to say something else when his cell phone rang. "Excuse me." He turned and walked into the kitchen of the little cabin.

Katya strained to hear his end of the conversation.

"You bastard, what have you done with my brother?" Pierce's expletive drew Katya into the kitchen, his privacy be damned.

Her pulse thundered in every vein, her heart banging against her chest. Maddox was in trouble.

Pierce paced the length of the small kitchen, the phone pressed to his ear with one hand, the other clenched in a tight fist by his side. "Where do you want to make the transfer?"

Katya's fingers twisted together and she bit down hard on her lip to keep it from trembling. What had happened to Maddox?

Pierce hit the Off button and reared back to throw the phone against the wall.

Katya caught his arm before he could let the device fly. "What happened to Maddox?"

"Fulton has him and wants to make a trade. We're to meet him at a warehouse close to the Port of St. Paul in an hour."

"He wants to trade me for Maddox?"

Pierce looked at her, his mouth set in a firm line. "Yeah. But I can't do that."

Katya nodded, every part of her body growing still. She knew what had to be done and didn't hesitate. "Yes, you can. We have to make the deal."

MADDOX PRESSED THE accelerator to the floor, pushing the rental car to its limit on the interstate between Minneapolis and Fargo. His little throwaway cell phone hadn't had reception since he left the Twin Cities.

The urge to turn around and go back fought with reason. He couldn't just go back to Minneapolis, find Katya and take her back under his wing. He wanted to force her to stay with him, even after all the danger died down. Thank God he'd insisted on taking her to the safe house himself. At least he knew how to find her.

What if Katya didn't want him to come?

She'd insisted that he leave her with the FBI. They knew better how to protect her. They were trained to man a safe house and provide the security needed to keep her out of Richard Fulton's sights. For all intents and purposes, *she* had rejected *him*. She had told him to leave.

Maddox had traveled nearly an hour away from the safe house before his resolve crumbled. He lifted his cell phone for the fifth time in as many minutes. Still no reception. Resisting the urge to throw the phone, he noticed an off ramp coming up. On this long stretch of interstate in Minnesota, they were few and far between. His foot slipped off the accelerator and the car veered off the road and onto the ramp. Maybe if he got to higher ground off the ramp he'd get a bar or two of reception.

He drove to the top of the ramp. The longer he was out of cell phone range, the more certain he was that something was wrong. He had to get hold of Pierce, even if it meant turning around and heading back to Minneapolis.

He checked his phone again. Still no bars. That

decided it. Without slowing, he barreled through the stop sign and flew across the overpass and onto the interstate, headed back east to Minneapolis. The sooner he was within range of a decent cell tower, the better. Once he talked to Pierce, he'd relax and return to the ranch.

As he neared Minneapolis and the turnoff to the safe house, four bars sprang up on his cell phone screen. Finally! He hit the speed-dial button for his brother and immediately got his answering machine. An hour out and just under an hour back since he'd left Katya and his brother at the safe house. Why he didn't trust them to keep Katya safe, he didn't know. But he couldn't just walk away. Not after the past two days of taking care of her. If something happened…

He tried his brother again. Still no answer.

Damn! Why wasn't he responding? A lump of lead weighed heavily in his gut. Was the safe house outside cell phone reception? Or could it be that Katya was once again in trouble?.

"MADDOX WOULDN'T WANT you to do this." Pierce held the door for Katya to climb into the SUV that would carry her to the warehouses located on the St. Paul side of the Mississippi River.

"Maddox cannot speak for himself. Because of me, he is a hostage of that murdering bastard." Katya stared straight ahead, calm, determined to face whatever lay ahead. Maddox had rescued her several times over the past couple days. If it was the last thing she did, she would make sure he came out of this fiasco alive.

Images of him holding her close in the sleeping bag in the cave kept playing through her mind. The dark

Native American with his long, straight black hair had hands that could crush, but were gentle. He had coaxed her away from a frozen death, given her a second chance to redeem her name, her country and her life. The least she could do was negotiate his freedom.

"I have a squad of agents moving into place around the warehouse. If Fulton shows, they'll nab him. Maybe even before you arrive."

She touched Pierce's arm. "No! You cannot let Fulton see them. If he suspects we are not alone, he might hurt Maddox."

"Don't worry. They are under strict instructions not to make a move until they know where Maddox is and have a clear shot at Fulton."

Bullets might fly and one might hit Maddox. "Can we just trade me for Maddox and leave all the bullets in the guns?"

Pierce smiled at her. "You really like the guy, don't you?"

She nodded. "He is a good man. He does not deserve to be caught in the cross fire."

"I agree. But we have to take Fulton out or you'll never be safe."

"I don't care about me."

"Consider that his next victim will not be safe."

"You're right."

Pierce dug a small disc out of his shirt pocket and handed it to her. "Put this in a pocket, somewhere that can't be found. A safe place where you won't lose it."

She turned the disc over. A plain shiny disc, it looked like a large watch battery. "What is it?"

"A gift from me and Maddox. In case things don't go according to plan."

She shrugged and shoved the disc into her pocket. "No, someplace no one would think to look."

Katya's brows pulled together. "Is this a GPS tracking device?"

Pierce grinned. "Smart as well as beautiful. Yes. That's exactly what it is. Just in case we get separated, we'll be able to find you."

She pulled the disc from her pocket and pulled the neckline of her sweater out enough so she could slide the disc into her bra. "Better?"

"Much." Pierce gulped. "Definitely smart as well as beautiful. Eyes on the road, Thunder Horse," he said beneath his breath.

The sedan in front of them slowed as they neared a T-intersection, crowded by trees and tall mounds of snow that had been pushed off the road.

As the car moved out into the road, a truck barreled at it from the south, slamming into the side of the sedan, sending it careening off the road and into a ditch.

Katya screamed.

The SUV driver slammed on the brakes and Katya hit the seat back in front of her, stunning her.

Before she knew what was happening her door jerked open and she was yanked from the SUV, a gun pointed at her head. "Don't try anything or I'll kill her," a deep male voice demanded.

"You kill her and you're a dead man." Pierce held his gun up in his hand, letting it dangle from the trigger guard. "Let the girl go."

"No can do. She's money."

"What have you done with Maddox?"

Fulton laughed. "Nothing. Not a damn thing. He's probably halfway to North Dakota by now. Move it,

Princess, we have an appointment to make." He grabbed her elbow and backed away from the vehicle, the gun pressing into her temple.

Despite the threat to her life, Katya couldn't stop the flood of relief from warming her insides. Maddox was safe. Fulton hadn't captured him.

The metal gun barrel bounced, slamming into her temple as Fulton forced her to walk backwards to the waiting truck with the smashed front end. The assassin slid into the driver's seat, pulling her in next to him, close enough that if anyone tried to shoot at them, they'd hit her as well. "Close the door."

Katya reached for the handle and pulled the door toward her. All the while Fulton kept his head close to hers, using her as a human shield.

He shifted the gun to his left hand and reached for the gearshift with his right. "Don't get any ideas. I can shoot equally well with both hands." With a quick tug, he had it in reverse, backing away from the FBI vehicles until they were out of range. Then he swung the truck around and hit the accelerator, rocketing the vehicle down the highway.

Katya let him take her without a fight. She wanted to get as far away from the agents as possible. Enough people had been hurt in this man's quest to capture her. This way Maddox's brother, Pierce, would be safe.

"You're a hired assassin, aren't you?" Katya asked.

"Not your business."

"When I'm the target, that makes it my business," she retorted.

Fulton laughed, driving one-handed. "The princess has a mouth on her."

"Who hired you to kill me?"

The man focused on navigating the road ahead. "Who said I was going to kill you?"

"You've shot enough bullets at me to take me out a couple times."

"If I'd wanted to hit you, trust me, I'd have hit you."

"You didn't answer me." She tried to turn her head to look at him, but he held the gun to her temple, pressing so hard she couldn't. "Who hired you?"

"Your future husband."

"What?" She tried again to turn her head. Cold, hard metal dug into her flesh. "What do you mean, my future husband?"

"You're a smart girl, figure it out." He slowed to negotiate a turn from the county road to a state highway. The truck shot forward, slipping sideways on a patch of ice.

Katya shook her head. "I don't have a future husband."

"You do now, and he was willing to pay big bucks for me to bring you back to Trejikistan to marry him."

"Trejikistan?" She searched her memory for anyone who had ever even hinted at wanting to marry her back in her country. She'd eavesdropped on a conversation between her father and… "Vladimir?"

"Bingo! Give the princess a prize."

"Vladimir wants to marry me? Why?"

"You're failing in my estimation, Princess, and I was beginning to think you were a smart cookie." Her captor shook his head. "The man thinks that by marrying you, he can build his case as the new ruler now that your father is out of the way."

Katya gasped. "Vladimir is responsible for my father's death?"

"Not for me to say—you'll have to ask him. I don't like to brag about my work." His eyes narrowed, the gun pressing harder into her temple. "You've slipped through my fingers too often lately. Makes me look bad."

Rage boiled up inside her. This man had killed her father. "You murdering bastard. You can rot in hell for all the people you've murdered, and for what? A few dollars?"

"More than a few."

Katya stared at the road ahead, her blood pounding in her veins. She wanted to kill this man who'd taken her father from her, to make him hurt as much as he'd hurt her father and her family. "You're a coward, a lowlife murderer. You'll pay for this. I promise you."

"You need to shut up." He swerved, flinging her head against the window.

Katya blinked back the pain, refusing to show this man an ounce of fear. "How much is he paying you?"

"Enough. More if I bring you back alive. That's the beauty of it. I get paid either way. Dead or alive."

"If it's all the same to you. I'd prefer to be dead than to marry Vladimir." She grabbed the steering wheel and yanked it to the left.

Richard Fulton jammed his foot on the brakes, let go of the gun and used both hands to regain control of the vehicle. The truck veered off the road and into the ditch filled with mounds of snow.

Katya shoved the door open, jumped out and ran.

"Damn woman. Stop!" Footsteps pounded on the ground behind her.

She didn't look back, pushing harder to reach the

road. She had to get away from this killer and warn her country about Vladimir's plan. As she reached the top of the ditch, her feet slipped out from under her on a patch of ice and she went down hard, her head hitting the pavement.

Richard Fulton stood over her, his gun pointed at her head. "I should have killed you back in that canyon."

Blackness consumed her.

Chapter Sixteen

Maddox took the turn, skidding sideways and almost running into an SUV that barreled into the intersection—the SUV that had taken Katya to the safe house. What was it doing out here?

He blocked the road with his rental car and leaped out.

Pierce dropped down from the driver's seat and ran toward Maddox. "Fulton has her."

Maddox ground to a halt, all the air leaving his lungs in a rush as though he'd been sucker punched. "What?"

"Fulton set up an ambush and grabbed Katya before we realized what was happening." Pierce jerked his head toward the other agent who'd been in the SUV with him. "Move the car." He grabbed Maddox's arm. "Ride with us. We have a tracking device on her. He won't get far with her."

"If he doesn't kill her first." Maddox stated, his feet like lead as he forced himself to move toward the vehicle. He couldn't bear to find her dead. He'd been through that once with Susan.

"She's not dead. He'd have killed her on the spot, not taken her hostage. Hell, he'd have killed her a long time ago if he really wanted her dead. He's a paid assassin. They don't miss unless they want to."

Maddox climbed into the passenger seat of the SUV. Pierce climbed in beside him and tossed a device with a screen on it. "Follow the moving dot. That's Katya's tracking device."

"How did he find her? I thought safe houses were supposed to be secret."

"All we can figure is that he might have an insider in the FBI feeding him information."

"He knew where to find us when we were out at the hunting cabin." Maddox stared ahead as they pulled around the rental car and picked up the agent. "He knew where to find us in Medora. He was always there."

"It's as though he has his own tracking device on her."

"Her necklace," Maddox said. "Katya said her father gave it to her so that he'd always know she was safe. He must have had a tracking device embedded in it."

"And Fulton knew it. Someone from Katya's country had to have given him that information." Pierce shook his head. "She would never have been safe as long as she had that necklace on her. We should have taken all of her belongings away before we brought her to the safe house. Sorry, Maddox."

"She wouldn't have given it up easily." It was her last gift from her father. Maddox's teeth ground together at the thought of Katya in Fulton's hands. "The main thing is to get her back before Fulton does something stupid."

"That's the plan. I've mobilized a task force. They have the tracking device up on their screens and will converge on Fulton, wherever he takes her."

"As long as they don't hurt Katya."

"What, and start an international incident?" Pierce shot a look at Maddox. "I put out strict instructions not to harm a hair on her pretty head."

"Good." Maddox sat back, clenching and unclenching his fist. He'd feel a whole lot better when he saw Katya again. Alive. "They're headed for Minneapolis."

"We'll keep a safe distance from them until they come to a halt."

Minutes dragged by. Maddox's hands gripped the tracker, the knuckles growing whiter the longer they trailed the killer. What was happening to Katya? Was she still alive? The only thing they knew for certain was that she was with the killer. Would he never stop? "At what point will you try to force him off the road?"

"We won't. He'll have to stop sooner or later, if for nothing else, fuel. We follow until he does so."

"If we don't run out of gas before he does." Maddox stole a look at the gas gauge.

"Don't worry. We're full and there's a backup tank."

Maddox's attention returned to the tracker. "Wait. I think they've stopped." He leaned closer. Was it true? Yes. The dot on the screen had stopped.

"Where?"

Maddox zoomed in on the tracking device and gave Pierce the address.

"That's near the port. What's he doing there?"

"Wherever he thinks he's going, he's not taking Katya with him." Maddox stared ahead.

Pierce relayed the information to the other agents. They agreed to set up operations two blocks from the tracker location and move in on foot. When he got off the radio, he stared across at Maddox. "You need to stay with the SUV. I can't risk having a civilian involved if shots are fired."

"Like hell."

"Maddox, I need to concentrate on saving Katya. Not you."

"I can't sit back and do nothing."

"You damn sure can."

Maddox clenched his teeth to keep from saying anything else.

"Promise you won't interfere?" Pierce insisted.

He nodded.

Two blocks from Katya's GPS location, the vehicles pulled together. Pierce joined the team and weapons were distributed—everything from Sig Sauer pistols to high-powered rifles only sharpshooters would know how to use correctly.

Darkness had fallen, the streetlights casting beams of light out into the street and shadows consuming all else.

As soon as the team set off, Maddox counted to ten and followed. He had promised not to interfere, but he didn't promise not to follow. Wherever Katya was, he wanted to be.

"GET UP!" FULTON SHOOK HER until her teeth rattled and her eyes opened.

Pain sliced through the back of her head as she stared up at her captor. "Where are we?"

For an answer, he yanked her to her feet and shoved her ahead of him toward a dark building that looked like a warehouse. The place smelled of rank water and diesel fumes.

"Where are we going?" she whispered, so careful not to speak too loudly that her voice echoed in her head. Her feet caught on an old cardboard box and she fell flat on her chest, the wind knocked from her lungs.

"Get up!" Fulton grabbed her by her hair and jerked her to her feet.

She got up quickly, standing on her toes to loosen his pull on her hair. His unrelenting hold brought unwanted tears to her eyes. "Okay, okay. I am coming." She hurried to keep up, all the while feeling for the tracking device she'd stuffed in her bra. She couldn't feel the little metal disc. The more she patted her chest, the more desperate she became. If she didn't have the disc, Pierce and the FBI would never find her. She could be tossed on a ship, or left somewhere to die, while they scratched their heads and wondered where Fulton had taken her.

Fulton yanked on her arm, forcing her ahead of him.

"What is your hurry, anyway?" she asked.

"The sooner I get you on the boat, the sooner I get paid." He reached the end of the alley and crossed a street to another equally dreary warehouse that appeared as though it hadn't been used in a decade. Windows, high on the brick walls, gaped open like faces frozen in horror, the glass broken, shadowy darkness revealing nothing within.

"I'm going on a boat?"

"On a container ship. In a container."

Katya sucked in a deep breath in an attempt to ease the panic rising in her throat. "How much is my cousin paying you?"

"Shut up."

"He doesn't actually have access to any money in Trejikistan without my—or my brother's—permission. Did you know that?"

Fulton came to an abrupt halt and glared down at her. "You'd better hope he has the money he promised to pay. If not, you'll both die."

She waited until Fulton resumed his breakneck pace, knowing she had scored with her previous comment. Maybe she could get him so distracted that she could escape. "Did you know that my cousin is a habitual liar? He once promised to buy a yacht from an English duke, but after testing it for six months, he backed out of the deal, claiming it was damaged."

"Shut up, woman!" Fulton jerked her to a halt and slammed her up against a brick wall. "Your mouth will get you killed. One more comment, and I'm through messing with you."

Katya clamped her lips closed on her next retort. Fulton was distracted. Now she just had to look for an opportunity to trip him or pull free of his hold on her.

Her father's killer took off again, headed for the back of the vacant warehouse. They had to pass by a stack of broken pallets to get to the backdoor.

As they came alongside the pallets, Katya faked tripping, falling to her hands and knees.

"I should just shoot you now." He pointed his gun at her head, his breathing harsh and strained like a bull in a rage.

"Maybe you should," Katya taunted, her fingers closing around a single slat with nails protruding from the opposite end.

When he leaned forward to grab for her hair, she

stood up, swinging the board at the hand holding the weapon.

The nails jabbed into his wrist. Fulton screamed, flinging the gun to the ground.

"You bit—"

He didn't finish the word before Katya swung back around with the board, this time catching the side of his face. The nails dug into the skin and ripped a long bloody path across his cheek. He screamed again, grabbing for his face.

Katya flung the board at him and ran the other way as fast as she could. If she could only make it to the end of the building and duck down another alley, she might lose him.

Her heart raced, her breathing came in ragged gasps, but she pressed on, moving as fast as her feet would carry her in snow boots.

Feet pounded on the pavement behind her, sharp curses flung at her from the angry man. "When I catch you…"

She reached the corner and spun to the right, running all out. The buildings were too long to give her any cover or concealment. Her only hope was to outrun him. Given his height and athletic ability, that didn't seem likely. He'd brought her to the oldest warehouses imaginable. Most appeared abandoned. She was on her own, with no one to rescue her. If she planned to survive, she'd have to rescue herself.

She amazed herself when she rounded the end of the next building and ducked down a back alley. This one contained a rusty trash Dumpster and old metal barrels. Before Fulton appeared around the corner, Katya hid behind a barrel, as she searched the trash-strewn ground for something she could use as a weapon. She grabbed a broken beer bottle from the ground and held it in front of her as she peered between the barrels at the man moving toward her.

"You might as well come out," he said. "I'll find you sooner or later."

She kept still, her pulse banging so loudly against her eardrums she was afraid she wouldn't hear him when he made his next move.

"If you escape from me, I'll only go after your boyfriend," he taunted. "Do you want me to kill your boyfriend?"

Katya's breath caught in her throat. She wanted to jump out and stab the murderer in the face. He had killed her father, he had tried to kill her and Tuck, and now he was threatening Maddox. Enough was enough.

She tamped down her raging anger and waited until he stepped in front of the barrel behind which she hid. When he did, she leaped from her hiding place, screaming as loud as she could and thrusting the broken bottle into Fulton's face.

THE FBI TOOK THE direct route toward the blip on the GPS tracking screen. Maddox had seen the screen and had a general idea of the layout of the streets. He hoped to get close enough to Katya to be there if she needed him.

Maddox ran from building to building, working his way closer to the last blip he'd seen on the screen. Fulton had been moving Katya toward the river. Hopefully, he didn't plan to toss her in. Maddox didn't know whether or not Katya could swim. There were a lot of things he didn't know about Katya and, *dammit,* he wanted to find out. All he needed was a little more time with her.

A scream ripped through the night, firing his adrenaline. He ran in the direction of the sound, hoping it hadn't echoed off the buildings from the opposite direction. Running full tilt, he skidded around a corner and into an alley filled with trash, barrels and an abandoned Dumpster.

There among the debris were two shadowy figures struggling in the darkness.

"Katya!"

"Stay back or I'll kill her!" Fulton shouted, twisting his hands in her hair and yanking so hard, her feet left the ground.

Katya yelped and kicked out, landing a boot against his shins. "He isn't armed!" she yelled.

Maddox didn't slow down, didn't stop to think, his entire body in reaction mode to the danger Katya was in. He charged the two like a raging lion, roaring at the top of his lungs.

He hit Fulton on the side, flinging him up into the air. The man slammed into the heavy metal Dumpster, dragging Katya by the hair.

Thrown off balance, she hit the ground next to the assassin, but came up fighting, twisting and kicking.

As distracted by Katya as he was, Fulton didn't see Maddox's second advance until too late.

Maddox balled his fist and rammed it into the killer's face. Bones snapped and blood gushed from Fulton's nose.

Katya pulled free and flung herself out of the way.

The assassin pushed to his feet and lunged at Maddox,

hitting him in the gut. The two men fell to the ground, Fulton landing on top of Maddox.

Maddox bucked and fought to get his hands free, but remained pinned to the ground by the trained assassin. No matter how hard he tried, he couldn't shake free.

A loud crack rent the air and Fulton fell to the side, stunned.

Maddox leaped onto him and held him down.

Katya stood over the two men, holding a four-foot-long two-by-four like a warrior, ready to take on an entire army.

Suddenly the alley filled with men carrying weapons, one of them Pierce.

Momentarily distracted, Maddox wasn't prepared when Fulton rolled to the side and out from under him. The assassin leaped to his feet and ran.

Pierce and every other agent on the FBI assault team raced after him. He didn't get to the end of the warehouse building before Pierce caught up with him and slammed him to the ground in a flying tackle.

Four assault rifles pointed at the fugitive as Pierce yanked the man's hands behind his back and handcuffed him. "You have the right to remain silent..."

As Pierce read the man his rights, Maddox stood and looked around for Katya. More FBI special agents had arrived in the alley and Maddox couldn't find her among them. His heart skipped several beats. Panic made him push through the men standing around until he spotted the dark-haired woman, his chest tightening at the sight of her.

She sat on the pavement, her arms wrapped around her knees, her shoulders shaking. She looked like an abandoned child, her hair tousled, her face streaked with dirt. But she was the most beautiful woman Maddox had ever seen.

He sat beside her and pulled her into his arms. For a long moment, they leaned against each other.

Pressing his lips into her hair, he whispered, "Thanks for rescuing me."

She gave a shaky laugh and looked up into his face. "I should be thanking you."

The dark alley couldn't dim the light in her pale blue eyes. She smiled. "You're my hero."

"And you are mine. He had me until you came at him like a warrior." He smoothed the hair out of her face. "Where'd you learn to fight dirty like that?"

She cupped his face with her hand and leaned forward to brush a kiss across his lips. "I did what I had to." She kissed him again.

This time Maddox didn't let her off so lightly. His arms tightened around her and he deepened the kiss, his tongue pushing past her teeth to toy with hers.

She gave back, pressing into him, her hands circling his neck, bringing him closer. When she broke contact, she whispered against his lips. "I wish we could stay like this."

Maddox chuckled against her lips. "What, in an alley sitting on the cold hard ground?"

She sighed, nestling into his embrace. "In your arms. It is as close to heaven as I have ever imagined."

Maddox's hands closed on her shoulders and he pushed her far enough away to look down into her face. "Then stay with me. Don't go back to Trejikistan."

Her chin drooped and she pressed her forehead to his chest. "I cannot."

"Can't—or won't?" His tone hardened. When he'd

left her with Pierce, he'd known it was one of the biggest mistakes of his life. "Katya, in the short time I've known you, you've become such an amazing part of my life. You reminded me how good it feels to be alive." He tipped her chin up and gazed down into her eyes. "Stay," he said, his tone low, uncaring if the one word sounded like begging. He'd get down on his knees if he thought it would help.

A single tear rolled from the corner of her eye. "I have to go back. I have to do what has to be done."

Before he could question her further, an ambulance arrived, the sirens blaring and the lights flashing in their eyes.

Emergency medical personnel dropped down from the vehicle.

Pierce appeared before them. "I called the EMTs. Fulton needs attention, and I want them to have a look at you both."

Right behind the ambulance, a news van skidded to a stop, followed by another and another. Soon the alley looked like a celebrity mob scene.

The EMTs insisted on checking out Katya and Maddox. Between the reporters and the EMTs, Katya and Maddox were separated.

Maddox wanted to go to her, to protect her from the onslaught of the media.

A reporter stuck a microphone in Katya's face. "Is it true? You're not a terrorist? The weapons found in your apartment were planted by someone else?"

"Yes," Katya answered, standing on her toes, her gaze panning the crowd until she captured Maddox's.

Maddox mouthed the words, "Are you okay?"

She shrugged, a weak, unconvincing smile curling her lips.

People crowded around her, pressing so close, her eyes rounded, her hands coming up in a protective gesture.

Maddox shoved an EMT aside. "Thanks, but I'll live." He had to get to Katya.

As he pushed through the media, a reporter yelled out over the others, "Katya Ivanov, we have it from a good source that you are actually royalty from Trejikistan, Princess Alexi Katya Ivanov, next in line for the throne now that your father is dead and your brother is missing. Is that true?"

Katya gasped, tears welling in her eyes. She looked toward Maddox and back to the reporter. "No comment." She ducked her head, letting her hair fall over her face.

Maddox froze in place. Princess? Katya was a princess? How had he not known that? Surely the reporter had his facts wrong.

"Princess Alexi," another reporter pushed her way through the crowd gathering around Katya. "Are you seeking asylum in the United States since your government has been taken over in a military coup?"

Yet another reporter pressed in with his camera and microphone. "Princess, are you abandoning your country just when the people were on the verge of conducting their first democratic election?"

Maddox remained frozen in place, staring over the cameras and reporters to the woman trapped in the middle. Who was she? Did he even know?

Katya's head came up and she pushed her shoulders back. "I am not abandoning my country. As soon as I can get cleared to travel, I will return to Trejikistan and lead my people until the elections and the new democratic government is in place."

Pierce muscled his way beside Maddox. "We need to get her out of here."

When Maddox didn't move, Pierce frowned. "She didn't tell you, did she?"

All Maddox could do was shake his head. The woman he'd made love to, the woman he'd raced across the prairie with on the back of a snowmobile was a princess? "You knew?"

Pierce nodded. "She didn't want you to know. For what it's worth, she thought it would make you treat her differently. Does it change the way you feel about her?"

"Damn right."

"Take some time to digest it, brother. Don't do anything stupid." Pierce left his brother and pushed through the crowd. "Show's over. Leave the lady alone, she's been through enough."

Katya was loaded into an ambulance, Pierce climbing in beside her. Richard Fulton, under heavy FBI guard, left in another ambulance.

Maddox stayed where he was long after the ambulances and the press left the scene.

"Can I drop you off somewhere?" One of the remaining agents touched Maddox on the arm.

Until then, his mind had been somersaulting over everything that had happened in the past few days. When the agent brought him back to the present, his thoughts came together, one thing becoming crystal clear. He wanted to be with Katya. "Can you drop me off at the hospital?"

"Which one?"

"Whichever one they took the princess to." He ran toward the agent's vehicle and jumped in. When the agent didn't get right in, Maddox opened the door and called out. "Are you coming?"

The agent chuckled, sliding into the driver's seat. "Suddenly you're a man on a mission?"

"Damn right." A mission to find his princess.

Chapter Seventeen

"Thank God, you're alive!" Katya cried out in her native language. Propped against pillows in a sterile white hospital bed, she held Pierce's cell phone to her ear, tears of joy sliding down her cheeks.

"Yes, sister, I returned from Africa as soon as I could find transportation out," Dmitri said. "Vladimir had the armed forces mobilized to declare a military dictatorship, claiming the country would fall apart if he didn't take immediate action."

"Oh, Dmitri. What a horrible mess to come home to. I should have been there."

"Not to worry," he assured her. "I was able to avert disaster. As for the elections, everything is back on track."

"I am truly happy that you are alive and well." She dabbed at yet more tears. "Did you find out what really happened to Father?"

Dmitri paused. "Katya, Father was murdered. Cousin Vladimir is in prison. He confessed to hiring an assassin to murder our father."

"I know." Katya's fingers twisted her fingers around the pendant containing the tracking device that had almost gotten her killed. She had yet to give it up, and might never if she could find a way to destroy the device her father had implanted inside it to keep her safe. "They captured the assassin here."

"Excellent news."

"It's hard to believe Vladimir would kill his family for a throne," Katya said softly.

"I know." Her brother cleared his throat. "Speaking of news, word has come to us via the paparazzi that you have been busy yourself. What's this about your being a terrorist?"

Katya laughed. "It's a long story that I'll tell you all about when I arrive home. For now, I'm clear of all charges and free to leave whenever I get out of this hospital."

"Hospital? Are you well? Should I come to the United States to rescue you?"

"No, I am fine, just a few scratches and bruises, I promise I'll tell you all about it. If all goes well, I should be home in the next couple of days."

"Why?"

"Why? Don't you need me in Trejikistan?" She sat up, her brows furrowing.

"You are always wanted and needed, but everything is under control here. I do not know what you could add by returning. Father's funeral was today. The elections will take place soon and the monarchy will no longer be needed. If you want to stay in the United States, do so. I know it has always been your dream to lead a 'normal' life. Katya, this is your chance."

His words made her hands shake. "Are you sure?" Could it be that she would be free to lead her life just like anyone else? Free to choose where she could go?

Free of political functions and dull, formal meetings? Free to choose who she wanted to be with?

"Yes, Katya, my dear."

"What about you?" she asked. "What will you do?"

"I will be here until our people are comfortable with their new government. Then?" He laughed. "Perhaps I will join you."

Katya laughed, too, her heartbeat erratic, joy, elation and hope playing havoc with her ability to think. "I have to go."

"I love you, sister."

"And I love you." She pressed the End button and held the phone to her chest to keep her heart from jumping out.

Pierce Thunder Horse appeared in the doorway. "Good news?"

"The best!" When he reached for the phone, she couldn't help but hug him. "Thank you."

"For what? The use of my phone?"

"Yes!" She hugged herself and closed her eyes, afraid she was still dreaming and she'd wake up. She had to find Maddox. Katya opened her eyes and tossed the sheet off.

"Whoa, what's this?"

"I have to get out of here."

"You can't go anywhere."

"Am I still considered a terrorist suspect?"

"No, between the videos and Fulton's confession, you're off the hook."

She stood, holding the back of her hospital gown together. "Where are my clothes?"

"In the closet. But don't you think you should wait until the doctor releases you?"

"I can't wait." She ran for the closet, hauling her dirty clothes from the shelf.

Pierce captured her hands, clothes and all. "Could you wait at least until after one more visit?"

"I don't need another doctor to tell me what I already know. I'm fine. And I'll be even better when—"

"Not a doctor, a friend." Pierce turned her toward the door.

Maddox stood with a bouquet of deep red roses in his hand, a strangely shy expression on his face. "Katya." He stepped into the room, his gaze locked on hers.

"Maddox." Katya's breath lodged in her throat, her heart banging against her rib cage. She let Pierce take the clothes from her nerveless fingers and place them back on the shelf as she stood rooted to the floor.

"I see you two have a lot to talk about. I'll just leave you alone." Pierce pushed past Maddox and shut the door behind him.

When he didn't say anything, Katya cleared her throat and tried to tell herself not to get too excited. "What are you doing here? I thought you'd be on your way back to the ranch."

"No. I'm here to see you."

"The doctor did not find anything wrong. I can leave as soon as he signs my release papers."

Maddox took another step toward her, still holding the flowers. "That's what I wanted to talk to you about."

He was close enough for her to see the lines next to his eyes. Maddox looked tired and she wanted to reach out and stroke away the frown tugging his brows downward. "Did you want to talk about the doctor or my leaving?"

"Your leaving."

She swallowed, wondering how she could tell him she was not going back home without throwing herself in his arms and making a complete fool of herself. "About that..."

He closed the distance between them and pressed a finger to her lips. "No, let me have my say, then you can throw me out if you want."

"But I don't—"

He pressed his finger over her lips again. "Just listen."

She nodded and his hand dropped to his side. "I'm not sure how things work in your country. I don't speak the language and I'm not familiar with your protocol, but I'm willing to learn."

"Why are—"

"Shh, let me finish." He paced the floor, still carrying the bouquet in his hands. "What I'm trying to tell you...no, asking you...ah, hell." He stopped in front of her and held out the roses. "I want to be your bodyguard, or whatever it takes to be close to you. Don't you sce? I want to get to know you. How you became a princess, your favorite color, when you lost your first tooth. Everything."

Tears welled up in Katya's eyes. Of all things he could have said, she'd never expected this, and she couldn't force words past the lump in her throat.

Maddox reached out to her, apparently realizing that he still held the roses. "These are for you."

She took the bouquet and held it up to sniff the fragrant petals.

His hands free, he wrapped thcm around her waist and pulled her close. "Don't you see? Crazy as it seems, I think I'm falling in love with you. Not the princess, not the political figure that could skate circles around my knowledge of protocol, but the passionate woman I first came to know in the cave. The warrior so much like my ancestors who's smart enough to know when to clobber a criminal with a two-by-four." He laughed. "So what do you think? Do you need another bodyguard? Think I could cut it in Trejikistan? I'm willing to go wherever you go."

Katya smiled and cupped his chin with her empty hand. "Maddox, look at me." When she had his attention, she told him her good news, "I'm not leaving."

His eyes widened. "You're not?"

"No. My brother is alive and well in Trejikistan. He'll take over all royal responsibilities. I'm not needed back home."

Maddox closed his eyes, sucked in a deep breath and let it out slowly. When he opened his eyes, a grin spread across his face. "Thank God. I really stink at foreign languages."

"Now that I'm not in line for the throne, I don't think I'll be needing a bodyguard, either."

His grin disappeared. "No?"

"No."

"Would you consider going on a real date with me?"

"To get to know you? Although we have been together pretty much nonstop for the past couple days, I do not know a lot about you." She smiled, her world a brighter place because of Maddox Thunder Horse. "I would be delighted to go on a date with you…on one condition."

His grin returned. "Name it."

"Don't call me Princess."

"Deal."

His dark eyes blazed, and he stood tall, his carriage that of a proud Lakota warrior. Then he bent to kiss her, his lips brushing gently against hers. "*Wankatanka yuha yuwakape miye.* The Great Spirit has blessed me."

* * * * *

Colby Brass

Debra Webb

Mills & Boon™
pure reading pleasure

ABOUT THE AUTHOR

Debra Webb wrote her first story at age nine and her first romance at thirteen. It wasn't until she spent three years working for the military behind the Iron Curtain and within the confining political walls of Berlin, Germany, that she realised her true calling. A five-year stint with NASA on the Space Shuttle Program reinforced her love of the endless possibilities within her grasp as a storyteller. A collision course between suspense and romance was set. Debra has been writing romantic suspense and action-packed romantic thrillers since. Visit her at www.DebraWebb.com or write to her at P.O. Box 4889, Huntsville, AL 35815.

DEDICATION

This book is dedicated to a man
I did not have the privilege of knowing personally.
But his reputation is one no one hereabouts
is likely to forget. Jerry Crabtree, a man
who did the thing he loved, police work,
until the day he died. Thank you, Jerry,
for a lifetime of commitment to serving
and protecting your fellow man.

CAST OF CHARACTERS

Evonne "Von" Cassidy—Von is a former Equalizer. She is focused and determined, but emotionally off-limits. She loved a man once, but refuses to admit that love still survives deep in her battered heart.

Trinity Barrett—Trinity is a protector. He will do anything to protect those he cares about. Can he save the woman he still loves?

Wanda Larkin—She has been seriously injured by her ex-husband, and her little girl, Lily, is missing.

Dennis Lane—He's a lowlife, but he's the one link they have to what Wanda Larkin's husband did with their daughter, Lily.

Waylon Robinson—He promises to cooperate. He knows where the children are...where Von is. But can he be trusted?

Special Agent George White—Simon's FBI contact, who has been investigating the human trafficking network spanning from Chicago to Alabama.

Victoria Colby-Camp—As head of the agency, Victoria sees only a bright future now that the Equalizers are fully merged with the Colby Agency.

Jim Colby—Jim wants his mother to be happy, no matter what it takes.

Simon Ruhl—A second-in-command at the Colby Agency. As a former special agent in the FBI, he has deep contacts with the Bureau.

Ian Michaels—As Victoria's other second-in-command, Ian is a stabilizing force within the staff.

Chapter One

Chicago, Tuesday, December 22, 2009, 2:05 p.m.

Only three days until Christmas.

Victoria Colby-Camp smiled as she watched the rush of last-minute shoppers along the sidewalks of Chicago's Miracle Mile.

Lunch with a longtime friend just two blocks from the office provided a nice stroll in the gently falling snow. Though many only endured Chicago's harsh winters, Victoria loved this time of year. It was filled with countless reasons to be joyous and to celebrate. Just six years ago she had celebrated her first Christmas with her son after more than twenty years of not knowing whether he was dead or alive.

Now she not only had her son, Jim, back, she also had gained a wonderful daughter, his wife Tasha, and two amazing grandchildren. A darling granddaughter, Jamie, and five-month-old Luke, Lucas James Colby. James would be so proud. The memory of her beloved late first husband brought a smile to Victoria's lips. He would very much approve of how far she and Jim had come despite the many obstacles life had thrown in their paths.

Victoria paused a moment to consider the building that had become home to the Colby Agency after the original building had been destroyed. Despite the state-of-the-art security, evil still found a way to touch those inside. Certainty chased away the niggling worry. No matter how hard their enemies fought to bring down the Colby Agency, somehow Victoria and her staff overcame the seemingly insurmountable to not only survive but also to thrive.

For this she was immensely thankful.

The chilly wind blew a wisp of hair against her cheek. Victoria swept it away, tucking the strands back into the French twist she'd so meticulously arranged that morning. Not so easy to do with gloved fingers. Sentimentality flowed inside her as she considered the numerous miracles she had observed firsthand over the past two-plus decades. The good somehow always outweighed the bad. She owed much to those who continued to persevere alongside her at the agency and fight the good fight.

Some had moved on to begin new lives elsewhere, but most remained invaluable assets, both as friends and as business contacts. The Colby staff was the best of the best. Victoria appreciated each one for his or her unique qualities. This year she and Jim had decided upon distinctly generous bonuses for every member of the staff.

Another smile spread across her lips. It was the

least she could do given the enormous sacrifices each had made through their continued dedication and loyalty during the ups and downs and changes with the agency.

A rush of pedestrians drew Victoria from her tender, affectionate musings.

"Did you see that?" a woman asked another as the two, headed in Victoria's direction, glanced back then hurried forward.

Victoria didn't hear the rest of the conversation since the women moved by so quickly. A group of pedestrians farther up the sidewalk drew her attention there.

A woman stood alone.

Victoria was first taken aback by her lack of suitable attire considering the freezing weather conditions. No coat…no hat or gloves. Dear God, no shoes. The woman stood, staring across the street, as if she expected someone or something to appear in her line of vision.

Then she turned, facing Victoria's direction, and trudged forward, her bare feet faltering clumsily through the ankle-deep snow.

Victoria's lips parted with a sharply indrawn breath.

The front of the woman's yellow blouse was stained a deep crimson. Droplets of that same startling color dripped from the fingertips of her right hand and onto the newly fallen snow, leaving a horrifying atlas of her jagged path.

Victoria's gloved hand slid into her coat pocket, wrapped around her cell phone even as a sort of shock held her unable to look away…unable to properly react. Who was this woman? What had happened to her?

She stumbled closer. "Can you help me?" Her lips were cracked from exposure and her skin was deathly pale from the icy cold.

Instinct kicking aside the shock, Victoria bolted forward just in time for the woman to collapse into her arms.

"Help me," she begged, her eyes wide with fear and glassy with whatever physical trauma she had suffered. Her left cheek was swollen. Blood had trickled from her nose and coagulated on her skin.

Victoria hit speed dial for the office as she lowered the woman onto the cold blanket of snow. "Mildred," she said before her personal assistant could launch into her practiced greeting, "I need paramedics. Now! I'm on the street in front of the office. I have a female, mid-to-late twenties, who is injured and bleeding."

Victoria surveyed the woman. The bleeding appeared to start at her left shoulder. "Make the call and get me some help out here!"

Tossing the cell phone aside, Victoria opened the bloody yellow blouse to assess the injury. A penetrating wound on the left shoulder. Deep. Still oozing precious blood.

"Please," the woman urged, her voice scarcely a gasp. "Help me."

"I've called for help," Victoria assured her as she shrugged off her coat and ripped the scarf from around her neck. With one hand she pressed the scarf over the wound to staunch the bleeding while spreading the coat over the woman's body with the other.

A sharply indrawn breath jerked Victoria's attention upward. A man, cell phone in hand, stared at the startling sight.

"Take off your coat," Victoria ordered him, "wrap it around her feet and legs."

Still frozen, the man blinked.

"Do it!" Victoria demanded.

His movements stilted, the man shouldered out of his heavy winter coat and moved to do as he had been instructed. "What…what happened?" he asked.

"I don't know," Victoria told him. "Help is on the way." To the woman whose lips were still moving with inaudible words, Victoria said, "Can you tell me your name?"

A weak gaze locked with Victoria's. "Help me," she murmured.

"You have my word," Victoria promised. "But I need your name." Sirens wailed in the distance, providing some amount of relief. Help was on the way. Thank God.

"My baby…" The rest of the woman's words were thready, indistinct whispers. "He took my Lily."

Victoria leaned closer. "Please, tell me your name." She wanted desperately to pursue the subject of the baby, Lily, but she needed the woman's name first.

"Wanda..." She moistened her cracked lips. "Larkin."

"What happened?" Victoria's son crouched on the other side of Wanda.

As if a shot of adrenaline had renewed her, Wanda Larkin frantically grabbed at Jim's shirt with her right hand. "He took my little girl," she cried. "You have to help me!"

Victoria's gaze collided with Jim's for an instant before returning to the woman's.

"Who took your baby?" Jim asked, his voice gentle.

"The paramedics as well as Chicago's finest are here."

Victoria glanced up at Trinity Barrett, a member of her staff. Like Jim, he hadn't taken the time to grab his coat before rushing out into the harsh weather. Victoria nodded, thankful the slippery streets hadn't slowed down the arrival of emergency services.

"Who took your baby?" Jim repeated a bit more firmly.

"My ex-husband," Wanda murmured. "He took my baby." Tears leaked from her glazed eyes. "I tried to stop him. Outside the toy...store." She gestured feebly in the direction from which she'd come.

As Trinity filled in the paramedics, Jim prompted more answers from the victim. Where did she live? What was the name of the toy store where the attack and abduction had taken place?

Victoria cleared her mind and took mental note of

the information Wanda managed to provide before her ability to listen and respond faded further. Victoria grabbed her phone from the snow and put through another call to Mildred with instructions to send Von Cassidy to the major toy store only a few blocks away. It was the only one in the direction Wanda had indicated. Every moment that passed lessened the likelihood of finding witnesses to the incident. There was no time to wait for the police to react.

Victoria and Jim moved aside as the paramedics took over care of the victim. While the police attempted to question Wanda, Jim gave Trinity a nod and they both slipped away. Victoria covered for them when the questioning turned to her and the man who'd reluctantly helped by giving up his coat.

By the time the paramedics had taken Wanda away in the waiting ambulance and the police had gone with a warning that there would likely be additional questions, Victoria was freezing. "Thank you," she said to the man whose name she couldn't immediately call to mind.

"I'm just sorry you had to ask for my help." He shook his head and offered a bewildered shrug. "You see these things on the news…in the movies…" He shook his head again. "But you never expect to be the one…"

"You reacted commendably," Victoria assured him before he trudged away. She surveyed the sidewalks where those who'd stood by watching now went on about the business of hurrying to their destinations.

When, she wondered, had helping one's fellowman become more a spectator's sport than a call to action?

She peered at the bloody snow where the victim had lain, then up at the sky. Victoria closed her eyes and let the falling snow sting her cold cheeks. Who was this woman? This Wanda Larkin?

Was the incident related to a custody battle?

Or was this something far more sinister?

Either way…a child was missing.

Whatever the motive behind the act—Victoria shifted her gaze to the building where her staff waited—the Colby Agency would find the missing child.

And the man responsible for this unthinkable tragedy.

Chapter Two

Humboldt Park, 3:30 p.m. (2 hours missing)

Trinity Barrett surveyed the block surrounding the apartment building where Wanda Larkin lived. Jim Colby reached for the unsecured door leading into the building. Trinity followed his boss inside the dingy stairwell. The wails of an infant somewhere above the first floor were underscored by at least one blaring television. A woman shouting at someone who had evidently made her unhappy drowned out the rest of the cacophony.

Jim studied the row of mailboxes on the wall to the left of the entry door. "Third floor, 306."

Wanda Larkin had given them the street address, but the apartment number she'd murmured had been inaudible.

Three flights of stairs later, Trinity approached Larkin's apartment first. A metal number six identified the unit.

Jim held up a hand for Trinity to wait as he moved to the right side of the door and knocked loudly.

No response from the interior. No distinguishable sound.

Prompted by Jim's second round of knocking, somewhere on the fourth floor a dog barked.

Jim nodded his approval and Trinity reached for the doorknob.

Technically they were entering unlawfully, but the woman had given her address when Jim asked—which could be loosely construed as authorization to enter the premises. The cops hadn't arrived just yet, which meant Trinity and Jim would need to proceed with caution. Tampering with evidence could impede the investigation as well as get them in serious hot water with the authorities.

The latch released with nothing more than a single turn of the knob. Trinity pushed the door inward and drew back, staying to the left and clear of the opening.

Seconds ticked by with no reaction.

Jim moved into the doorway, then entered the apparently deserted apartment.

Trinity followed.

The place was neat and clean despite the worn-out furnishings.

No sign of a struggle.

The scent of recently baked cookies permeated the air. A small Christmas tree sat on the table in one corner, the decorations mostly homemade.

Jim headed for the small hall that likely led to the bedrooms and bath. Trinity moved around the living room. A couple of framed photos sat on a table in front of the window overlooking the unkempt street. No curtains, just the open slats of yellowed blinds.

Trinity picked up a photo of the woman, Wanda Larkin, and a small girl, six or seven years old, maybe. Cute kid with blond hair and brown eyes like her mother. His chest tightened at the idea that the child may have been harmed…or worse. He picked up another framed photo, this one probably taken at school. Her name, Lily, was stamped in gold lettering across the bottom of the photo. Using his cell phone, he snapped a close-up of the photo.

"Two bedrooms, one bath," Jim announced as he strode back into the room. "All are clean. If there's been any trouble here, there's no indication."

Trinity passed the framed photo of Lily to his boss. "I'll check the kitchen."

The kitchen was actually a part of the living room, the two spaces divided only by a breakfast bar. A plate of cookies decorated for Christmas sat on the counter. The little girl's artwork and more photos were displayed on the fridge.

Lily. Trinity touched the name scrawled on a pink piece of construction paper, then traced the cut-and-pasted Christmas tree the child had drawn. An innocent child…that was now in danger.

He shook off the troubling thoughts and focused on the details. Fridge and cabinets were painfully bare of provisions. Clearly the mother struggled financially, but the cleanliness of the apartment as well as the Christmas decorations and cookies indicated how hard she tried. A schedule printed on computer paper was taped to the side of the fridge. Trinity studied the document.

"She works at Mercy General," Trinity said aloud. The schedule gave no indication of the position she held, only the hours scheduled to work each day.

Jim joined him in the kitchen. "She scheduled to work today?"

Trinity shook his head. "Tomorrow afternoon." The numerous night shifts made him wonder who kept the girl, Lily, while her mother worked.

"I'm calling the police!"

Trinity and Jim turned simultaneously. An elderly woman waved a cordless phone receiver in her right hand while sporting what appeared to be a can of pepper spray in the left.

Jim's hands went up surrender style. "No need to call the police, ma'am," he assured her. "We're from the Colby Agency. We're here to help Ms. Larkin."

Trinity lifted his hands in the same fashion. "Are you a neighbor of Ms. Larkin's?"

The woman pursed her lips and narrowed her gaze. "If you're here to help her, why isn't she here, too?" she demanded, promptly ignoring Trinity's question. "Since she's not, that means you're here illegally."

Unfortunately, Trinity considered, the lady had a valid point.

"I'm Jim Colby," Jim explained, "and this is my

colleague Trinity Barrett." Jim gestured to his coat. "If you'll allow me, I'll gladly show you my ID."

The woman cocked her head. "Open that coat up so I can see if there's a gun under there."

Smart lady, Trinity decided.

Jim obliged, gingerly tugging open his coat using his thumbs and forefingers.

The woman nodded, a frizzy gray curl slipped loose from her haphazard ponytail. "You, too," she instructed Trinity.

Trinity did the same. Jacy Kelley, the agency's new receptionist, had appeared in the parking garage with Trinity and Jim's coats before they headed here.

"Come on over here where I can see." The neighbor wasn't stepping away from the open doorway.

Moving cautiously, Trinity and his boss again complied with her demand.

When they'd reached the center of the living room, she said, "That's close enough right there."

Both displayed their credentials.

After leaning forward to check out the IDs they offered, she eyed first Jim then Trinity with marginally less suspicion. "Where's Wanda and Lily?" Fury tightened her lips. "Has something happened?"

Jim explained the circumstances that brought them to Larkin's apartment, leaving out the part about the missing child. They needed this woman cooperative, not hysterical. Her face paled and her eyes widened at the few details Jim provided.

"I knew that no-good bum would do something

like this eventually." She shoved the canister of pepper spray into the pocket of her baggy jeans, shifted the phone to her left hand and extended her right toward Jim. "I'm Teresa Boles. I live cross the hall. I take care of Lily after school." As Jim shook her hand, she added, "He should've gone to jail for good the last time he knocked Wanda around."

"Ms. Boles," Trinity began as he, too, accepted a brisk handshake from the lady. Her grip was a heck of a lot stronger than he'd expected. "We'll need the ex-husband's name, phone number and address. Can you help us with that?"

"Kobi Larkin." Teresa wagged her head. "I haven't seen him in months. Not since he broke Wanda's jaw." She muttered a curse under her breath. "I helped her take out a restraining order and he hasn't been back. I hoped we'd seen the last of him." She suddenly frowned. "Wait." She looked from Jim to Trinity and back. "You said Wanda was at the hospital. Where's Lily?"

Trinity and Jim exchanged a look. "Ms. Boles," Jim said gently, "we don't know where Lily is. Bear in mind that Wanda was seriously injured and we can't be certain her story was accurate."

"Where's the baby?" Boles demanded, anger overtaking the fear in her voice. "Did that lowdown fool do something to Lily?"

"Ms. Larkin," Trinity took up where Jim had left off, "stated that her ex-husband had taken Lily. Do you have any idea where he might have taken her? Where he lives or works?"

"Why aren't the police doing something?" she shrieked. "There's no telling what he'll do! He's a dopehead! A no-good son of a bitch!"

"Ms. Boles," Trinity said coolly, hoping his rational tone would calm her, "the police are at the hospital with Wanda. They'll probably be here soon. We're trying to get a head start on finding the little girl. We promised Wanda we would find her. Anything you can do to help us will help Lily."

"We need as much information about him as you can provide," Jim reiterated.

She trembled, took a deep, shaky breath and squared her shoulders. "Kobi lives on the street, as far as I know. Don't have a job or a phone. But," she said when Jim would have interrupted, "the one thing I know for sure is that he hangs around with some other troublemakers over in Rogers Park." She shook her head. "I don't know any names of his friends," she added before Trinity could ask. "I heard Wanda say something about his friends in Rogers Park when she was yelling at him the last time he had the nerve to show up here. Before he broke her jaw. A couple of months ago."

"We'll check it out." Jim pulled a business card from his jacket pocket. "Ms. Boles, please call us if you think of anything else or hear anything related to Mr. Larkin or Lily."

Boles accepted the card, stared at it a long moment.

"What about the police?" She looked to Jim first, then to Trinity. "Won't they come here, too? Aren't you working with them? Do they understand that he's capable of anything? Just because he's Lily's father doesn't mean he'll take care of her."

"Yes, ma'am," Trinity answered, "the police will likely be here soon and have questions for you, as well. As we explained, we're trying to get a head start with locating the father so we can help Lily."

"Every second we waste," Jim said, his tone dull, emotionless, "may be the one that could have made the difference in how this turns out. You have my word that we'll do everything possible." He moved around the bewildered woman and headed for the door. "Call if you think of anything at all."

"Thank you, Ms. Boles." Trinity tried to reassure her with his eyes. "We'll find Lily." He started for the door.

"If it's not too late already," Ms. Boles called after him. "Kobi's crazy. He could do anything."

Trinity didn't slow his momentum.

Jim was right.

Every second counted.

Chapter Three

Toy World, 3:40 p.m.

The police arrived at the toy store a full three minutes after Von, forcing her to adopt a different strategy for questioning employees.

In the past fifteen minutes they had taken four employees, one at a time, into the manager's office for questioning. Von couldn't eavesdrop so she had initiated her own approach.

First she'd visually examined the sidewalk and street in front of the toy store. No blood. Didn't make sense. The woman had been bleeding. Quite possibly her coat, assuming she had been wearing one at the time, had soaked up the initial blood lost. But where was her coat?

According to Victoria, the incident had taken place on the sidewalk in front of the store. Since the checkout counter and the restrooms were at the back of the store, it made sense to Von that any employee who'd witnessed the confrontation would have been working the aisles at the front of the store.

Von wandered the action figure aisle, the end closest to the two-story glass store front, and watched for the red apron the employees wore. The last-minute shoppers were out in full force. The thick crowd helped her to blend in. She glanced at the street beyond the heavily decorated wall of glass. Von doubted the two police cruisers parked out front were discouraging business since Christmas was just three days away. Some parents would walk over hot coals or dodge flying bullets to fulfill their kids' Christmas wishes.

Which was dumb in Von's opinion. Christmas was a waste of energy and resources.

A young guy, younger than her twenty-eight, rolled a float stacked high with boxes onto the aisle where Von waited. Depending on how long he'd been stocking these shelves he may have witnessed the confrontation between Larkin and her ex.

Half a dozen steps and she stood right behind the store clerk. "Excuse me."

He didn't turn around or acknowledge her presence.

She tapped him on the shoulder.

He jumped.

Then she saw the reason he hadn't heard her. His shoulder-length hair hid the wire extending from his ear to his MP3 player.

He snatched the earbud free and jammed it into his apron pocket. "Can I help you?" He cleared his throat. "I mean, sorry." He forced a smile. "How may I help you, ma'am?"

The distinct flicker of worry in his eyes warned that he'd committed this transgression before and wanted no part of that kind of trouble again.

"Have you been stocking on this aisle all afternoon?" Might as well get straight to the point.

He glanced past her, then searched her face a moment as if attempting to determine if she was a spy for management. "Since about one."

She hitched a thumb toward the front window. "My best friend had a big fight right outside with her ex. Did you see it happen?"

He stiffened. "I already talked to the police. I told 'em everything I know."

Von produced a trembling smile. "I can't get the police to tell me anything and I'm really worried. She's at the hospital and her ex took her little girl." Von shrugged. "I really want to find that bastard before he does something even more stupid."

The clerk licked his lips, checked both directions of the aisle. "I wish I could help you." He shrugged. "I really do. But I really did tell the cops all I know." He gestured to the floor to ceiling, wall to wall window. "I could see them arguing but I couldn't hear what they were saying. The dude grabbed the kid's hand and walked off. The woman ran after him. Looked like she was yelling but I couldn't hear what she was saying."

"Which way did they go?"

He pointed left and shrugged again. "That's all I know."

Von gave him a grateful smile. "Thanks."

The police would continue questioning employees until they were certain no one had seen or heard anything. Von had other plans.

If the violent part of the confrontation hadn't happened in front of the store, then it had to have occurred after the ex walked away with the kid in tow. Von moved out the front entrance and turned left.

Concentrating on the snowy sidewalk, she passed a restaurant, a bookstore and a pharmacy. When she reached the end of the block she turned around and retraced her steps.

No blood. Just the slush of snow beaten down by foot traffic.

How far had Larkin and her ex gone before the physical confrontation occurred? The Colby Agency was five blocks away. A street over and four blocks down. The woman had been bleeding profusely. Wherever she was attacked, presumably with a knife, there would be blood close by. If not on the sidewalk near the toy store…if not in front of witnesses who surely would have called the police— It had to be in a more secluded place. Some place no one would look on a busy afternoon only a few shopping days from Christmas.

Von checked the wide alley between the pharmacy and the bookstore. Some trash, a few empty boxes and a Dumpster but no blood. Double-checking as she retraced her steps, she returned to the sidewalk and moved on to the next possibility.

Between the restaurant and the toy store was another alley, this one too narrow for the city's garbage truck. Again there were empty boxes. A couple of garbage cans and not much else.

"Damn it." Had Wanda Larkin gotten disoriented and confused the location of the confrontation? Maybe she'd followed the jerk a considerable distance from the toy store.

Von ventured deeper into the alley. As she neared the end where the alley gave way to another sidewalk and street, her gaze snagged on a dark spot. Not mud or other grime. This was distinctly rusty in color. The snow was a slushy mess from the foot traffic but there was something…

She touched the spot, assessed the smudge on her fingertip.

Definitely blood.

Her heart rate accelerated as anticipation fired in her veins.

At the intersection of the alley and the parallel street that ran behind the toy store another stack of boxes were overturned and scattered.

More blood.

Von dragged box after box aside…a woman's coat had been wadded into a ball and tossed to the side. Von cautiously unrolled the coat. The lining was bloodstained. Fur-lined ankle boots were hidden behind more boxes…and socks—all bloodstained.

Judging by the amount of blood on the ground, Von estimated that Wanda Larkin had been immobile and hemorrhaging heavily for several minutes. Lying on the frigid ground with no coat and no shoes.

Fury roared through Von as she pieced together the story the elements of the scene revealed.

The ex had meant for Wanda to die.

Von sat back on her haunches and surveyed the scene once more. Larkin had stabbed his ex-wife or slashed at her with the knife. Von inspected the coat, noted the hole in the garment. Not an extended tear in the fabric, a distinct hole. No slash. He'd stabbed her. He'd hit her or pushed her hard enough to knock her unconscious or stun her, at least for a few minutes. Then he'd stripped off her coat and boots, tried to camouflage her body and walked away.

Leaving her to die.

Exposure to the extreme cold would have hastened the outcome.

"Bastard." Von pushed to her feet and double-timed it back to the toy store. She tracked down the guy she'd questioned before. "Do me a favor." The clerk didn't look too gung-ho, but Von went on, "Tell the police there's blood in the alley between this store and the restaurant next door."

The guy's eyes rounded. "Blood?"

"Tell them!" Von ordered as she backed down the aisle toward the exit. "Tell them *now*."

She didn't wait around to get caught up in questioning. Her SUV was in the parking garage down the block and across the street. On the way, she put in a call to Victoria and explained what she'd discovered near the toy store.

"Von, I want you to rendezvous with Jim and Trinity," Victoria instructed. "They're en route to Rogers Park. The ex-husband reportedly lives or spends time in the area."

"Do we have his name or a description?" Von asked, pushing aside the automatic reaction that had nothing to do with this case.

"His name is Kobi Larkin. Research is sending a DMV photo to your phones now. Also, Trinity obtained a photo of the child at the mother's apartment. He'll forward that to you as well." Victoria hesitated. "And, Von, tread cautiously," she warned. "Keep me posted. I'll follow up with Chicago PD."

"On my way," Von assured the chief of the Colby Agency as she sprinted to her SUV. Her mind raced ahead of her…to Rogers Park.

To *him*.

Trinity Barrett.

Living in the same city with him wasn't the end of the world. Not at all. Chicago was plenty big enough that running into each other wasn't exactly that big of an issue. He'd worked in the high-class section of the city; she'd worked on the fringes. Hadn't been a problem…until this year.

From the moment Jim Colby had told her the Equalizers were merging with the Colby Agency, Von had known this moment might come.

But she'd hoped.

She'd even prayed.

Well, sort of.

Now the nightmare she'd wished to avoid was becoming reality.

She would be forced to work with Trinity Barrett, her ex-husband.

After hitting the key fob and climbing into the driver's seat of her SUV, she jammed the key into the ignition and started the engine. She took a slow, deep breath and relaxed to the degree possible.

She could do this.

It wasn't the end of the world, Von reminded herself. Not really. Yes, it would be awkward and annoying and damned frustrating working with him. But there was every reason to anticipate that she would certainly survive the challenge.

He, however, might not.

Chapter Four

Rogers Park, 4:30 p.m. (3 hours missing)

Trinity waited at the corner of the block, the rendezvous point.

She was almost here.

Evonne Cassidy. *Von.* His ex-wife.

Trinity hiked his shoulders in an effort to relieve some of the stress. He should have resigned ten months ago when Victoria announced that the Equalizers were merging with the Colby Agency. But Trinity loved his work at the Colby Agency. He'd hoped that Von would do the right thing and decide not to come onboard at the agency.

But she'd done exactly the opposite.

Five years ago they had made the decision to end their volatile relationship. Problem was, neither of them had been willing to leave Chicago. Determined to make a fresh start Trinity had, in time, signed on with the Colby Agency. A couple years later he'd heard through mutual friends that Von had taken a position at another PI type firm, but he hadn't known until a few days later that it was Victoria Colby's son's firm.

That fact hadn't been a problem until this year.

Until then, Trinity and Von hadn't spoken since the divorce finalized, not for any reason. Shortly after the announced merger earlier this year, they'd had a face-to-face meeting in neutral territory. A decision to keep their history private had been reached. There had been no need to drag their tumultuous shared past into the present. They would be cordial to each other at work and if they were lucky, a mutual assignment wouldn't come up.

So much for luck.

He watched her SUV roll to a stop at the curb. This was it. No turning back.

They were professionals. They were both dedicated to their work. There was no time to deal with personal issues under the circumstances.

A child was in danger.

Von slid from behind the wheel, shoved the door shut with her hip and hit the key fob to initiate the vehicle's security system. Her trendy slacks and matching coat were signature Von. She liked being comfortable, but she never sacrificed fashion to make it happen. Somehow she always looked like she'd just stepped off a runway in the most casual of clothes.

Trinity swallowed hard as she marched toward him. He'd seen her every single weekday this year at the office. No matter, each time his internal reaction was the same—uncertainty, yearning…frustration.

Fool he was, even five years hadn't changed the way just watching her move made him feel. One thing was an absolute certainty, he would take that particular secret with him to his grave.

Giving her the satisfaction of knowing that she had the upper hand on his heart was one humiliation he had no desire to experience.

"Just received word from Simon that there are two possible addresses where Larkin has been known to hang out," she announced as she strode toward Trinity's position on the sidewalk.

Simon Ruhl was one of Victoria and Jim's seconds in command. Possessing deep connections within the FBI, Simon could generally reach out to his contacts for swift and relevant information.

"Excellent," Trinity acknowledged the news. It was a starting point. Rogers Park had more than its share of less than savory characters and locations. Wasting time sifting through them all was less than optimum under the circumstances.

Glancing past Trinity, then in the other direction, Von asked, "Where's Jim?"

Jim Colby was the former head of the Equalizers. It had taken time, but the crew who'd come onboard from the Equalizers and the staff at the Colby Agency had learned to consider both Jim and Victoria "the boss." Trinity doubted Von's question about Jim had anything to do with her considering him her *actual* boss. Most likely she had hoped a third party would be around to provide a buffer between the two of them. Trinity had hoped for the same. Just another example of how luck had deserted him completely today.

"He's on the phone with Chicago PD." Trinity pulled the collar of his coat up around his neck. "They're not too happy that we got the jump on their investigation. Larkin's neighbor mentioned we'd been in the apartment. Jim's doing damage control."

Von made a disapproving face. "That's ridiculous. Who cares who got the jump? Finding the kid is the goal here."

Her lack of patience with the rules was a leftover of Equalizer methodology. That tactic had slowly but surely been overcome in recent months. Von, like the others, had learned the Colby way of conducting an investigation. Granted, this situation called for swift, decisive action, still some amount of interfacing was necessary when boundaries were breached.

Enemies were easy to make. Allies were far more difficult to attain and even harder to keep. The Colby Agency prided itself on cultivating and maintaining strong allies.

"Where to first?" she prompted.

Trinity kicked aside the distractions and gestured to the apartment building to their right. "Kobi Larkin has a sister who lives on the second floor. The sister, according to neighbors, has refused to speak to him since he and Wanda divorced. We're hoping she can point us in the right direction."

"Larkin may be scum," Von commented as they

crossed the street, "but he's still the woman's brother." She shook her head as she surveyed both ends of the block once more. "In my experience a perp's family is rarely any real help so I wouldn't hold my breath."

Trinity couldn't cite any recent examples to dispute her assertion. But they had to try every avenue, no matter how remote.

Like the building where Wanda Larkin lived, this one was rundown and dingy. Despite the cold, four teenage males loitered on the steps leading to the front entrance. Von ignored their lewd comments. Trinity stared from one to the other, long enough to make them squirm. The door closed behind Von who hadn't hung around to watch his protective maneuver.

He caught up with her on the stairs leading to the second floor. She didn't bother glancing back. Von Cassidy could take care of herself and she didn't like anyone indicating otherwise—in word or deed.

Fixing his gaze someplace besides on her swaying hips was a task. Trinity was glad when they reached the second-floor corridor.

"Two-fifteen," he said as he led the way along the cluttered hall. Apparently tomorrow was trash pickup day. Most of the doors were flanked by bags of what had the look and smell of household garbage.

At apartment 215, he stopped and rapped on the door, careful to keep to the left in the event whoever was inside opted to take a shot at whoever had dared to knock. Von waited on the other side of the door.

"Who is it?"

The voice inside was female and distinctly unfriendly.

"Maggie Clemmons," Trinity began, "my name is Trinity Barrett. I'm an investigator looking into the disappearance of your brother, Kobi Larkin, and I have a few questions for you. I'd appreciate it if you'd open the door and cooperate."

Von arrowed him a look of approval. Nothing he'd said had been a flat-out lie, but he'd left out some relevant info like the fact that he wasn't a cop.

"I don't know anything about him or his friends," the woman claimed. "I haven't heard from that no-account bum in months."

"Ma'am," Trinity pressed, "just a few moments of your time will be greatly appreciated. This is a matter of the utmost importance."

Silence.

Von raised her eyebrows in question at Trinity.

He wasn't giving up just yet. "Ma'am?"

"I told you I don't know anything," came through the door.

"He took Lily," Trinity added since the concept that her brother was missing hadn't done the trick.

Trinity's gaze locked with Von's. If the child being in danger didn't get through to the woman…likely nothing would. Maybe Von had been right in her assessment. Blood was thicker than water.

Grinding metal echoed from turning locks, providing the response they had hoped for. Relief flared in Trinity's chest.

The door opened and a woman who'd obviously just saturated her hair with a color treatment looked from Trinity to Von and back. "He wouldn't have taken Lily." She shook her head adamantly as if that would make her words so. "No way."

"May we come in, ma'am?" Trinity didn't want to have this conversation in the corridor. Not with several doors cracked open just enough for nosy neighbors to see and hear too much already.

With a swipe to her brow with the towel dangling around her neck, the woman opened the door wider. "There's got to be a mistake."

Once Trinity and Von were inside, she closed the door. "Did Wanda say Kobi took Lily?"

"Ms. Clemmons, have you heard from your brother today?" Von asked.

Clemmons glared at Von, then blinked repeatedly. Apparently the pungent smell of the chemical hair treatment was getting to her. "I told you I haven't heard from Kobi in months." She blinked twice more. "Where's Wanda? Why didn't she come if what you're saying is so? She wouldn't just send somebody around saying such things."

"Wanda is at Mercy General," Trinity explained. "According to an update I received from my superior just a few minutes ago, she survived surgery and is currently in guarded condition." Victoria had called just before Von arrived. He probably should have mentioned that to her as well. But he'd been too busy worrying about how they would manage to work together without killing each other.

The woman hugged her arms around her waist. "He swore to me that he didn't hurt her. Is Wanda gonna be all right?"

So much for telling the truth.

"If Wanda pulls through with no permanent damage," Von answered the question, "she'll be very lucky. Kobi stabbed her, stripped her coat and boots off and left her to die in the snow beneath a stack of empty boxes in an alley where no one would find her."

"Dear God," Clemmons murmured.

"When did you speak to Kobi?" Trinity pressed, hoping to get the truth before Clemmons had time to rethink her position.

"About two o'clock, I guess." She dabbed at her forehead with the towel again. "He said they'd had a big fight, but that everything was gonna be okay. He said he was going away for a while. To get himself together." She turned her palms up in an earnest manner. "That's why he called. After all this time, he just wanted to say bye before he left." Her head wagged side to side. "He's pushed her around from time to time but he never hurt her...like this."

Not so according to the neighbor, but Trinity wasn't arguing the point. He needed this woman to keep talking.

"Did he give you any idea where he might be

planning to go?" Von demanded before Trinity could, keeping the pressure on.

Maggie Clemmons shrugged. "He just said he was owed some money and he was gonna use it to do the right thing…finally."

"Do you have reason to believe he planned to, as you say, get himself together?" Trinity hoped the man had perhaps gone into hiding with his child and meant no harm to her. Finding a scumbag like him wouldn't be that difficult. So far, he hadn't proven that smart. "To do the right thing?"

Clemmons heaved a weary sigh. "No. He's said that before. He probably took the money and got more drugs. That's what he usually does." She divided her attention between Trinity and Von. "That's why I know he wouldn't have taken Lily with him. He don't care about much but he does want her to have a better life. He's always said she deserves better than he or Wanda could give her."

"The fact of the matter is," Trinity said somberly, "he did take Lily, after leaving Wanda for dead. It doesn't sound like he has Lily's best interests at heart just now."

"We have to find him," Von added. "Before he allows any harm to come to the child…before the police find him. If you care about your brother you need to help us. You know what they do to people who hurt children."

Silence screamed in the room for two beats. Trinity hoped Von's strategy worked. A plea from woman to woman—one that included hope for the brother.

"Charlie Jones," Clemmons said with a confirming nod. "I don't know where he is. But Charlie knows Kobi better than anyone. He'll know how to find him."

"How do we find Charlie?" Trinity asked. "We have to hurry. There's no time for tracking him down. Not if you can give us that information."

Clemmons hurried over to the end table next to her sofa. She scribbled something on a pad of paper, then ripped the page free and brought it to Trinity. "This is his address. I don't know his phone number. But you'll find him here. If anyone knows where Kobi is, it's Charlie."

While Von thanked Ms. Clemmons, Trinity made his way into the corridor and put through a call to Simon Ruhl. By the time they reached the stairwell, Trinity had relayed the name and address to Simon for intelligence gathering. Any info available from any and all sources could prove useful in their approach.

Trinity dropped his cell phone into his jacket pocket. "Simon will call us if he finds anything." Since the address was only fifteen or so minutes away the preliminary info might be minimal, but they couldn't wait around for additional details.

Von put her hand out to push through the door of the building's front exit. "If we're—"

She abruptly whirled around. Shoved Trinity against the wall. And kissed him.

His fingers tightened in her coat with the intention of pushing her away…but they relaxed instantly as the reality that *Von* was kissing him sank into his brain. His eyes closed as the feel of her hot mouth moving over his trumped all other senses.

Vaguely he was aware that the door opened and people entered the building. He heard the shuffling of boots, the hushed exchange of male voices. Trinity wanted to open his eyes and assess the new arrivals but her tongue slid along his and all other thought vanished.

Her arms went around his neck and he promptly forgot the past five years…the hurt…the arguments… the loneliness he'd felt so many, many nights along with anyone or anything else he should have been thinking about just now.

"Get a room," a male voice grunted.

Male laughter faded along with the heavy footfalls tromping up the stairs.

Von suddenly drew away. "Let's go."

Trinity blinked. Grappled with the concept of what had just happened.

Von pushed out the door.

He swiped his still burning mouth with the back of his hand. "What the hell?" With a bewildered glance up the stairs, he shuffled out the door to catch up with her.

"You mind explaining what that was about?"

he demanded when he caught up with her hurried stride.

She jerked her head toward the street and the dark sedan illegally parked in a red zone. "Cops."

Trinity stopped. He stared at the sedan then back at the apartment building.

"Come on," Von called back. "We're wasting time."

Since Trinity had arrived in the neighborhood with Jim Colby, he didn't have much choice but to go wherever he went from here with Von.

He climbed into the passenger seat of her SUV.

His lips still tingled from the unexpected kiss.

It hadn't meant anything, he reminded that truly stupid part of himself that wanted to be psyched about the fact that she had kissed him for any reason.

Von would do whatever it took to get the job done.

Even kissing a guy she disliked…her ex-husband.

Trinity's cell phone vibrated. He pulled it from his pocket to check the screen. A text from Simon.

Proceed with extreme caution.

Target is dangerous.

More details to come.

Trinity confirmed that he had received the information. He slid his phone back into his jacket pocket and checked the weapon at his waist.

"Got your weapon?" he asked the driver.

Von sent him a sidelong glance. "Have you ever known me to be without it?"

An avalanche of memories twisted his gut.

At that moment Trinity wasn't so sure Charlie Jones was going to be the most dangerous aspect of this investigation.

He swallowed back the doubt.

Whatever he had to face…the top priority was finding that little girl and bringing her safely back to her mother.

Chapter Five

5:40 p.m. (four hours missing)

Von studied the photo of Charlie Jones sent via a multimedia message to her phone by Simon. Forty years of age, according to the stats accompanying the photo, long, stringy brown hair, cocaine-skinny with an extra long rap sheet. A real dirtbag.

Even worse, this was a friend of Lily Larkin's father—the man who had disappeared with her after stabbing and leaving her mother for dead.

Not good.

A snowman, leaning precariously to one side, adorned one of the postage-stamp-sized yards of rundown duplexes.

Only one streetlight worked and that was on the end opposite of where Von had opted to park, allowing for the possibility of trouble getting damned close without warning. The up side was that the dark provided good cover for her black SUV.

Lily Larkin had been missing approximately four

hours. Every additional moment that passed was one too many. Von wanted to find that little girl.

"The cops will be right behind us," Trinity commented. "If they get to Jones first, we'll be at an impasse."

"Then what're we waiting for?" Von had wanted to move as soon as they pulled to the curb. Her partner was the one who'd insisted they hold off.

Colby rules—the investigator with the most seniority at the agency was lead.

"That," Trinity said, his attention fixed on the row of housing "is what we waited for."

Two men exited the front door of the duplex suspected as being the hangout of Jones and his friends. The interior light disappeared as soon as the front door closed behind them but not before Von got a decent look at the man with long, stringy brown hair.

"He got a heads-up that the police are asking questions about him," Von said, voicing the realization that barged into her brain a few seconds later than it had her reluctant partner's.

"Can you stay on him without him noticing?" Trinity turned to her. "We can't risk losing him."

Von didn't justify his question with a response. She shook her head as she started the SUV's engine. They were married for three years, during which time she and Trinity had tracked down numerous bail jumpers as well as varied and sundry bad guys.

He knew her driving and surveillance abilities.

"Lots of things can change in five years," he noted as if that explained everything.

Another remark she wasn't going to bother rejoining.

She gave Jones a half a block head start before easing away from the curb. The sparse traffic made getting any closer dicey at best.

"He's taking the upcoming left."

Like she couldn't see the luxury silver SUV easing toward the center line. "Looks that way."

Von drove past the street the target had taken.

Trinity didn't say a word. He didn't have to. She felt his tension radiating across the center console. He would have chosen a different strategy. Tough, he wasn't driving.

She took the next left. Drove the short block and braked for the stop sign at the subsequent intersection. "And there he goes," she noted aloud as the silver SUV drove past their position.

Trinity said nothing as she made the right turn and followed the target.

Truth was, she couldn't read minds and the target could just as easily have gone in the opposite direction. That, too, would have been fine. She would have seen his taillights and followed. This neighborhood was pretty barren.

This street was flanked by rundown shops that had long ago closed for business. Scarcely any streetlights still worked. Jones was playing it safe, keeping a low profile in a deserted area where anyone watching was likely up to no good as well. And would be easily spotted.

Von's choice to take a different route had been a simple diversion tactic that had a fifty percent chance of success.

Brake lights abruptly lit the night as the SUV skidded to a sideways stop in the street.

Fifty percent chance of failure.

"Back up!"

Von had already hit the brakes and jammed the gearshift into Reverse before Trinity issued the order.

Something in her peripheral vision caused her to stall. She blinked as she watched the two men climbing out of the silver SUV. "They're running."

She hadn't realized she'd said the words out loud until Trinity bolted from the vehicle.

Von hissed a curse. The man was going to get himself shot jumping out in the middle of the street like this with two known scumbags already running scared.

She rammed the gearshift back into Drive and barreled around the SUV they'd left blocking the street, using the sidewalk for passage.

One of the men darted to the right into an alley.

Von braked. Her SUV slid to an abrupt stop and she jammed into Park.

Trinity overtook the man still running down the middle of the street.

Von released her seat belt and burst out of the

vehicle. She headed after the man who'd charged into the alley.

She reached beneath her jacket and wrapped her fingers around the butt of her weapon.

Her target body slammed a door in an attempt to break into the building to the right. The door didn't budge. He lunged forward once more.

Von was close enough to hear him panting for breath.

That was the thing about bad guys. They took lots of risks but didn't bother staying in shape.

She dove forward. Grabbed his jacket. Her momentum sent him stumbling forward, face-first onto the pavement. He tried to buck her off.

Clamping her thighs around his waist, Von shoved the muzzle of her weapon into the back of his skull. "Don't move." She grabbed a handful of stringy brown hair when his right hand continued to fumble around beneath him. "If that's a weapon you're going for, don't bother." She nudged his scalp a little harder with the business end of her .9 mm. He stilled.

"Slowly," she warned, "draw your hands from under you and spread them above your head." When he'd done as she instructed, she released his hair and reached beneath him. "No wonder you didn't pull it out sooner." His weapon had slid deep into his pants. For now, it was basically out of his reach, as well as hers.

"Charlie Jones?" she asked. Looked like him,

but it was pretty damned dark in this alley and she couldn't be certain.

"Who's asking?" he snarled.

She jabbed the muzzle deeper. "A friend." No wallet in his back pockets. She doubted he carried any ID. "Are you Charlie Jones?"

"Maybe. You a cop?"

"Look." She revised her strategy. "I'm not a cop. And I don't really care who you are or what you've done, I just want some answers about an associate of yours. Then you can be on your way."

Several seconds ticked off. "So ask. Maybe I'll answer."

Since she hadn't heard any gunfire she assumed Trinity's situation was under control.

"Kobi Larkin," Von said. "Where is he?"

The scumbag kissing the asphalt barked a laugh. "How the hell am I supposed to know?"

"You know him, right?"

"Yeah, yeah. So what? I know a lot of people."

Von twisted her fingers in the guy's hair and pulled hard. He grunted. "Did you see him today?"

"Depends," he snarled.

"Did you see him?"

"Yeah, I saw him."

She loosened her grip on his oily hair. "Did he have a little girl with him?"

The bastard snorted. "Yeah. Sweet little thing."

Von barely restrained the need to pull the trigger. "Where's the little girl now?"

The wail of sirens split the night air.

Jones or whoever the hell he was tensed.

"If you want a head start," she warned, "you'd better talk fast."

"He wanted to make some money," the lowlife said. "He had a *real* need, you know what I mean?"

Yeah, she knew exactly what he meant. "You gave him money? For what?" Fear and disgust exploded in her heart at the idea that any scumbag could be a parent. A person had to have a license to drive a vehicle…but anyone could be a parent—no prerequisites or licenses required.

"No. Man, I ain't into that." He made a disgusted sound. "But I know people…who are."

"Who did you send him to?" Damn it all to hell. This couldn't be right. What father would do this?

"Another associate of mine."

"What's his name and how do I find him?"

The sirens were closer now.

"I don't know his name. Just his phone number. I call him and he gives a drop location."

Von's stomach waded into knots. "You called him on your cell?"

"Yeah."

She reached into his pocket, pulled out the cell phone she'd felt when checking for his weapon. "Which number?" She opened up the log of recent calls, matched the one he recited from memory. A very close associate if he knew the number by heart.

Von pushed aside the personal feelings. She had to focus. The time the call was made seemed right based on the mother's statement of events.

"What do you get out of the deal?" Von couldn't keep the revulsion out of her voice, didn't even try.

"Twenty percent."

"Twenty percent of what?"

"A good-looking little girl like that? Thirty-five hundred. Sometimes more." He sniggered. "You'd think even an idiot would know that changing your mind isn't an option."

"What the hell are you talking about?" Von demanded.

"We're done," Jones growled. "Get off me before—"

Doors slammed on the street where she'd left her vehicle.

"Get off me!" He started to buck again.

She burrowed the muzzle deep into his flesh and leaned forward to whisper in his nasty ear. "Does he keep the kids or does he auction them?"

"He sells 'em," he muttered. "You said you'd give me a head start."

"I lied." Von pressed hard on his carotid artery. He tried to throw her off, but the insistent pressure won the battle, rendering him unconscious.

She rolled him onto his back and fished the weapon from his crotch.

A glance toward the street told her she hadn't been spotted just yet.

She sprinted in the opposite direction, tossing the bastard's weapon into a Dumpster. Having him wake up and use it on a cop or anyone else was a possibility she wanted to avoid.

At the other end of the alley, she checked the street in both directions. Another police cruiser, sirens flashing and blaring, skidded into a left turn headed for where her vehicle as well as Jones's had been left. Two Chicago PD cruisers were parked in front of the duplex reportedly rented or leased by Jones.

Von needed cover until she could determine Trinity's status and find new wheels.

First she had to get across the street without being spotted. Shouldn't be too difficult considering the lack of working lights along the block.

She skimmed the offerings along the block, the warm glow pouring from the windows of most proclaiming inhabitants. Likely armed and unfriendly.

Just pick one.

One, only one, was dark as if no one was home or it was vacant.

Von took a breath and headed across the street. She took her time. Strolled leisurely. Walked right up the steps of the porch. No chairs or benches available.

Her heart pounding, she sat down on the top step.

From the corner of her eye she confirmed that no uniforms had headed her way.

She sent a text to Trinity.

Status?

While she waited for a response, she sent a text to Simon Ruhl with the number Jones claimed was his contact for the sale of Lily Larkin.

Von's stomach cramped at the thought.

Don't think about it. Just do what has to be done.

Von needed an address…anything to reach this bastard. This trafficker.

Bile burned the back of her throat.

What're you doing sitting down?

Relief rushed through Von's veins as she read the text from Trinity. She glanced around.

I'm two houses to your right.

Von stood, walked across the porch, climbed over the rickety railing and jumped down to the side yard. She moved through the backyard of the properties until she reached the one where Trinity waited.

He leaned against the side of the house. "The police have Jones and his pal in custody."

"Did you get anything?"

Trinity nodded. "Jones brokered a deal for Larkin." He looked away. "He sold his daughter, Von." After a few seconds his gaze locked with hers once more. Even in the darkness she could see—maybe she felt—his simmering fury. "He sold her to get money for drugs."

She held up the cell phone she'd taken from Jones. "I've got his cell and the number he uses to make contact with this broker."

"We need a ride now," Trinity said as he checked his phone. "Jim's sending someone to pick us up."

Von's chest tightened. The child had been taken from her mother nearly five hours ago. She could be anywhere by now.

The screen of Trinity's phone lit with an incoming text.

They had to find this bastard. There was no time to wait for the police to Mirandize their suspects and attempt to get the information necessary to stop this travesty. The lowlifes would lawyer up and hours and hours would be wasted.

"This way." Trinity gestured to the row of houses behind them. "Two streets over. Jim's waiting."

Von hurried to keep up with Trinity's long strides. Her mind reeled with scenarios for locating this scumbag. Maybe Simon would have some luck with the cell number she'd passed along.

A dog barked.

Lunged at them.

Von jumped. She swallowed back her heart when she recognized that the dog was chained.

Trinity had her by the arm tugging her forward through the darkness between houses. Rectangles of light beamed through the windows, providing enough illumination for them to make their way through the maze of shrubs and trees. Her mind wouldn't stay focused on her steps. She could only think of the little girl.

Jim's sedan sat at the corner. He flashed his headlights to ensure they spotted him.

Someone else was in the front passenger seat. Trinity opened the back door and let Von get in first. Then he climbed in and closed the door.

"You two okay?" Jim asked.

Von nodded. Trinity responded, "Yes."

Simon Ruhl, the other passenger, shook his head. "Kobi Larkin is dead."

"What?" Von didn't understand. "How?"

"One of my contacts in Chicago PD," Simon explained, "let me know that Larkin's body was discovered in the duplex where Jones lives."

Von and Trinity exchanged a look.

"Wait." Von replayed her interrogation of Jones. "Jones said something like 'You'd think even an idiot would know that changing your mind isn't an option.'"

"Larkin changed his mind," Trinity concluded. "Jones or one of his associates killed him when he wouldn't let it go."

Von had no sympathy for the dirtbag. "Too bad he didn't grow a conscience until it was too late." How could the man sell his own child?

"The number you sent Simon," Jim said, "we're running it down now but it's not going to be easy. The person it belongs to doesn't want to be discovered via that means. It'll take time."

They didn't have time. "We have to do something now," Von argued.

"It may be too late already," Trinity reiterated. "These brokers work fast. She could be on her way anywhere by now."

"We're doing all we can," Simon offered. "Larkin is dead. Jones and his associate are in police custody. We'll move forward as soon as—"

Von turned to Trinity. "Call him."

"What?" Trinity's face scrunched in confusion.

"Tell him you have some merchandise," Von said quickly, the idea taking shape. "A fifteen-year-old female. You need to get rid of her today. Now."

Jim and Simon spoke up simultaneously. Both tossing out reasons her suggestion wouldn't work.

The confusion cleared from Trinity's face as if he'd just grasped the idea. "That kind of move would require bait."

"Absolutely," Von agreed, tuning out the arguments coming from the front seat.

Realization dawned in Trinity's eyes and his head moved side to side. "No way."

"It's the only way," Von argued. She glared from one man to the other. "There's no time. Waiting isn't an option and we all know it. We have to move now."

"What you're suggesting is out of the question," Trinity challenged.

"What's the big deal, Barrett?" Von demanded. She wasn't fifteen but that fact could be disguised long enough to get the ball rolling. "I've been bait before."

The silence that followed confirmed what she knew with complete certainty. All in the vehicle understood that her proposal was the fastest, most logical and effective way to move forward.

Setting up some sort of deal with the buyer was the only way to save this child.

Chapter Six

Mercy General Hospital, 7:30 p.m. (6 hours missing)

The rhythmic sound of the numerous machines hooked to Wanda Larkin kept the silence at bay. But nothing abated the underlying sense of worry and doom induced by the smell of the room. No matter the technology used, there simply was no way to make a hospital smell "inviting" or "comforting."

Victoria wished there was something more she could do for the poor woman she'd found on the street. Hours had passed since Wanda's lifesaving surgery and still she had not regained consciousness for more than a moment or so. The doctors and nurses assigned to her weren't overly concerned as of yet. With the mental as well as physical trauma she had suffered, it wasn't unusual for a patient to want to stay asleep. It was a defense mechanism.

Perhaps, since Victoria had no good news to report regarding Wanda's missing child, it was for the best.

Even now Victoria waited for an update from Jim or Simon.

A missing child, no matter the circumstances, was horrifying enough, but, dear God, at this time of the year when celebrating life and love were on the minds of most…it was unusually cruel.

A soft moan drew Victoria from her troubling thoughts. She stood and moved closer to the bed. Wanda moaned again, her head moving side to side ever so slightly.

Victoria took her hand. "You're in the hospital," she explained gently. "The doctors are taking very good care of you, Wanda."

The patient's eyes opened. She blinked twice then stared into Victoria's. "You have to help me."

Victoria patted her hand. "Everything that can be is being done, I promise."

Tears welled in Wanda's eyes. "He took Lily." She moistened her dry lips. "He took my baby."

"We know," Victoria assured her, her heart breaking with the idea that they hadn't found the child already. "We're retracing his steps in hopes of locating Lily."

"You're the woman…" Wanda's voice faded and she cleared her throat.

Victoria put a bendable straw into the cup of water from the bedside table and offered Wanda a drink. When she had dampened her throat, she squeezed Victoria's hand. "You're the woman who helped me. I remember…just you. No one else."

A smile tugged at Victoria's lips. "I'm Victoria Colby-Camp. Yes, I called for help and tried to keep you warm until help arrived. My investigators from the Colby Agency are looking for Lily right now."

Wanda's brow furrowed and her lips trembled. "He tried to kill me."

Victoria wanted to tell her that the bastard was dead, that he'd gotten what he deserved and none too soon. Kobi Larkin had died the same way he'd lived, savagely and ruthlessly. But, no matter how he'd hurt Wanda, he had still been her husband once and was the father of her child. Victoria wasn't sure she could deal with that truth right now.

"He tried to hurt you," Victoria agreed, "that is true. But you're going to be fine. You'll be up and out of here in just a few days."

Wanda tried to lever herself into a sitting position. "I have to find my baby."

Alarm trickled through Victoria. "You have to lie still, my dear. For now, there's nothing you can do." She ushered the patient back down onto the bed. "You won't be any good at all to Lily if you don't allow yourself to heal properly. Getting well needs to be your priority while *we* find Lily."

Wanda swiped at her tears with thc hand not burdened with IV lines. "I can't just lie here while… he…" Her lips pinched with the fear widening her eyes, then quaked as she murmured, "I have to find her. He doesn't know how to love her like a father should."

"Following the doctor's orders is what you have to do," Victoria urged. "My agency and the police are doing all that can be done to find your daughter. There is nothing you could do even if you weren't stuck in this hospital bed. You must get well. Lily will need you when this is over."

"You swear?" she pleaded. "Swear to me that you'll find my baby."

Victoria knew better than to make a promise like that under any circumstances. There was no way to guarantee success, no matter how hard her people fought to make that happen. But the horror already haunting the poor woman's eyes tore at Victoria's resolve to maintain her professional boundaries.

"I swear," Victoria said, unable to hold back the promise. "We will find your daughter."

Chapter Seven

Warehouse District, 7:45 p.m.

Trinity had gotten his way.

It was a flat-out miracle.

Three years of marriage and never once had he won an argument with Von.

She wasn't happy about it, but she had thrown her hands up and given in. Rather than using Von as bait in a situation that could possibly have gone bad really fast, they had come up with a new plan that didn't involve bait at all. Rather, money was the sacrificial offering. Lots of money.

"If this guy doesn't show soon," she threatened, as if she'd read Trinity's mind, "we're going with the plan I suggested."

Trinity hunched his shoulders to draw the collar of his coat around his neck against the cold, then studied the dark street. "He'll show."

That was something Von would learn about the Colby Agency. If Simon Ruhl, Ian Michaels or Victoria Colby-Camp said it would be, then it would be.

This was a contact Simon had gotten from a former Bureau colleague—one Simon trusted. The contact would show.

This particular contact, a Dennis Lane, was not only connected to the Midwest human trafficking network, his number had also shown up on the downloaded list of calls to and from the number Charlie Jones claimed was his only means of contact with the buyer who'd purchased Lily Larkin. So far neither the agency nor the Bureau had been able to trace the number to a source, but Lane's number had popped out at Simon's Bureau colleague.

Now, Trinity and Von waited for Lane…hoping like hell he could make the connection to the dirtbag who had Lily.

Von folded her arms over her chest and leaned against the building. "Thirty minutes," she announced, her words a little muffled by the scarf wrapped around her shoulders and throat. "If he doesn't show in the next half hour, I'm out of here. I've got that junkie Charlie's contact number. I'm moving on it in thirty-one minutes."

Trinity didn't doubt her one little bit. Patience was not one of her virtues. Though she had a number of others. Not big as a minute. She stood a mere five-two and wouldn't weigh a hundred pounds soaking wet. But she wasn't afraid of anyone. His lips curled with amusement at the idea that an enemy might look at her and see a mere poodle facing off against a pit bull, but she rarely lost a battle, particularly one of wills.

She still kept her coal-black hair cut short. It hugged her face and neck in soft, silky wisps. And those eyes. Pure blue laser beams that could melt your heart or cut you in two. Her body was lean from plenty of cardio and well toned from pumping iron, but not so much so as to lessen the feminine qualities.

Those curves were firm and toned but, at the same time, soft and smooth. Not even five years had allowed him to forget.

"Are you finished?"

Trinity blinked, then quickly looked away. "I was just thinking." She'd caught him. Not good. And unfortunately it wasn't the first time.

"When are you going to stop doing that?" She pushed away from the wall and walked to the edge of the sidewalk to peer down the street, first one direction, then the other. She could never be still. "It's a waste of time," she added.

Anger instantly tangled in his gut. She did this every time. And he got ticked every single time. "Doing what?"

"Remembering." She sent that laser gaze in his direction. "The past is called the past for a reason. It's over. There's no going back."

"Oh, yeah." He shoved his hands into his pockets to prevent reaching out and shaking her. *"That."*

She wanted to pretend *they* never happened. Under

the ruse of moving on, she had tucked their three years of marriage into a tight little compartment and shoved it to the very back of her mind—never to be opened again. He hadn't been able to accomplish the feat. The memories were always with him…far too handy and completely unforgettable.

He couldn't move on. He was one hundred percent stuck in that past she proclaimed as over.

"Maybe that's our guy." She hitched her head to the right where a set of headlights bobbed as a dark sedan rolled over the potholed street.

Trinity resisted the urge to lean down and check the weapon in his ankle holster. No matter how dependable the contact, if he suspected trouble he wouldn't hesitate to protect himself from a perceived threat. Trinity tapped the communications device in his ear to ensure those listening understood that the target appeared to be approaching and the meet was going down.

Simon Ruhl and Jim Colby were parked in a nearby alley, monitoring the situation and providing intel as it became available. They would also provide any necessary backup.

The sedan eased to a stop in front of where they waited. The lack of working streetlamps prevented much in the way of visuals. The door opened, the momentary light from the interior allowed Trinity to visually confirm it was the expected contact.

"Barton?" the man asked.

Trinity nodded as he stepped forward. Myles Barton was his cover. "This is my wife, Louise."

Von, her arms still crossed over her chest, eyed the guy suspiciously. "I hope you aren't wasting our time, Mr. Lane. I don't like to be kept waiting."

"If memory serves," Lane said, his words directed at Von, "you called me, Mrs. Barton. Are you in the habit of calling on those you suspect incapable of accomplishing the goal?"

Von lifted her chin in that sassy manner that said she wasn't bested by the likes of this guy. "We'll see, won't we?"

Seemingly, unruffled, Lane shifted his attention to Trinity. "You're looking for a child in the three- to six-year range?"

"A girl," Von put in, taking a step in the direction of the men. "Blond hair," she looked to Trinity, "like her father."

Lane didn't like Von's pushiness; that much was obvious. But he also wasn't going to pass on the opportunity to make some extra cash. "These extra options can be expensive," he warned.

Fury tightened Trinity's gut. The bastard had just referred to a child as if it were an automobile. "I'm prepared to pay twenty for the child," Trinity pressed, careful to keep his disgust out of his face, "five extra for your trouble if you can make this happen in the next twenty-four hours."

Lane laughed. "Impossible. I'll need seventy-two

at the very least." He glanced at Von. "Especially if you're being picky."

"We're leaving for Texas on Friday morning," Trinity explained. "We haven't visited what's left of our families in seven years. We need the child with us. We want a minimum of twenty-four hours to orient the child…if you know what I mean."

Lane considered Trinity, then Von before shaking his head. "Your family believes you have a daughter?" He shook his head. "I don't even want to know."

"Good," Trinity cautioned, "because that's none of your business. Are we doing business or what? Time is wasting."

Lane shrugged. "Whatever. I've heard it all." His gaze narrowed then. "Seems strange that you waited till the last minute to do your *shopping*."

"You're our third contact," Von said with all the drama of a highly trained actress. "The others couldn't produce what we were looking for. I hope you're better than your competition."

Trinity's instincts went on alert. The guy's suspicion had mounted exponentially in the past minute. Pushing him any harder would have him backing out as surely as he'd just taken the step down from the curb putting him closer to his car.

"I might not be the right man for the job," he offered. "These transactions can be problematic. Frankly, overzealous buyers make me nervous."

Von's breath caught and her worried gaze landed on Trinity's. "You have to do something." She played extremely disappointed perfectly. "We're running out of time."

Trinity leveled his full attention on the man who had, for all intents and purposes, closed down his shop. "Fifty. I'm willing to go as high as fifty thousand for a girl and ten extra to you for making it happen *now.* Tonight with no further questions."

Lane hesitated only a second. "Sounds like you and your wife have a desperate situation."

"It's an inheritance thing," Trinity lied, "nothing you'd find interesting. But that's as high as I go," he warned when anticipation lit in Lane's eyes. "The time limit is nonnegotiable."

"Please, Myles." Von grabbed Trinity by the arm and played the part of the persistent and petulant wife. "She has to be blond."

Trinity could almost see the dollar signs flashing in Lane's expression. "Seventy-five. Total," he said flatly. "You bring me a little blond-haired girl meeting the right age criteria—tonight—and the money is yours. How you split it with your supplier is up to you."

"Brown eyes," Von piped up. She stared in feigned adoration at Trinity a moment before turning to the other man. "I want her to have blond hair and brown eyes. No substitutions."

The scumbag held up his hands. "I'll do what I can."

"If you can't do it," Trinity countered, "say so now. We'll move on to the next name on our list."

Lane's jaw hardened with something like anger. "I'll make it happen."

"When will we know?" Trinity pressed. "We have arrangements to make."

"I'll call you within the hour." Lane reached for the door of his vehicle, then hesitated. "Bring cash," he said with a blunt look at Trinity. "All of it."

"Cash," Trinity echoed. "Is there any other way to shop?" He gestured to his jacket. "May I?"

Another hesitation, then a nod.

Trinity pulled an envelope from an interior coat pocket and passed it to the man. "A little incentive to make up for the pressure we're no doubt causing."

Lane opened the envelope and fingered the cash. Five thousand in hundred dollar bills. He looked to Trinity with raised eyebrows. "You won't be disappointed." He got into the sedan and pulled away from the curb.

"He's suspicious," Von commented.

"He is," Trinity agreed. "But, I think his greed will override any lingering concerns he might have."

"It's cold."

She didn't look at him but he looked at her. He resisted the impulse to put his arm around her and pull her close, to warm her body with his.

But that would only make her angry.

"Let's go." He gestured for her to go ahead of him. "We can wait in the car or go to the coffee shop." The sedan they were using belonged to the Colby

Agency but was registered to a dummy corporation in the event the plates were run.

"I hate the waiting," she muttered as she reached for the door on the passenger side of the car.

"Yeah. Me, too."

That was the worst part of an investigation…the waiting. And the wondering. Was the little girl safe? Would they get to her in time? Would this elaborate ruse even accomplish their goal?

"Lane is making the call."

Trinity and Von's gazes locked as the words echoed through their communication links. Simon had just verified that Lane had made the call to the number Charlie Jones had insisted was the contact for the Lily Larkin buyer.

Trinity prayed they would get this lucky…that it would be this simple.

"Continue to the coffee house and wait for the call from Lane," Jim instructed via the com link. "We'll keep you advised."

Von acknowledged the instructions as she fastened her seatbelt.

Maggie's Coffee House was their destination. It was located directly across the street from the building that housed the Colby Agency. Simon and Jim would take up positions nearby as well.

The next few hours were far too crucial to leave anything to chance.

Von relaxed into her seat and remained uncharacteristically quiet during the drive across town. She usually had plenty to say, whatever the situation. Trinity started to make casual conversation but then the reality of the last few minutes hit him.

Von had made that remark about the past….

Trinity banged his head against the headrest. Simon would wonder about that, maybe even ask. When Trinity had come onboard at the agency that he'd been married before was in the background search. He hadn't attempted to hide it. There hadn't been any reason. Von hadn't hidden her past from Jim Colby—as if anyone could.

Their former marriage hadn't been relevant.

When the Equalizers had merged with the agency, new background checks hadn't been necessary for either staff. Jim's people had gone through rigorous security measures already as had the investigators at the agency.

Since Von had reclaimed her maiden name, evidently nothing had clicked. She and Trinity had opted to keep it that way. For better or worse.

This was something they would need to clear up when this investigation was over. Until now it hadn't felt relevant.

Trinity parked in the small lot on the Colby Agency side of the street.

"A meeting has been initiated with the Jones's contact," Jim advised via the com link.

Hope fired in Trinity's veins. "We'll be standing by." He wasn't sure where Simon and Jim would park. Possibly in the alley behind the coffee house.

Their sedan was nowhere in sight when he and Von emerged from theirs. Every precaution had to be taken to ensure this deal went down without a hitch.

"Careful," Trinity said as they crossed the street. Traffic was still fairly heavy with last-minute Christmas shoppers and the sidewalks remained treacherous with three days' worth of snow compacted and iced over in the less traveled areas.

Von marched across the street as if there wasn't a speck of snow or ice to be seen, much less traffic. Trinity took a bit more care. If he hadn't made the suggestion she would likely have moved more cautiously. She wasn't taking any orders or advice from him. He didn't know why he'd expected she would.

He supposed he deserved exactly the response he'd gotten. The break-up of their marriage was, to a large degree, his fault. He'd owned his mistakes. But nothing he'd said or done for a full year after the initial separation had changed her mind about the divorce.

Even after five years she hadn't forgiven him.

Maybe he hadn't forgiven her.

He moved ahead of her now to open the door to the coffee house. She indulged his need to play the gentleman, but she neither thanked him nor met his gaze.

It was too late to consider that working together on this case might be a mistake.

There was no going back.

"Coffee?" he asked.

"Definitely."

She didn't wait with him at the counter. Instead, she claimed a table away from the windows overlooking Chicago's famous Mag Mile.

He placed the order for two coffees. While he waited Jim and Simon entered and got in line behind him.

In the event anyone was watching, they didn't acknowledge Trinity or Von.

When Trinity had paid for the coffee, he walked past his colleagues without eye contact and joined Von at the table. He sat a steaming cup in front of her and took the seat across from her.

Trinity removed his coat and draped it over an empty chair. Before sipping his coffee he deactivated his com link.

As if she'd read his mind, Von did the same.

"There will be questions," he said.

"My mistake," she said.

Another first. Von rarely fessed up to mistakes. Then again, she rarely made them. She was very, very good at any endeavor she chose to undertake.

Good at a lot of things.

"I shouldn't have been staring," he admitted. It was true. If he hadn't been taking a trip down memory avenue she wouldn't have gotten annoyed…and the remark wouldn't have happened.

She leaned forward, braced her elbows on the

table. "This is too important for either of us to let the past be a distraction."

He nodded.

"I can hardly bear to think what that little girl might be going through." She closed her eyes and drew in a deep, steadying breath, then slowly released it.

Trinity couldn't help himself. He reached across the table and touched her hand. Her eyes opened instantly. "We'll get her back."

A small nod of agreement was her only response.

He knew what she was thinking, but he didn't dare say it. That would cross a line he wasn't prepared to risk crossing.

She blinked and the moment was over. As if he'd burned her with his hand she snatched hers away and straightened her back, putting as much distance between them as possible.

It was always the same.

There were things he wanted to say. But there was never a right time.

His cell phone vibrated.

He reached into his pocket and retrieved the phone, his gaze instantly settling on the screen. "It's Lane."

"I guess I misjudged him," Von said as she reactivated her com link.

Trinity slid the phone open. "Barton." He reactivated his own com link.

Lane provided an address in one of the city's suburbs. "Meet me there in one hour. Blond hair, brown eyes, six years old. She's ready to meet her new parents."

"We'll be there," Trinity assured him.

There was a moment's hesitation, then, "I checked you out, Barton."

Tension slid through Trinity. "I expected you would."

"Everything appears to be on the up-and-up," Lane allowed. "But, if you or your wife makes one wrong move. If I even get a whiff of a set-up, the deal is off. You got it?"

"Got it."

"One hour," Lane echoed.

"We'll be there," Trinity confirmed. He closed the phone and slid it into his pocket.

"We set?" Von's face reflected the worry she'd picked up on in his.

"All set." He glanced toward the table where Simon and Jim waited. Trinity repeated the address as much for Von's sake as for Jim and Simon's. "Anything feels wrong to him and the deal is off."

Von pushed her chair from the table and stood. "We'll just have to make sure nothing feels wrong."

Which meant backup would have to stay way, way back.

Just in case.

Chapter Eight

St. Patrick's Church, 9:33 p.m. (8 hours missing)

Just beyond Chicago's business district St. Patrick's Church stood tall and proud in the darkness. The two spires, as different as day and night, towered forbiddingly over the street.

St. Patrick's was the second oldest church in the city, one of the few structures to survive The Great Chicago Fire. Architecturally it was admirable, but Von had never been much of a churchgoer.

It had something to do with God abandoning her when she needed Him most. She let it go the first time it happened, when she was thirteen. But then… six years ago, He let her down again.

The past was the past, she reminded herself.

She shivered, though they sat in the relative comfort of the car. Just staring at the hulking structure of the church with the snow falling around it felt foreboding somehow. The holiday decorations were another sore spot with her.

Face it, girl, you have some serious baggage.

Trinity, of all people, should see that.

Whatever. This investigation had to be her total focus right now.

That they were to meet Lane—a man who profited from the sale of humans—was likely the underlying factor motivating her feeling as she'd been cast into some sort of sinister theater production.

The briefcase containing the money and two state-of-the-art tracking devices was in the backseat. Backup was stationed two blocks away, well outside possible enemy detection range. Von had strapped a .32 to her ankle, as had Trinity. Communication links were in place. Backup, Simon and Jim, would be aware of every word.

Once again Lane was running a few minutes behind.

Trinity reached into his jacket and withdrew his cell phone. He glanced at the screen, then at her. "It's Lane." After pressing the necessary buttons, Trinity said, "You're late. We had a deal, Lane."

The hesitation that crackled in the air warned that Lane understood he was on speaker.

"I have you on speaker," Trinity put in quickly, "my wife is here, *waiting,* with me."

"I'm very disappointed, Mr. Lane," Von managed to say though her mind still reeled with the idea that Trinity had called her his *wife.*

That was her role in this undercover operation.

She was Louise Barton, wife to Myles Barton.

But it felt…strange.

"There's been a change of plans."

An alarm wailed in the back of Von's brain.

"I'm paying you exceedingly well, Lane," Trinity reminded their contact. "You came highly recommended. I have no patience for games. You should have given me a straight up no before you took my money. This conversation is over."

"All is in order, Mr. Barton," Lane hastened to say. "We've changed the transaction location. That's all. I have what you want."

Trinity held Von's gaze. "I'm not happy about this, Lane." Trinity allowed a beat of thick silence. "But I'm prepared to move forward."

"Just one more thing," Lane said.

"Mr. Lane, this is becoming tedious."

Von's attention flew to the rearview mirror to the glare of headlights approaching from their rear. She clutched Trinity's sleeve and nodded to the rearview mirror. Three seconds later a gray sedan pulled up next to theirs. The dark tint on the windows concealed the driver as well as any passengers.

"I'm sure you understand what you need to do," Lane said.

"Lane—"

"This is ridiculous," Von snapped, cutting Trinity off. "We're supposed to get in this gray car you've sent and just go wherever it takes us?"

Lane had severed the telephone connection.

Von's door opened.

Her gaze collided first with the business end of a

weapon. "Get out," the masked man holding the gun demanded.

Behind her, Trinity was receiving a similar order.

"There's no need for guns," Trinity said. "I don't know what's—"

"Do as you're told and shut up," the man holding the weapon aimed at Trinity commanded.

Von climbed out, as did Trinity. Their escorts led them around to the gray sedan and ushered them into the backseat. Trinity's escort snatched the cell phone from his hand; Von's ripped the purse from hers.

After a quick search of her purse, he held out his hand. "I'll need your cell."

Von dragged the phone from her jacket pocket and placed it in his hand. "I just got that phone," she complained with the petulance that was a trait of her cover. And any info she could give to Jim and Simon via the com link, the better.

"Get in," the man roared, pushing her toward the open door of the gray sedan's back seat.

When she and Trinity were inside and the doors closed, the man who'd ushered her into the car dropped into the front passenger seat. He settled the briefcase containing the money in the seat between him and the driver. The tracking devices inside would ensure Jim and Simon were able to follow their movements despite the abrupt change in plans.

As soon as the doors closed, the sedan peeled away.

"Where are you taking us?" Trinity demanded. "What's going on here?"

"You'll have your answers soon," the guy in the passenger seat said with a glance toward Trinity.

Von settled back into her seat. She took Trinity's hand in hers to keep up the pretense of being his wife—who would unquestionably be frightened at the moment.

His fingers were stiff at first, but it wasn't long before they closed around her hand.

Von swallowed back the emotion that rose into her throat.

If he would just let it go.

Even after all this time, *he* tugged at her emotions. Just being near him…remembering. Despite the fact that she chastised him for remembering, she remembered.

All too well.

She wiggled her hand free of his.

This wasn't a good idea.

She remembered everything.

Von closed her eyes and cleared her head. She summoned the image of Lily Larkin and all other thought vanished.

Tonight…right now…nothing else mattered except finding that little girl.

They were headed away from the city.

Von's instincts bumped into hyperspeed. She didn't dare look back to see if backup could be spotted somewhere in the distance.

Jim and Simon were too good to be given the slip by these morons. She glared at the two masked men in the front seat. And there were the tracking devices. She and Trinity were covered. Not to mention they were both still armed, but playing this out in an attempt to get as much information as possible was necessary.

It was possible that their contact had opted to take extreme measures to ensure security, but Von had been in this business too long to hold out more than a fleeting hope on that score.

Lane had been suspicious all along.

The prospect of a highly lucrative deal had kept him from walking away…but, evidently, someone higher up the food chain had made him see the hastiness of his decision and made the final call.

There would be no deal tonight.

More likely she and Trinity would be taken somewhere and interrogated. It wouldn't be pretty. And, unless, backup intervened, they wouldn't likely survive. Lane would get the money either way.

Funny, she considered Trinity's profile, she'd started out in this business with him. He'd had that swagger down to a science. The cowboy boots and the worn soft jeans. He'd charmed her with one look. But that had been a long time ago. Now, after all they had survived, it looked as if they would be ending their careers together.

But it wouldn't be without a fight.

She crossed her legs, placed her right hand on her

knee, allowed her fingers to slip down to her ankle and trace the outline of the weapon strapped there.

As if his gaze had summoned her, she turned to the man at her side. His lips tilted upward just a fraction…just enough for her to know that he wasn't worried.

He wasn't going down without a fight, either.

Her heart bumped hard against her chest when his hand closed around hers once more.

They would get through this.

It wouldn't change things between them but at least they would be alive.

HALF AN HOUR OF SILENCE elapsed before they reached their destination.

The driver parked in front of a barnlike structure. Beyond the small clearing the area around the structure was wooded. The moonlight reflecting off the snow gave the place an eerie look. Two SUVs were parked to one side.

The men in front climbed out.

"Don't do anything until I say so," Trinity murmured to her a split second before their doors were wrenched open.

She nodded her understanding.

Not wanting to be dragged from the vehicle, Von emerged and started forward. The muzzle of her escort's handgun jammed into her back as a reminder that she should continue her submissive behavior.

Two SUVs were parked outside the building.

As they approached what she now realized was in fact a barn, the wide doors opened.

Inside was nothing at all like a barn. No stalls. No hayloft. There were concrete floors and fluorescent lights. Desks and chairs and two sofas. Several doors lined the far end of the structure. All were closed. No windows.

A transfer station.

Considering the goods Lane traded in and the out of the way location…definitely a transfer station.

This was where they brought the kids…where they kept them until they were shipped out.

Disgust twisted in her stomach.

There were four more men inside. None wore masks. All looked like average, run of the mill working guys. The two who'd escorted them here at gunpoint removed their masks.

Bad sign.

Any time the enemy didn't care if you saw their faces was bad.

It meant they weren't worried about their hostages giving away their descriptions or identities.

The hostages were going to be in no position to give away anything.

They would be dead.

Damn.

Von scanned the faces. Lane's wasn't among the group. Three were thirtysomethings, late twenties maybe, and appeared physically fit. The fourth was older and heavier with a bit of a bulge hanging over his belt.

"Put 'em in three for now," the guy with the bulge ordered.

None of the doors on the back side of the structure were visibly numbered. One of the men who'd brought them here hustled them toward the third door from the left. Von tried to get a closer look at the layout of the larger room, a command center obviously. A couple of computers. Her escort pushed her forward.

"Did you ensure they weren't armed?" the bulge guy asked.

Well damn. Then again, they'd been lucky to get this far without the subject coming up.

The surprise on their escort's face gave the answer to the man who'd asked. "Why would they be armed?"

Give the guy a "stupid criminal" award. Lane might have been suspicious but this guy clearly had swallowed the bait, hook, line and sinker.

"Do it," his chubby pal ordered. "Now." As if to reiterate his words, he strode up to Trinity and patted him down.

The dummy they'd come to this dance with, did the same to her.

The older guy shook his head as he stared at Trinity's .32. "Mr. Lane is not going to be happy about this."

"Self-protection," Trinity said pointedly. "I don't

go anywhere without it. Any man who does is a fool."

Their gazes held a moment longer, but the older guy didn't say anything in response.

Once they were shoved into room three, the door was slammed shut and they were left to wait for the next move. Unarmed and with a dead com link. Trinity had discreetly tapped his link several times with no response. Something was wrong with the link.

But they still had the hidden tracking devices in the briefcase.

Von wanted to rail about the deal going back to Trinity but he held a finger to his lips. He was right. The room could be and probably was bugged.

There was no furniture in the room. Not a single chair or a table. Only a plastic box filled with toys. She walked over and picked up a fuzzy bear. This was a holding facility, all right.

Lane hadn't just been suspicious, he had known. He wouldn't have brought a customer to a holding facility. He had known they were undercover operatives of some sort before he'd made the call tonight.

Now he would want to know who had hired them and what exactly they knew.

The money was irrelevant.

It was insured and marked for tracking purposes. Unless it was skillfully laundered first, anyone who tried to use it would be caught.

Von hoped she got to witness that part.

The door opened.

She and Trinity turned to face whatever came next.

A man rolled a utility cart into the room.

A second man carried two folding chairs. He placed them in the center of the room. “Sit,” he ordered.

“Where is Lane?” Trinity demanded, keeping with his cover. “We had a deal.”

“We won’t need him for this,” the man with the cart explained. He gestured to the chairs. “Have a seat.”

“This has gone far enough,” Trinity protested. “I demand that you take my wife and I back to our car. You clearly do not understand who you’re dealing with.”

“You’re right,” the one at the cart said as he picked up a roll of duct tape. “That’s what we’re going to find out.”

“What’s he talking about, Myles?” Von asked, feigning fear, which wasn’t that difficult.

“It’s all right.” Trinity hugged her. “We’ll get through this.”

“Sit,” the man who’d delivered the chairs roared yet again.

Trinity waited until Von had taken her seat and then settled into his. Their hands were taped behind them. Their ankles were bound and then a strip of tape was placed over their mouths.

How creative.

The men left the room.

If there was anything else on the cart besides duct

tape and what looked like a rope, she couldn't see it. Maybe the whole thing had been a scare tactic designed to get them primed for talking.

Von had already spotted two cameras. They were being watched. Any attempts they made to free themselves would be futile.

There was one thing she could do. Maybe their captors would even expect her to do it.

She bounced up and down in her chair, scooting it closer to Trinity. When she'd gotten close enough she placed her head on his shoulder and blinked rapidly as if holding back tears.

He smelled good. The same sexy scent he'd always worn. It reminded her of other scents and sensations. Like salty sea air and the spray of the ocean's wild, crashing waves. If she closed her eyes she could conjure up the feel of sand between her toes…and the wind on her face. They'd taken their honeymoon in the Bahamas. Warm, beautiful…the most amazing week of her life.

Too bad it hadn't lasted.

The door suddenly opened and two men entered once more.

Lane was one of them.

Von felt the tension in Trinity's posture.

Lane turned to his colleague. "Bring the woman first." He glanced at Von before walking out.

Trinity struggled with his bindings as the man approached her.

The man manacled her arm and jerked her to her feet. "Let's see how long it takes you to talk."

Since she couldn't exactly walk with her ankles taped together he pitched her over his shoulder and started for the door.

Trinity broke the folding chair getting out of it, but then fell face-first onto the floor.

There was nothing he could do.

The door slammed shut, cutting him off from her view.

The bastard carrying her hefted her into another chair, this one in the main space of the building.

Lane stared at her for a long moment, then said, "Start with the toes. If she doesn't talk, move to the fingers. I want to know exactly who they are."

Von had two options. She could just tell the truth, spill the beans, right up front and die quickly. Or she could attempt to hold out, maybe come up with something that would keep both her and Trinity alive.

The tape was ripped from her lips. She winced.

"Do you want to talk now?" the man in charge of her interrogation asked. "Or." He cut loose the tape around her ankles. "Lose a little toe?"

"We have money," she offered with all the uncertainty and fear she could muster. "A lot more than what's in the briefcase." That should give them something to think about.

The guy braced a hand on each arm of the chair and leaned in, putting his face close to hers. "You trying to buy time, lady?"

"Just trying to save us both some time," Von explained. "My husband and I are in a time crunch of our own. We need that little girl."

The bastard trailed a finger down her cheek.

She drew away from his touch.

"How much money?" he asked as he traced that same finger down her throat.

She resisted the urge to kick him in the crotch. He was in the perfect position. And he had cut the tape on her ankles. But she would play it this way for a bit and see what happened.

"Maybe three times that much at my husband's office in a safe. Even more in the bank." If she was going to lie, she might as well make it good. Not only did she not have a safe in her little apartment, she also felt reasonably certain Trinity didn't, either. Not unless his rich uncle had died since they divorced.

Then again, she was relatively certain he didn't have a rich uncle.

"Let's see what the boss has to say about that." The man straightened away from her. "Lane!"

Lane looked up from his cell phone conversation and held up a hand indicating he needed a moment or two.

While they waited, Von surveyed the movements of the others on site. She had counted four men besides their two escorts when they'd arrived. Six, altogether. Lane made seven. All were accounted for except two as far as she could see. She stretched her neck and considered the four doors across the back of the building. Number three from the left was where Trinity was. That left three other rooms. Were there prisoners in those rooms? Abducted children? Maybe Lily Larkin?

Wait…if there were cameras in the room where she and Trinity were held, surely there were monitors out here somewhere. Maybe she could get a glimpse of who or what was in the other three rooms.

She saw no monitors displaying scenes or spaces like the room she had been in. One computer screen displayed a map. Making out the details of the map was impossible from where she sat. The other computer screen was also a map, this one constantly moving like a weather map.

How were these dimwits monitoring the cameras in the rooms? Then she knew. Unless these guys carried some sort of personal, handheld monitoring systems, the cameras were nothing more than inoperable visual deterrents.

She couldn't be absolutely certain but it was a strong possibility. Good to know in the event she survived the next few minutes. Testing her theory wouldn't be that difficult.

Lane finished his call and strode over to where she and her would-be interrogator waited.

"She says there's three times what's in the briefcase at her husband's office in a safe."

Lane eyed her speculatively. "I don't believe you and your husband are who you say you are. Why would I believe this?"

Von remembered to look and sound afraid. "We just want a little girl. We have some very important business to take care of in Texas. It's about money. And..." She looked away. "I want a child."

Lane snickered. "You really expect me to believe that if we let you go right now, with a kid to call your own, that you'll forget this whole thing happened?"

Von blinked several times for effect. "My husband will lose his inheritance if we don't show." Before Lane could interrupt, she added, "Two million dollars."

Now both bastards appeared interested.

"Tax free," she went on, "But there has to be an heir for him to collect. It's one of his crazy grandfather's stipulations. He has to be married and have an heir. We've been traveling extensively the past few years. We haven't been home. Mainly because my husband and his father had a falling out. Anyway, we claimed there was a child. A little girl. We've never sent pictures. Never really talked about her. The estrangement made it easy to pull off." She leveled her gaze on Lane's. "But that's all changed now. His grandfather is dying. We have to have that little girl."

Lane continued to analyze her a few moments more, then he said to his pal, "Bring the husband to me."

Von hoped she had bought them some time.

The man returned with Trinity whose hands and mouth were still secured with the tape.

"You and I," Lane announced, "are going to pick up something from your safe at home." He gestured to Von. "Your lovely wife will wait here for our return. Need I remind you that her continued well-being will be solely dependent upon your complete cooperation and satisfying results?"

Lane ripped the tape from Trinity's mouth and stuck it to his shirtfront. Unlike Von, Trinity didn't wince. He glared at the man.

"What did you do?" Trinity demanded of Von as if furious with her.

Although they had a cover and had gone over the details she had just passed along to Lane, confirmation was necessary.

"I told them about the money in the safe," she explained. "And—" she swallowed as if nervous "—exactly what's at stake."

Trinity shook his head, then arrowed a furious gaze at Lane. "We had a deal. You reneged on that deal. And now you want more money?"

Lane shrugged. "Only if you want your wife to remain breathing. We'll get the money, return here, and you and your wife will be free to go."

"What about the child?" Von demanded. "The little girl?"

Lane gave another of those nonchalant shrugs. "You can have her." He smiled at Von, then at Trinity. "We had a deal, after all."

He was lying. She and Trinity would be dead as soon as the possibility of making any more money was off the table. This bastard had never intended to do business with them. Simon's contact didn't know this guy nearly as well as he'd thought.

"Mr. Barton and I will be back," Lane said to the others in the room. "Be prepared to move out as scheduled." He gestured for the man who'd driven them here to follow him.

Trinity glanced back at her as Lane ushered him toward the door.

He was worried.

Von couldn't say she wasn't.

But at least one of them was out of here.

Trinity would take care of Lane and his henchman. She'd just given Trinity his ticket out of here.

Von surveyed the room and the five other men milling around. All she had to do was create her own exodus, though there wasn't a single window and the only exterior door she'd confirmed was the one they had entered. There would be a way. All she had to do was find it and then she was out of here.

But not until she knew who or what was in those other rooms.

If there was even one child in this building, she wasn't leaving without him or her.

What she needed was an opportunity.

She couldn't wait for opportunity to knock.

"Excuse me," she announced to the room at large, "I need to use the restroom."

It was a ploy as old as time, but it was a tried-and-true one.

One of the men glanced at the escort who'd brought her here. "You take care of her. We have final preparations to make."

She was hoisted up and dragged to one of the doors at the back of the room, the second from the left. The goon opened the door and gestured for her to go in.

It was a bathroom, two stalls, one sink.

She turned her back to the guy and wiggled her hands. "You'll have to cut me loose."

With a heavy sigh, he cut her hands loose and then pushed her toward the door. "Make it fast."

Von shut the door in his face and quickly did her business. The request had been a ploy, but she wasn't going to pass up the opportunity to relieve herself. Before flushing the toilet, she pressed her ear to the wall that separated this room from the first room. She closed her eyes and listened hard.

Nothing.

Wait…a whimper?

Then she heard it clearly.

Crying.

Whoever was in the first room from the left was crying.

Sounded like a child.

Fury whipped through Von.

That solidified her determination. She wasn't leaving here without the child…or children.

Chapter Nine

Colby Agency, 11:50 p.m. (10 hours missing)

"There must be security or traffic cameras somewhere in the nearby vicinity," Jim argued with Simon's Bureau contact who was present via the teleconferencing system. "St. Patrick's is barely outside the downtown business district."

Simon and Victoria sat at the conference table in her office. But Jim couldn't sit. Von and Trinity were out there…somewhere. Their sedan had been found on Adams Street near St. Patrick's church. At the rendezvous location. Jim and Simon had been a mere two blocks away. The moment communications were severed they had moved to the rendezvous location.

Only to find an empty sedan, front doors standing open.

The last verbal exchange captured by the communications link was of Von demanding to know where they were going.

Jim and Simon had determined that the vehicle to which Von and Trinity were transferred had been equipped with jamming devices, disabling the communications link as well as the tracking devices in the briefcase as soon as the doors were closed.

Damn it!

Simon had touched base with his contact for any additional information and support. At this point their only hope was to pick up via security or traffic cams the gray sedan leaving the area of the church.

It was a long shot, but it was the only one they had.

George White, Simon's contact, had been more than patient. Jim recognized that he had about half an hour ago crossed the line of reason.

"There are a number of cameras in the downtown area," White agreed, "but no silver or grayish sedan was picked on any of them between the time you heard the exchange and you arrived to discover your investigators' deserted vehicle. These men were obviously versed in the streets and blocks to avoid."

The telephone on Victoria's desk buzzed. She hurried to answer it.

"White, this contact of yours can't be pressured into revealing any details he perhaps has held back regarding this Lane character?"

"He insists he knows nothing more," White explained via the speakers of the conference table's teleconferencing system. "He can't name Lane's buyers or his contacts in the trafficking world. Lane once worked in the drug smuggling business with my contact. He moved on, it seems, to a different kind of cargo. My investigation into this human trafficking network is just getting its legs. We have a long ways to go."

Jim shook his head. This was getting them nowhere.

"Mr. White." Victoria had returned to the head of the conference table. "Please let us know if you learn anything at all that might be useful to our investigation. We appreciate your assistance."

White assured Victoria that he would and the call ended.

"What's going on?" Jim asked his mother. White was the only contact to Lane they had. Cutting off communications with him for the moment had to mean there had been a significant development.

"That was security," Victoria said, her voice quivering just a bit. "Trinity Barrett is on his way up in the elevator."

Jim didn't bother asking how that was possible. Victoria, Simon and he rushed into the corridor and on to the reception area to await the elevator's arrival.

A soft chime announced the car's stop on their floor, then the doors slid apart.

Trinity stepped forward. "I don't have much time."

Chapter Ten

"Lane and one of his men are waiting in the car in the alley less than a block from here," Trinity explained. He hated this part. He needed to get what he'd come for and get out of here…get back to Von. "I have five minutes to exit the building."

"Where is Von?" Jim Colby demanded.

Trinity swiped a hand over his face. He felt numb. Leaving her had been one of the hardest things he'd ever done. "She's at the transfer facility—or what appears to be a transfer facility. She's okay for now. The facility is about thirty minutes south of the city. We didn't take 94 and I'm not completely certain I can find my way back. The dark window tinting prevented me from monitoring the road signs. I'll need Lane to get me there."

"Why did he bring you here?" Simon asked.

"Money," Trinity said flatly. "To buy time, Von told them that we had more money at my office. I think she's attempting to persuade Lane that our quest to get a child is real and that we don't care how much it costs or what they're doing."

"You understand," Victoria said in that calm tone that spoke of unending strength and hard-earned wisdom, "that you're beyond that point now. Whatever else you and Von do, this man intends to kill you both."

Trinity nodded. "I know. Right now I need weapons I can conceal from these bastards and I need money." He reached inside his jacket and peeled the duct tape off his shirt. "This has Lane's prints on it."

Simon carefully accepted the tape. "I'll bag this and have it processed."

"I'll take care of the weapons," Jim said. "Come with me."

Victoria nodded. "Simon and I will prepare the money for transport."

Trinity inhaled his first deep breath since leaving Von in the hands of those bastards. He followed Jim down the corridor to the supply room. Trinity had no idea how much money the agency kept in the safe, but it would have to do.

Jim pressed his thumb to the scanner on the massive walk-in safe that was the arms room and then entered the pass code. The door opened and he and Trinity entered.

The arms room was a new addition to the Colby Agency offices. It had been added in the rebuild after the original offices were destroyed a few years back. In Victoria's office, a smaller version was camouflaged behind a paneled wall. Money and other negotiable assets were kept there. Swift and decisive action was only accomplished when fully prepared for most any scenario.

"Not even the smallest handgun we have will work," Jim said as he surveyed the offerings.

"I'm well versed in the use of knives," Trinity reminded him.

Jim selected a lightweight but lethal-looking switchblade. He passed it to Trinity. "Open the lining of your interior jacket pocket and drop the knife into the bulk between the lining and the leather."

Trinity used the knife to slit the pocket's lining, then carefully burrowed the knife in the material inside. "Done."

Jim gestured to Trinity's left wrist. "Take off your watch."

Trinity removed the watch and accepted the one Jim handed him.

Jim tapped the crystal face of the watch. "Crush it against your opponent's throat. A small dose of tranquilizer will be injected into the skin when the crystal breaks. He'll be out for the better part of an hour."

With the watch on his wrist, Trinity waited for the next tool.

A silver pen. "Press the top down as if you're preparing to use the pen for writing, then jab it into your opponent. This tranquilizer will put an elephant down."

"That'll work." Trinity placed the pen in his right jacket side pocket.

"Let's see if Simon and Victoria have the money ready to go."

They moved back toward Victoria's office, but Trinity hesitated before entering. "I told Lane my office was on the third floor. He can't see the front of the building from the alley, but I don't want to risk that he or his pal might be watching from another vantage point." A large wall of windows in Victoria's office overlooked the street. With the lights on, movement could be spotted from the street.

"Of course." Jim went to the door and asked his mother and Simon to join them in the corridor.

"There's one hundred thousand in here," Simon confirmed as he passed the portfolio type case to Trinity. "That's all we have readily available."

It wouldn't be enough, but it could work until he had subdued the enemy. He grasped the leather handle of the case in his right hand.

"Negotiate," Jim suggested. "Tell Lane you'll give him more once Von and the child he promised are with you and safely away from the place you were held." Jim handed him a tiny round disk. "Place this anywhere on the exterior of the car, it's magnetic, and we'll be able to track you. We couldn't track you before because there appeared to be a jamming device in the sedan that transported you from Adams Street to the transfer facility. Putting this one outside should alleviate that concern."

Trinity had presumed as much. He kept the small disk in his left hand. "Lane is smart," Trinity related. "Don't get too close." And that was assuming Trinity got the opportunity to place the device at all. "If I make any calls or summon help in any detectable manner, Von dies."

"There are security cameras all along the Mag Mile," Simon advised. "Whatever happens with the tracking device, we can capture your movements for some distance in that manner."

Victoria followed Trinity back to the elevator while Jim and Simon hurried down the stairwell to reach the basement garage and their vehicle in hopes of tracking Trinity's departure with Lane.

"Be careful," Victoria urged.

Trinity nodded then pressed the button for the lobby.

Her worried gaze remained on him until he was in the elevator and the doors slid closed.

Trinity squeezed his eyes shut as the car moved downward. He sent a silent plea heavenward that he could do whatever necessary to ensure Von's safety.

She had given him this shot at freedom. He had to make it count.

"Night, Mr. Barrett," the security guard called to his back as Trinity hurried across the lobby.

Trinity hesitated, then walked back to the security desk. He reached across the desk and tapped the notepad on the counter. "Make a note that I won't be in the rest of the week," he said. "In case anyone asks."

The bewildered guard nodded. "Yes, sir."

"Thank you." Trinity turned and headed for the exit. Inside, where the security guard couldn't see, he was shaking.

He couldn't let Von down.

Once before he'd done that and he'd lost her.

He couldn't let that happen again. Losing her had been bad enough, but letting her die…no way.

AS HE'D SUSPECTED Lane met him on the sidewalk before Trinity reached the alley.

"I thought you said your office was on the third floor. I didn't see any lights go on."

"My office is an interior one," Trinity explained. "You wouldn't have seen the light. I didn't bother turning one on in the reception area."

"What's on the fourth floor?" Lane asked, suspicious as usual.

"More offices," Trinity said, allowing his frustration and impatience to show. "Accounting, I believe. But I've never been up there so I really don't know."

"Their lights were on," Lane countered. "I saw at least one person pass a window up there."

"It's almost the end of the year," Trinity tossed back at him. "They're likely preparing for tax season. Who knows?"

That seemed to satisfy Lane for the moment. "Give me the bag."

Trinity passed him the portfolio. Its weight made the bastard smile.

"You know the way," Lane said, gesturing for him to go first.

When they reached the alley, the sedan's engine revved to life but the headlights remained dark.

"Let's see what's in the case," Lane suggested. He motioned to his colleague who got out of the vehicle. "Pat him down," Lane ordered his driver.

Trinity held his hands away from his sides to facilitate the man's pat down, then held his breath, again praying that the guy wouldn't find the knife or the pen. He would need both when the time came.

Lane placed the case on the hood of the car and opened it. It wouldn't take him long to see that there was only a hundred thou inside.

The guy doing the pat down found the pen and shoved it into his own jacket pocket. Trinity noted that it was in his left pocket.

Thankfully the scumbag didn't notice the knife. Trinity had been wearing a watch previously so he didn't pay any attention to that.

"There's only a hundred thou here," Lane said, anger simmering in his tone. "Your wife indicated there was a lot more than this."

Time to play the tough guy. "That's right," Trinity said. "We go get my wife and the child you promised us and I'll give you another hundred thousand. I'm no fool, Lane. You've already double-crossed me once tonight."

Lane's associate slammed Trinity against the wall of the building behind him. "You're in no position to dictate conditions. We want it now."

Trinity shook his head. "Not until you hold up your end of the bargain."

"Kill him," Lane ordered.

Trinity laughed. "That would be a mistake."

Lane stormed up to him and shoved the muzzle of a weapon into his face. "How do you figure that, smart guy? You don't seem to have any advantage at the moment. They'll find your body in the snow tomorrow morning. Just another holiday mugging. People get desperate around the holidays."

"I left a note with the security guard. If anything happens to me, they're to look for you, Lane." Trinity grinned. "I provided a very detailed description and your fingerprints."

Lane's gaze narrowed. "You're lying."

"You didn't see me talk to the security guard." Lane had been watching. Trinity knew he had.

"You couldn't have left my prints," Lane argued.

"The duct tape," Trinity reminded him. "You ripped it off my mouth and shoved it on my shirt. I've seen it on television a thousand times. Can you be certain your prints aren't salvageable from the tape? All I want is my wife back and the child you promised us. Why would I contact the police then?

Buying children is a crime, isn't it? I have no desire to go to jail."

"Put him in the car," Lane roared. He strode back to the car, grabbed the portfolio and climbed into the front passenger seat.

"You think you're pretty smart, don't you?" the scumbag still holding Trinity against the brick wall jeered.

Trinity shook his head. "Just desperate, that's all."

The bastard pulled Trinity away from the wall and slammed him into the car. The tracking disk flew from his hand. There was no opportunity to see where it landed before the bastard shoved Trinity into the backseat.

Well, there went any chance of Jim and Simon tracking the vehicle.

Trinity wasn't going to sweat whether he had backup or not for the moment. He was prepared to take control of the situation and then he would contact backup.

Right now he needed to watch what he could see of the passing landscape through the front windshield and when he felt confident that he was close enough to find his way back to Von's location hc would make his move.

He could handle the current odds. Back at the transfer facility his chances were less than optimal.

He studied Lane. Greedy bastard. That greed and

Von's quick thinking were the only reasons either of them was still alive.

That was the thing about bad guys. Even when they were smart enough and ballsy enough to pull off near-perfect crimes, their greed or need for power always got them in the end.

Lane's would get him.

Twenty minutes into the ride Trinity recognized the deer crossing sign they passed on the long stretch of deserted road. Someone had painted a red *X* on the sign. One of the few landmarks he'd been able to note. They were close. Eight or ten minutes, no more.

"We need to pull over." Trinity clamped his hand over his mouth.

Lane twisted around to glare at him. "What's the problem?"

"I'm…" Trinity grabbed at the door latch. "I'm ill," he muttered.

"Don't move," Lane growled and aimed his weapon into the backseat.

Ignoring the threat, Trinity released the lock on his door and pulled at the handle. Cold air rushed in around the partially open door.

"Shut that door!" Lane shouted.

The driver swerved as he attempted to determine what was going on in the back seat.

Trinity opened the door a little farther. "Can't…" He heaved, making it as authentic as possible.

"Pull over," Lane instructed the driver.

The car braked hard and rolled to a stop onto the shoulder of the road.

Trinity rammed his upper body out the door and made more sounds of having to empty his stomach.

Lane jerked Trinity's door open. Trinity scrambled out of the car and moved on all fours into the darkness. He kept up the fake heaving and groaning.

"What the hell's wrong with him?" the driver demanded as he came up alongside Lane.

"Who knows?"

Trinity mentally prepared a plan, then slowed the gagging and groaning.

"Get him back in the car," Lane ordered his subordinate.

Trinity braced.

The driver stalked over, reached down and grabbed Trinity by the left arm and hauled him to his feet. "Let's go."

A car door slammed, indicating Lane had already climbed back inside.

Trinity shook loose from the guy's hold and bent down to brace his hands on his thighs as if he might be sick again.

The driver opened the back passenger side door and came back to usher Trinity inside, grabbing him by the arm once more.

Trinity rammed the back of his free hand and wrist into the guy's throat, crushing the watch crystal with the impact. The guy let go of Trinity and stumbled back. He reached for his throat with one hand and his weapon with the other.

Lane was out of the car before Trinity could go for the knife in the lining of his coat or go after the special pen the other guy had shoved into his own pocket.

Trinity shoved upward the barrel of the weapon that leveled in his direction. He threw his full body weight into Lane, pinning him against the car.

Lane headbutted him. Shoved him backward. They tumbled to the ground where the other guy lay crumpled and unmoving.

Trinity fought to gain control of the weapon. Lane wasn't letting go. They rolled, alternately gaining and then losing the upper hand.

One shot, then two and three expelled from the weapon Lane attempted to turn toward Trinity. Fighting equally hard to keep the muzzle away from his person, Trinity finally got Lane on his back and began to beat the hand clasped around the butt of the weapon against the pavement. Somehow they'd managed to roll right up next to the front bumper of the car.

Two more shots fired off. Trinity dared to shift his attention to the guy's head. He slammed it into the pavement instead of the weapon. He slammed it hard, then harder.

The grip on the weapon loosened.

Trinity drew back his fist and punched him in the

jaw. Lane's eyes lolled back in his head. He stopped struggling.

Taking a second to catch his breath, Trinity pulled the weapon from Lane's slack fingers and shoved it into his waistband. He pushed to his feet and staggered over to the other guy to retrieve his weapon as well as the tranquillizer pen.

He made his way to the driver's side of the car and got the keys. When he'd opened the trunk he loaded Lane, and then his buddy inside. Trinity shot a couple of holes into the raised lid of the trunk just in case. He didn't want the bastards to suffocate. Even if they deserved no better.

Lane's cell phone wasn't in any of his pockets. The other guy's was but the keypad was locked. Trinity threw the phone into the woods, snagged the guy's weapon, then shut the trunk lid.

Stretching his neck after the rolling around on the ground, he made his way to the driver's seat and dropped into it. He shoved the key into the ignition and gave it a twist.

Nothing happened.

Not a sound.

He tried again.

Still nothing.

Trinity exhaled a frustrated breath. He pulled the hood release and then got out.

Nothing appeared to be wrong under the hood.

Then the engine should start.

A bad feeling niggling in the back of his brain,

Trinity walked around to the side of the car where the scuffling had taken place.

Most of the rounds that had gotten pulled off from Lane's handgun had gone into the side of the vehicle between the wheel and the passenger compartment.

Trinity shook his head.

He didn't know what one or more of the bullets could have hit and it had to be a one in a thousand possibility, but something about the vehicle's electrical system had apparently been damaged.

The engine would not turn over. The interior lights wouldn't come on. No heat. No radio. Nothing.

Trinity searched for Lane's cell phone, starting with the first place they'd fallen to the cold, frozen grass. After a minutes' frustration, he found it on the ground a few feet from the car.

"Blast it!" He tried a number of different combinations to unlock the keypad. None worked. The fifth attempt disabled the phone entirely.

"Perfect." He tossed it deep into the woods as well.

Trinity stared down the dark, desolate road. He knew the way from here. But it was quite a distance when measured in steps. He'd just have to run it. If he was lucky there would be a house along the way.

If he was even luckier Simon and Jim would pick up their route on one or more of the city's traffic cams and maybe, just maybe they would come in this direction.

Until then, he was on his own.

On foot.

Chapter Eleven

Wednesday, December 23rd, 12:01 a.m.

Von rubbed her hip and stared at the ceiling.

She'd almost made it that time.

But that worthless folding chair kept *folding* at just the wrong moment and throwing her off balance.

"One more time."

The guys in the other room surely had heard her bumping around in here but no one had come to see what she was doing.

Maybe they didn't care as long as they knew she was in here and more money was on the way.

Whatever.

She'd pushed the metal cart against the wall, then braced one of the folding chairs beneath its wheels to ensure it didn't roll away. The second chair she'd stacked on top of the cart to give her the height she needed to reach the drop-style ceiling. This close to the wall the support system would be well braced and she should be able to move a tile aside and climb up there.

Her goal was to move across the ceiling and see what was in the room to her right. The bathroom was to her left. No point looking there first.

The cart had more duct tape and rope and nothing else. She'd wrapped a length of rope around her waist in case she needed it and pocketed a roll of duct tape. Then she'd taped the heck out of the chair in hopes of preventing it from folding.

She climbed onto the cart. Took a breath and stepped up onto the seat of the rickety chair.

She could reach the tile directly over her head with her hands and had successfully pushed it out of the way the last go around. But pulling herself up there was proving the difficulty.

Her gloves had so far prevented the metal of the brace work from cutting into her palms. She grabbed on and closed her eyes.

Pull.

Her arms shook with exhaustion from the previous three attempts.

"Don't give up. Don't give up," she murmured.

Be strong! Pull!

Her head and shoulders rose above the brace work. She dared to release her hold with her left hand and swing her arm over the support beam.

Take a breath.

Relax a second.

She was halfway there.

It was dark as pitch up there. She let go with her right hand and wrapped that arm around the broad support beam that ran atop the wall that separated her room from the next one.

If she could get up onto the beam, she could slide a tile away on the other side of the dividing wall just enough to see who or what was in there.

She leaned forward with her upper torso, snaked her right leg upward. Getting her leg and booted foot through the opening and swung up onto the beam was a major hurdle…but she made it.

With a little more effort she was lying facedown along the length of the beam.

Lights were on in the neighboring room. She reached down and lifted the corner of the nearest acoustic ceiling tile.

Slowly…don't make a sound.

The room appeared to be empty…at least what she could see of it.

She leaned her head down. Dared to raise the tile a little higher.

Something darted across the room.

Von blinked.

What the…?

She lifted the tile higher still.

Her heart stumbled.

Six children, all small girls, huddled against the wall farthest from her.

Dear God.

Tiny gasps echoed in the room.

Six sets of eyes were suddenly focused on the ceiling.

Von hadn't realized she'd said the words out loud.

She managed to get a finger to her lips in the universal gesture for quiet.

With effort she slid the tile completely aside, leaving an opening about eighteen inches by thirty-six inches, the same as the one she'd climbed up through. The only difference was there wouldn't be a chair or cart on this side of the wall for her to drop down onto.

Couldn't be helped.

She had to get down there.

Holding her breath and fighting her quivering muscles, she eased one leg, then the other over the edge of the beam and through the opening.

She hung onto the beam with both arms wrapped around it.

Next she had to ease downward until she was holding on with nothing but her fingers.

From there it would be a four foot or so drop.

Good thing she hadn't worn high heels.

"Who are you?"

The gasp she heard then was her own. She took a breath, told her pulse rate to slow. "My name is Von. I'm here to help you."

Lots of whispering and moving about below her.

Von tried to see what was going on, but all she could see was the children gathered somewhere beneath her.

"You need to move so I can drop down," she whispered as loudly as she dared.

More whispering and a couple of groans.

"Here." Something touched Von's foot.

As best she could tell the children had made a support bridge of sorts and were attempting to help her down.

"I might hurt you," Von argued softly. "You should move."

"Just let go," a small voice urged.

Von held her breath and forced her fingers to release from the steel beam.

She slid down the wall.

Literally.

Little hands and bodies kept her pressed against the wall so she landed upright and on her feet.

Other than a stinging cheek, she was okay.

When she turned around, six small girls were huddled a few feet away, wide eyes staring at her.

"Did the police send you?" the girl who looked to be the oldest, maybe ten, asked.

"No," another whispered gruffly. "God sent her, silly."

Von held her finger to her lips once more, then hurried over to the door to listen. The men were talking, arguing maybe. She couldn't make out the words, but they were definitely having a fierce discussion.

She turned and surveyed the room that was all white and square just exactly as hers had been only without the cart and folding chairs.

How the heck was she going to get these kids out of here?

She moved toward the huddle of girls. Terror lit in their eyes.

"Are there others here?"

"See," a little red-haired girl grumbled, "she's not an angel. If she was she'd know that."

Her status had just dropped several notches. "We don't have time to talk about that now. Just tell me how many others are here."

The oldest stepped forward. "I saw six others."

Twelve. For Pete's sake. "Are you all okay?" She surveyed the small faces. "I mean, are you hurt in any way? Cut? Bruised? Bleeding?"

Heads wagged side to side.

"Good." Von moistened her lips. "What about the others?"

"One little girl was crying a lot," the oldest said.

"Way more than the rest of us," the redhead added.

Could be scared. Could be hurt. "You didn't see any injury? No blood or anything?"

Heads wagged in unison once more.

"Okay." What next? "What're your names?"

"Tara," said the oldest.

"April." The redhead.

They went down the line from there. Janey had blond hair. Katie, brown. Sophie had coal-black hair. And Lydia had brown corkscrew curls. They ranged in age from seven to ten.

All lived in Chicago or nearby towns.

There were a lot of questions Von would have liked to ask, but she had to focus on finding a way out.

Maybe if she could get them up into the ceiling cavity, their captors would think they had escaped.

It might work.

Except, as far as Von could see, there was no way to escape. Yet, hiding was the only step she could take to protect them. She couldn't do nothing.

But then how would she get up there? Being found in this room would be a surefire indication of exactly what had gone down.

Her hands settled on her waist.

She looked down.

The rope.

Inspiration had adrenaline firing in her veins.

"I need you to help me get back up there," she said to the oldest.

Renewed terror flashed in six sets of eyes.

She touched the rope at her waist. "I'm going to pull each of you up, too. But I have to get up there first."

Lips quivered and tears flowed down the cheeks of two of the girls.

Tara turned to the clutch of girls. "Listen," she whispered fiercely. "Von's here to help us. We have to listen to her. Okay?"

Little heads bobbed up and down.

Tara turned back to Von. "Tell me what to do."

It wasn't an easy task, but Von figured it out. She used the biggest of the little girls, made a pyramid/

ladder of sorts and then climbed up, trying her level best not to hurt anyone.

Once Von was on the beam, she laid down lengthwise. After snugging her legs on either side of the steel and curling one arm around it, she reached down with her right hand.

Tara, with the help of April, hefted the smallest girl up within Von's reach.

Slowly, but surely she pulled four little girls up to the beam. Her entire body was shaking with exhaustion. She'd lined the little girls up on the beam, impressing upon each one how important it was not to move. She explained how the tiles would give way if they fell against them and then they would fall to the floor.

Each sat like a little stone statue, not moving a muscle.

Von tied one end of the rope around her waist and lowered the other down to the room. It didn't quite reach the floor, but low enough that April could grab on. She climbed part of the way and Von pulled her up the rest of the way. She joined the other little ones lining the steel beam.

Tara's turn.

She was older and heavier than the others and Von was really tired but she would die before she'd leave a single child in that room.

Tara climbed as far as she could. Von pulled. The rope slipped once. But somehow Von managed to haul the child through the opening.

Before she dared to relax, Von righted the ceiling tile, careful to ensure it was exactly the way she'd found it.

It was very dark with the tile back in place. The children were terrified. But Tara did an excellent job of keeping them calm.

Von couldn't rest her muscles as long as she wanted to. She had to get moving.

"I'm going to the other room and get the rest of the children," she told Tara. "Whatever happens, don't move and don't make a sound. Do you understand me?"

Tara nodded enthusiastically.

Using the steel beam that ran across the main wall that divided the small square rooms from the large room where the captors were, Von made her way past her room and the bathroom. When she reached room number one, the first from the left, she moved onto the beam that cut across the dividing wall.

Once again, she carefully moved a ceiling tile. Again, the children huddled in fear as she attempted to lower herself into the room.

She wasn't so lucky this time. None came to her aid. There wasn't a Tara in this group.

But there was a Lily.

Relief expanded in her chest when she recognized the little girl.

She explained who she was and what she was doing to help the girls. The oldest, Jenny, finally stepped up to the plate and showed similar leadership skills as Tara had.

Climbing back up into the ceiling cavity wasn't so easy this time, either. Two of the girls were very small, including Lily. But Von finally made it.

The smallest girls were lifted up first, then the rest. Finally Jenny.

"I have to go back down now," Von explained to Jenny. "Those bad men will find me, but you must be absolutely quiet no matter what you hear happening. If they can't find you, you'll be safe."

Jenny promised to stay quiet and to keep the girls quiet.

Von shimmied back across the main beam and explained the same to Tara.

"They'll hurt you," Tara protested.

There was no time for this.

"Maybe," Von acknowledged. "But I can't help you if you don't do as I say."

Finally Tara relented and made the same promise Jenny had.

Von lowered back down onto the rickety chair. She put the ceiling tile in place, then climbed down to the floor. Moving quickly, she dismantled her climbing apparatus and put all back just as it was.

The duct tape she had used she stuck to the bottom of the cart, out of sight. The rope she placed on the cart's lowest shelf.

She brushed off her clothes. Took a breath and waited. The cameras obviously weren't operable. Not only had no one come rushing in while she went through this little rescue exercise, but she also hadn't noticed any monitors with realtime video feed in the large room.

They were in the middle of nowhere. These were children. The bastards clearly thought they had nothing to worry about.

Trinity should be back by now.

Von started to pace. She had no way of knowing what time it was, but it felt as if it had been hours.

The men's voices were louder now. Definitely arguing.

The door to her room burst open.

"You," one of the men, the older, chubby one, demanded, "get out here."

Von squared her shoulders and walked out the door, fully expecting to find Trinity and Lane back.

No Trinity.

No Lane.

Only the men who'd been here when they arrived. Judging by their expressions all were ticked off. Wait, there was one newcomer. Middle-aged. Dressed in a distinguished suit. Nothing like the others.

Was he the buyer?

"The truck is ready."

Von's gaze shifted to the female voice that had made the announcement. A young woman, twenty-two or -three at most, had entered the building and now walked quickly across the room. She glanced at

Von and then tiptoed to whisper something in Suit Guy's ear.

Blond hair…slender build…the woman looked familiar. When she turned to walk back out of the building Von studied her profile. Something about the curve of her cheek…her profile.

Von knew this woman from somewhere.

"Your husband and Lane aren't back yet," the older man with the bulging belly roared.

That was obvious. "Where are they?" she asked in a small voice. She had to remember that she was a victim here. She had to act like one. As the gazes stared holes through her, she hugged her arms around herself and tried to look frightened.

"We're going to assume that your husband caused trouble and that Lane and Robinson won't be coming back," he snapped.

Von wouldn't bank on that. "My husband would never leave me here like this. You're wrong." She tilted her chin defiantly. "I know my husband."

"Well, I don't." The older, chubby man bellied up to her. "I'm going with the theory that we've been made and we're moving now, instead of later."

This was going to get ugly.

"Let me call home," she offered in the most pitiful voice she could muster. "Or his office." She shook her head. "I'm telling you he wouldn't do this."

"No time," he snarled. "We're ready to move."

It wasn't until he made the statement that she noticed the changes in the room. There was nothing.

The desks and computers, the chairs, even the sofas. All of it was gone. Nothing but concrete floors, white walls and cheap fluorescent lights dangling from the ceilings.

"But what about the money?" Von asked. "Don't you want my husband's money?"

"Get the brats," the chubby guy ordered, ignoring her questions.

Von held her breath.

The others hurried to do as they were told.

Doors opened.

Scrambling around…surprised voices tossed questions back and forth.

Finally the announcement she'd been expecting echoed: "They're gone!"

Chubby Guy moved closer and glared at Von. "Where are they?"

She blinked, tried to look bewildered. "What're you talking about? You've had me locked in that room all this time. Where is my husband?"

"Where…are…the…children?" Each word was spat at her through clenched teeth.

"I told you I don't know what you're talking about."

"Get me those bolt cutters," he roared.

A man grabbed Von from behind.

Time to stop playing.

She whirled around and landed the heel of her hand into his throat. He stumbled back, gagging.

Another reached for her. She kicked his feet out from under him and twisted away from him.

Vicious fingers dug into her flesh, hauled her up against a hard body just as the muzzle of a weapon bored into her temple. "You've been holding out on me, missy," this one snarled.

"Tear this place apart," Chubby Guy shouted to his minions. "Find those brats. They're in here somewhere. They have to be."

It didn't take the bastards long to figure out that up was the only way to go.

Von closed her eyes at the sound of the children wailing in terror.

"I think we should let the kiddies watch you die," Chubby growled in her ear.

"Let her go."

Von's gaze shot to the man who had spoken. The guy in the pricey suit. Suit Guy.

"She and her husband have caused a lot of trouble," Chubby argued.

Suit Guy shook his head. "Nothing we can do about that now. If Lane had stuck to his agenda, this wouldn't have happened. Let her go. Now," he reiterated when his underling hesitated.

Chubby released her and Von took a challenging step toward the man in the suit. "I'm not going anywhere without those kids."

He smiled. "You may be more right than you know. Take off your coat."

Her eyes narrowed. “I don’t think so.” She wasn’t doing anything this perv told her to do.

He nodded to his henchmen. Roughs hands peeled the coat off her shoulders and down her arms. It landed on the floor behind her.

Suit Guy walked all the way around her, The silence in the building was deafening.

He suddenly stopped and turned to Chubby. “She goes with us. She’ll bring a nice sum in the gaming auction.” He smiled at Von. “They love women like you. Those prepared to fight to the death.”

Fury blasted any reason right out of Von’s head. “I’m not going anywhere with you unless you let the children go.”

“How nice,” he mused aloud, “a woman willing to sacrifice herself for others. Such a rare trait.”

Von lunged for the bastard.

Savage hands grabbed her back.

“You’ll find out,” she threatened, “just how rare I am.”

A needle pierced her skin on the back of her shoulder.

Von whirled around to fight off her attacker.

She staggered as the room kept spinning.

The children were her final thought before the blackness descended.

Chapter Twelve

12:58 a.m. (11 hours missing)

Trinity's heart pounded hard enough to burst through the wall of his chest.

The house he'd spotted was a good half mile off the road.

He hadn't slowed down since he'd left Lane and his pal in the trunk of their sedan.

Not a single vehicle…not the first sign of a house until now.

Barking greeted him as he neared the house.

Two dogs, their growls several levels below friendly, circled him.

Trinity ignored the animals.

He climbed the steps, his lungs burning with the need for air, and crossed the porch. With no compunction as to the time, he banged hard enough on the door to shake the Christmas wreath hanging there and to wake the dead.

The dogs stayed close, growling and snarling.

No sound inside the house.

Trinity banged again, harder still.

A light came on inside.

Thank God.

The overhead porch light blinked on next.

With a heavy creak the door flew inward and the black muzzle of a double barrel shotgun came within inches of Trinity's face.

"What do you want?" The pajama-clad man had obviously awakened from a deep sleep. His hair was mussed and his face was grim.

That was the first time Trinity noticed exactly how cold it was. The chill leached into his bones and exhaustion clawed at him.

"I need to call for help," Trinity explained. "My wife's been abducted."

The man's gaze narrowed even more. "What do you mean abducted?"

"These men took her…. They tried to kill me." Trinity hoped that part would get this guy's full attention a little more rapidly. He needed a damned phone!

The man looked past Trinity then hitched his head in invitation. "Come on in. Ingrid!" he shouted over his shoulder. "Make some coffee."

Trinity was barely inside the door when the man gestured to the table next to the sofa. "There's the phone."

Trinity put through a call to Jim Colby and gave his location. The man with the shotgun provided specific road numbers and directions from the city.

Jim assured Trinity that he and Simon, as well as Simon's Bureau contact, were en route.

Trinity replaced the receiver and tried not to sway. Seemed the warmer he got on the outside the colder he felt on the inside.

"This'll warm you up." A woman, the wife, Ingrid, Trinity supposed, offered him a mug of steaming coffee.

"Thank you." He cradled the hot cup in his hands. As soon as he'd caught his breath he would keep going to try and find that damned barn. He couldn't wait for Simon and Jim to arrive.

Ingrid tied the sash of her robe a little more tightly. "What happened to your wife?"

Jessie, the husband, had taken a seat on the couch, but the shotgun remained propped against his leg. He sipped his coffee and eyed Trinity with slowly receding suspicion.

"We were looking for a missing child—"

"Your child is missing, too?" Ingrid asked, her voice as well as her expression loaded with disbelief.

"She's not our little girl," he explained. "She's the daughter of a friend. We were trying to help find her. The men responsible for her abduction are using what looks like a barn in the woods." He shook his head. "It can't be much farther up the road."

"You talking about the old Crosby place?" Jessie set his coffee mug on the table next to him.

Trinity shrugged. "I'm not familiar with this area.

But it looks like a barn. I didn't see a house. It's a good distance off the paved road."

"Get my coat," Jessie said to his wife. "I know the place you're talking about. I'll take you there right now. Ingrid'll tell the police or whoever you called where to go when they get here."

Trinity set his cup aside as well. "Do you have a cell phone we can take with us?"

Jessie shook his head as he shouldered into the coat Ingrid rushed to him. "But I got this shotgun and a four-wheel drive truck."

Trinity managed a smile. "That'll work."

LESS THAN TEN MINUTES on the dark road and Jessie turned on his left blinker. "This is the old Crosby place."

"This is it." Trinity recognized the big oak tree that loomed close to the narrow dirt road that cut into the woods. The oak was long dead. It was a miracle it hadn't already fallen.

"Couple months ago I was down this way and saw a truck waiting to pull out on the road," Jessie said. "I figured the place had been sold. Never bothered to come over here and see what was going on or ask nobody."

"Let's take it a little slow," Trinity suggested.

Jessie cut the headlights. "No use warning 'em that we're coming."

The narrow road gave way to a clearing and what looked like an old barn stood beneath the moonlight, surrounded by snow—snow that had been heavily marred by tire tracks.

The SUVs he'd noticed here before were gone.

"Stop," Trinity said, desperation aching in his chest.

He hoped out of the truck and bounded through the snow. The big double doors opened with no resistance. The barn was dark but Trinity could feel the emptiness.

They were gone.

He motioned for Jessie to pull closer then shouted, "Turn on your headlights."

The twin beams of light split through the dark interior of the building. The desks, chairs…everything was gone.

Trinity found the wall switch and turned on the fluorescent lights. The harsh glare reflected against the white walls and bare cement floor.

He moved from door to door at the far end of the building. Each was empty, but oddly in shambles. The ceiling tiles were pulled down here and there. He had a feeling that Von had something to do with that.

The place was completely deserted.

He turned back to Jessie. "Did you say your truck is four-wheel drive?"

"Yes, sir."

"I need you to drive me around the building…" Trinity exhaled a breath of sheer misery. "So I can see if there's anything out there."

"Got spotlights, too," Jessie explained as they hustled back to his truck.

He drove slowly around the clearing, shining his spotlights and headlights so that Trinity could search for anything…or anyone left behind.

Nothing.

Simon and Jim would likely be here any minute.

Trinity couldn't wait.

"Can you take me one more place?" he asked Jessie.

"THAT IT?" JESSIE ASKED.

"That's it."

Lane's car.

"Pull over here and leave your emergency flashers on." Since he didn't have a cell phone he needed to catch Jim and Simon's attention when they passed. Since they hadn't met a single vehicle on the road, Trinity could safely assume they were still en route.

Trinity bounded out of the truck and snagged the keys from the car's ignition.

Jessie shut down the truck's engine but left the lights on as well as the flashers. Trinity could hear the men kicking at the trunk and swearing at each other.

"Friends of yours?" Jessie asked.

Trinity shook his head. "They know who took my wife." He kept calling Von his wife even though that cover was no longer necessary…but the truth was he'd always thought of her as his wife.

"They armed?"

He shook his head again and opened his jacket. "I have their weapons."

Jessie pulled the shotgun away from his shoulder where he had it propped and aimed the barrel at the trunk. "Open'er up and let's see what they got to say."

"My thoughts exactly." Trinity drew the weapon with the most ammo in the clip with his right hand and unlocked the trunk with his left.

Both men attempted to sit up.

"Don't move," Trinity warned.

"You're a dead man," Lane challenged.

"You might want to reassess that conclusion," Jessie suggested.

Trinity liked this guy better all the time.

"Get out," Trinity ordered.

When both men attempted to do so, Trinity aimed the weapon at Lane. "Not you."

The other guy scrambled out over his boss.

Trinity slammed the trunk lid closed and turned to the man whose teeth were chattering from the cold. "What's your name?"

"Waylon Robinson."

"Okay, Robinson," Trinity said, "on your knees."

"Look, man," the guy whined, "I'll tell you whatever you want to know. Just don't do this."

"You heard him," Jessie echoed. "On the ground."

The guy lowered to his knees, fear seeping from his pores like sweat.

"Where did they take my wife?"

The idiot's eyes went even wider. "They left?"

"Yes." Trinity rammed the muzzle into his forehead. "Where did they go? They must've had a plan. A route. A rendezvous with a buyer. Tell me now. This is the only chance you'll get."

"Okay, okay. I don't know about your wife, but they have to get the kids to New Orleans by Christmas morning. The buyer takes them by boat from there. I don't know where to. I swear to God." He closed his eyes and shook his head. "That's all I know. I just do what I'm told."

Trinity felt sick to his stomach that these bastards would be doing this disgusting work at all, but especially at Christmas. "I need to know what they're traveling in and the route."

The guy's eyes opened wide. "Sometimes it's a panel truck. Sometimes a van. It was always different, just like the route."

Lane's ranting inside the trunk grew increasingly louder.

Had to be a good eighteen hours from here to New Orleans. "They make any regular stops?"

"Just one." His face turned somber.

"Where?"

"I'll show you, but I'm not telling you."

Well, damn. The scumbag had grown a brain in the last five minutes. Great.

"I'd just go ahead and shoot him," Jessie suggested, the aim of his double barrel centered on the man's head. "He don't seem worth saving to me."

"You're probably right," Trinity agreed. "But I would like to get my wife back before Christmas."

"I can take you straight there. If we hurry, we'll beat them there and we can take 'em by surprise. There'll only be two in the truck. We got time to get there first before anyone shows."

"Since they've left already," Trinity wondered, "why didn't they stop and pick up you and Lane? They surely would've recognized your vehicle. It's not like there's much traffic on this stretch of road."

He shook his head adamantly. "They never leave in this direction." He hitched his head south. "They take the back roads to the interstate."

"What's the purpose of this one stop they make?" Trinity still wasn't convinced.

"To pick up more merchandise. They got two streams of supply. One here and one down south. They'll meet up with their counterparts down there and then you'll be seriously outnumbered."

Headlights coming from the north cut through the darkness.

"Think maybe that's your friends?" Jessie asked.

"Hope so." Trinity turned to watch the car approach.

As it slowed to a stop he recognized Simon Ruhl behind the wheel. Relief made his knees weak.

WHEN SIMON, JIM, AND FBI AGENT George White were brought up to speed, Trinity suggested a strategy.

"Robinson will take me to the next pick up location—the only other stop between here and New Orleans—and I'll intercept with the help of local law enforcement, if necessary."

White was shaking his head before Trinity finished his statement. "I can't let you do this without the Bureau. This is a federal crime, Colby," he said to Jim. "The Bureau has jurisdiction."

Trinity wasn't wasting time arguing. "Then you'll go with us."

"Wait!" Robinson argued. "I said I'd take you. I'm not taking no fed."

"First of all—" White countered Trinity, ignoring Robinson all together "—we should have notified the local authorities already. The lives of twelve minors are at stake. We're all in violation of at least a half dozen laws."

Jim held up his hands before anyone else could speak. "Agent White is absolutely right." When Trinity would have balked, Jim went on, "However, we need a head start if we're going to ensure the safety of these children as well as Von."

"What do you have in mind?" White asked, clearly still unconvinced.

"Simon," Jim turned to the man at his side, "call Ian and have him bring an SUV with everything Barrett will need. We need it here ASAP. And call your contact at the paper and see if we can slip in a last-minute bit of breaking news in the morning edition. We want whoever is behind this to believe Lane and Robinson didn't survive to be interrogated by authorities."

Simon pulled his cell phone from his jacket and stepped aside to make the calls.

Lane started to grunt and groan around the glove that had been stuffed into his mouth. He'd been taken from the trunk and set on the ground until a decision was made.

"What're you up to, Colby?" White demanded.

"You and Barrett will get on the road with your guide here and intercept these bastards. So that they won't change their strategy, we'll make sure the news mentions that a car with two unidentified dead bodies was discovered in the wee hours of the morning."

White nodded. "I see where you're going."

"All we need is thirty-six hours," Trinity said. "Once we've intercepted the cargo, White can have the New Orleans field office set a trap for the buyer at the port. There won't be any collateral damage and the Bureau gets a big break in this operation."

White held up his hands. "All right." He exhaled a heavy breath. "That I'll agree to. But only because I can write it up as part of my ongoing investigation."

"What about him?" Trinity nodded toward Lane.

"I'm certain my friends at Chicago PD can figure out something to do with him for the next thirty-six hours," Jim offered. "And you," he said to Robinson, "may get full immunity for your cooperation."

Lane started that emphatic grunting and groaning again. Jim nodded to Trinity who removed the man's gag.

"I'll cooperate," he said. "I waive my right to counsel just like Robinson. I want to help."

"Considering the delicacy and shortness of time," White said, "I will allow you to remain in Mr. Colby and Mr. Ruhl's custody for the next thirty-six hours. During which time you will be represented by counsel and will give a full accounting of all you know related to this operation. That's how you can help, Lane."

"Anything," Lane pleaded.

"Be aware," White reminded both men, "that I do not have the authority to grant either of you immunity, but I can vouch for your cooperation and if we're successful in returning these children unharmed, I believe your efforts will be recognized."

"Close enough," Lane agreed.

Simon stepped back into the circle. "Ian is making the necessary preparations and I've made the calls to ensure the media works to our advantage."

Trinity wasn't sure he could stand waiting another minute.

Jim turned to him. "You find Von and bring her and those children back here unharmed."

Trinity nodded. "Yes, sir."

He would do it or die trying.

Chapter Thirteen

The roar of the wheels on the asphalt had finally lulled the children to sleep.

The tranquillizer they'd used on Von had worn off an hour or so ago. Since then she'd dozed once or twice but she'd jerked awake each time the momentum of the vehicle changed.

The bastards had provided blankets and pillows. Otherwise they lay on the cold steel bed of the panel truck. A case of bottled water and a small portable toilet had been provided.

More frightening, they were smashed into a small area near the cab while office furniture filled the end nearest the side-by-side cargo doors. The furniture appeared to be attached to the walls of the cargo area, but if any of it came loose and the driver made a sudden stop the children could be… She didn't even want to think about it.

The risks these people took with the lives of these children were appalling. What was she thinking? They had no sense of compassion for these children. These little girls were commodities.

She and the children had been warned that if they tried anything or made any noise, especially when the vehicle was stopped, they would all die. Von looked around the walls and ceiling of the cargo area in an attempt to see through the semi-darkness. The driver had warned that explosives were rigged in the cargo area. If she and the children failed to behave…they would be remotely activated.

Von hoped she lived long enough to personally beat the attitude out of at least one of these scumbags. Preferably the guy in the suit.

Trinity.

She wouldn't believe he was dead.

He was far too resourceful for that.

Knowing him, he was hot on the trail of this damned truck right now.

Except he didn't know what kind of vehicle they were in or what route they had taken. Or their destination, for that matter.

No one beyond the people involved in this heinous act did.

Maybe Lane or his cohort knew, but expecting either one of them to talk, assuming they were still alive, was likely wishful thinking.

If they were dead…Trinity might be alive.

An ache swelled in her chest.

She didn't love him anymore. The very idea, after five years, would be ridiculous. But she didn't want anything bad to happen to him.

But they were over. Way over.

After five years she had come to the conclusion that what happened was not his fault any more than it was hers. They had been young…it had just happened.

She'd lost the baby. Three months pregnant and… she'd lost it. He hadn't forced her to go to work that day. It had been her decision. That he'd gotten caught in traffic and hadn't made the rendezvous in time hadn't been his fault. She had known it then but it had been a lot easier to blame him than to blame herself. And in all likelihood it was just random bad luck.

Her entire life, everything she'd loved had been taken from her. Her father in a freak car accident when she was five and then her mother from cancer when Von had only been thirteen. On Christmas Eve, at that.

Where had God been when she'd needed him?

Time had passed and she'd let it go. It hadn't been God's fault. It just was. Von had made up her mind that it was best not to let herself care too much about anything. No risk involved that way.

Then she'd met Trinity. She'd fallen so hard for him. She'd been eighteen and full of eagerness to explore every aspect of life.

Two weeks later they had gotten married. So, painfully young. So very much in love.

They'd worked for a friend of Trinity's in the bail bonding business. Von had loved her work…loved even more that she worked most of the time with Trinity.

She shouldn't haven taken the same old risks after discovering she was pregnant. She should have been more careful.

Her hand went to her abdomen as if, even now, she could feel the pain. God had let her down again. She hadn't trusted Him since.

Just stop.

Von cleared the past from her mind and summoned the image of the blonde from back at the transfer facility. Von knew that face. But for the life of her she couldn't think from where.

A whimper drew her attention to Lily. The lighting was dim, but Von's eyes had adjusted hours ago.

The whimpers evolved into sobs and Von crawled over to where she lay. If the other girls woke, she'd have a real problem on her hands.

"Hey." She swept a wisp of blond hair from the little girl's damp cheek. "You can't sleep?" Von knew that considering all the child had been through with her insane father and then these criminals it was no wonder she was having nightmares.

Lily shook her head. "I'm scared the bombs'll go off."

Bastards. "We're okay right now. Here." Von scooted in next to her and pulled the child against her chest. "Maybe we can go to sleep together."

"I want my mommy," Lily murmured.

Von swiped the tears from Lily's cheek. "Well, I just happen to know that your mommy's looking forward to seeing you, too. She'll be waiting for you when we get back home."

"What about the bad men?" Lily whispered. "They said we can't go back home."

"You don't worry about what those bad men say," Von said firmly. "I'm taking all of you home. Now, let's go to sleep."

"Tell me a story?"

Von wanted to say no. She'd put children's stories and all that stuff out of her mind a long time ago.

"Please, Miss Von," another little voice said. "Tell us a story."

"My stories aren't very good," Von hedged. How the heck had she gotten into a situation like this? She didn't even like kids. Not really. She'd made the decision after losing her baby. It made life simpler. Besides, she was a career-focused single woman.

And she liked it that way.

Pleas echoed around the group that was supposed to be sleeping.

She was outnumbered.

"Fine, fine," Von surrendered. "I'll tell you a story, but then someone has to tell me a story."

One that involved Trinity showing up to save the day.

Now where had that thought come from?

"Once upon a time," she began.

"Not that kind of story," Tara protested.

Now they were going to tell her how to *tell* the story?

"When I was a kid," Von cautioned the girls, "all good stories started with once upon a time."

"We want to hear your story," April said.

"Did the bad men ever take you when you were a little girl?" another asked.

She could tell them the one her aunt had told her, that God had taken Von's mother on Christmas Eve because he needed another angel. Or the one about how Von couldn't stay with her aunt and cousins because they didn't have enough room. Foster homes were far better for little orphaned girls.

Or maybe she should tell the one about how she'd lost the one thing she'd wanted more than anything else in this whole wide world—her baby.

How life wasn't fair.

How no one could be trusted with your heart.

"Miss Von?"

Von blinked away the bad memories. "Okay. How about I tell you about my adventures as Von the superhero?"

"You're a superhero?" Tara asked.

"Like in the movies?" Lily wanted to know.

"Maybe not that super," Von confessed, "but I've had my share of adventures where I rescued someone in trouble." She'd failed as a daughter and a wife and a mother. But she was damned good as a rescuer.

"Like when you tried to hide us from the bad men?" April asked.

"Yeah," Von said. "And like I'm here with you

right now. I'm not leaving you. I'll keep trying to rescue you until I get the job done."

And she would.

No matter how badly her childhood, or any other aspect of her life, had stunk. Von Cassidy was a good guy—gal. She rescued those who needed rescuing.

That was her job.

If she were really, really lucky, Trinity would show up to give her a hand.

"There was a little girl named Evonne," she began. "She couldn't spell her name so her mom shortened it to Von."

Giggles rippled around the group.

"When she was only six years old and in first grade she had to rescue a white rabbit."

A dozen questions bombarded her. What was the rabbit's name? Where did she go to kindergarten? How big was the rabbit? Did the rabbit have a mom and dad? And so on.

As Von lost herself to the silly story of the last week of first grade, she couldn't help thinking that her poor old teacher had about lost her mind trying to find that darned rabbit.

Maybe some parts of her childhood weren't so bad.

If she lived through this she would have to tell Trinity the rabbit story.

Chapter Fourteen

Colby Agency, Chicago, 10:01 a.m.

"Jim."

Jim roused from a deep sleep, the first he'd had in twenty-four hours. He straightened and blinked. He'd fallen asleep at his desk. "What's wrong? Have we heard from Barrett or Von?"

"Nothing yet." Ian Michaels stood at his door. "But we may have a situation."

Jim had known Ian Michaels for a long time. He and Simon Ruhl were seconds in command here at the agency. A former U.S. Marshal, Ian was as dark and mysterious as was Simon, former FBI, but both men were the best in the business of private investigations. If Ian thought they had a situation, then they had a serious situation.

"We need you in the conference room."

Jim jumped from his chair and strode across the room. When he'd come to his office for some shut-eye, Simon Ruhl had still been interrogating Lane.

Apparently he'd learned something new. "What's going on?"

"Lane claims he has some additional information that he'd forgotten until now."

Jim shook his head. "Yeah, right. Has Simon had any sleep?"

"Very little. He's had misgivings about Lane's statement from the beginning. At this point, he's quite frustrated."

Jim was aware that Simon wasn't convinced of the man's story. He'd left Simon with the job of digging the truth out of him. "I guess we'll find out what Lane's been hiding."

In the conference room, Simon sat at the long table with Lane. "He refused to talk," Simon explained, "until you were in the room." The frustration Ian had spoken of vibrated in his tone.

Jim pulled out a chair and sat down. Ian did the same. "All right, Lane. You have our attention. What is it you have to add that's so important?"

"I've been thinking about the activities of the past few months." Lane pursed his lips and appeared to give his next words deep thought before continuing. "There have been times during the past few operations that I felt the orders I received were influenced by someone who has an in with law enforcement."

An alarm triggered deep inside Jim. "You have three seconds to get to the point, Lane, or this will not end well. You have my word on that."

Ian and Simon exchanged a look of concern but neither objected.

They should be worried. Jim would not play games with this lowlife. He could either come clean now or Jim would be cleaning the floor with his face.

"I believe my superior was notified when and how certain attempts to bring down our operation would be carried out. It seemed to me that we always brushed right past any such attempts."

"Someone in Chicago PD?" Jim prompted.

Lane stared straight into Jim's eyes. "I want full immunity. I know your agency. You have the power and influence to make that happen."

Jim shifted his attention to Simon and Ian. "Would you gentlemen excuse us for a moment?"

"Jim," Ian said, "we should—"

"Now," Jim interrupted. He wanted no witnesses to what he was about to do and say. He definitely didn't want to involve Ian or Simon in his decision to cross the line. And he was definitely about to cross the line.

With obvious reluctance, the two men stood and left the room, closing the door behind them.

Jim pushed up from his chair and walked around to Lane's side of the table.

To say the man's cocky attitude had melted into one of nervous uncertainty would be an understatement.

In one swift, fluid motion, Jim shoved Lane's head against the polished mahogany table. He withdrew the weapon from his waistband and rammed it into the man's skull. "If you know something that affects the well-being of my two investigators you'd better tell me now."

"It's the fed," Lane croaked hoarsely. "Agent White. He's the inside guy. I guarantee the only reason he went along with this whole thing was so he could ensure your people failed. He's the one who told me this Barton couple's intention to buy a kid was a setup. If he doesn't kill them, he'll make sure someone else does."

Jim leaned down close and whispered in Lane's ear. "You'd better pray that you haven't waited too long to come clean. I'd hate for housecleaning to have to scrape your brains off my mother's shiny conference table."

Jim shoved the weapon back into his waistband and reached for the phone.

Maybe it wasn't too late to warn Trinity.

Chapter Fifteen

I-65 South, 10:05 a.m.

Twenty miles to Huntsville, Alabama.

Trinity had broken the speed limit by fifteen to twenty miles per hour for most of the trip.

Robinson was asleep in the passenger seat. White sat in the backseat and, like Trinity, had refused to take his eyes off the road or his attention off the operation.

His cell phone had died hours ago. He'd been using Trinity's most of the morning since he had charging capabilities. Giving the guy grace, White hadn't had someone like Ian Michaels making trip preparations for him. Ian had pretty much thought of everything.

Trinity gave Robinson a shake. "Wake up, man. I think the next exit is ours."

Robinson sat up straighter and rubbed a hand over his face. "Yeah, that's it." He pointed to the upcoming exit. Then he peered at the time on the dash. "We should be running just ahead of the truck. They can't risk speeding, for obvious reasons."

Trinity slowed for the exit, merged onto the 565 interchange and accelerated. He couldn't get there fast enough. Determination to get Von back from those bastards and to rescue the children was all that had kept him going the past eight hours when sleep and exhaustion had relentlessly haunted him.

Finding her safe and getting her back to Chicago, along with the children, was his top priority. He would not fail her or those kids.

"The pickup location is a condemned mill," Robinson said. "It's in an old, rundown part of town. Don't have to worry about anybody getting in your business around there."

"We just stay out of sight until the truck or van arrives?" Trinity couldn't get right with the idea that those in charge were going to move forward with their game plan despite last night's glitch.

The organization was tightly run. They hadn't been caught yet and there was a reason for that.

They didn't make stupid mistakes.

Something was off kilter.

"Yeah. When they arrive, there will be a delay before moving out again," Robinson explained. "They'll wait until after midnight."

"Why wait that late?" That didn't add up considering their current movements, if the cover of darkness was the point. "They've been on the road all morning."

"We usually get on the road earlier so we're on location by dawn. Last night was off because Lane wanted to make some extra cash. He gave the boss an excuse about not being prepared." Robinson stretched his back as best he could within the confines of the vehicle. "We don't usually take this kind of risk. The middle of the night is way better. Traffic's light and cops are usually sleeping in their cars."

White received another call. Trinity glanced in the rearview mirror. The agent appeared in deep conversation.

Whether it was sleep deprivation or paranoia motivated by exhaustion and worry, this just didn't feel right to Trinity. That feeling was escalating with every passing hour. Getting on the road after the bastards who had Von and the kids had been his sole goal after midnight last night. But now, maybe because the adrenaline had slowed, his instincts were screaming at him.

"That was Simon," White said. "Lane has given a very detailed statement. His story confirms what Robinson has told us thus far."

Trinity felt some amount of relief at hearing from Simon. "Did you bring him up to speed on our progress?"

"I did. We're to give him a heads-up when we get into position."

Robinson leaned forward. "We got a few more minutes before we get to the next exit. I need a restroom and some coffee."

"That wouldn't be a bad idea," White agreed. "Get that part over before we reach our destination."

Trinity didn't want to stop, didn't want to take the time. So far they'd only gotten off the road for fuel, taking relief breaks at the same time. But time was on their side at this point. A rest stop couldn't hurt. He needed to be ready to act once they were in position at the target location.

"Take the next exit," Robinson said as he pulled the gloves from his coat pockets and tucked them into place. "It's a truck stop. Always plenty of traffic. Makes it easy to remain anonymous." He picked up the scarf hanging loosely on his shoulders and wrapped it around his throat as if he expected icy winds.

Frustration creeping under his skin, Trinity took the exit. It was a good twenty degrees warmer here, he didn't see any reason for gloves or a scarf. But then, he was obsessing on insignificant details.

"That one," Robinson said, "on the right."

The truck stop was massive. Thirteen or fourteen pump islands surrounded a large building. Like Robinson said it was plenty crowded. "You been here before," Trinity ventured.

"Lots of times."

When Trinity's booted feet hit the ground, he took a moment to stretch. Almost nine hours behind the wheel had stiffened his muscles.

Not about to let Robinson out of his sight, Trinity followed the guy and White through the building's main entrance. Just inside the double doors there were two more sets of double doors, one to the convenience store on the left and the other to a restaurant on the right, a narrow corridor leading to the restrooms cut straight through the middle.

"I gotta hit the john first," Robinson said, heading into the corridor.

White nodded, going in the same direction.

Though a large cup of coffee would be damned good right now, Trinity hesitated a moment—he preferred to stick with Robinson. He couldn't afford to risk losing him. Right now, the sleaze was Trinity's only connection to getting Von back. And the children.

Inside the men's room was the usual equipment with numerous stalls and a couple of showers. For the truckers, he supposed. White was taking care of business at one of the urinals already.

Trinity checked the bottom of the stalls until he saw Robinson's shoes, then chose the urinal closest to the exit so he'd be between Robinson and the exit when he emerged from his stall.

White strolled over to the row of sinks and Robinson stepped out of the stall. The fact that he didn't flush caused Trinity to hesitate before taking care of his own needs.

Robinson pulled his scarf higher on his face as he walked up behind White.

"Robinson, what—?"

He grabbed the agent around the neck.

Trinity lunged in that direction.

Robinson snatched White's weapon from his shoulder holster and fired a round into the agent's temple. The muffled ping echoed in the room.

Trinity reached for the weapon in his waistband.

Robinson released the agent's body and thrust the muzzle of the weapon in Trinity's face. "Think before you act, Barrett."

Trinity glared at him. "What the hell have you done?" Ignoring his own safety, he lowered to a crouch and checked White's carotid artery. Damn. Half the man's skull was missing.

Robinson kicked White's shoulder. "Don't waste your time. He's dead."

Fury and shock making his movements stilted, Trinity searched White's pockets for his cell phone.

Where the hell was it?

The sound of paper towels being torn from the roll jerked Trinity's attention upward. He leveled a bead on Robinson. "Put the gun down, you son of a bitch."

Robinson wiped the blood splatters from his hands and tossed the soiled paper towel as well as the weapon to the floor. More blood and tissue clung to the wall and mirror above the sink.

"We don't have time to play this game." Gone was the frightened hired helper who just wanted immunity or a lighter sentence. The man staring at Trinity had the look and sound of a ruthless killer. He unwound the scarf from his neck and poked it into the trash bin.

"You killed a federal agent," Trinity roared. He snatched up the weapon Robinson had tossed. "You're not going anywhere but into official custody."

Robinson laughed. "You won't do that."

"Watch me." Trinity pushed to his feet. All he had to do was walk into the convenience store or the restaurant and have someone—anyone—call the police. Robinson was out of his mind if he thought Trinity was going to let him get away with this. He wouldn't kill him because he needed him.

"You can't save your friend and all those children if you kill me or have me locked up."

Robinson started for the door, turning his back to Trinity and the weapon leveled on him. The man definitely had to be insane. "Stop," Trinity ordered.

A hand on the door, Robinson turned back to him. "You see that?" He nodded to the weapon he'd used to kill White. "Why do you suppose Agent White put a silencer on his weapon? You don't have one on yours."

Trinity hadn't missed the silencer. He hadn't seen White attach the silencer. Hadn't heard him mention needing one. It certainly wasn't standard issue.

"He's one of them," Robinson said. "He was going to kill you when we got to the location. Me, too, probably. Now, let's go."

"I can't leave him here." Trinity shook his head. "I

have to call the police. You will give me the location and then I'm calling the police."

Robinson shrugged. "Go ahead. Then you'll be detained and questioned. God only knows how long that will take. Not to mention—" he nodded to the weapon once more "—it has your prints on it, not mine." He held up a gloved hand. "Meanwhile your lady friend and those children will disappear." He smiled, the expression patronizing. "I know these people, Barrett. You won't ever find her. That's assuming you aren't rotting away in prison for murdering a federal agent."

"Why should I trust you?" Trinity didn't have to mention that there was a dead man lying on the dingy tile floor that seemed to indicate otherwise. The voice of justice and morality was screaming in his brain…but Von…and those children…needed him.

"Because I don't care about you," Robinson said, "or the people you're trying to stop. I know where Lane hid the 80k you gave him. He has his own special savings account. Since he won't need it, I plan to use it for a very long, very tropical vacation."

Trinity glanced down at White once more. How could he be sure Robinson was right about him? And even if he was, this was wrong…to walk away and leave him here was unconscionable.

"He would've left you here on the floor," Robinson said, as if reading Trinity's mind. "If not here, at our next stop. The bad guys would get away. You and I would be dead and White would have been wounded.

Not to mention whatever tidy sums he received under the table for his cooperation. On top of all that, he'd be a hero for trying to stop this thing from going down. They give agents merit badges for that sort of thing, don't they?"

"Let's go." Trinity swallowed back the bitter bile of self-disgust as he put first one then the other weapon in his waistband beneath his coat.

His heart pounded so hard the blood roared in his ears as they exited that long narrow corridor. The sun seemed to spotlight Trinity as he approached the SUV. He kept expecting someone to scream and fingers to point.

They reached the SUV and Robinson held out his hand. The gloves were gone. Trinity hadn't noticed him taking them off.

"Give me the keys. I'll take it from here," Robinson said. "I know the way and you don't look your best just now."

Trinity handed him the keys and climbed into the passenger seat.

What difference did it make?

He'd crossed a line that no man on the side of right should ever cross.

Robinson pulled out onto the road and took the ramp back to the interchange. "We'll be there in less than twenty minutes. You should have plenty of time to get into position before they arrive."

Trinity shook himself. He had to contact Simon. "I

need my cell." He unfastened his seatbelt and twisted around to dig around in the backseat.

"I doubt you'll find it." Robinson snickered. "White isn't that dumb."

White's phone lay on the seat. The battery was fully charged. Fury tightened Trinity's lips. He tapped a few keys. "Damn it." Had to have a pass code.

Trinity collapsed into his seat. Robinson was probably right. Trinity's phone would be missing. White had likely disposed of it in the men's room back there before Trinity came in. He should have thought of that.

But why?

He'd had no reason to believe White was a traitor.

"What proof do you have that White was the inside man for this organization?" Trinity's voice echoed hollowly in the vehicle.

"I've seen him in secret meetings with Lane. He's the way we avoided law enforcement." Robinson slowed for an exit. "But you don't have to take my word for it. Lane has kept a file on White. He thought he might need it sometime. He can give you all the proof you need. Besides, how do you think we knew you and your wife weren't real buyers?"

Trinity couldn't help staring at the man. He wanted to rip him apart with his bare hands. "How do you sleep at night? These are children? All you care about is the money?"

"Look." Robinson shot him a glare. "I'm doing the

right thing this time. Yeah, I'm taking the money and I'm going far away. But you don't get it." He braked for the intersection at the bottom of the ramp. "This isn't the kind of job you give notice and walk away from. I've been involved in this group for three years and the only people I've seen leave have been with a bullet in the back of their skulls."

Trinity had no sympathy for him.

"Three years?" he asked. "You've watched a lot of kids snatched from their families."

Robinson had nothing to say to that.

Trinity stared out at the rundown and abandoned houses flanking the narrow street Robinson had turned onto.

Tomorrow was Christmas Eve.

Agent White was dead, whether he deserved it or not. His family would be devastated.

Twelve children from the Chicago area were missing, their parents frantic.

And Von… She might not even be alive.

She couldn't die like this. God wouldn't do that twice.

Chapter Sixteen

The truck stopped.

Von snapped to attention. She'd been dozing. The girls had all fallen asleep again and Von had surrendered to the need herself.

She'd told stories for hours. She'd even talked each of the girls into telling a story of her own.

A door slammed.

Von's breath caught.

It had been hours since they had stopped for fuel. She'd smelled petroleum fumes so she had suspected the two stops had been for fuel.

But she didn't smell anything now.

She wanted to move but two of the girls' heads were resting in her lap.

Another door slammed.

With the engine of the truck shutoff, the cargo area was dark. Really dark.

If the girls awoke now, they would be terrified.

Von licked her lips. She needed more water but she'd resisted the urge to drink her fill so the kids would have all they wanted. Still, it wasn't enough. Two bottles for each child. Very little was left.

The silence tugged at her attention.

Where were they?

They'd been on the road for a long time. Eight or more hours, she felt certain.

Had they reached their destination?

Von could sit here in fear…or she could do something.

Do something had always been her preferred choice.

If there actually were explosives rigged in this space, then she was dooming the children to sudden death. If she sat here and did nothing she was sentencing them to a fate perhaps far worse.

One at a time, Von eased the sleeping children away from her lap. She couldn't see anything. What she had been able to see when the dim lighting had been on was basically nothing. The lighting had been focused on the floor area, leaving the overhead area in total darkness.

Feeling her way, she crept to the wall of furniture that separated their compartment from the door. She pushed at it. It didn't budge.

Tracing with her fingers, she found narrow gaps and ledges. This was actual furniture put together to conceal what was behind it. She tiptoed, reached as high as possible and found a little ledge. Then she climbed, putting the toe of her shoe into a lower gap and using her fingers to pull upward from the higher ledge.

The stack of furniture didn't go all the way to the top of the cargo area. There was maybe fourteen or so inches of space.

She hauled herself up on top of the stack. Grabbed on with both arms when she almost rolled off the other side. If she made herself very straight, keeping her arms tight against her sides, she could lay there and maybe not be seen by anyone opening the cargo doors.

Something heavy moved.

A metal on metal grind pierced the air.

Von stilled. She urged her breathing and her heart to be quiet.

The side-by-side cargo doors swung outward.

The girls started to whimper and cry out for her.

Von's chest ached.

Did she go to the girls or be still?

The beam of two flashlights shone into the truck.

Von held her breath.

"Get the woman," one of the guys said. "Let's have some fun."

More creaking and scraping accompanied the moving of the portion of the stacked furniture that served as a door. Thankfully the part she wasn't lying on. These guys had gone to a lot of trouble to make it look like they were hauling a load of office furniture.

One of the men moved into the space with the girls.

Von could scarcely bear their cries.

"She's not here!" the guy stumbling around the girls shouted.

"Are you blind?" the other guy demanded as he climbed into the truck. "She has to be in there!"

Both were in the compartment with the girls.

The girls wailed. The men swore and stumbled around.

Von lowered herself down the front side of the wall of furniture and scrambled out of the truck.

It was dark.

Light tried to creep in through cracks in high walls.

No time to figure it out.

She ducked under the truck, hid behind the rear wheels on the driver's side.

The ground was dusty…not ground, she realized. Concrete.

They were in some sort of huge building.

It smelled old and burned…like charred wood.

The sobbing and wailing in the truck ripped her heart to shreds. Von put her hands over her ears to try and block the sound. She bit down on her lip, hard, to distract her brain from the horrifying sounds.

More ranting from the men.

When they came out of the truck looking for her… it wouldn't take them long to find her.

She felt over her head. Metal…caked dirt. She

crept toward the center of the vehicle. A long, round pole-like object ran down the center. Why hadn't she studied auto mechanics in high school instead of stupid home economics?

Holding her breath once more, she grabbed something that felt like metal and pulled her body lengthwise onto the long thing that extended along a good portion of the center of the vehicle.

Boots hit the concrete.

Von concentrated hard on holding on to whatever was overhead with her hands and maintaining balance on the pole.

Flashlight beams roamed, bouncing on the floor.

If she could just stay still…just be absolutely quiet…

"Idiot, you left the side door open!" one of the men growled.

What door? Von hadn't seen any door.

"I didn't leave the door open," the other argued. The statement was followed by a string of profanities from the accuser.

"Look around outside. If she gets away we're dead meat."

One of the men remained close. She heard his every step. He didn't seem concerned with stealth.

Light roved the floor beneath her.

The air evaporated in her lungs.

Don't move. Don't breathe.

The yellow beam moved away.

Von dared to breathe.

More cursing echoed in the darkness.

The truck shifted.

He was climbing back into the cargo area.

The children began to shriek and cry again.

Von closed her eyes and fought the emotions tearing at her. She had to stay still…had to make them believe she had gotten away.

Something slammed in the truck.

Remaining still was one of the hardest things Von had ever done.

Boots hit the ground again, then stormed away from the truck.

"She's not in here," one of the men shouted.

Von could hear them arguing outside.

Did she dare move?

Not yet.

A minute more…see what happened next.

Then she knew what to do…or what to try to do.

She counted backward from one hundred…then she dropped her feet to the floor and rolled off the pole. Listening for the return of the men, she scrambled from beneath the truck and headed for the cab. The door opened with no resistance. Thankfully the dome light didn't glow to life.

Her fingers went immediately to the ignition…not on the steering column. Her heart rocketed into her throat. She felt around on the dash…found it.

The key was in the ignition on the dash.

Von climbed into the seat, eased the door shut and

locked it. She scrambled across the seat and locked the passenger door as well.

Once she started the engine there would be no turning back. She had to assume that, based on the way the truck was parked, they had pulled into the building. Which meant the doorway was behind her.

As old and decrepit as this building smelled, surely the door wouldn't be that difficult to break down.

She checked the emergency brake. It was released. Stretching her legs, she checked the pedals. Brake pedal. Accelerator. Relief jangled through her. She didn't want to deal with a clutch.

"This is it," she mumbled.

As soon as they heard the engine they would run back inside, guns blazing.

Von pumped the accelerator for good measure.

She twisted the key in the ignition.

The engine growled to life.

With a yank she pulled the gearshift into Reverse, then slammed her right foot down on the accelerator.

The truck jerked backward.

Shouting.

She couldn't understand the words but she heard shouting.

The truck hit something…bounced a little. She pressed harder on the accelerator. The tires spun.

"Go, damn you!" she muttered.

The windshield shattered.

She jerked.

Her fingers scrambled across the dash for the light switch. She pulled. The lights blared on, blinding the men with the guns.

The doors hadn't given way.

To hell with it.

She let off the gas and simultaneously jerked the gearshift into Drive.

Von stomped the accelerator.

The truck jolted forward.

The men scattered.

Wall.

Damn.

She hit the brake, slammed back into Reverse, rammed the accelerator.

The truck whined but roared backward.

She hit what she hoped were the doors.

Metal groaned. Wood splintered.

The vehicle broke through the barrier and barreled backward into the open.

Sunlight blinded her for a moment.

Squinting, she tried to inventory her surroundings.

She slammed on the brakes.

Parking lot.

She was in a parking lot outside a massive rundown building.

Where were the two goons?

Too quiet.

Von shifted into Drive.

Movement.

Someone in the building.

She hit the gas and bolted across the parking lot. The turn onto the street that ran parallel to the lot almost tipped the truck over. Von didn't slow down. She had to get away.

Save the children.

What time was it? Where the hell was she? Could they really blow the truck up? They'd claimed to have explosives planted in the cargo area.

She kept driving.

More closed and dilapidated businesses flanked the narrow street.

No people.

No houses.

In the distance she could see taller buildings, not quite skyscrapers but taller than these rundown businesses. How did she get there?

She worked up the nerve to glance at her side mirrors. The street behind her was clear.

Her immediate need was a phone.

Call the police. Call the agency.

Check on Trinity.

Her heart knocked against her sternum.

The kids were probably scared to death but she didn't dare stop to explain what was happening.

Not until she was either on official police property or surrounded by police cruisers.

A big orange-and-white-striped guardrail crossed the street a block ahead.

The street ended.

"No way!"

She checked her mirrors again. Still clear.

She'd passed the last of the businesses a half a block back. Turning this big panel truck around on this narrow street without getting off the pavement wasn't going to be easy but she had to try. She couldn't risk getting stuck in the grass. No snow but damp-looking. Water was puddled here and there.

Rolling her window down, she craned her neck to keep watch. She cut the steering wheel hard to the left, not an easy task. Eased back as far as she dared, then cut hard to the right and eased forward at the same time. Again and again she repeated this maneuver until the truck was facing the opposite direction.

Her arms shook with the effort.

Still no one ran toward her…no vehicle approached.

Where the hell were those guys?

Okay. Now all she had to do was drive past the old warehouse or whatever the huge building was.

If she got up some speed and just kept going no matter what…she'd be okay.

She glanced around the interior of the cab. What she would give for a cell phone just now. Then she surveyed the street.

The men had to be somewhere.

Von tightened her grip on the steering wheel and pressed down on the accelerator.

By the time she reached the building she'd escaped the speedometer read forty-five miles per hour, which was damned fast on this narrow, potholed street.

Relief melted her spine when no shots were fired and no one ran after her.

No orange-and-white-stripped signs for as far as she could see.

"Good to go."

She didn't bother slowing down. If she got picked up on traffic radar that was all the better. The next best thing to having a cell phone right now would be having a cop blue light her.

A black dot appeared in the side mirror.

Von blinked, looked again to make sure she wasn't seeing things.

It was a vehicle.

"No!"

She pressed harder on the accelerator.

How much farther to a populated street?

The approaching vehicle suddenly charged past her.

Her foot eased off the accelerator.

What if that SUV wasn't about her and the children? Could be someone from one of the closed businesses or from some street she didn't know how to get to. It didn't have to be trouble for her.

Her pulse skittered with the burn of adrenaline.

She knew better. This was trouble.

At the end of the block the vehicle skidded to a sideways stop in the road, cutting off her path.

Oh, yeah.

Von hit the brake. The driver's door of the SUV opened. She rammed into Reverse and charged backward, watching her side mirrors but doing a poor job of staying in one lane. The truck swerved.

The SUV straightened and came after her.

The idea that she would pass that building again had a lump of worry clogging her throat.

There was no choice. She had to keep going.

But the street ended.

Panic swelled that lump in her throat.

There was nowhere else to go.

She slammed on the brake.

The truck came to a screeching, jarring stop.

She grimaced when she thought of the girls.

Something hit her foot.

Von looked down. A handgun lay at her feet.

She stretched, reached the weapon.

With her feet on the brake, she grasped the weapon in both hands and braced it on the steering wheel. She closed one eye and zeroed in with the other on the vehicle heading toward her.

Just let them come after her.

Whoever climbed out of that vehicle and started toward the truck…was dead.

Chapter Seventeen

Colby Agency, Chicago, 12:30 p.m. (23 hours missing)

Simon and Ian entered Victoria's office. Simon, in deep conversation on his cell, remained near the door.

She and Jim had been waiting for word…any word on Trinity or Von…and the children.

Since Lane's revelation, Simon had contacted the local Bureau field office. Simon still had difficulty believing that White was on the take. The two had known each other for years.

Ian was working the DA end of things. Lane had been turned over to Chicago PD's custody just over an hour ago.

"District Attorney Brian Ford just called," Ian announced. "Lane lawyered up and isn't talking. He refuses to relate any additional details regarding the drop-off or transfer location without the guarantee of immunity."

Victoria shook her head. "He, of all people, is very much aware of the shortness of time."

"He is. We know," Ian explained, "based on our GPS system that Barrett is in Huntsville, Alabama. As of five minutes ago he was still moving so we don't as of yet have a location of where the next pick-up occurs."

"That's where the good news ends," Simon cut in as he stepped toward Victoria's desk. "At ten-forty-five this morning Agent White's body was discovered in the men's room of a fueling station just off Interchange 565. He was shot point-blank."

"Dear God." Victoria put a hand to her chest. "Nothing on Trinity or Robinson?"

"Nothing," Simon confirmed. "But it gets worse."

"What else?" Jim asked.

Victoria's son looked exhausted. He'd had little sleep. None of them had had more than cat naps. And the situation continued to escalate out of control.

"Since White was with Barrett and Robinson," Simon explained, "APBs have been issued for both."

"If they're detained," Ian went on, "there's no way to know what will become of Von or the children. Not only is their safety still unknown and at risk, there is the issue of the second stream of cargo Lane spoke of. There is no way to get anyone in place to intercede if Barrett and Robinson are in custody."

"It's all happening in the next few hours," Victoria

said, her mind racing to come up with some feasible solution.

"There's nothing law enforcement or the Bureau in Huntsville can do since we don't have a location for the trafficking transaction." Simon shook his head. "If we give them Barrett's location then he'll be taken into custody. And we can't be sure of Robinson's status at this point."

"Our hands are tied until we hear something from Barrett," Jim suggested, uncharacteristic defeat in his tone.

Victoria was having none of that. They were all exhausted, but the Colby Agency never gave up. "Simon, if you can persuade a contact at the Bureau to go with you to Huntsville—via the agency jet—the two of you will be there to work the situation and provide backup to Trinity and Von in real time."

Simon chuckled wearily. "I can try. But keep in mind that the last agent who accompanied one of our people on this investigation was murdered."

"I'll go as well," Ian offered. "Simon will need to work the politics of this delicate situation. I can handle the operational logistics."

Jim stood. "No, I'll go. I should have seen through Lane hours before he made his declaration. It's my shortcoming. I'll make it right."

Victoria held her hands up surrender style. "You gentlemen make the decision. We want Trinity, Von and those children safety returned to us. Lily's mother is conscious and well on her way to recovery, but she needs to hear good news. I have complete faith that the three of you will get the job done."

If it wasn't too late already.

Mildred, Victoria's longtime personal assistant, appeared at her door. "Trinity called. He's discovered the location where Von and the children are supposed to be. Robinson is still cooperating. That's all he had time to tell me."

Victoria felt the first smile in several days. Hope bloomed despite everything. Trinity was alive.

Chapter Eighteen

Von snugged her finger around the trigger as the driver's side door opened.

She wasn't going to let these bastards get their hands on these kids again.

A man emerged from the SUV.

Von blinked.

Trinity.

An audible ache burst from her throat.

She rammed the gearshift into Park and scrambled out of the truck.

They collided in the street between the vehicles.

He hugged her so tightly she couldn't breathe and she didn't care.

He was alive.

When she drew back at last she pounded him on the shoulder. "What took you so damned long?"

"There's a lot we need to talk about," he said, "but right now we have to get off the street." He glanced around as if he feared someone might be watching. "Are the kids okay?"

The kids. She'd probably turned them upside down

and every other way. "Unless my reckless driving caused any injuries."

"We'll check on them as soon as we're out of sight. Drive back to the mill warehouse. We'll take cover there for the moment."

Before she could ask him if he'd lost his mind, he explained, "I neutralized any threat there."

Von couldn't remember ever feeling so relieved. She waited until Trinity turned his vehicle around and then she followed in the truck.

Despite knowing he had neutralized the two goons, anticipation burned in her veins as they approached the old mill warehouse.

Trinity drove his vehicle into the building, she did the same.

They'd made a hell of a lot of noise, couple of gunshots, shattering windshield, bursting through those doors.

But there was apparently no one around to hear.

"Let's check on the kids," Trinity said as soon as Von had climbed out of the truck.

She followed him around to the back and they opened up the truck. It worried her that she hadn't heard any wailing or crying out of her name from back there.

Von showed him how the hidden door in the faux stacked furniture operated. The light from the open doors shone into the back of the truck.

Tousled heads and wide eyes stared out.

Von smiled. "Come on, girls. You don't have to be afraid now."

One by one, the twelve children climbed out of the truck with Tara and Von assisting.

They all veered clear of Trinity until Von explained that he was their friend.

Von had never in her whole life been so happy to see anyone as she was to see Trinity.

If nothing else ever went right in her life again, this would be enough.

"There's a long-wheel base panel van hidden over here," Trinity explained once the little girls were unloaded and reassured.

Using the flashlights the kidnappers had dropped, he directed Von to the far corner of the building where the van was parked and covered. He pulled the drape from the vehicle, revealing the advertisement painted on the side. Premier Roadside Assistance.

Von turned back to look at the truck she'd ridden in across country. "With trying to escape I hadn't noticed that." She gestured to the advertisement painted on it. Southern Family Movers.

"We need to get the girls loaded into the van," Trinity said, drawing her attention back to him. "We have to contact the agency, but first and foremost we have to get out of here so nothing looks amiss."

"You're going to have to explain what exactly is going on," Von said as they moved back to where the girls were huddled.

"Load the girls," he said, "then I'll explain." He

gave her a look that said we can't talk about it in front of the children.

While Von loaded the girls, Trinity moved his SUV to another dark recess of the building. Then, he got the two scumbags who'd driven Von and the girls here and loaded them into the back of the truck. They grunted and groaned, but the tape on their mouths prevented them from saying anything. Once they were in the truck, he taped their ankles together and reinforced the bonds around their wrists.

Trinity went to his SUV and ensured the weapon Robinson had used to murder White was secured. Then he dragged Robinson to the truck to join his colleagues. Once he was secured, Trinity closed them up in the back of the truck just as they had done Von and those sweet little children.

He took the truck keys from the ignition and pocketed them and checked for any other telltale evidence of a scuffle he might have missed.

The drive-through doors were a different story. He wasn't sure what he could do for them after Von's great escape, but he had to try.

When Von had pulled the panel van out of the building, Trinity closed the damaged doors as best he could. They looked like hell but they would have to do.

When he climbed into the passenger seat of the van, Von asked, "What're we doing now?"

Trinity glanced back at the girls seated around

the cargo bay. "We're going to lay low until this is over."

"What about the others?"

"I'll explain—" he nodded toward the kids "—later."

"Where to?"

"Someplace safe."

2:40 p.m.

THE DRIVE TO MONTE SANO MOUNTAIN took twenty minutes. Mildred had relayed that Victoria had personally seen to the arrangements. A three-bedroom cabin, deep in the woods, high atop a mountain.

Bliss, considering what these children had been through. Not to mention Von.

She had spoken to Victoria en route and passed along the girls' names and the names of their parents as well as their addresses. It was a shame to have to keep the girls from the reunion with their parents even for another minute. But until this thing played out, it was the only way to intercept the other children who had been abducted. Robinson had insisted, as had Lane, that more children would be brought to this location for transfer to New Orleans.

Trinity didn't like using one of the scumbag's phones, but it was necessary for the moment. He couldn't risk turning it off and removing the battery in the event there was contact related to the next phase of the operation. He'd contacted the agency as soon as he'd taken it back at the mill warehouse, but only for long enough to relay that he was alive and on track.

"This is it." Trinity turned back to the girls. "We'll be safe here for a while until we can get you home to your families."

Small smiles and weak cheers were his response. The kids were tired and hungry and likely still a little terrified that they would never see their families again. He'd have to find a way to take their minds off those horrors for a little while.

The key was under the mat just as Victoria had said it would be.

Once the girls were inside exploring, Trinity ushered Von to the kitchen and gave her an update.

"Robinson murdered Agent White right in front of you? Are you serious?" she asked, her expression cluttered with disbelief.

Trinity nodded. "These people are ruthless."

Von shook her head and started searching through cabinets for food. Unfortunately the supplies were limited to the essentials. Bare essentials.

"One of the men who drove the truck you were in received a text message that the additional cargo would be delayed. Midnight. With a tentative departure from here immediately thereafter. We have to stay put until midnight at the very least. Or risk losing out on recovering those children."

Von turned to face him and leaned against the

counter. "If anything at all feels off, they could hurt those kids." She shrugged. "Or just keep going."

"Exactly."

"Not to mention you have to stay out of sight," Von reminded him. "It'll take time to get that part straightened out. Until then, you're a wanted man. And I need you."

"I know." Trinity wasn't about to waste time feeling sorry for himself on that count. These were the risks that went with the job. Robinson likely wouldn't confess what he'd done but truth was on Trinity's side. As Von said, it would take time, but justice would prevail.

Besides, he had the Colby Agency on his side.

"Okay, look." Von pushed away from the cabinets. "We need food. And clothes." She looked Trinity straight in the eye. "I'm going shopping. You keep the girls occupied until I get back."

Trinity held up both hands stop-sign fashion. "Whoa. I don't think that's a good idea."

Von braced her hands on her hips. "I'm not the one with the APB sporting my description. I'll be fine. There was a supercenter in the valley right before we started up the mountain. I'll be back in less than an hour."

There was no arguing with Von Cassidy when she made up her mind. Trinity gave her the cash he'd brought with him and the agency credit card.

And she was off.

He strolled into the great room where the girls were piled around the television.

So long as no one was bleeding or crying, he was happy.

THE SUPERCENTER WAS PACKED.

Christmas stuff was everywhere.

Von was always relieved when the holiday was over.

Those last-minute shoppers just wouldn't give up until the bitter end.

Von shook her head as she guided her cart through the masses of bodies. Didn't people have better things to do?

Since she wasn't exactly sure of the girls' sizes, she'd selected stretchy sweat shirts and sweat pants in children's smalls and mediums and a couple of larges and in a variety of colors. Undies. And a pink set of the same in her size. A new shirt for Trinity.

Pizza. Lots of pizza and chips and soft drinks.

Cookies, and more cookies.

After what these kids had been through, they deserved all the junk food they wanted.

Since she didn't want to use the cash or answer any questions and show ID, Von used the self-checkout line. It took a little longer, but she managed.

Once she'd swiped the credit card and signed off, she was ready to bag her goods and get out of this zoo.

If she hadn't plopped a bag in the cart at just that

moment or hadn't glanced at the Santa for charity bell ringer outside the entrance doors, she wouldn't have seen her.

But she did.

The blonde…the one Von had seen back at the barn transfer location in Chicago.

She was outside the store speaking on her cell phone. A big, broad-shouldered man stood close by.

Could be coincidence.

Huntsville was a fair-sized town, but still small compared to Chicago.

Von loaded her purchases into her cart and pretended to check the bags one last time. With her head down, she scanned the front of the store to see what the blonde would do next.

The man with her headed back out to the parking lot, his cell phone pressed to his ear.

Von's heart seemed to stop beating as she watched the man walk directly to the slot where she'd parked the van. He circled it, all the while in deep conversation on his cell.

They had tracked the van here.

Something else she should have thought of.

The blonde entered the store and surveyed the crowd.

Von bent forward and tucked a bag on the bottom rack of the cart.

She had to get out of here, had to call Trinity.

There was no back way out of the supercenter. Only the main entrance and exit at the front.

Von was going to have to get creative.

She left her cart near the video rental kiosk and walked to the ladies room.

Inside, she checked the stalls to ensure all were vacant.

She pulled the cell phone Trinity had insisted she take with her from her pocket and called the cabin. There was no way to know for certain if they had tracked her here using the van or the phone, but this call had to be made.

"Hello."

Trinity didn't identify himself but Von knew his voice as well as she knew her own. "Get the children out of there now."

"What's going on, Von?"

"They've tracked the van or the cell." She shook her head. "I don't know. But if they know I'm in this store, they know I've been at the cabin. Get them out." She tried to think what they'd passed on the road to the cabin. "The church," she blurted. "There was a church a mile or so from there. Walk them through the woods until you reach the church."

"Von," Trinity said when she would have ended the call.

"Yeah?"

"What're you going to do?"

She laughed softly. "You know me. I always figure something out. See you in a bit." She closed the phone before he could say anything else. On her way out the restroom door she dropped it into the trash bin.

Strangely her cart still sat by the exit when she moved in that direction. The blonde was obviously combing the store searching for Von.

Right now, Von needed a ride.

Since the guy who'd been hanging around the blonde hadn't looked familiar to Von, she was going to assume they had never met.

Because he was still outside, loitering around the van.

Von pushed her cart alongside a man's who was exiting at the same time.

"Looks like another Christmas without snow," she commented with a big smile. She had no idea what else to chat about. She wasn't one to keep up with sports and she knew absolutely nothing about hunting.

"If you live here long enough," the man said with an answering smile, "you get used to that."

Keeping a wary eye on the man near the van, Von just keep walking right alongside her new friend. He was regaling her with the advantages of being a schoolteacher and having the holidays off. She was nodding and making agreeable sounds.

They could have been any other couple in town.

"Have a merry Christmas," he said as he stopped at the trunk of what was presumably his car.

"You, too!" Von called, moving two cars over.

While he loaded his goods, she searched her pockets. "Oh, no!"

The man looked up from closing his trunk.

"I've locked my keys in my car." She held her hands palms up.

He pushed his cart aside and started in her direction. "Is there anything I can do?"

She hurried away from the car with her own cart in tow. "I've done this before. My husband's going to kill me. I guess I'll have to call him to come get me."

"That's a shame." The man shook his head.

"He'll have to drag the twins out," she said when her last comment didn't do it.

"Twins?"

She nodded. "Only three months old."

His face puckered with concern. "Well I'd hate for him to have to do that. You live nearby?"

"Just up the road."

"Fine," he offered with a nod. "I'll give you a ride then. It's practically Christmas but it's the neighborly thing to do in any season."

With her purchases loaded, Von sank into the seat and relaxed as he pulled out of the supercenter parking lot.

Her nerves were shot.

Any more close calls like this and she was going to have to think about changing careers.

Her Good Samaritan looked at her a little strangely

when Von told him she lived in the house behind the church.

"Reverend Hardin's house?"

Not good. He knew the place. "Yes. He's my uncle. My husband and I are staying there until we find our own place. We just moved down from Chicago. He was transferred with his job. Are you a member of my uncle's church?"

The driver shook his head. "I should be, I suppose." He flashed a smile. "Not much of a churchgoer."

Von had to bite her tongue.

He offered to help with the bags, but she insisted he hurry on home. His family was probably waiting. It was almost Christmas Eve, after all.

When he'd driven away, Von stood there surrounded by blue plastic bags.

The cold whipped around her and she felt ready to collapse. It was getting dark, this day was almost over. But the battle was just beginning.

Since there hadn't been anyone at the front of the church, she walked around to the back. No one outside but there was a door that appeared to lead into the back of the church or more accurately a closed in porch of sorts. Von opened the door and stepped inside. A long, narrow room, the walls lined with windows and benches, the benches lined with little girls. Trinity turned toward Von and their gazes locked.

"You okay?"

She nodded. She was tired. Emotion welled in her throat. She was so glad he was here.

Trinity walked over and tilted her chin up to get a better look at her face and the breakdown she was trying really hard to hide. “Don’t worry,” he said softly. “We’re safe and that’s all that matters.”

She nodded jerkily. What he said was right. She knew. She was just too tired to cope at the moment.

“Come.” He ushered her over to a bench to sit next to the girls. “Stay put. I’ll figure this out.”

Chapter Nineteen

4:51 p.m.

Trinity approached the house behind the church. There were no lights on inside and one vehicle parked in the drive, a minivan.

Could be someone home despite the lack of lights as night approached.

The house was likely the church parsonage and it was almost Christmas Eve. Surely if there was someone home they wouldn't turn away twelve little girls.

Silent inside. Trinity knocked on the door. Still quiet. The occasional vehicle passing on the street in front of the church was the only sound.

A couple more knocks and he felt convinced that no one was home.

He checked under the welcome mat, then the little concrete angel sitting near the door. The house key was under the angel.

People in the south could usually be counted on for leaving a house key handy.

There were no signs announcing one security system or the other protected the house. Trinity hoped he wasn't about to alert the police to his location.

No beeps, whistles or bells sounded when he opened the door. He felt on the wall for a light switch and turned on the overhead fixture. The lack of a keypad near the door signaled that a security system was not part of the home's amenities.

Trinity walked through the house, from the kitchen through the three bedrooms and home office. No sign of anyone. Most telling was that there was no milk in the refrigerator and no gifts under the Christmas tree. Kids lived here and the absence of milk and gifts was a good sign that the family wasn't home and wouldn't be back for a few days.

Headed for the door to go after Von and the kids, the telephone rang, stopping Trinity in his tracks. On the third ring the answering machine was activated.

Hello, you've reached the Hardin family. Be back for services Christmas Eve night. Leave us a message or call our cell phone. God bless.

They had the house for the night.

Some of Trinity's tension eased. He hurried back to the church. They could all use a few hours of unguarded relaxation.

He opened the back door of the church and stuck his head inside. "Come on. We have a place for the night." He grinned. "The preacher and his family are away until tomorrow."

Von released a big puff of air. "Great." She stood. "Come on, girls."

Trinity held the door as the girls marched out. He had to smile as he watched Von leading the troop toward the parsonage.

And she'd thought she wouldn't make a good mother after losing the baby.

Trinity shook his head. She would make a great mother.

Von supervised a dozen showers while Trinity prepared pizza. Lots of pizza. And green beans. Kids needed something green with each meal, his mother had always insisted. With no salad fixings available, he'd opened the three cans of green beans he found in the cupboard. He doubted the girls would be overjoyed, but at least the beans were green.

There was no milk in the house but there were fruit drinks. While the oven took care of dinner, Trinity put in a call to the agency. Victoria needed to be aware of this latest turn of events.

The news from her end was not encouraging.

By the time the pizzas were sliced and the green beans in a serving bowl on the counter, twelve little angels appeared, each dressed in new sweats. Pinks, blues and greens.

The Hardins had paper plates and disposable cups

which would make for easier clean up. Trinity passed around a roll of paper towels for napkins.

Stretched out on the floor in front of the television, the girls gobbled down their pizza and picked at their beans. Trinity brought Von up to speed while they consumed their equally appetizing dinner.

"Victoria, along with the Bureau liaison, are contacting all the girls' parents to let them know their children are safe and will be home by tomorrow."

"I'm certain there are some relieved parents in the Chicago area tonight. Wow." Von cast a lingering glance at the girls. "The idea that these children could have been lost forever..." She visibly shuddered. "It's just unthinkable." She met Trinity's eyes. "I talked to each of the girls and none seems to have been harmed in any way, other than being mentally terrorized. I didn't see any indication of physical abuse. No bruises or scrapes of any kind."

"Thank God," Trinity said, his heart relieved. "There's more," he went on with his update. "Robinson and the others are dead." He imagined Von wouldn't suffer any regrets over that aspect of this horrific business.

She shook her head. "That's a shame but it's hard to feel any sympathy for guys like that." She met Trinity's gaze. "So whoever's running this operation knows."

Trinity nodded. "Some homeless people seeking shelter went into the old mill warehouse and discovered the bodies. The moving truck and the SUV were still inside. The local authorities are hounding Victoria as to my whereabouts."

Von rubbed her forehead. "This just gets worse and worse."

"Jim, Ian and Simon, along with some other agent from the Bureau are here."

That surprised Von. "In Huntsville?"

"Landed maybe an hour ago. They're trying to straighten out this mess with the local authorities. We're to stay put until morning. Victoria said the mill warehouse is under surveillance, but I don't think that'll help at this point."

"Definitely not." Von picked up the paper plate and tossed the remains of her dinner into the trash. She turned back to Trinity. "They know their rendezvous location here has been compromised, as have their operatives who they obviously terminated. Their cargo is missing and the plan for getting these kids to New Orleans is dead in the water. I just hope someone can find the other kids that were supposed to be picked up here."

"It would make sense," Trinity said, the idea jelling in his head, "that if the bad guys are still trying to track us down...then everything's at a standstill."

"Possibly," Von agreed. "The blonde." She plowed her fingers through her hair. "I know that blonde girl from somewhere. She was with the man in charge. He wore the kind of suit you don't find on the racks at department stores."

Trinity surveyed the girls scattered on the living

room floor. "I know this is a big financial loss to him and his operation, but why risk getting caught over one lost shipment? This operation is too well executed, too sophisticated to take that kind of risk."

Von braced her hands on the counter and considered his words. "Maybe," she said, "this guy just doesn't like to lose." She met Trinity's gaze. "He was going to auction me for those deadly fight matches."

Trinity's gut twisted at the idea. "The agency needs to stop that bastard." The idea that White had been an insider outraged Trinity all over again.

"Why don't you take a shower first?" Von suggested. "I'll get the girls settled and then," she grinned, "I'm going to have a long soak in that big tub I saw in the master bathroom."

Trinity tried to suppress the images her words prompted. Didn't work. "Sounds good to me."

He hesitated before going for that shower. "Thanks for the shirt, by the way."

"There are toiletries and…ah…underwear, too." Her cheeks pinked.

He had to grin. "Are you blushing?"

She shook her head. "Absolutely not! I got what we all needed. It's no big deal."

"Uh-huh."

"Just go, Barrett," she scolded firmly, but the laugh that followed was genuine.

It was good to hear her laugh.

It had been way too long.

* * *

7:05 p.m.

"MY TURN." VON GAVE Trinity a high five as she passed him in the hallway outside the bedrooms. "The girls are down for the count." It was early but they were all exhausted and well fed for the first time in at least a couple of days.

Von turned, moving backward very slowly, to watch Trinity walk away. He looked really good in that white shirt and the jeans. His feet were bare and his hair was still a little damp.

She smiled when he stopped at the first bedroom door. He stood there a moment, then moved on to the next one. Von had tucked the girls into the queen-sized beds, six to a room. With three girls at the head and three at the foot of each bed, it worked out nicely. Except for the pillow situation. She'd had a heck of a time tracking down enough pillows. Leaving a bedside lamp on to keep the darkness at bay had satisfied the children.

Each one had insisted on a good-night kiss. Von shook her head. She never made it a habit of kissing children. Tonight she'd kissed twelve, one right after the other. Her chest tightened. They were safe…for now.

How could a person have a child and ever let them out of their sight?

Von didn't see how parents did it.

The worry…the sheer terror…of just dropping them off at school.

Maybe that was why she'd lost the baby. Maybe she wasn't cut out for being a parent.

Okay, she needed a bath. A long, hot bath.

The master bathroom was a little small but there was a nice-sized tub. That was all Von needed. She started the water running and then dug around under the sink for soaking oils or bubble bath. Anything to cleanse away the stench of scumbags.

"Aha!" It wasn't a luxurious soaking oil but it was a nicely scented bubble bath that promised to relax her muscles. Von poured a couple of capfuls into the bath water and rounded up two towels.

She started to slip off her clothes, then remembered the sweats and undies she'd bought for herself. Back in the bedroom she snagged the bag and closed herself in the bathroom once more.

Leaving her two-day-old attire on the tile floor, she sank into the wonderfully warm water and relaxed.

It felt so good.

So, so, so good.

She closed her eyes and allowed her muscles to relax.

Slowly the insanity of the past twenty-four hours dissolved.

Somewhere on the fringes of sleep, images whispered through her mind. Trinity touching her…his lips moving over her body. Her body shivered. *I love you…*

Von's eyes snapped open. She sat up. Shivered. The water had cooled.

She climbed out, drained and rinsed the tub, then slowly dried her body. Her skin was sensitive to her own touch. Her insides still quivering from the dreams of Trinity touching her.

When she'd discarded her old clothes—which she never wanted to see again—into the store bag, she dressed in the new items she'd purchased.

The house was quiet as she made her way down the hall. The girls were all sleeping soundly. *Good.* She put her bag of trashed clothes next to the others, the girls' discarded clothes and the dinner trash, then she frowned. The sofa now blocked the front door. Good move, but…

Where was Trinity?

She wandered into the kitchen. The two rooms were open to each other, divided by a long bar. She was halfway across the big kitchen when the back door opened.

Von jumped, put her hand over her mouth but not quickly enough to stifle the gasp.

"Sorry." Trinity tinkered with the door, then pushed it closed and locked it. He slid a cabinet, kind of like a small china cabinet, in front of the back door. "Just taking a few precautions."

He was worried that whoever had killed Robinson and his cronies would still come after the kids…and the two people responsible for rescuing them.

Shouldering out of his coat, he gifted her with a

reassuring smile. "Don't worry. We're going to be fine."

The weapon in the waistband of his jeans reminded her that they were armed. She'd tucked the weapon he gave her under the mattress in the master bedroom.

"I know." She shivered in spite of her assertion. "I'm just tired."

He tossed his coat onto the bar. "Come on." He draped an arm around her shoulders. "You need sleep." He ushered her down the hall to the bedroom.

She stood there, staring at him as he drew the covers back. He was right. She understood that. But she didn't want to be alone.

"I'll take the couch," he said. "Victoria has the number here. If there are any developments she'll contact us. Otherwise we're to stay put until we receive new orders."

All true. And him sleeping on the couch was a good idea. She completely agreed.

But it wasn't what she wanted him to do at this moment.

She looked up at him, wondered why on earth she hadn't recognized what a mistake she'd made five years ago before now. It hadn't been his fault they'd lost the baby. That he'd wanted to try again, later when they were older and more financially secure, had been smart. But she'd been too damaged to be reasonable. She'd lost everything that ever mattered to her. Her parents…her baby… She couldn't bear to have him die on her, too. So she'd made him go. She'd forced him out of her life…so she couldn't lose him that way.

She'd been crazy with hurt…too young to cope.

Was it too late to fix that now?

"I want you here…" She moistened her lips, mostly to buy time and to shore up her courage. "With me."

Trinity didn't question her. Didn't argue. He closed the door softly, turned the knob to lock it. Then he reached for her.

His boots and their clothes landed in a pile on the floor. When her body was skin-to-skin with his she felt as if she were home for the first time in five years.

He lowered her to the bed, his lips working that magic that only Trinity Barrett could work on her. Despite the urgency she felt in his body, he took his time. He lavished every part of her with attention until she felt ready to scream with need. She bit her lips together, didn't want to wake the girls…didn't want anything but him touching her like this…forever.

When he sank into her…she was complete.

Time stopped and there was nothing but his touch…his soft whispers…and the incredible sensation of ecstasy.

TRINITY'S ENTIRE BODY shuddered with the climax that only Von could bring in him. He'd wanted no other woman except her. She was his soul mate… his wife no matter that legal documents indicated otherwise.

She was his…there would never be anyone else.

He held her close, was terrified by the prospect of letting go.

Von kissed his chest. "When this is over," she murmured, "we're going to have that talk you've been asking about."

A smile tugged at his lips even as emotion burned his eyes. "'Bout time," he whispered.

She nodded, her cheek caressing his skin. "Definitely."

He kissed the top of her head, relished the feel of her silky hair. "Sleep. I'll keep watch."

As badly as he hated to, he untangled himself from her sweet, warm body and pulled on his clothes and boots.

He gathered her clothes and placed them on the bed before kissing her cheek. "Just in case." He patted her clothes.

They had to be prepared…just in case.

Thursday, December 24th, 12:03 a.m.

VON HEARD A BELL.

She sat up. Blinked.

"Put the girls under the beds."

Her gaze flew to Trinity's. He pressed a finger to

his lips before she could ask the question on the tip of her tongue, then he disappeared down the hall.

Trouble was here.

Von reached under the mattress and got the weapon she'd stashed there. Staying low, she crept into the first bedroom and awakened Tara.

"Shh." She put her fingers against the girl's mouth. "Quiet: I need all of you under the bed. Now."

Tara nodded, her eyes still cluttered with sleep.

It took a full minute, but Von and Tara finally got the girls under the bed.

Von moved on to the next room.

This time it wasn't so easy.

There were plaster containers of toys stashed under the bed. Von pushed the containers into the closet while April helped the others get under the bed.

Something crashed in the kitchen.

The cabinet, she realized.

Damn.

Gunshots shattered the silence.

Cries echoed from beneath the bed.

Von hunkered down next to the bed. "Stay quiet," she whispered. "And don't move."

She crawled to the door, checked the hall and then hurried to the next bedroom. More sobbing. She moved close to the bed and grabbed Tara's hand. "We'll be okay. But we have to stay very still and very quiet."

Tara nodded.

The sobbing stopped but another crash echoed from the living room-kitchen area.

Maintaining a crouch, Von moved in that direction, her weapon palmed and ready.

Trinity had one man down and was taking on a second.

Von eased closer, not daring to stand and make herself a target in front of the many windows.

The man was working hard to pull the muzzle of his weapon down to Trinity's face. Trinity was working equally hard to keep it away.

Von lowered onto her belly and braced her elbows on the floor. She took aim…held her breath…and fired.

The bastard's knee buckled as the bullet passed through his thigh.

A scream rent the air. He released his weapon and crumpled to the floor, curling into a ball of agony.

Trinity snatched up the dropped weapon and shouted to her, "Get back! There's more of them out there."

A window crashed and something tumbled onto the floor.

Canister.

"Gas!" Trinity shouted at the same instant Von recognized the danger.

She jumped to her feet and rushed back into the hall. "Don't come out," she shouted to the girls as she slammed the first bedroom door. She dove into the second bedroom and shoved the door shut.

"What's happening?" Tara poked her head from under the bed.

"Stay under the bed," Von urged. She wanted to open the windows but that would only announce their exact location to the enemy.

Instead, she slowed her breathing and tried not to inhale the fumes leaking under the door.

"Don't be afraid," Von whispered, her head already spinning. "It's Christmas Eve..."

Nothing bad could happen...not today.

Chapter Twenty

Huntsville Women and Children's Hospital, 4:15 a.m.

Von wasn't sitting in this damned room another second.

She hopped off the exam table and walked out in the not-so-attractive hospital gown. Who cared?

Jim Colby, obviously deep in conversation with two men Von didn't recognize, turned toward her. "There's one of our heroes." Jim waved her over. "Let me introduce you to Special Agent in Charge Vince Latham and his deputy, Special Agent Melvin Wells. They represent the Huntsville field office."

Von shook hands. "Thank you." She wondered which of them had given the order to gas the parsonage. At the time, no one had known how many of the enemy was inside…seemed like the thing to do if anyone was going to be saved when backup showed up on the scene.

Thankfully Jim and Ian had been close by, just waiting for the enemy to show.

"Thank you," Latham insisted. "You and Mr. Barrett saved those children."

"What about the others?" Von turned to Jim. "There was supposed to be another pickup here."

"One of the men captured this morning broke at two-thirty," Jim assured her. "Four other children were recovered and are here as well."

"Are they okay?" Von's heart bumped into a faster rhythm.

"They're fine. Like the others, the examinations were merely a precaution."

Von still had a bit of a headache from the sleeping gas. "Where's Trinity?"

Jim pointed to the room next to the one Von had exited. "The doctor's still with him, but he should be out soon."

Von nodded. "The kids?"

"I'll show you," Wells spoke up.

Jim gave her a final pat on the shoulder before she followed the agent down the wide corridor. They passed several treatment rooms, but he didn't stop until they reached the last door.

Inside was one big treatment room with several beds. Numerous gurneys had been pulled into the room to facilitate the girls.

"They wanted to be together," Wells explained.

"Miss Von!"

Von lost count of the times she was hugged. The girls' sweats had been exchanged for little hospital gowns printed with cartoon characters and animals. Not nearly so ugly as the one Von wore.

The best part was that they were all fine.

Just fine.

"Their parents should be arriving from the airport any minute now," Wells told her when the girls had wandered back to the coloring books and crayons provided by the staff.

"Wow." Von was surprised. "That's fast."

"This Victoria Colby-Camp person is something," Wells said with admiration. "She, apparently, got on the phone with some of the rich folks she knows in Chicago. Three private planes were scrambled within the hour to bring the parents of all twelve children here." He shrugged. "It is Christmas Eve, you know."

"It is," Von said, tears welling in her eyes despite her best efforts to hold them back.

Before she could tell the girls she would be back in a bit, the door opened and people crowded in.

Not just people, she realized, the *parents.* The last to enter was Wanda Larkin, wheelchair-bound but here nonetheless. Jolie Ruhl, Simon's wife, pushed the wheelchair. She flashed a smile at Von.

Von and Wells stepped back and watched the incredible reunion. It was the most remarkable thing Von had ever witnessed.

It was truly a Christmas miracle.

This, Von admitted, was what Christmas was really about.

She turned to leave the room, giving the families the privacy they deserved, and Trinity waited in the doorway for her. He wasn't wearing an ugly gown like she was. He had on those rugged jeans and cowboy boots, along with the white shirt she'd bought him.

She rushed into his arms. He hugged her tight.

"Come on, let's find your clothes." He ushered her into the corridor. "We have a debriefing."

"Already?" Von was surprised. "Here?"

He nodded. "It can't wait."

4:40 a.m.

THE HOSPITAL HAD PROVIDED a conference room used by the doctors. Jim Colby, Simon Ruhl, and Ian Michaels were all present. Victoria and the special agent in charge of the Chicago field office had been tied in via a teleconferencing system. Agents Latham and Wells, Madison County Police Chief Chet Crabtree and three other detectives were also included.

"Four men are dead," Latham began. "All a part of the trafficking organization responsible for the abduction of the girls we are pleased to say are all unharmed."

Applause swelled around the room.

"Three of this organization have been taken into custody and are currently being interrogated. Only one has broken his silence and we are most thankful for that since four more children were recovered."

More applause. As exhausted as Von felt, she wanted to jump up and down and cheer. They had won. The children were safe.

Trinity couldn't help himself, he reached for Von's hand under the table. She didn't resist. In fact, she smiled up at him. His heart did some crazy fluttering.

"But," Latham said somberly, "we have some hard work ahead of us. This is only the tip of the iceberg. We believe this organization is one of the largest human trafficking networks in this country. They must be stopped." He looked around the room. "It will take all our combined forces to make that happen. This morning SAIC, Special Agent in Charge, Bream of Chicago and I were authorized to create a special task force including detectives from numerous jurisdictions between Chicago and New Orleans." Like a fire and brimstone preacher, Latham flattened his palms on the table and eyed each person seated for an intense moment. "We will stop this evil."

Von raised her hand, the one Trinity wasn't holding.

Latham pointed to her. "Miss Cassidy." He gestured to the room at large. "I believe everyone here is aware that Miss Cassidy and her colleague, Mr. Barrett, were pivotal in this significant break."

The applause was deafening this time. Trinity gave a nod of acknowledgement.

"You have something to share, Miss Cassidy," Latham said when the applause had diminished.

"While I was being held in the Chicago location," Von began, "and then again here in Huntsville, I saw a young woman I'm certain I recognized."

Utter silence fell over the assembled group.

"Blonde, maybe twenty-three or -four." Von shook her head. "I'm convinced she was an abduction victim about six years back. It was highly publicized. All over the news for months. She was on a high school graduation trip. Her name was Tina…or Terri." Von shook her head in frustration. "Something like that."

"Tessa Woods," one of the detectives said. "From Purvis, Mississippi."

"That's her." Von nodded, sat up straighter. "I'm nearly certain it was her."

Latham turned to his deputy. "Wells, get us a photo of Miss Woods."

The debrief continued from there with an underlying anticipation that throbbed with hope. When the photo of Tessa Woods was sent to Agent Wells's phone, Von confirmed that the woman she had seen working with these bastards was indeed Tessa Woods or, at least, a woman who looked exactly like her.

When the meeting concluded, Trinity and Von followed Jim and the other Colby folks into the corridor.

"We're finished here," Jim said. "The agency jet is prepared for takeoff. Jolie, Wanda and Lily Larkin, will be flying back to Chicago with us. The other parents and children have transportation at their disposal to do the same. What about you two? Are you ready to return or do you need a few days to decompress?"

"Excuse me," Simon interrupted with a wave of his cell phone before stepping away.

Trinity turned to Von. "You need a vacation?"

She exhaled. "Definitely."

Simon approached the huddle. "Pardon me again," he said, looking first at Trinity and then Von, "Victoria would like to speak to the two of you privately." He passed the phone to Trinity. "You can use the conference room since it's clear now." He smiled. "Put the phone on speaker."

Trinity and Von exchanged a look of confusion.

"Don't worry," Jim said knowingly, "we'll wait."

Inside the conference room, Trinity pressed the speaker button on the phone and placed it on the conference table. "Yes, Victoria. Von and I are both here."

"I think the two of you need some time off," Victoria said, cutting straight to the chase. "I've taken the liberty, with Mildred's help, of reserving a lovely mountain retreat for the two of you in Gatlinburg. It's only a few hours' drive from Huntsville. They tell me the snow is lovely just now."

Judging by the look on Von's face she didn't know what to say any more than Trinity did. "That's not necessary, Victoria. We..." We what? He wanted to do this more than words could convey...but did Von? He looked to her and shrugged.

"We...know we have final reports to turn in," Von said. "And..." She turned her palms up with the same *I dunno* look.

"Let's not pretend we don't all know the facts," Victoria said pointedly. "Here at the Colby Agency, we know our people. We support our people. You two have a second chance here. Take it."

Trinity smiled. "I do believe that's a direct order."

"It most definitely is," Victoria confirmed.

"Well then," Von said hesitantly, "I guess we'll be taking a vacation."

"There's a rental waiting in the parking lot," Victoria informed them. "Mildred will forward your reservation information to Simon's phone—which you'll be using until you return to Chicago."

Von and Trinity recited, "Yes, ma'am," in unison.

Trinity closed the phone, ending the call. He looked Von up and down. "I think our first order of business is a shopping spree."

Von shook her head. "I hate last-minute shoppers."

Trinity pulled her into his arms. “Or maybe we won’t need any clothes.”

“I like the way you think, Barrett.”

They finalized their negotiations with a kiss.

It was almost Christmas…anything was possible.

Chapter Twenty-One

Chicago, Christmas Day

Victoria watched as her granddaughter opened more presents. She imagined that Lily Larkin was having a similarly happy Christmas. The Colby Agency had showered the Larkin apartment with gifts for both mother and daughter.

The day was perfect. Victoria looked around her son's living room. They were all together. Safe and happy.

As if reading her mind, Lucas pulled her close and kissed her cheek. "I have a special Christmas present for you, darling."

She looked up at him, breathless. He still did that to her, even after all these years. "And what's that?" As if he hadn't already given her the world.

"Day before yesterday I officially retired."

Victoria felt her eyes widen. "What?" That was impossible. Lucas Camp retired?

He nodded. "From now on, I'm working with you

at the Colby Agency." He grinned. "You'll be my only boss."

Then he placed a soft, lingering kiss on her lips.

Clapping and whistling from across the room interrupted their sweet celebration.

"Now there's something worth celebrating," Jim said.

"Hear, hear," Tasha added, baby Luke in her arms.

Victoria blinked back the emotion in her eyes. "This truly is a magical Christmas."

"Jim has news as well," Tasha announced with a nudge of her handsome husband.

"Do tell," Lucas encouraged.

"I'm meeting with a buyer for the brownstone next week," Jim said. "He's interested in purchasing the building and the name, the Equalizers. According to his attorney, he intends to start a similar shop of his own."

"That's great news," Victoria said, very pleased. "You and Tasha can start looking for that country home you've been talking about."

Tasha grinned. "I've already gotten in touch with a Realtor."

Jim and Tasha had been considering purchasing a large country estate. The sale of the brownstone would go a long way in making that purchase. Victoria had offered to buy a property for them, but her son would have no part in it. He was doing this on his own.

That was the Colby in him. Undying determination and fearless independence.

Christmas miracles, Victoria decided. The past few days had been filled with that magic.

Another year was behind them and the Colby legacy continued to thrive.

* * * * *

Don't miss the stories in this mini series!

COLBY AGENCY: CHRISTMAS MIRACLES

Colby Brass
DEBRA WEBB
January 2011

Colby Core
DEBRA WEBB
February 2011

Mills & Boon™
6 Brand New Stories
Each Month
INTRIGUE™
edge-of-your-seat suspense
ignited by passion
INTRIG_2